TRUDI CANAVAN

MAKER'S CURSE

Book Four of Millennium's Rule

orbit

www.orbitbooks.net

ORBIT

First published in Great Britain in 2020 by Orbit

This paperback edition published in Great Britain in 2021 by Orbit

A CIP catalogue record for this book is available from the British Library.

ISBN 978-0-356-51076-7

Typeset in Garamond by Palimpsest Book Production Limited, Falkirk, Stirlingshire
Printed and bound in Great Britain by Clays Ltd, Elcograf S.p.A.

Papers used by Orbit are from well-managed
forests and other responsible sources.

Orbit
An imprint of
Little, Brown Book Group
Carmelite House
50 Victoria Embankment
London EC4Y 0DZ

An Hachette UK Company
www.hachette.co.uk

www.orbitbooks.net

PART ONE

RIELLE

CHAPTER 1

The arrival place was surrounded by three low walls, each a little higher than the last, as if they were seating around a performance area. A large slab of rock dominated the centre. As Rielle moved sideways within the place between worlds, so that her legs would not fuse with the slab when she arrived, she stared at the dark stain covering the top and tried not to imagine it was blood. When air surrounded her, she breathed in, and her heart sank at a familiar scent.

It *was* blood.

Shivering, she looked around. The land around her was flat, and divided into fields. The road leading to the arrival place – or was it a sacrificial altar now? – was empty of travellers, and weeds were encroaching on either side. The fields were occupied by workers, however. None had seen her yet. She did not recognise the crop, and the cool air held none of the scent of the plants she had helped harvest last time she had been in this world. Her senses told her that there was very little magic about. That did not worry her. She'd brought enough with her that becoming stranded was very unlikely.

She had not been to this world for five cycles – a cycle being the measurement of time similar to a year in most worlds. When she had left it, she'd forged a new path, but it was unlikely any trace would remain after so much time. The most reliable way to find her way back here had been to follow the traces of what had once been well used as a route; then, on arrival, seek out the area she had lived in before.

Judging by the plant species, she'd arrived in a very different part of the world to the one she remembered.

She had learned that the sudden removal of power could have unpredictable effects on civilisations, with violence and chaos all too common. Without magic to call upon, the local sorcerers would be no threat to her. Nor would ordinary people. Yet she'd hesitated to return here, fearing that her brief visit might have changed this world for the worse, and that the inhabitants would blame her for those changes.

Because she *was* to blame.

She had been chasing Qall, the young man whose body was meant to hold the mind of the Raen, former ruler of all the worlds. The ruler's most loyal servant, Dahli, wanted to attempt another resurrection and had sent out his followers to find and abduct Qall. When one did, Qall had chosen to cooperate with his enemy in the hopes of finding a way to resolve the situation. To stop Rielle following and complicating the situation, he'd removed all the magic of a world in order to trap her there.

But the people of that world didn't know that. All they knew was that she had arrived at about the same time. The more sensitive of them might have felt the flood of magic she had created several days later, when she had given up agelessness in order to become a Maker again, so that she could generate the magic needed to escape this world. They'd have sensed someone take that magic, and the workers and managers of the clothing factory saw her fade out of sight straight after. It wouldn't have taken much for the local sorcerers to work out she'd had something to do with it.

Taking hold of the lozenge-shaped pendant that hung on a chain around her neck, she twirled it between her fingers. She'd had to replace the bristles of the brush concealed inside three times since she'd begun restoring worlds, wearing them out while painting

4

in order to generate magic. Thinking back to the image she'd made in the grime of the fumigation room at the factory, she sighed. She had depicted the workers living free and prosperous instead of held in near-slavery by sorcerers. Sympathy and anger had moved her to paint it, but she had regretted it every day since. If the workers had rebelled, it was likely that violence had followed. Though the sorcerers among them had no magic, they still had physical methods of persuasion and punishment. She looked down at the stained slab. It was unlikely they'd have given up their power without spilling blood.

Meddling in the affairs of worlds was dangerous. She and Tyen had learned that when they'd attempted to negotiate peace between the two worlds of Murai and Doum. They'd discovered their task had been designed to distract them as the leaders of Doum planned their invasion of Murai. They'd both decided never to become involved in the affairs of a world again.

And then she had, here, in the world she now knew was called Infae.

A shout brought her attention back to her surroundings. One of the workers had seen her, and was pointing in her direction. She sought his mind but found nothing. A certain amount of magic must imbue an area in order for minds within it to be accessible. She could release enough of it to be able to, but the closer she was to a person the less magic was required. So she moved to the edge of the circle, stepped over the stone walls, and started towards them.

The workers were gathering together. The way they hoisted their harvesting tools spoke of determination and defensiveness. At a signal from one, they began walking towards her, fanning out to surround her. She did not have to see their faces to know they meant to do her harm.

She stopped, let magic spill out and read their minds.

Her breath caught in her throat. They had decided she was a sorcerer by her strange clothing and because she had appeared within the stone circle. Sorcerers were to be killed – sacrificed to the goddess Rel, who had stripped Infae of magic.

The goddess Rel?

The group were afraid as well as determined. They knew she could have arrived carrying magic. Sorcerers didn't submit to being sacrificed without a fight. She couldn't help admiring their bravery, even as she felt horror that this world had come to this. They knew if they failed, the priestesses and priests in the nearby city would deal with her. If not . . . they would be paid well when they brought this woman's head to them.

Rielle's stomach turned. She drew a deep breath, pushed out of the world and, as the first of the deadly harvesting scythes passed through the air she had occupied a moment before, skimmed away.

A sense of the direction the city lay in had been in their minds. She headed for it, moving herself higher so she could see the area better. The land was flat in all directions, except where outcrops of rock thrust up from the earth. Quite different to the landscape she had visited the last time she had entered Infae, five cycles ago. The local city was definitely not the one she had known, sprawling around a delta river system. Here, one particularly large outcrop dominated the plain, its surface covered in buildings and roads.

She increased her speed, deciding she would not emerge in the world to breathe before arriving in the city. Descending to the rooftops from above, she positioned herself over the top of an empty circular tower built of bricks so dark they were almost black.

The air that surrounded her was humid and tinged with smoke. As her feet touched the tower roof, a wave of dizziness told her she had spent longer out of the world than she had realised. No physical sensation could be felt in the airless place between worlds, so she could never tell how close she was to suffocating. Having given up the ability to pattern-shift – to heal her body with magic

– in order to become a Maker again, she could not survive there any longer than she could hold her breath.

A muffled sound of shouting drew her attention down to the streets. Nearby, smoke and flames were billowing from the half-collapsed roof of a large building. Where streets were visible she could see people carrying buckets of water up the hill in a seemingly futile effort to quench the fire. Bright orange lights caught her attention, and she glimpsed a group of twenty or more people carrying torches striding past an alley entrance, their manner full of satisfaction and threat. It sent a chill down her spine as she stretched forth her senses to look for the source.

She found nothing, of course. Though she could sense some magic here, it was too thinly spread. Some patches did exist that might be strong enough to allow thought reading, however.

Releasing magic while on the tower would draw attention to her, so she pushed a little way out of the world and skimmed down to the alley the torch-bearers had passed. It was within one of the areas of stronger magic. The crowd's stragglers were still passing. Seeking minds, she caught fragments of thoughts.

. . . know better than to hide sorcerers in their . . .

No more sorcerers! No more sorcerers!

. . . said there was nobody inside but I'm sure I heard . . .

. . . knew who would be next so they robbed them the night before, which was enough warning that they got away . . .

. . . hope they never work out that I can use magic, or I'm dead and all my family and . . .

When the marchers had passed, she peered out of the alley. Blackened ruins lay where three more houses had once stood. The street was eerily quiet. She caught sight of a few people looking through the curtained windows of their homes, and detected the minds of several within the closest houses, full of fear and relief that the Followers of Rel had not targeted them this time.

Rielle moved back into the deeper shadows of the alleyway.

They've turned me into a god that hates sorcerers. The irony of that

7

development would have been amusing, if not for the deadly consequences. *What can I do? Is there any way I can convince them I'm not a god? Or, failing that, persuade them not to kill in my name?*

She needed to know more. Pushing out of the world as far as she could while still being able to see enough of the city to navigate by, she skimmed over the rooftops, hoping nobody would look up and see her ghostly figure flying past. She needed to find a quiet place close to one of the patches of stronger magic from which she could observe more people. Inspecting the garbage within another alley told her it was a promising location. It was full of offcuts of cloth, wire and other materials. Where objects were made, magic would be generated, imbuing the area with it.

Descending into the alley, she was not surprised to see the local buildings housed carpenters, tailors and hatmakers. It was a busy area, making it likely someone would enter the alley and see her here. She'd noted that both men and women wore patterned knee-length wrap skirts over a loose, sleeveless top. Unwrapping her scarf from her head, she wrapped it around her waist, covering the bottom half of her shift dress.

There was magic here, but not as much as she needed. She let some of what she carried flow gently outwards. It slowly intensified the local patch of stronger magic, and soon she was able to detect the thoughts of people nearby.

What was that? came the thoughts of a woman, pausing in her work. The flow of magic had come from close by, but not within the building. The woman glanced around the room and saw that none of the other hatmakers had looked up from their stitching. Her son's back was stiff, however, and as she met his gaze she felt a wave of affection. *Toyr is more sensitive than most*, she reminded herself. *He may not be a Maker, but he can sense them working better than all the priestesses of Rel. If he finds a new one and nobody else has reported them, the reward might be enough to buy us a better workshop.*

"Go on," she told him. "But no further than two buildings from here."

The boy leapt up and ran out of the room, excited by the prospect of earning his family money.

There was no sense of menace in this search the woman had sent him on. Makers weren't hated as sorcerers were. They were considered to have a godlike skill, as Rel had created magic before she'd emptied Infae of it. Rielle had stopped releasing magic, so the boy would not detect her, but he might note her strange appearance. Rising, she continued reading his mind as she walked down the alley, travelling in the opposite direction as he was.

It's probably someone the priestesses already know about, Toyr was thinking. A new cloth-maker had moved in a couple of days ago and was looking to hire weavers. *Three streets away, though. Further than Mother said I could go.* He headed for the area anyway. *But she wouldn't mind if I found a Maker and we got the reward.*

A pang of envy followed the thought. To be one of the rare sorcerers who generated plentiful magic when creating would be wonderful. They were given anything they wanted, as long as they spent their days making things. They got to make whatever they desired to. His mother constantly told him he should be thankful that the priestesses had freed all the artisans of the city from bondage, and ensured they were paid a fair wage, but making hats was boring. If he were a Maker he would never have to make a hat again. What he'd make instead he had no idea, but he was sure he'd find something he liked doing.

The boy's thoughts were fading as he moved out of the magically enhanced area Rielle had created. She reached the end of the alley. Shops selling all manner of garments, shoes and hats faced the street beyond. Sensing another patch of stronger magic in the alley across it, she slipped out of the world and skimmed quickly across the street. Arriving again, she walked down the second alley to the end, from where she looked out upon a small open space ringed by food vendors. Letting more of her magic strengthen what was here, she sought the minds of three young men talking nearby.

. . . ending slavery was a good thing, but this is going a bit too far,
one was thinking. "Do you think they'll come here?" he asked his
friends. "What if they decide to burn shops as well?"

"They won't," the taller of the youngsters replied. "We've always
been family businesses. We paid people well."

"I heard family workshops were burned in Defka city," the third
pointed out.

"Why?" the first young man asked.

"For making their children work, I heard."

"But how's a person going to have the skills they need by the
time they're grown if they don't start young?"

"Teaching is all right," the tall one said. "It's making them
work without pay that's—"

"Who *are* you?"

The voice cut over the youth's chatter, coming from closer behind
her. She turned to see a young man a few steps away, his body tense
as if he were ready to flee at any moment. Which he was, she read.
He had come to find the source of the sudden surges of magic in
the area, as he had been ordered to do by the Followers of Rel. He
was a sorcerer, and the Followers had only let him live because
he was a close friend of one of the priests, who had pointed out
that Annad was a gentle scholar and healer, and had never employed
even a servant, let alone used his magic to rule over others.

He was worried, now that he had found the source of the magic,
that he would have to turn her over to the Followers. She was
clearly a stranger, if not to this world then to this part of it. But
if she was a Maker she might be safe . . .

He was thinking all this deliberately, using the Traveller
language that his mentor had taught him, as it was known by
sorcerers who moved between worlds, hoping she would see she
was in danger and have time to flee.

"I am in no danger," she assured him. "But I do not want to
cause trouble. Is there somewhere we can talk?"

He considered. It was a risk. Probably too great a risk. But she deserved an explanation. If she could get to his late mentor's rooms unseen . . .

She moved closer and held out a hand. He looked at it dubiously. As she began to withdraw it, curiosity overcame his fears, and he took it.

Pushing out of the world, she took them far enough into the space between worlds that the city almost disappeared. Enough details remained visible that she could navigate, skimming high over the city. Annad's eyes widened, but his surprise was quickly replaced by fascination. He knew about world travelling, she guessed, though perhaps not how to.

She took them back towards the world so they could see more of the city's streets and buildings.

"*Where are your mentor's rooms?*" she asked.

He pointed. "*The highest room of the tower with the five-panelled roof.*"

No other roof fitted that description. She skimmed down, through the roof and into a circular room. To her relief it was unoccupied. She did not want to make his situation any more complicated and dangerous.

As they arrived she let go of his hand. "I am Rielle," she told him.

"I am Annad," he replied.

"What happened in this world?"

He told her about the loss of magic. Foreign sorcerers had been blamed for it, and many of them murdered. After they had died or fled, the Followers of Rel had arrived, spreading their tales of a goddess who had taken all the magic of Infae, disgusted with the way sorcerers enslaved and exploited non-sorcerers. Now it was the local sorcerers who were murdered, and while he had survived so far, Annad did not like to think about his chances of living out the year if his friend lost influence among the Followers.

"But they do not kill Makers," he assured her. "You are a powerful Maker?"

"Yes. But I am also a sorcerer."

"How long have you been here?" he asked.

"I arrived in this world today."

His eyebrows rose in surprise. At the same time he felt a rush of excitement as he realised she must be powerful to have travelled all the way to other worlds through the place between. "You did not know this was a dead world?"

"I knew."

"Then why did you enter?"

"To see what has happened since the magic was taken."

He frowned. "How did you know it was taken?"

She sighed. "Because I was here when it happened."

He stared at her, recalling what the priestesses believed. *Is this her? Is this Rel? The Followers say she will return. If we are better, if all are free, she will restore the world.*

Rielle shook her head. "I am no god. I did not mean for this to happen, but it is my fault. I should have come back sooner. I was . . ." She sighed. "I should not have meddled."

Annad stared at her silently. He did not see the goddess the Followers spoke of. He saw a powerful sorcerer and Maker in obvious distress. He thought back to his mentor, Sentah, who had been strong enough not just to travel between worlds, but to become ageless. When the magic had left the world, Sentah had been unable to heal himself when yellowlung spread through the city. But he had welcomed that death, saying he had lived far too long. His only regret was not being able to teach Annad everything he knew.

"I'm sorry," Rielle said.

He shook his head. "It is not your fault he caught yellowlung."

Nor was it entirely her fault that the old man had been unable to heal himself. The magic she'd made, then taken, before leaving Infae would not have spread this far.

"So . . . what will you do now?" he asked.

She drew in a deep breath and straightened. "Decide whether

or not to restore this world. I think, before I do so, I will need to find out more about the Followers. Where are they based?"

"Vohenn."

The delta city. She nodded. "Then I will go there."

Annad crossed his arms. "By restore, do you mean fill Infae with magic?"

"Yes. I am a Maker. A particularly strong one."

He nodded. "That's what Sentah believed. He'd said Makers couldn't be gods, since they could not become ageless. Not without breaking the worlds. It was the price they paid for their ability."

She blinked in surprise. "You know of Maker's Curse?"

Annad straightened, glowing with pride that she should be impressed by his knowledge of magic. "Sentah told me of it."

"How did he know about it?"

"He was a member of a secret library, so I expect he read about it there."

She felt a flash of hope. "Where is this library?"

Annad grimaced. "Lost. Sentah's membership was revoked many cycles ago, and all of those who belonged to it have died since. He gave me clues to its location when he was dying, saying if I could work them out I was worthy of its treasures, but it is not in this world." The young man shrugged. "And even if this world was restored, I don't know how to travel between worlds."

Rielle considered him. *I could teach him. If I decide not to restore Infae's magic I'll have to take him out of this world first.* Then go with him on his search? *But what of restoring worlds?*

She'd decide later, after she had sorted out matters here.

"Where is Vohenn?" she asked.

A vague idea of the city's location flitted through his mind, his knowledge based on Sentah's maps.

"May I see the maps?"

He nodded, then hurried over to a cupboard and, with hands shaking, opened it and rifled though a multitude of scrolls, packets and loose sheafs of paper. Drawing out a large roll, he moved to a table and pushed aside the dirty utensils and crockery of several past meals to make space for the unrolled map.

Rielle watched his mind as he pointed out details. Vohenn was half a world away. It had only taken five cycles – nearly seven years in Infae's measure of time – for the Cult of Rel to spread so far.

She touched the map. "Can I take this?"

"If you take me with you," Annad replied.

Rielle looked up at him. "If I have to leave this world suddenly, you will be stranded on the other side of it."

His shoulders lifted. "I am willing to take that risk." *Not just for the fame of being her guide*, he told himself, *but if she is here to decide whether to restore magic, I must speak on behalf of sorcerers.* "It's not like there's anything to keep me here now."

"Then pack a bag. Even if I restore magic, you won't survive with nothing to trade."

She picked up the map and examined it as he rushed about packing. He did not take long, pausing only to write two quick notes, one for the landlord and the other for a friend. When he was done, she held out a hand. He took it gingerly.

"Take a deep breath."

As he did so, she sucked in one herself, then pushed them both out of the world and began skimming upwards. The land below shrank, and soon she was able to recognise local features on the map. Having got her bearings, she sent them shooting off towards the nearest coastline. Following it would take longer than going directly to Vohenn, but a large ocean lay between them and their destination, with no features to get her bearings from.

She stopped several times to breathe, Annad coping with standing on an invisible surface high above the world remarkably well. He had travelled with his mentor using this method once or twice, though never so high above the ground, and never so far from home. At last a delta city appeared. The waterways glistened brightly, the reflection of the dawn sky making the water appear clean rather than the waste-tainted filth she remembered. Taking them downwards, she realised that the illusion was not entirely false. The waters were much less polluted now and no slick of wastes stretched to the horizon.

The city was still a shambles, but at the centre a shining new building was under construction. Rielle had seen plenty of temples before and it was clear this was to be one. Stopping high above the city, she brought them into the world again to consider her next move.

To her surprise, plenty of magic surrounded them. It emanated from the city below like a comforting mist, spreading a little way out into the countryside. The sources were numerous, but one in particular was stronger than the rest and she traced it back to a building in the temple complex. She sought minds.

A man was resuming his carving of a sculpture, taking advantage of the quiet of early morning to get some work done before the rest of the Makers arrived. This was where the Cult of Rel housed the Makers it had attracted with the promise of good living conditions. Many were working on the temple decorations, their professions ranging from carvers to painters to weavers. They were overseen by a priestess named Bel.

Rielle recognised the face in the carver's mind. The youngest and most shy of the three young women who had helped Rielle, Bel was now full of confidence and purpose. She liked working with the artisans, and they looked up to her as one of the three who the goddess had judged worthy, and whose likeness Rel had painted in *The Promise*.

Rielle winced. As she feared, they'd taken the images she'd made of them on the factory wall as a kind of prophecy and order. They believed they must make the scene of prosperity and equality happen before she returned.

How had this translated to killing sorcerers? Looking around the city, she saw no sign of burned houses. She skimmed across minds until she found a sorcerer enjoying a morning meal with his family. He nursed no fear of being murdered. Searching further, she found no sign that sorcerers were being attacked here. Many were not as wealthy as they had been before, but few had fallen on hard times. Enough magic existed that they could trade small services for payment. Several had joined the temple and become priests and priestesses.

Turning back to the temple, Rielle searched the minds there. She found young priests and priestesses gathering for their morning class.

"Sorcerers aren't being killed here," she observed.

"They call themselves the Cult of Rel," Annad observed. "Not the Followers."

Rielle looked into the minds of people within the centre of the temple. A familiar name caught her attention. She handed the map to Annad, pushed out of the world and sent them downwards.

"Time to find out what's going on."

They passed through the temple roof into a large room. A young woman stood before a mirror adjusting her plain white high-priestess robes. Rielle let go of Annad's hand and walked over to the young woman.

"Solicitations, High Priestess Bel," Rielle said.

The young woman looked up at the mirror, blinked as she saw Rielle's reflection, then spun around. Rielle smiled as disbelief fought recognition in the woman's mind and lost.

"It's you!" Bel exclaimed. "It's really you!" She put a hand to her mouth in amazement, covering a grin. The young woman considered what would be appropriate behaviour, then decided she must prostrate herself.

"No," Rielle said quickly, catching Bel's hands. "Do not lower yourself before me. I am not . . . We are friends. And we have much to discuss." She let go of the girl's hands. "Are Mai and Vai here too?"

Bel nodded. "I'll send for them." She moved to the door and, opening it a crack, spoke to someone beyond. "Find High Priestesses Mai and Vai and tell them to meet me here immediately." She closed the door, then glanced at Rielle's companion.

"This is Annad," Rielle explained. "I arrived on the other side of the world and he offered to be my guide."

Bel smiled at him. "Welcome to the Temple of Rel, Annad. You have travelled a long way."

He shrugged. "Yes. Thank you," he replied haltingly, unfamiliar with her language but able to understand and answer because he could read her mind.

Bel paused, deliberating whether she should send someone for food. She was saved from deciding by the door opening. They all turned to see Mai entering.

"Rel! You came back!" The young woman beamed and hurried towards Rielle, then stopped abruptly. "I mean . . . goddess Rel, welcome back." Her knees began to bend.

"Thank you," Rielle replied. "Please don't do that."

Mai froze, then straightened and continued the rest of the way to Rielle, her steps measured and her face calm despite the multitude of emotions vibrating within her. Fear, delight, even a little guilt. She, Vai and Bel had presumed so much by starting all of this, not because they believed Rielle was a god, but because they knew she wasn't.

"Then why tell people I am?" Rielle asked.

Mai paled. "Ah . . ."

"We didn't think you'd come back," Bel replied. "The whole idea that you might return wasn't ours. We wanted people to fix their own problems, not wait for you. That's why we seek out Makers and pay them well in exchange for creating things. We believe we can bring back the magic ourselves."

"But people are so excited by the idea of a goddess visiting our world. They want to meet you themselves," Mai explained. "They want it so badly that when we suggested you wouldn't return, they lost interest in fighting for freedom."

Bel smiled. "And you were clearly so powerful you might well have been a goddess."

Rielle shook her head. "Gods don't make mistakes. I do."

"All gods do," Mai told her, frowning. "How could anyone believe in gods that were infallible, when they see how imperfect the world is?"

Rielle could not answer that.

"Why did you leave that picture?" Bel asked.

Before Rielle could reply, the door opened again. Vai stepped into the room and, seeing Rielle, stopped to stare.

"Yes," Rielle said. "I'm back. I'd have come sooner, but . . ." What could she say? That she had avoided coming for fear of what her interference might have led to?

"You don't need to have an excuse," Mai said. "Why have you returned?"

Rielle sighed and turned to Bel. "The picture was . . . I wished you had a better life. I wanted to show you that you deserved to be treated with fairness and dignity. It was a way to say thank you for all the help you gave me." She paused. "But . . . to be honest, I did hope you and the other workers would be inspired to make a change, even as I worried that my interference would lead to strife. And it did." She glanced at Annad. "I arrived on the other side of the world and found that the Followers of Rel were killing sorcerers in my name."

"Ah," Vai said, her voice darkening. "The Followers."

"They disagreed with us," Bel explained. "And formed their own cult."

"It wasn't easy, in the beginning." Vai came forward to join them, now recovered from the shock of seeing Rielle. She had always been the most confident and pragmatic of the three. "People didn't know if what you drew was a promise or an instruction. Or meant anything. We and the other workers decided that it must mean *something*. We wouldn't let it mean nothing, so we refused to work."

"It wasn't easy." Mai shuddered. "The factory managers didn't have magic, but they had other weapons. Beatings. Withholding pay. Throwing the children out of the compounds and keeping their parents within. But the factory owners weren't going to make any money if we didn't work, so they had to give in eventually."

"The controllers who saw you disappear told others about you, before the managers ordered them to silence," Bel added. "As word spread that we were visited by a goddess, many controllers refused to deal out the beatings, or joined us. One had made a copy of the painting you left by pressing cloth against the wall, so that others could see and replicate it."

"By the time the owners were ready to negotiate, it was too late," Vai finished. "It was out of their control. Out of everyone's. People looked to us for answers. They didn't like that we didn't have any, so we had to start making things up. To make rules and give orders. We managed to stop things going completely crazy."

"There's no stopping the current, so we stick to steering the boat," Bel added, in a tone that suggested she'd used the saying many times before.

"That all seems like a long time ago," Mai said. "We've been in control here for a few years now. Elsewhere . . . unfortunately the other side of the world is too far away for us to influence. One day we will be strong enough to deal with the Followers, but not right now."

"Are you . . . are you unhappy with what we've tried to do?" Bel asked.

Rielle glanced from face to face. The women were holding their breath. She realised she was frowning and relaxed her expression.

"No. I'm amazed you have achieved so much. And yet . . ." Rielle hesitated, trying to put words to the nagging doubt she felt.

"What?" Vai asked.

Rielle spread her hands. "I am troubled, that it is all built on a lie. I am not a god."

They bowed their heads.

"Would you have us undo everything?" Mai asked.

Rielle sighed. "No. The truth might be as dangerous as the lie." She grimaced. "Though it might stop the Followers."

"Could you pretend to be a god in order to stop them?"

Rielle winced. "If I had to, I suppose I could." She looked at Annad. "What do you think, Annad?"

He shook his head. "I think they would fight to retain their power. They would declare you a fake − a sorcerer pretending to be Rel."

"Even if I restored the magic of this world?"

He shrugged. "Then perhaps you wouldn't have to convince them of anything, because the sorcerers could defend themselves again."

Rielle turned to the girls. "People here obey you and made hard changes because you let them believe I would return and restore the magic of this world. That was a risk. I might never have returned. But I am here, and that means you face another dilemma: if I do restore this world, I will be putting power back into the hands of those who oppressed you."

Mai shook her head. "If they go back to their old ways, they will not find people as willing to bend to their demands."

"So you don't mean to restore the magic?" Bel asked, turning back to Rielle. "Or do you need to be completely sure it won't do harm first?"

Rielle shook her head. "I doubt I would ever be completely sure. Perhaps if I were a god I would be able to predict the future, but I am not. And since I am not a god, and not of this world, the decision is not mine to make."

Annad took a step towards her, opening his mouth ready to list the reasons he wanted to give in favour of restoring magic, but the three women frowned at him in a warning against interrupting and he bit back the words, bowing his head respectfully.

"Whose decision is it?" Vai asked.

"The people of Infae." Rielle smiled. "But since it would take too long to ask them all . . . their representatives."

"Would we suffice as those representatives?" Bel asked. "We and your guide together."

"You have the good of all people at the heart of what you do. That seems the best qualification I can think of." Rielle looked at Annad. "And my guide speaks for sorcerers from the other side of Infae. I think we can tell what he wishes." She turned back. "What do you want me to do?"

The trio exchanged glances. Rielle saw from their thoughts and doubtful faces that they had discussed many times what might happen when magic returned to Infae, though they had figured it would happen slowly over many centuries. They'd considered many possible consequences, both good and bad. They'd consulted men and women whose wisdom they respected, and debated their advice.

Bel regarded Rielle thoughtfully. "You've restored worlds before, haven't you?"

"Yes. Many times." Always at the behest of another. This was the first time that burden of that decision had shifted to her, and here she was fobbing it off onto these three young women. Yet it felt like the right thing to do. "I have seen enough to know I can't predict what will happen. All I am certain of is that it brings great change."

"Then . . ." Mai glanced at her two friends. "I say we should do it. We've weathered one change. We will survive another. There is much good in magic. We may need it, when we deal with the Followers. And we *will* deal with them. They sprang from our actions, and we must be the ones to stop them."

Vai nodded. "I agree. We have built the foundations of a fairer world. I've been cynical about the chances of it staying that way, magic or no magic. People will always try to take advantage of others. So we may as well have magic."

"Then we are united," Bel said. She didn't elaborate, just smiled and turned to Rielle. "I ask, humbly, for you to return magic to our world."

Rielle bowed her head. "I will do so."

A cheer erupted from Annad, earning him looks of amusement from the women.

"Do . . . you need us to bring you anything?" Bel asked.

"No, I came prepared." Rielle started towards the centre of the room. Shrugging off her pack, she opened it and drew out a board, a sheaf of paper and a drawing stick. The materials always seemed too humble in the face of the task she would be performing, but she handled them reverently, glad for this chance to exercise her skills.

"I think another portrait will do," she said. "In those chairs over there, where the light is good."

As they obeyed, she drew a deep breath, composed a picture in her mind and began to transfer their likenesses to paper.

CHAPTER 2

"That's all I can teach you," Rielle told Annad late the next day. "Remember my warnings and take every precaution, but my strongest advice is to find someone with experience travelling between the worlds to give you more guidance, and show you the signs and clues that indicate you are about to enter an uninhabitable or dead world."

Annad placed a hand on his heart in a gesture of thanks. "Thank you, Rielle. I will be careful. I am in your debt. If I find the library, I will send a message through the Restorers."

She smiled. "If I find it, I will seek you out and take you there. But I doubt I will be free to search for it any time soon. There are still many more worlds in need of restoration."

Annad nodded. "I will visit the temple as often as I can to check if you have left any messages for me."

"Farewell, Annad." Taking a step back, Rielle inhaled deeply, let a breath out, then drew in another and held it. Pushing out of the world, she skimmed upwards, located the tower roof on which she had first arrived in Annad's city and sped towards it. Once there, she immediately pushed out of the world, following her own path back to the arrival place with its bloodied altar, then straight into the whiteness of the place between.

The arrival place she had travelled from towards Infae began to reappear. She placed herself in the middle, arriving a little higher than the ground where the plants she had trampled had begun to recover and stand upright again. After a quick pause to fill her lungs, she pushed onwards to the next world.

She hadn't thought she would miss being able to pattern-shift, but she did every time she travelled between worlds. Using it, she could have stayed in the place between for as long as she needed without suffocating. *Well, that's not entirely true. I'd have died eventually when I ran out of magic.*

The other times she had missed it were when she caught a common cough or cut herself on a sharp object. So far she hadn't suffered greater injuries or illnesses, since she could use magic to shield herself from most dangers, but many times she had regretted not being able to heal someone else.

The knowledge that she was no longer ageless did not bother her much. She would age and die, but so did most humans. When she started to feel the effects of age, she would probably feel the loss more, but for now there was no point dwelling on it. Especially since she could always sacrifice her Maker ability and become ageless again.

But not yet. Her Maker ability was unique and, as she'd said to Annad, many more worlds needed to be restored. She had always left choosing which was next up to Baluka, since he was the Restorers' leader; Infae was the first world she had decided to restore without his direction.

Doing so brought a sense of completion she had craved for a long time. Not only because of the way she had left the world five cycles ago, but also because of *why* she had been able to.

When she'd first visited Infae, she had been ageless, having lost her natural Maker ability when she'd learned pattern-shifting. While trapped in Infae, she had used the last of the magic she had carried not only to remove her pattern-shifting ability and restore her Maker gift, but also to enhance that gift far beyond its former strength, until she could easily and quickly restore entire worlds. So she felt strangely indebted to Infae, because but for her time there she would not be able to restore other worlds. She'd owed it that same help.

One day there would be no more worlds needing her help, and she would swap her Maker ability for pattern-shifting and become ageless again. The worlds that had been drained of magic in the battles of the last ten cycles would be restored: from those that had suffered in the chaos after the Raen, the ruler of all worlds, had died, to those affected by the confrontation between Dahli and the Restorers. The latter were close to the location of the conflict, but other dead worlds – emptied of magic when sorcerers, no longer restrained by the Raen's laws, had attempted to learn pattern-shifting – were scattered throughout the known worlds.

Refugees from these worlds had made their way to Baluka over the cycles to beg for help, each waiting to have their home world restored. Some had waited many cycles for that help. Thinking about that brought a sense of urgency. Her visit to Infae had been spontaneous – she'd recognised a world near to it and realised she had a rare chance to visit. She didn't regret taking the opportunity – or for spending time teaching Annad – but it meant she would be late returning to Baluka, and her next restoration. The Restorers' efforts to maintain peace often depended on good timing, and for Baluka to have his most valuable tool disappear for a few days could upset any number of plans. Still, if she travelled efficiently, she might cut that back to a day.

The arrival place in the next world was a raised dais within a city square, watched over by street urchins hoping to earn a gemstone or slip of precious metal in exchange for providing information about their world or descriptions of travellers who had passed that day. This was a common kind of arrival place in a living city – wide and open so that large or simultaneous groups could enter the world with space to spare.

The next world's arrival place was a glade within a forest. Locations with no sign of human habitation nearby were common, too. They were often connected to a city arrival place. Chances were low for a path leading directly out of a city in one world to

25

lead somewhere perfectly suited to human settlement in the next. Sometimes cities arose where that path arrived that relied entirely on travel between worlds for their existence, but they were always more vulnerable to abandonment and ruin.

The following arrival place was another ruin. Ruins were the most common setting of all. Civilisations rose and fell, but the paths that connected them remained in use if they still made convenient, safe links between worlds.

Less common locations for arrival places included temples, and she passed through one next. It was no surprise that the materialisation and disappearance of people of varied and sometimes strange appearance gave arrival places an aura of mystery and mysticism. People living near one not of their making might consider their visitors deities, but they did not remain uneducated in the ways of sorcerers and worlds for long. Though the truth was more humble, the habit of attributing divinity to supernatural occurrences was hard to break.

Rielle had come to accept the probability that the Angels of her world had been sorcerers, who long ago set down the rules of the religion she'd grown up with in the hope that her world would recover from the great wars that had stripped it of magic. But though she believed this was the likely truth, she still felt a superstitious fear whenever she thought about it, and wondered if she would be struck down by angry Angels if she ever returned to her home.

Maybe that was the true reason she did not like people thinking of her as a god.

Pushing that thought aside, Rielle travelled on until exhaustion dulled her concentration. By then, the feeling of hunger that returned whenever she arrived in a world was intense. She stopped in a world used to catering to sorcerous visitors to buy food and accommodation, arriving in the middle of the night and resuming her journey not long after dawn with her body still aching with tiredness. Dozens of worlds later, she slowed again when dizziness forced her to stop and breathe for a while.

At last she arrived in the Restorers' base world, Affen. As always, her appearance at nearby arrival places had been noted and messengers sent to inform Baluka. He was waiting for her in the large main hall of the Restorers' headquarters.

"Rielle," he said, stepping away from a small group of sorcerers who had taken the opportunity to talk to their leader. "You're late."

She nodded. "I had a little private business to attend to on the way back."

He frowned, the lines between his brows deepening. *But it isn't time yet*, he thought. Once every cycle she disappeared for several days, always refusing to explain why. *Did she go early this time?* When she met his gaze and remained silent, he put his questions aside, frustrated but respecting her right to have a private life outside of working for the Restorers. He hoped her silence meant she wasn't reading his mind.

She almost blushed. She had promised him that she wouldn't, but some habits were hard to break. Withdrawing her senses, she looked at the sorcerers he'd been speaking to.

"Do you want me to come and see you later?"

He shook his head. "No, I've rearranged my schedule. Let's go down to the planning room."

"Another world to restore?" she asked.

"No. There is something else I'd like you to do."

Rielle reined in her curiosity and fell into step beside him as he started towards the stairs that led down to the building's numerous underground levels. Baluka glanced at her and paused before beginning the descent.

"You look tired."

"I haven't had much sleep over the last few days," she replied. The concept of days was vague, when every world's cycles of time were different. The period between one sunrise and another could be as short as a few hours by her world's measure, or as long as a year. How did one measure a day when there were two suns, or more? And many worlds had moons – a phenomenon she had never experienced before she left her world.

World-travelling sorcerers measured longer stretches of time by cycles, which was the length of time it took the Travellers, an ancient race of merchant sorcerers, to do a circuit through the worlds they traded in. The Traveller tongue, their unifying language, was also the common language among sorcerers. Baluka had once been a Traveller. She glanced at him, recalling the young man who had found her, stranded in a desert world. Now the curious lines the Travellers imprinted under their skin were faded, and new creases emphasised his mouth and eyes. He looked older than he ought to. The constant hard work and demands of leading the force that maintained peace in the worlds had aged him. In appearance he reminded her, more and more, of his father, Lejikh, though he was still of a very different nature.

"I'm not sure I can give you time to rest," Baluka said apologetically.

"This task is urgent, then?"

"Somewhat."

They had descended five floors. Baluka led her through an open doorway into a familiar meeting room, closing it behind him. Collapsing into one of the large, cushioned chairs, Rielle sighed at the simple comfort of resting a tired body. Moving to a chair that faced hers, Baluka perched on the edge.

"Do you remember restoring a world called Prama?" he asked. She shook her head.

"It was more than two cycles ago. Prama was drained by a sorcerer seeking to become immortal. He failed, twice."

"Ah, that's right. He took all the magic of one side of the world in the first attempt, then travelled to the other and tried again, even though it was obvious that he would be gathering less magic the second time, since it had spread out around the world while he was travelling."

28

"Magic ability doesn't guarantee intelligence." Baluka smiled wryly.

"I brought him to you, at the request of Prama's leaders," she recalled. "They knew he'd try again once I'd restored their world, and they didn't want to execute him."

Baluka nodded. "We put him in Dearn."

Along with many hundreds of other sorcerers who had stripped worlds for their own gain. Rielle often wondered what it was like there now, populated by a mix of foolish and greedy sorcerers with no access to magic.

"Prama has given us trouble since we restored their world," Baluka told her. "They had regarded one of their neighbouring worlds, Whun, as an enemy for hundreds of years. For the last three quarter-cycles they've threatened to attack Whun over petty grievances. We have assured both sides that we will not allow the other to harm them. Now the Pramans have made good on their threat, claiming that if they hadn't attacked Whun, the Whuns would have attacked them first." He shook his head. "We need to made good on our promises to protect and punish."

Rielle frowned. "You want me to protect the Whuns? Surely your generals can deal with this."

"The Restorer armies are stretched thin, as always." He shook his head. "There is a simpler solution. I want you to strip Prama again."

"Strip . . ." Rielle stared at him. "You can't be serious."

His gaze was hard but his expression was regretful. "I am. I know this is not the sort of task you offered to do for us, but it is a better alternative than sending in fighters, for us and for the Pramans. Nobody would be killed or harmed."

"Except people whose livelihoods rely on magic, whose sick-nesses and injuries are being tended by sorcerers, or whose defence depends on magic."

"There will be far more sick, injured and besieged if we inter-vene with force, or allow the two worlds to descend into war."

Rielle pushed herself out of the chair, her legs protesting, but her weariness seemed insignificant compared to what Baluka was asking her to do. He made it sound so reasonable, but . . .

"This is not what I do, Baluka. This is the opposite of what I do. I restore worlds. I don't wreck them."

"You won't be wrecking this one; you'll be subduing it."

If she agreed to this once, he would ask again. And again. Perhaps she would be doing good, ultimately. Perhaps once Prama had learned its lesson she could restore it again. She didn't have to see Baluka's thoughts to guess that this was his hope and intention. Withdraw magic to control rogue worlds. Restore it to those who cooperate.

I'm just a tool, she told herself. *Well then, if I don't get to choose my actions, I don't have to shoulder the responsibility for the lives they affect. Baluka does.*

But the thought was not convincing. She was more than a tool. She was a person, with a conscience and reputation she must live with. Passively allowing herself to become a weapon was no different to actively becoming one. She shook her head.

"No. I won't start down this path. I can't."

He radiated disappointment and acceptance. She caught the snatch of a thought: *There are other ways.* He would send several sorcerers to Prama to strip it. *Using Rielle would have been faster and involved no risk . . .*

She turned away, both physically and mentally, to hide her scowl. No risk? Had he forgotten that she could no longer pattern-shift? A wound could still kill her. Suffocation between worlds was a constant danger, and if an unexpected threat caused her to use all of her stored magic in a dead world before she could create more, she would be as vulnerable as any non-sorcerer.

"I have another world for you to strengthen," he said. "If you are willing."

She nodded, then returned to her seat and drew out her notebook from her pack. "Where?"

As he began to describe it and the route to take there, she wrote down everything. To her relief, the task was a simple one – no local politics to deal with. She would travel close to the world of her former mentor, Tarren, too. Perhaps she could visit him.

"I need a few good sleeps," she told Baluka.

"There is no urgency. Let's make it your final restoration before you take time off. You will still be needing several days' break?"

She smiled. "Yes."

"Then I'll see you afterwards."

"You don't want me to report back?"

"Send messages when you're done so I can tick that world off my list."

"I will. I hope Prama comes to its senses, and you can tick that problem off your list."

"I hope so too."

CHAPTER 3

Rielle knew within moments of emerging from the place between worlds that her approach had been noted. Students were watching her through the glass that separated the arrival place from the study rooms that surrounded it. She scanned the minds in the area and immediately found one of a student hurrying to inform Tarren he had a guest.

Her former mentor's new home was within an abandoned city. The metropolis had been carved into the surface of a flat plain of rock, linking with natural underground rivers, most of them intermittent. The complex of tunnels, corridors and thoroughfares – and the remains of the mines that had once supported the city's existence – formed an immense labyrinth. Tarren had taken up residence in the most comfortable area. Shafts to the surface let in air, and mirrors bounced light downwards. Pipes brought clean water and carried away waste. In places, rooms were open to the sky, both naturally and carved so by the previous occupants, and the students had turned these spaces into places to grow food.

The arrival place was one of these gardens. Glass walls faced it on all sides, allowing Tarren's students to keep an eye out for visitors, welcome or not. Though it was night, it was early enough that the rooms were still occupied. Most of the students watching her smiled when she waved. They knew who she was, or rather, they knew *what* she was: the Maker, and one of Tarren's powerful friends.

If they hadn't heard the rumours and stories that spread so effectively through the worlds via travelling sorcerers, they would have learned all about her from Tarren. Even if the old man hadn't been a terrible gossip, some of his students were more powerful than he and could read his mind.

Walking to the main door of the building, Rielle stepped from icy air into warmth. Two of the young women came over. Both were of the same world and race, their hair and eyes a pale pink and their skin white. Their colouring was not common in the worlds. Tarren had trouble telling them apart sometimes, but Rielle had noted that the younger, Dilleh, had a slight dip in the centre of her hairline, and a habit of biting her lip when listening. It was harder to identify them when they were outside, however, as both tended to wear voluminous, translucent veils to protect their eyes and skin from bright light.

"Rielle," the older of the two, Mwei, said.

"Are you well?" Dilleh asked.

Rielle nodded. "Good. A little tired. How is Tarren?"

Mwei shrugged. "His usual self."

"He worries," Dilleh added, "since . . . you know."

"I worry, too," Rielle told them. A few cycles ago, Tarren's home had been invaded and ransacked. The old man and his students had fled and none were harmed. The attackers hadn't focused their attention on the occupants, instead looting and destroying. "Has anyone worked out who they were, and why they did it?"

Mwei's face wrinkled. "We're certain they were from Liftre, but Tarren doesn't agree. There is a rumour they are trying to stop other sorcerers running schools."

"But we have no proof," Dilleh finished.

"Ah! Rielle! It *is* you."

Rielle turned to see Tarren entering the room. "Yes, it *is* me," she replied. "Did you have reason to doubt your messenger?"

He pretended to pout. "Well, it has been a while. Some of us might have forgotten what you look like."

She shook her head. "It hasn't been *that* long."

"It feels like it." The old man smiled and beckoned. "Stop distracting my charges and come join me for dinner."

Rielle smiled at the two women in farewell and followed Tarren out of the room and down a corridor that curved around the study rooms.

"How are your students?"

"Mostly reasonably well," he replied. "None are a match to Min and Goggendan." He sighed as he remembered his two most promising students, who had left after the attack, their studies unfinished. "Min has mated and has twins to look after now, so I don't think he'll be back, but I still have hope Goggendan will overcome her fear and join us again." He glanced through a window at another study room. "I have two new young ones. Both have particularly strong powers, but one is spoilt and lazy and a bad influence on the other."

Tarren continued chatting as he led her through sprawling, interconnected circular rooms to his private suite. The walls were mud rendered, handprints still visible here and there. The roof was woven grass plastered with more mud. It was all decorative rather than functional, designed to remind him of the home he had grown up in. Which was very different to the buildings clinging atop a spire of rock that he had occupied when she'd first met him.

"Here we are," Tarren said, ushering her through a door and over to one of several circular tables standing between curved benches built into the wall. A servant was setting out a second set of cutlery and crockery on one of the tables. "Take a seat," Tarren bade. He settled onto a cushion before a half-eaten meal.

Rielle obeyed, setting down her pack and helping herself to the contents of a steaming pot in the centre of the table. She braced herself for the burn of the spices Tarren enjoyed and tucked in.

"So how many worlds have you restored since we last met?" he asked.

"I'm not sure. Many hundreds. Baluka would know exactly." She paused. "Though not correctly. My last was the world Qall trapped me in, all those cycles ago. I'm not going to tell him about that one."

He nodded, recalling her tale of the workers who had helped her, and her transformation from an ageless sorcerer back into a Maker. "Had it changed for the worse, or better?"

"That depends if you think them making me a god is good or bad."

He chuckled. "One of the benefits of having godlike powers."

"Which they never benefited from."

"Except to gain a role model and inspiration for change, am I right?"

"Yes. Luckily, good changes. Well, mostly. On the other side of the world they're sacrificing sorcerers to the goddess Rel, but hopefully the return of magic will put a stop to that."

"Oh dear." His smile eased into sympathy. "Your discomfort with having power over others, even unintentional power, is one of your admirable traits, Rielle, but you should not let it prevent you from helping people when you can."

She sighed. "I know. I'm just . . . I'm afraid that what I do will harm more than help. Like in Murai and Doum." She frowned as she recalled her and Tyen's attempts to prevent war between the two worlds. "It's safer for the worlds to let Baluka decide which I restore." She frowned as she recalled Baluka's request. "Though now I'm wondering if I can trust him to make all the decisions."

"Why is that?"

She told him of Baluka's request that she strip a world she had restored. His brows lowered as he listened, and he nodded when she was done. "It disturbs me that he is willing to use such measures," she finished.

"Why?"

"It seems so ruthless." She shook her head. "Maybe only because it seems so coming from Baluka."

Tarren spread his hands. "He is a man charged with maintaining peace in the worlds. Why wouldn't he use all the tools at his disposal, if they reduce or avoid bloodshed?"

Her stomach sank. "So you think I should have agreed?"

His expression softened. "No. You were right to refuse. Though it is likely his intentions were good, as you believe, it would indeed make you a weapon. You cannot be the Maker if you are also destroying worlds."

Rielle winced as his words reminded her of Maker's Curse. "Unless I become ageless and retain my Maker ability. Then I'll destroy all the worlds."

"You don't know if that's true," Tarren told her. "For all you know, the curse refers to the possibility that a sorcerer will strip a world of magic when learning pattern-shifting. It is old, this idea. It might come from a time when sorcerers becoming ageless was rare and the consequences were more of a shock than now."

"Well, there's a chance the answer to that question exists," she said, then told him of Annad's mentor and the clues to the location of a secret library.

Tarren rolled his eyes. "What a pointless and cruel thing for a mentor to do to his charge! Why couldn't he just tell him where it was?"

She grimaced. "Perhaps he was addled on his deathbed. Perhaps he guessed that Annad, having never left his world, wouldn't recognise the landmarks a world traveller would use, so he tried to use ones he would. Perhaps he was guarding against others reading Annad's mind by giving him clues only he could interpret."

"Perhaps, perhaps, perhaps." Tarren pursed his lips. "Perhaps we'd have a better chance at following the clues than Annad. Did you memorise them?"

"I wrote them down in my notebook. Do you want to see them?"

"Yes . . . but don't show them to me. If the sorcerers who ransacked my former house are truly seeking to gather and hoard knowledge, they might seek me out again. If they find me, they'll read my mind. As long as only you and Annad know the clues, the chances are you'll find the library before they do."

Rielle had started to reach for her pack, but now she straightened and muttered a curse. "I shouldn't have told you about it."

"Possibly not."

"I was hoping for your help."

Tarren shook his head. "You're on your own with this one. Unless . . . unless you approach your friend, Tyen."

Rielle considered the old man's suggestion, and his description of Tyen as her "friend". Tarren hadn't given up on the possibility that she and Tyen might resume a romantic relationship, but he now thought it unlikely. While she hadn't dismissed the idea entirely, a part of her still resisted it. Her distrust of Tyen had sprung from believing he had been trying to resurrect Valhan for selfish reasons, despite knowing that the Raen would kill her. Though she had since learned that Tyen had been playing a dangerous game of double-spy, cooperating with Dahli's plans of resurrection so that the man didn't find someone else to do it, and hoping to give her and Qall time to find a safe home far away, she was wary of letting herself grow fond of him again. Or anyone, really. Especially not when she had worlds to save. She'd been unable to commit her heart to anyone before, due to her promise to protect Qall. Now she was even less free to.

Tyen *was* the most obvious source of help to find the library, though. Nobody but Qall could read his mind. Although he did not have Vella, the sentient book containing centuries of knowledge, to consult any more, he was smart and well used to accessing information from libraries. He even had a school of sorts, though it had no official location.

"Tyen is too busy to spend time hunting for information about an ancient myth," she pointed out.

Tarren grimaced. "Yes, you are right about that."

According to Tarren, Liftre's new management had made it clear they disapproved of Tyen running a school. It wasn't clear if this was due to Tyen's role as a spy in two major conflicts in the worlds, or simply because Tyen wanted to stop the production of war machines, whereas Liftre was profiting from making them. Whenever they learned where Tyen and his students had settled, they manipulated the people of the world into demanding he leave. They used threats and blackmail to persuade his students to abandon their training, and made it clear that Liftre would have no association with anyone who sought his teaching. He had only a small group of pupils, all fiercely loyal.

She frowned. "Do you still think Liftre wasn't behind the attack on your previous home?"

Tarren waved a hand dismissively. "If they were, they only wanted the records I took when I left Liftre, and anything else I might have gathered since. They've never demanded I stop teaching."

"Not yet."

"And if they do, I will ignore them." He tapped his forehead. "My greatest treasure is knowledge and a knack for teaching. They can't take that from me."

Rielle smiled. "What more does anyone need?" She drummed her fingers on the table edge and considered his earlier suggestion. If she did visit Tyen it would have to be after she had restored the next world and visited Qall. Though if Qall had decided it was time to leave her home world she had no idea what she would be doing next.

She doubted he would leave, though. Last time she'd visited him, he had been certain he needed to stay there a couple more cycles. She had seen no troubling changes in him, only the expected ones of someone growing up and gaining in maturity and wisdom, but if he thought there was still a danger the Raen's memories would overtake his mind, she must believe it was possible. Since she could not read his mind, he was the only person who knew what was going on in his head.

"But there's no proof it *was* Liftre behind the attack," Tarren added.

"Who else could it be?" she asked, bringing her thoughts back to the present.

"Dahli's former followers?"

She shrugged. "Possibly."

She and Tyen had let people assume that they'd killed Dahli after what was now known as the Resurrection Battle. She couldn't tell Tarren that they had let the Raen's former Most Loyal live. They had done so, so that he could find Zeke, his new lover and a talented machine maker, and the two of them dedicate themselves to inventing ways to eliminate war machines. If others learned this from Tarren's mind, the news would spread quickly throughout the worlds, causing chaos.

Whenever she thought of Dahli it was with a mix of sadness, worry and anger. When angry about the deaths he'd caused – not the least being that of her friend, Ulma – she remembered that Dahli had acted out of a mad, distorted love and grief for the Raen. She hoped that he had found Zeke and mended the rift between them.

It wouldn't be easy, she thought. *When Dahli killed half of the Restorer's army, Zeke saw the monster he became. My lingering distrust of Tyen must be nothing compared to what Zeke would have to overcome to trust and desire Dahli again.*

And then she would worry that she and Tyen had made the wrong decision, and Dahli would return to wreak havoc in the worlds again.

"Tyen would be delighted to see you," Tarren said.

Rielle looked up to see him watching her closely, a gleam of mischief in his eyes. She shook a finger at him.

"I told you, no more matchmaking."

He grinned. "Can you blame me? It's my greatest wish to see the two of you together again before I die."

"Die?" She made a disbelieving sound. "I doubt any of your ageless former students are going to let your body deteriorate enough to succumb to old age, and your current students can protect you very well."

He chuckled. "Yes. I am more concerned they won't let me go when I'm ready."

She reached out and squeezed his arm. "I hope that you are never ready."

He patted her hand. "So do I."

CHAPTER 4

A strange forest surrounded Rielle. The trees formed a maze of trunks leaning at all angles except vertical. Droplet-shaped leaves appeared to strain upwards and a network of fine roots descended from the branches to the ground – which was perfectly flat and glossy, suggesting opaque water, or mud.

Adjusting her position within the space between worlds, Rielle rose above the trees. As she arrived, air surrounded her, and she quickly stilled a disc of it below her feet. Looking down through this invisible support, she marvelled at the pattern spread below her. The forest was one single plant, connected by arching branches. Where each limb touched the ground, another cluster of branches sprouted. The collective effect was a pattern that echoed a river delta or fan-shaped coral, originating somewhere past the horizon.

Incredible, she thought. No matter how far she travelled in the worlds, she still encountered new and remarkable phenomena. Whether the product of human endeavour, living things adapting to an environment or natural forces sculpting the land, the worlds seemed capable of producing endless variety and spectacle.

But she was not here to see the sights; she was here to restore this world – the world of Telemna-vo. Once again, she sought the minds of other humans, before remembering that thoughts could not be read in worlds with little or no magic. Extending other senses, she sought magic instead . . .

. . . and exhaled in surprise and frustration. This was no dead world. It wasn't even a weak world. It could not be Telemna-vo.

She shook her head. Perhaps she'd misunderstood Baluka's directions and arrived in the wrong world. Thinking back, all the landmarks he'd described for the last nine or ten worlds had been present and obvious. It did not seem likely she had misinterpreted them. It was possible Baluka had been repeating directions given to him by another Restorer or a representative of Telemna-vo and a mistake had crept in.

She would have to go back and inspect every location closely, seeking the place where she had taken a wrong path. The mistake must have happened in the last few worlds, as it was highly unlikely that a second route would contain the same sequence of landmarks. If that was right, Telemna-vo was probably a neighbour to this one.

Taking a deep breath, she pushed out of the world and retraced her steps. She could not see how she could have gone astray in the last world, so she retreated to the next. And the next. Finally, after she had reversed through five worlds, she headed back to the world of the forest, reassured that she had followed the directions correctly, and the error was Baluka's, not hers.

Her next option was to search around the local worlds in the hope she was close to her destination. The people in this world might know where Telemna-vo was located or, if they didn't recognise the name, have heard of a neighbouring world that had been stripped of magic in the last five to ten cycles.

Those people must be far away, as she was sensing only distant, vague thoughts. She sought magic again, seeking a current in it. Magic tended to flow away from the source of its creation: people. Scanning the horizon, she sensed a slow but steady drift from the direction of the giant tree's source.

She took a couple of deep breaths, then held in the last one and pushed out of the world. Propelling herself sideways, she skimmed just outside the world. Two other major trunks of the plant were visible now, and in the distance they joined to form a thicker one. But not long after they joined, the enormous plant came to an abrupt and shocking end.

Blackened vegetation continued in ghostly traces of the dead plant for a few hundred paces, then a monochromatic patchwork of fields removed all trace. Smoke arose from an area of the forest to her left. Changing direction to inspect this, Rielle found a line of fire eating away at the vegetation, watched over by the tiny forms of distant humans holding torches.

A sadness crept over her as she hovered. Another natural wonder was slowly being destroyed to make way for crops. She had seen it countless times. People must eat, but often they did not anticipate the consequences of turning wild land to domestication. When living systems that had developed over countless millennia were broken, the land soon became depleted of fertility. Would the soil here sustain the population for long without the plant, or be a wasteland in a few generations?

She turned her attention to the fields. They formed a grid-like pattern very different to that of the plant. Mud from the fields had been dredged to the edges of each to form a dry ridge. Tracks followed the crest of each ridge, allowing passage for both people and domestic animals. These joined and grew broader to allow more traffic wherever they headed towards clusters of buildings on higher ground. These groups of buildings grew larger as she followed the ever-widening thoroughfares. Signs of greater human interference appeared. Channels directed water to small rectangular lakes, allowing areas of dry-land crops. Other roads in the distance zigzagged nearer to the one she followed, some joining with it, some leading to the same destination: a hill smothered in roofs and walls and streets.

This city was made up of circular buildings, each crowned by a domed roof topped with a spire. Some of the buildings were linked by straight walls, forming a courtyard between them. At the top of the hill, rising from a cluster of many small linked towers, rose an enormous gold dome that gleamed brightly in the sunlight. It matched exactly the description of the city Baluka's directions indicated she would find at her destination in Telemna-vo.

Rielle emerged into the world to breathe. If this was Telemna-vo, why would Baluka ask her to create magic in a world that already contained it?

Have the Telemnans found some other way to strengthen their world since they made the arrangement with Baluka? she wondered. Perhaps another Maker of unusually strong ability had been born or had visited from another world. That thought brought a mild, unexpected pang of jealousy, followed by a stronger and more sensible hope. To share the burden of restoring worlds would be a great relief.

This other Maker might not want to work for the Restorers, however. They might have been a friend of Valhan or prefer to work independently. Rielle's ability helped the Restorers gain the gratitude and loyalty of worlds, keep alliances and maintain peace. Another Maker could weaken these links and efforts, or even give strength to worlds that became enemies of the Restorers.

Rielle pushed aside a feeling of foreboding. The chance that two Makers of her strength had emerged in the same era was slim. More likely, the Telemnans thought their world was in a weaker condition than it was. With a sigh, she descended towards the city and sought the hexagonal building within which Baluka had said she would meet the world's most powerful sorcerers. It was at exactly the location she'd been given. A few men and women were present in the courtyard, some sitting on benches, others walking across the space. All wore long, many-layered robes, each layer a slightly lighter shade than the one beneath, and the darkest extending to closely cover their heads. The effect was conveniently similar to her simple shift and head scarf, so she did not need to adjust her appearance to avoid seeming oddly or improperly dressed to the locals.

She descended into the courtyard. The people noticed her shadow and stopped whatever they were doing to stare at her. When she arrived, they did not approach, and she read from their minds that they were waiting for someone of appropriate status to greet the visitor.

After a long moment a tall man with unruly white hair emerged from a door and approached her. From him she read that he had been told to expect a woman sorcerer of her description to visit.

"Welcome to Ka, Rielle the Maker," he said in hesitant Traveller tongue.

"It is an honour to my soul to be here," she replied in Telemnan, reading the traditional response of his people from his mind. Several more phrases were exchanged, and she curbed her impatience even as she perceived that he was using the shorter Telemnan ceremony of greeting.

"You will find Oier, Head Sorcerer, in the fire tower," he told her. "Ascend to the top. He awaits you." Turning, he gestured gracefully to a red-painted door in one of the five towers. Rielle pressed her palms together in thanks, then touched her forehead to indicate she understood.

"I will walk the way with gratitude," she replied.

He remained where he was and watched as she approached the door. She placed a hand on the fire symbol painted on the door, then stepped inside, sensing his relief that she had seen their custom in his mind. To not acknowledge the fire spirit would be to invite bad luck to this place, perhaps to the whole city.

Inside the tower, all was illuminated by red light filtering through small stained-glass windows. She made her way up a narrow, curved stair that hugged the wall and arrived at the open door of a room with larger, clear windows facing out towards the city. Setting down her pack, she patiently followed the longer ritual of greeting with a man who seemed surprisingly young for the leader of a guild of sorcery. Oier was barely older than she had been when she had left her home world. The Sorcerers' Guild chose their leaders by strength, she read, so each year there was the potential for a new leader to emerge from the graduates of schools around the world. To maintain stability, most decisions were made by vote in a council of masters.

By the time the welcoming ritual was over, Rielle had found answers to most of her questions from the Head Sorcerer's mind. This was, indeed, the world that had appealed to Baluka for restoration. It was not a dead world but had grown dramatically weaker in the recent past. Several reasons had been considered for the weakening, but none had been proven. Most Telemnans blamed the neighbouring world, Woperi.

"Why would the Peri take magic from your world?" she asked.

"We have been caught up in a feud for many years," Oier admitted, "after they brought a plant into this world knowing it would spread rapidly and render much of our land unusable. You may have seen it, not too far outside this city."

"I did. So Telemna-vo retaliated?"

"Yes. Our sorcerers bred and released an insect into the other world that would ruin their crops. They then struck back by introducing a disease that blinded a species of domesticated animals we eat." He spread his hands in a gesture of futility and acceptance. "We have continued this battle for over seventy cycles. It has brought famine and poverty to both worlds, though no attack has ever been directed at people, and neither side has marred the sanctity of magic by using it for warfare."

She frowned. "You do not consider famine and poverty an attack on people?"

He grimaced. "Not a direct attack."

Resisting the urge to sigh, she nudged the subject back to what she needed to know. "Would stripping magic from this world be considered a direct attack?"

"No."

"Is removing magic harming its sanctity?"

He hesitated. "That depends whether it is then being used for warfare."

"And if it was?"

His expression darkened. "Then we are free to respond like for like."

Magical warfare. Now she didn't resist a sigh. They had no proof the weakening was an attack by the Peri, and thankfully they were reluctant enough to begin a war to be very careful of confirming such an offence.

"Why did you ask for your world to be restored?"

Oier looked confused. "To make us strong again."

"But if this weakening continues, you will lose all that I give you again within a few years. Would it not be better to discover the cause first?"

He nodded. "I would rather we did, but I was outvoted on the matter. Many of us do not want to know the truth."

In case it *was* an attack by the Peri. The council's reluctance to go to war would be admirable, if it wasn't as foolish as this feud was to begin with. Oier was frustrated. Battle training was not taught in Telemna-vo. Their enemy had the same belief about the sanctity of magic and were not warriors either. Oier feared that if this had changed in Woperi, his people would need to adapt quickly. Either way, to have any chance of surviving a magical attack, they needed a world strong in magic.

She considered him carefully. "I restore dead worlds, not half-depleted ones," she told him. "I am a Maker, not a negotiator or problem fixer."

He winced and nodded.

Rielle looked away so he would not think her frown was directed at him. Baluka should not have sent her here. Either he had done so knowing the world wasn't depleted, or the Sorcerers' Guild had deceived him – which they could only do by sending someone to the Restorers to ask for help who believed this world was weaker than it was.

If the former, why would Baluka send her here? Did he want her to find the cause of the weakening? Did he expect her to deal with what she found? His request that she strip worlds had made her wary. *Is he trying to persuade me to get more involved in the decision-making behind restoring worlds? To shoulder some of the burden of controlling them?*

The possibility set anger simmering within her. She ought to leave and confront Baluka. She ought to refuse this world's request for magic. Too many dead worlds still waited for help, isolated and empty of magic, to justify her getting involved in this local problem. Strengthening Telemna-vo was a waste of her ability.

And yet she found she could not tell this young man she wouldn't help him. Not without giving him, and his people, a chance to avoid the magical warfare they feared.

"Would it help if I demanded you send sorcerers to seek the reason for the weakening before I restored this world?"

He nodded. "Not many of us are capable of travelling between worlds, however."

Which they would need to be, to cover distances quickly. "A few is better than none. What of the messenger you sent to the Restorers?"

"Our strongest member. Do you want her to search again?"

Rielle shook her head. "No. Send her to me. I need her to take the Restorers a message. While she is gone, I suggest your guild begin negotiations with the Peri to end this foolish cycle of revenge. Tell them I am here to strengthen your world. Tell them if they refuse to negotiate, I will not restore their world if it is depleted again." She sighed. "It is likely I will have to stay until Baluka's reply to my message arrives, so I will need accommodation also."

As she spoke, Oier had cringed a little at the thought of ordering the guild sorcerers about, then relaxed as he realised he could truly tell them he had no choice. Then his eyes widened with fear as he understood that his world and the next were going to confront each other directly. Only in negotiations for now, but that could as easily lead to war. He tried to gather his thoughts enough to begin the elaborate ritual for welcoming a guest who will be staying in someone's house, but she raised a hand to stop him.

"Forgive me, but I do not have the time for formalities," she told him. "As soon as I dispatch my messenger, I will be leaving."

"Where are you going?" he asked.

"To start my own investigations in Woperi."

He pressed his palms to his chest in respect. "I thank you on behalf of Telemna-vo. Please enjoy the comforts of this room while I make the arrangements."

Then he hurried away. As the sound of his footsteps echoed from the stairwell, Rielle looked around. The room was furnished both as a space to meet visitors and as a place to work. Shelves lined the walls, and both books and objects filled them. She picked up her pack, moved to one of the chairs facing Oier's desk and sat down.

Hopefully their messenger could travel fast. The longer they took to reach Baluka and return, the greater the chance her visit to Qall would be delayed. She considered the distance from Telemna-vo to Affen, the Restorers' home world. If their messenger was likely to travel slowly, she could give the woman directions to a closer Restorers' outpost, with a request for a faster messenger to continue on to Baluka.

But she wanted to be sure Baluka received her message, and the only way to do that was for the Telemnan messenger to meet him personally. Then, when they returned, she would see Baluka's response in the messenger's memory, and perhaps see a hint of his true intentions.

She would go herself, but after she had investigated the situation in Woperi, she wanted to seek the reason for the weakening of this world. It might be something simple and easily resolved. Perhaps it didn't have anything to do with the Peri. Perhaps an otherworld sorcerer had taken up residence in Telemna-vo and was attempting to learn pattern-shifting.

Whatever the reason, I'll hand the task of dealing with it to Baluka.

It's not my place to interfere in the politics of worlds. She had already involved herself more than she ought to by demanding these worlds begin negotiations. *I will do no more*, she decided. *My failed negotiations in Doum and Murai taught me that no matter how powerful I am, I don't have the expertise or knowledge to be a negotiator. I can so easily do harm when I think I have done good. Baluka has thousands of generals and experts to call upon for advice.*

And she was not going to be tricked into doing Baluka's job for him. As Tarren had said, she was the Maker. Not the Negotiator, or the Warrior, or the World Problem Fixer. Crossing her arms, she scowled at the doorway, only to find a young woman staring back at her.

Leaping to her feet, Rielle managed to smile, and invited the messenger into the room.

CHAPTER 5

B aluka had once told her it was easier to deal with a world if all or most of the people in it were united under one form of leadership and administration. That made negotiating peace simpler, and punishing the culprits if agreements were broken more effective. Worlds that were considered unified were not as rare as Rielle had expected, partly because they were considered so even if some of the people within were in rebellion against the leadership. Since the usual way a world became unified was by one country or empire conquering the rest, some sort of resistance always existed, but ultimately nothing convinced enemies within a world to cooperate with each other like an external threat.

Unfortunately, Woperi was not a united world. Most of the humans populating it didn't even call it "Woperi" – which meant "good soil" in the language of the Peri, the country that had started the cycle of revenge with Telemna-vo. The non-Peri occupants Rielle had seen so far lived a basic tribal existence on land dominated by gigantic plants like the one she had seen on arrival in the neighbouring world. The Peri were the most sophisticated of the peoples she had found.

Their laws ensured that the growth and removal of the giant plants were controlled. Areas were cleared for crops, the wood put to good use, then allowed to go wild again when the soil's nutrients were depleted. This had made the Peri prosperous, giving them time to spend on activities other than meeting their basic needs. They had a society of sorcerers that had, perhaps ironically, been founded by a woman from Telemna-vo centuries before.

Rielle had learned this and much more by skimming minds while sitting on a ridge outside the main city. She didn't want to meet the locals. They might assume she was there to help them against the Telemnans. It was up to the Telemnans to make contact and seek peace with the Peri. She was not here to play negotiator.

The local sorcerers had their Telemnan counterparts on their mind a great deal at the moment. Partly this was because the Telemnan sorcerers *had* begun negotiations, but also because the Peri suspected their neighbours of stealing magic from their world. They'd been more active in seeking the source of their world's weakening than had the Telemnans, but all but two of their sorcerers were too weak for world travelling, so their investigations involved long journeys through the plant-tangled wilds.

Rielle had spent each day since her arrival in Woperi looking for the place from which the magic had been taken, then returning to spy on the evening meetings of the Peri sorcerers. She'd barely slept, frustration keeping her awake when she did attempt to rest. Better to spend that time searching, she reasoned, so her responsibilities would be taken care of as soon as possible. Now, as twin moons rose over the forest and the latest meeting was called to an end, she stood, shouldered her pack, drew in a deep breath and began skimming across the world.

Each time she'd explored Woperi, she'd travelled in a different direction. The previous day she'd skimmed over an ocean and arrived in a continent too dry to support the enormous plants. To her surprise, the third city she'd found was familiar, and she realised she had visited this world a few cycles ago on their way to another. The sorcerers here had also noticed a lessening of magic recently, and were deliberating whether to contact the Restorers. They, like her, suspected an otherworld sorcerer had tried to become ageless in their world. Rielle had wondered if the Peri sorcerers were imagining the depletion of their world, but now she knew it to be true. Their world had been strong during her last visit, and it would take considerable sorcerous activity to reduce it to the current level.

At every city she found, she stopped to read minds and look for currents in the magic. It would have been an easy way to find the place magic had been taken from if there had been no people in this world generating it. The outflow of magic from cities and towns overwhelmed all but the strongest currents.

But it was unlikely she'd find evidence of someone learning pattern-shifting in cities anyway. Sorcerers attempting to become ageless in a populated world tended to do so away from people. While the Restorers did not disallow sorcerers learning to pattern-shift, they had outlawed doing so in worlds where people lived. Few empty worlds contained enough magic to achieve it, however, so the punishment for breaking that law hadn't deterred sorcerers, only made them more careful about concealing their attempts.

The sun seemed to reverse as she travelled, rising before her and illuminating the land. The plant grew taller, becoming a tangle of branches piled upon branches. She stopped to catch her breath regularly, searching for minds each time, but finding only small tribal villages. When she found a group of hunters deep under the mass of vegetation, she paused to read their minds more closely.

A group of seven men, from fit elders to adolescents, walked through the natural labyrinth of tunnels formed by the branches. They were returning home from a long journey made every cycle to teach the youngest where to find rare minerals and gemstones. She was about to draw her attention away when she saw something bright through one of the young men's eyes and felt his envy. It was a pendant hanging against an older man's chest. Circular and metallic, its outer edge was notched more neatly than any tribesman could achieve with such a hard substance.

A cog, she thought. *A machine part*. A chill pricked her skin. If someone had brought war machines to this world, a far greater

disaster might befall both it and Telemna-vo than magical depletion. The young man looked at other shiny articles the older men
wore: a cylinder with six-sided holes at each end, a delicate bunch
of springs and what looked like an eye fashioned of metal and
glass. One of the elders noticed the young man staring and assured
him he would have a talisman when he had come of age.

She shifted to the old man's mind and saw a flash of memory,
of a burned patch of forest littered with strange and precious objects.
It was a long trek from their home, through other tribes' territory,
and as he traced the path in his mind, Rielle murmured a curse.
The landmarks he recalled were only visible under the vegetation.
Then one caught her attention, and she searched the landscape for
it: a plateau. In the direction she had been travelling, she found a
shadow that might be the place. The site was on top. The area had
been burned, so it would be easy to find from above.

She pushed back into the place between worlds and propelled
herself towards the shadow. As she neared, her admiration for the
hunters grew. They'd travelled a long way to the plateau base,
then climbed the steep walls to its top. The upper area was not
large, so it was no surprise that the men had found the site. The
blackened patch marring the otherwise green covering was obvious
from above. She descended towards it.

From her vantage point, the outlines of a human-created structure were obvious. A building of moderate size had been destroyed,
and not just by the fire. It looked as though it had exploded from
within, scattering stones from the walls in all directions. Large
broken slabs of rock lay in the middle, their position suggesting
they had fallen into place when the walls were blown outwards
from beneath them.

One smaller piece was not stained with soot and lay further
from the centre of the ruin. Perhaps the hunters had flipped it
over to see what lay beneath. Rielle brought herself down to hover
above the clearing. As she moved to the stone, she sensed something between worlds and stopped.

It was a path, leading deeper into the place between worlds. A sorcerer had left the world from this place. The path felt recent, but not fresh. She guessed it had been made many days before, but not as much as a quarter-cycle.

Rielle emerged into the world, heated a speck of air to create a floating light and began examining the site closely. Had the occupant destroyed it, or had it been destroyed by an enemy? She closed her eyes and sought magic. It was much weaker here. She felt no sense of its drift, except . . .

Some deep instinct stirred, setting her nerves vibrating. It took a moment before she realised why. Magic was moving towards her, slowly and steadily. From all directions.

This was the place from which it had been taken.

Her insides grew cold as suspicions grew and bloomed. Moving to the stone that had been flipped over since the fire, she examined the ground. Soil and ash covered all and a few seedlings had sprouted, but in one area this covering looked disturbed. She pushed it aside with magic and found what the hunters had discovered and hidden.

Broken pieces of machinery glinted in the light. As she uncovered more, her heart sank. Parts of war machines and the squashed walls of their outer hulls appeared. She squatted and picked up a few items, examining them. Other than some distortion from being flattened, they looked new. None of them were fully formed machines, however.

Was this a workshop? If it was, then it had been abandoned too quickly for the machine maker to take these parts with them. Were they a war-machine maker? *Or was this Zeke and Dahli's hideaway?*

Her mood lifted a little at that last thought. While she had many reasons to hate Dahli, she found she could not. The advantage – or disadvantage – of being able to read minds was that it was all too easy to see what drove a person, and sympathise. While she was still angry with Dahli for what he'd done, she also understood he'd done it out of grief and love, and the belief that without the Raen the worlds would descend into chaos and war.

She'd met too many people motivated by greed and a lust for power over others to truly damn Dahli for his actions. But it was hard to forgive what he'd done: attempting to destroy an innocent young man in order to give the Raen a new body, luring the Restorers into a battle with his followers to force Qall into absorbing Valhan's memories, killing those Restorers in the most cruel and painful way she could imagine.

The memory of that last battle started to replay again. Knowing that a sorcerer would, as he or she materialised in a world, merge with any object in the way, Dahli had sprung a trap that caused rods to fall into the space the Restorer army had arrived in. Hundreds of sorcerers had died as their bodies fused with the metal, including the only ageless Traveller, Rielle's friend, Ulma.

If Rielle had known that Ulma had died in this way before she and Qall had lured Dahli away from the battle to confront him on his own, she might not have been so willing to set him free. It was fortunate for him that she only discovered it later, when she had returned to the site of the battle.

Pushing the memories away, Rielle considered what to do next. If this had, indeed, been Dahli's lair, should she follow the path? What if she found him? Would her anger overwhelm her sympathy towards him, and make her do something she'd regret later? Fear of that regret tempted her to ignore the path, but if war-machine makers were targeting these two worlds, Baluka needed to know. And once she had informed him of the true reason for these worlds' magical depletion, she would be free to travel to her own world and check on Qall.

Swallowing her reluctance, she slipped a few machine parts into her pack, drew in a deep breath and pushed out of the world. The ruins and charred forest faded to white as she started along the faint path, then new shadows formed, gained a hint of colour and coalesced into shapes. Soon she could see a bleached scene very different to the one she had left. She would arrive in a rocky gully, the only vegetation a scattering of dark tussock grass. As more details became clear, she realised the grass wasn't dark by nature but blackened, and the rocks around her were piled and scattered in a way that suggested they'd been blown outwards. Finally, as she drew even closer to the world, streaks of ash became discernible.

Air surrounded her, and she drew in a deep breath, the warmth of it filling her lungs. At the same time, she created a shield around herself in case the machine makers were close by and spooked by her arrival. To her relief, a search for minds found none. A scan for magic told her this place was weak, but the further she stretched the stronger it was. As in the ruins of the last world, magic was flowing towards her from all directions.

The landscape and building materials might be different, but the site was otherwise the same as the ruin she had just left. Scuffing the ground with the toe of her shoe, she wasn't surprised when she uncovered a metallic shine. She crouched to examine the ground, digging up more machine parts. These were partly melted. She slipped some into a different pocket of her pack. Examining a nearby rock, she discovered that the side facing the house glistened as if lightly polished. The blast that had destroyed this place had been very hot indeed.

She could not discern whether it had been loosed by the occupants or an attacker. The leftover machine parts suggested a hasty exit, but then they might have been of such low value that they weren't worth the hassle of transporting them. Whatever the reason for their exit, the magic flowing towards her suggested the depletion of these two worlds had occurred at the ruins.

The amount of magic used was far more than would be needed to destroy the buildings or make and run machines. Tyen had told her that mechanical magic was very efficient, requiring little power. This was why war machines were so appealing to non-sorcerers. It gave them a way to use magic despite having no or little magical ability. Unfortunately, since most sorcerers could easily defend against them, war machines were more often used on defenceless humans than on sorcerers.

Had these two buildings been factories for making war machines? They seemed too small for that. Perhaps instead they had been the workshops of inventers. Had their operations been discovered, forcing their hasty abandonment? Or had they been levelled when the occupants left, to hide signs of their presence? Were the machines made here now attacking innocent people somewhere else in the worlds? Rielle pushed out of the world, disturbed by the thought. Another path led away, leaving Telemna-vo. Should she follow it?

No, she decided. *I've spent too long here already. This is for Baluka to investigate. I will send him another message informing him of the sites.*

She skimmed upwards, searching for familiar landmarks. The Telemnan sorcerers had provided her with maps of their world when she'd first arrived, and soon enough she recognised the shape of a coastline. Navigating by the direction of the sun's light, she shot off in the direction of their city.

Fortunately for the peoples of Woperi and Telemna-vo, the machine makers were gone. Whatever they'd been doing to weaken the worlds had stopped. Hopefully that news wouldn't bring an end to the two worlds' negotiations for peace. After stopping three times to breathe, she reached the forest and soon afterwards found the city of Ka.

Descending to the guild building, she materialised in Oier's room, causing him to jump.

"Maker Rielle," he said. "Welcome back."

"Thank you. I have found the source of the weakening. Call a meeting of the Masters and invite the Perian representatives – they are still here?"

"Yes." He called out for messengers, and two young apprentices hurried into the room, listening intently to his instructions to find the council members and prepare the meeting hall.

As the pair hurried away, Rielle considered what she would tell the sorcerers. She drew one of the machine parts out of her pack. It was flat and circular, with a hole in the centre. One side had melted into a nubbly straight edge. Perhaps the chance they might face a machine army in future would persuade the people of both worlds to continue cooperating. A common threat could unite neighbouring worlds, too.

A single set of footsteps echoed in the stairwell. Rielle turned to see the messenger she had sent to Baluka enter the room. The woman pressed her palms together.

"Maker Rielle," she said. "I have delivered your message and I bear a reply."

Rielle's heart skipped. "Please relay it now, unless it is for my ears only."

"It is not," the young woman said. "Baluka, Leader of the Restorers, says his instructions have not changed. You are to strengthen Telemna-vo."

Looking into the woman's mind, Rielle saw no further clue to Baluka's intentions in her memories of their meeting. He had merely listened to her message and stated the reply she'd just delivered. Suppressing the urge to sigh, Rielle nodded, and gave the young woman the melted cog, together with instructions to find a nearby Restorer base and leave a new message, which would be passed on to Baluka through the usual channels.

His decision annoyed her, but she would deal with that later. For now, it was more important to consider the repercussions of strengthening Telemna-vo and not Woperi. Would the Telemnans take advantage of their stronger position against Peri? Rielle rubbed a finger against the molten edge of the metal disc. *Probably, but it won't mean warfare. They have no battle experience or training and they don't like direct confrontation. The Peri are the same. Still, people can change their minds and ways.* Doum had taught her that.

She nodded to herself as she decided what she would do: restore Telemna-vo *and* Woperi. Encouraging both worlds to form an alliance in case of attack by machines, too. Baluka might not like her strengthening the Peri's world without consulting him, but she had told him when she had begun working for him that she would, occasionally, restore a world if she judged it beneficial. If he objected, she'd remind him of that, and perhaps he'd be a bit more considerate of the situations he put her in.

Within a few hours she'd be free to go. What was supposed to have been a simple visit to restore a world had delayed her by a couple of days. She could only hope Qall wasn't relying on her to arrive exactly a cycle since her last visit.

CHAPTER 6

The heat of the sand seeped up through the soles of Rielle's shoes. Warm, dry air filled her lungs. It held a scent that was familiar, unique to this place and stirring both longing and a near forgotten fear. Breathing in deeply, she looked down on the city of her birth.

Five cycles ago it hadn't occurred to her to wonder how Qall had known exactly where to enter her world to arrive so near Fyre. Other matters had crowded her thoughts, like whether he had become Valhan and was going to kill her, if Baluka and the Restorers were being slaughtered back at the site of the battle, and wondering whose side Tyen was really on. A cycle later, at their first reunion, Qall had explained that it was the place where Valhan had entered her world. The Raen had arrived very near her home, before she'd even existed.

It was a strange coincidence, but when she considered that Valhan had visited many places within countless worlds in his thousand-year-long life, she realised it wasn't. He may have known of her world before the war that stripped it of magic many centuries ago. He might even have visited Tyen's world before it became magically depleted.

She had noted that, while the sorcerers in Telemna-vo and the Peri knew of the Raen, neither people had worshipped him as a god. He was the ruler of all worlds and the few times he had visited he'd been obeyed without question, but they neither grieved nor were relieved that he was dead. They had accepted the Restorers' rule in his place with the same passivity. When a world was used to a powerful but distant otherworld ruler being in charge of matters that didn't concern them most of the time, they didn't see anything strange in new otherworlders replacing them.

It was now Baluka's job to encourage the two worlds to come to a peace agreement. She'd sent him a report outlining all she had done and learned, and the locations of the two ruined buildings containing evidence of machine construction. It was up to him to investigate the reason for the weakening of both worlds. Finding the source had delayed her too much already.

She could not help speculating, however. Tyen had told her that his home was weak thanks to the overuse of machines. The sheer number of them was the problem rather than the amount of magic each used, along with the fact that they now did many of the creative jobs that people used to do, so less magic was generated. There could not have been many machines at the two ruined buildings, so they couldn't be the source of the worlds' weakening. More likely it was the work of one powerful sorcerer, or several moderately strong ones.

As Rielle turned her mind to her destination, she mused that machines were never going to be a threat to her home world. What point was there in invading with very little magic?

I guess someone might, if there were natural resources to take, she thought. Visitors would have to carry enough magic to be able to enter and then leave her world again, but that wasn't hard for a strong sorcerer. It was running out of his store of magic that had stranded Valhan here, not just that very little magic existed to replace it.

Only one sorcerer was needed to take an entire army into a world. And in a near-dead world the locals had almost no magic to fight back with. If a powerful sorcerer learned of her world's existence and had reason to invade, nothing would stop them.

She shuddered. Over the cycles since Valhan's death she had witnessed countless ways that humans could be cruel to humans.

Conquest, slavery, brutal rulers, exploitation. The more she understood how and why these things could happen the more she worried
that just knowing about such evils could change her for the worse.
Was that how Valhan had became so callous? Did he simply grow
used to it? Yet she feared ignorance. *You can't avoid a disaster if
you can't recognise the signs it's coming.*

Looking at the city of Fyre, she asked herself yet again if she
missed her home.

No.

Would she care if her world was invaded and enslaved?

Yes. She had many reasons to dislike her world, but she would
not wish such horrors on anyone.

Not her parents, who hadn't been particularly warm or caring
towards her, their main concern that she marry for their social
advantage even if that meant to a degenerate or cruel member of
the city's great families.

Not the citizens of Fyre, who had rejected her for using magic,
though she had been tricked into it by a "corruptor".

Not even the priests, who had sent her to an isolated prison
where they believed she would be forced to bear magically talented
children – and where she might still be if Valhan, posing as an
Angel, hadn't secretly taken it over many years before and sent
the magic users to places where they could spend their lives
generating magic in penance for their sins.

And not all of the people she had known had been heartless.
Not Narmah, her aunt, who had taught her to paint and provided
love and support when Rielle's parents hadn't. Not Izare, her first
love. Not his friends, who had welcomed her unconditionally to
their circle. Not Sa-Mica, the priest who had helped her start a
new life. Not Betzi, and the Schpetan weavers she had lived among
for five years. Not the countless other people she had never met,
who had never heard of her, who hadn't even been born yet.

She began walking. Slipping the straps of her pack off her
shoulders, she unclipped them from the sides and linked them

together into one handle, slung over her shoulder. She took her scarf from around her neck and draped it over her head, tossing each end, weighted with beads, over the opposite shoulder. The previous four times she had visited her home she had worried needlessly that she would be recognised. Her family had moved to another city, as had Izare. The priests who had cared for the city were gone. It was easy to forget that fifteen cycles had passed since she had been exiled, and while she had aged for five of them, the ten she had spent ageless had given her the health of youth without the adolescent softness. She was physically only about five cycles older than when she'd left.

That, oddly, provided the best disguise. Once, two cycles before, Rielle had passed one of the girls she had attended temple classes with. Now a mother of two young children, Tareme had looked twice when she'd seen Rielle, then shook her head and averted her eyes politely. Curious, Rielle had followed her to a house, then released enough magic to imbue the building so she could read the woman's mind. She saw that Tareme was thinking that the stranger had reminded her of the dyeworker's daughter, but couldn't be. Rielle would be much older, if she hadn't died years before.

That, and the absence of anyone Rielle had been close to, made it feel as though the city of her childhood was now populated by strangers. Though it was a melancholy place to her now, at least this made it easier to visit. The distance it gave her allowed the part of her that had been wounded by the rejection of her people to heal.

She'd heard other rumours about herself from Qall, many of them amusing. Sa-Mica had returned to his homeland with tales of an Angel who took a Fyrian woman with him when he returned to his realm. Some priests thought it nonsense, and that Mica was half-crazed. Others thought the Angel hadn't taken Rielle with him but had torn her soul apart as was supposed to happen to users of magic. In a few places in her world, people believed Rielle had become an Angel. Considering that Valhan had never been an Angel, but a powerful sorcerer, that could be considered a truth of sorts.

Her shoes met the start of stone pavement. A bridge stretched before her. She crossed, as always feeling a chill as she remembered when she had walked the other way in chains, covered in bruises and rotting matter from the citizens who had gathered to see off the latest "tainted" magic user. On the other side lay the main road that spiralled inwards to the city centre. She followed this for a short while, passing the location of the dyeworks that had been her home, now demolished and replaced by housing.

Turning off the main road, she entered the artisan quarter. Little had changed here since she had walked these streets as a young woman caught in a secret, and then defiant, love affair with a famous artist. The area she headed for was nowhere near the vibrant one she had lived in, however. Closer to the houses of the merchants, it was a place where a woman in exotic, fine clothes would not be out of place. Here she found a little temple, barely bigger than her family's shop had been, and stepped inside.

The shadows within were cool and welcoming. She moved to a seat and settled down. The priest would soon notice her and bring her a message from Qall letting her know where she would find him.

It did not take long. The man emerged to greet the visitor, stopped as he recognised her, then inclined his head respectfully and retreated.

She waited.

And waited.

She was about to rise and seek him out when someone entered from the main door. Turning, she saw an old woman hurry into the temple and look around. As this visitor saw Rielle, she gasped.

"It *is* you!"

At the voice, Rielle leapt to her feet. "Narmah?"

"Yes!"

Her aunt hurried forward. She had aged significantly, but her eyes were bright with vitality. Rielle stiffened as Narmah threw her arms around her, then she relaxed in the woman's embrace. It had been a long time since anyone had been this close and familiar. Too long.

"Sit," Rielle urged, gently pulling away. Narmah obeyed, her gaze never leaving Rielle's face. "Tell me, what have you been doing?"

Her aunt laughed. "Nothing as exciting as your life since you left here!" When Rielle paused to consider how to respond to that, Narmah tilted her head to one side. "Not all exciting, I suppose. You can fill me in on the details in a bit." She patted Rielle's arm and grew serious. "First I can tell you your parents and brother are doing well. Rumours of scandal still cling to them, but the people in Palper don't know the details and they like your family's products too much to shun them. Your family isn't as rich as it once was, but it's comfortable enough."

"Including you?"

Narmah scowled. "Not at first. They blamed me, you know. I blamed myself for a long time, but when I got the message from your friend last year, he told me the truth. I wasn't able to tolerate your parents' scorn any longer, so I took up his offer of a home in Fyre in exchange for watching for you."

"You mean Qall?"

"Yes. He arranged a small apartment for me so that I could be here when you returned, as he wasn't sure that he would be."

"I see. And what were you to do once I arrived?"

"Tell you where to find him. Tell you he is ready to leave this world."

A thrill ran through Rielle's body, part excitement, part fear. She would no longer need to worry about him, trapped here with little magic to call upon for his defence. Unless Valhan's memories had somehow overwhelmed his personality in the last cycle. How could she be sure they hadn't? She would not know for sure until she looked into his mind. Would he let her?

If he did, and Valhan hadn't taken over his mind, what then? What would Qall do next? If he wanted her help, she would give it. If he didn't, she would let him find his own way in the worlds. *Either way*, she thought ruefully, *I will still worry about him.*

"So . . . where is he?" she asked.

"Dothu," Narmah replied. "Though that's where he expected to be three days ago. You are a little late."

"Yes." Rielle scowled. "I was delayed."

"I suppose you must go straight away, as a result." Narmah sounded sad.

Rielle shrugged. "I'm sure he can spare us a little time to catch up."

Her aunt's mouth stretched into a broad smile. "I have wanted this meeting for so long, and more so since Qall hinted at your adventures. Tell me everything!"

"That *would* take too long." Rielle chuckled. "So let's start by you telling me what Qall has told you, then I'll add what I can to that."

Nodding, Narmah drew a deep breath and began.

CHAPTER 7

D espite Qall having already told Narmah tales of other worlds and what sorcerers could do, the woman's eyes widened with astonishment when Rielle began to fade from sight. Surprise was definitely better than horror, Rielle mused. She had always expected Narmah would, at the least, disapprove if she heard that her niece had not only learned to use magic, but embraced it. Whatever Qall had told the woman had overridden the repulsion that people of this world felt towards the "tainted".

When Rielle judged herself far enough away that people would have to concentrate hard to see her, she gave her aunt a final wave, then propelled herself up through the roof of the temple. Once she was high into the sky, she brought herself closer to the world so that she could see it better. Getting her bearings from the landmarks below, she skimmed north.

Dothu was a small village on the other side of the mountain range in which the Mountain Temple was located, where she had been sent as punishment for using magic. It had grown up around another isolated temple, but one in which priests received training in magic. Learning that Qall had taken her advice and found a more secretive place to live had brought her a great deal of relief. He had made some unwise decisions when he'd first settled in her world, and always seemed to be scrambling to survive the consequences.

When she had first left him, four cycles before, he had headed into Fyre. Having changed his appearance so he looked like an Angel, his presence had caused quite a stir. He'd admitted to Rielle later that he'd had nothing more than vague plans for what to do next, but had assumed that if Valhan could pass as an Angel then so would he.

He was right, but he'd underestimated the complications of appearing as an Angel to an entire city of believers. As he'd arrived, the citizens of Fyre had been too astonished to do more than follow and stare, none daring to approach him. He'd arrived at the temple unmolested. The priests were frozen by astonishment and terror, unsure what to do with him, so he'd requested quiet rooms for contemplation. They gave him the Head Priest's surprisingly luxurious quarters, where he'd had time to consider what to do next.

He'd decided belatedly that announcing his presence to all had been a mistake. With little magic to call upon, he could not perform the miracles the people would expect. He was vulnerable, too. He'd assumed the priests would protect him without question, but when he let out enough magic to allow him to read minds, he saw that some were sceptical, believing him to be a faker.

But they left him alone, which gave him time to come up with a story that the doubters would go along with. He told them that the Angels had decided that one of their number must live among humans every few generations to best judge whether this world was ready to be restored to full magical strength. This was supported by the Angel who had visited previously – Valhan – who they believed had found the world unworthy and stripped it of all magic before leaving. Now Qall added a warning: the Angels would destroy the soul of anyone who deliberately harmed him or stood in the way of his task.

This the priests accepted. Some realised that full restoration of the world's magic would rob them of the power they had over people. They dared not obstruct him, but instead tried to show him the worst of the world to convince him it was not ready. Some showed him criminals and the state of the poor; others introduced him to the wealthy and powerful; both meant to show him how corrupt humans were.

The sceptics expected him to seek power. Instead he spent part of his time observing the world and the rest in "contemplation". He gave equal attention to all that he was shown, be it humble or sophisticated, virtuous or corrupt. During the time he spent alone, he accessed Valhan's memories and knowledge – which had been transferred from the man's desiccated finger to Vella, Tyen's sentient book. He had discovered his true identity – the boy he'd been before Valhan had removed his memories in preparation for imprinting his own. He learned he had been nobody significant despite his strong magical ability, since he'd been too young to have made an impression on his world, let alone all the worlds.

Rielle had assumed he'd seek everything Valhan had known about her, since he needed as much insight into the people of her home world as possible. But what the Raen had known about her was of limited use. She had not truly lived among the rich, powerful families of Fyre who sought Qall's attention now. Neither had Valhan. Qall could only learn about them through his own experiences.

He soon discovered that mingling with them had risks, and as hard as he tried, he could not always avoid being drawn into political games. He'd eventually decided to escape by travelling the world – something the priests were all too willing to facilitate by then. This did not make it difficult for Rielle to find him, as he'd always ensured that he sent a message to the priest of the little temple containing his expected location on the day she arrived.

Rielle paused to breathe at the base of the mountains, then pushed on. As the jagged peaks passed below her, she wondered if Qall was truly ready to be released from her world. During her visits they had talked about devising a test to confirm that Valhan hadn't taken over his mind, but they had never settled on what it would involve.

Among the many obvious reasons to hope he was ready to leave was her discomfort with him pretending to be an Angel. It wasn't that it offended her beliefs, since she had cast them aside, but it was still a deception. Given the choice between honesty and his safety, however, she would always choose to protect him.

Deep, winding valleys twisted back and forth down to a scrubby plain, the river that had shaped them converging into three main arteries that emptied into a flat blue sea. One contained a small lake and it was to this that she headed. Walls ringed the edges of the largest island within the lake. Inside them lay hulking stone buildings in a cluster at one side, and cultivated lines of greenery on the other.

Rielle did not descend into the temple grounds, but instead veered towards the small village that squeezed itself between steep valley walls and the lake's edge. Both village and temple were known as Dothu, so Qall could be in either. More likely the temple, though, if he was still pretending to be an Angel.

Habit had her searching for a quiet, out-of-the-way place to arrive unnoticed. She found it in a shelter for domesticated animals, currently empty as the occupants were out on the steep slopes behind it, grazing. Air surrounded her, heavily fragrant with dust and animal smells. Her breath caught in her throat and she resisted the urge to cough. When she had recovered her composure and her lungs were refreshed, she let out a little magic and searched for minds.

The closest were the couple who owned the barn and animals, working in a house nearby. Next nearest was their son, watching over the beasts. As her magic spread, she caught the minds of several more villagers. One, a middle-aged woman of means, sensed the wave of magic wash into the area and grew both curious and wary. She did not know what it meant, but it had happened several times in the last half-year.

Something the priests are doing, on their island, the woman guessed. *Though this time it's not coming from the direction of the temple.* She'd wondered if the occurrences had been the doing of that strange young priest who'd arrived about the same time. *The unnervingly pale one – though very handsome despite that. The young women think he looks like an Angel.*

But he was gone now, so it couldn't be him. Maybe it never was. The woman wanted to get up and seek out the source, but a well-honed sense of self-preservation kept her sitting in her chair, fingers automatically guiding the fibres of the animal fleece in her hands as it was drawn and twisted into the spinning wheel.

Rielle frowned. The face in the woman's mind looked much like Qall's, and people of his colouring were unusual in this part of the world, yet this strange priest was not here. How long he had been gone, Rielle couldn't see. The woman's thoughts had not been precise on timing. Several days was the only impression she'd given.

Stretching her senses out further, Rielle let out enough magic to reach the island temple. Sweeping across several minds, she noted a general feeling of calm and boredom after a time of excitement. One mind stood out, the misery and anger within it a stark contrast. The owner was a young priest named Gere. Rielle concentrated on his thoughts.

And nearly shied away again. Memories of moments with his lover flashed between angry, heartbroken resentment at those who had parted them. Watching recollections of lovemaking always felt as rude and inappropriate as secretly doing so in person. A few facts were immediately clear: Gere's lover, Sa-Kal, was a man, was handsome and an Angel . . .

Sa-Kal? Kal? Qall?

Rielle blinked in surprise. Was she mistaken? Watching the priest's spiralling thoughts, she became ever more certain. Nobody else here looked anything like Qall.

The last time Qall showed interest in anyone, it was a rich young woman, Rielle recalled. It was one of the reasons the priests had been happy when Qall decided to travel. Though the family knew their daughter was not chaste, they wanted her to settle down and marry, and a dalliance with an Angel who would eventually return to his realm did not suit their plans at all.

Gere was revealing more as he stewed on Sa-Kal's departure. He had been told his lover had left, but he nursed a suspicion that it had not been willingly. Something in the manner of Gere's superior had suggested it.

Now Gere was worrying, and Rielle in turn could not help joining him. What would the priesthood do to Sa-Kal? Surely nobody would risk harming him. He was an Angel. He'd warned them that the other Angels would destroy the soul of anyone who did. But Gere could see ways around this. Someone whose soul was already forfeit, perhaps because they had used magic, might be persuaded to kill Sa-Kal if the reward was attractive enough. Whoever arranged for them to harm Sa-Kal might still attract the Angel's punishment, but perhaps not if they didn't know that Sa-Kal was an Angel.

His fears were doing nothing to ease Rielle's anxiety. She moved away from Gere and sought other minds, hoping to find out where Qall had gone or been taken, and why. A fruitless search for the Head Priest followed. Most minds were now focused on a ceremony. From those observing the proceedings she learned that the High Priest Sa-Wan had left with Sa-Kal. They did not know where the pair had gone. They did not even know that Sa-Kal claimed to be an Angel.

The rest of the priests were too involved in the ceremony to let their minds wander to recent events. Rielle resigned herself to waiting and watching. Then, just as one of the senior priests thought that his duties would soon be done, she heard a sound close by. Bringing her attention back to her immediate surroundings, she looked around, seeking the source of the noise. Shadows flickered beyond the door of the barn, and she heard the scrape of a rusty latch.

Taking a quick, deep breath, she pushed out of the world. The building faded to a grey shadow. A rectangle of white appeared, a vague shape moving within it. The farmer's son had returned, she guessed. With her hiding spot compromised, she propelled herself upwards and hovered over the village.

She sought another place in the village, then changed her mind. The closer she was to the minds she wanted to read, the less magic she needed to release. She skimmed over to the island and emerged in the world above the temple, hovering on a support of stilled air. Using her eyes and the minds of those below, she pieced together the gist of the interior layout, seeking a secluded place to arrive. The ceremony had ended, and most of the occupants were leaving the main hall. Novices headed towards their quarters or to lessons. Priests scattered to begin a variety of tasks. The only two people that weren't moving were in isolation as punishment for a sin or small crime: Gere in order to prevent him chasing after Qall, and another novice for stealing.

They occupied only two of eight isolation rooms. Rielle pushed out of the world and skimmed down into one. Once in place, she released a little more magic and sought the minds of the senior priests again.

One was standing in for the High Priest, so she watched him closely. He wondered for some time how Sa-Wan kept everything running smoothly, then at last he paused to reflect that he didn't envy the man his current task, and she saw the true reason for Qall's departure.

The senior priests had been sceptical about Qall's claim to be an Angel, and when the young man's dalliance with Gere had been discovered, they'd seen it as proof he wasn't. Not because Gere was a man, but because Angels weren't supposed to be base and lustful. It was possible, they'd realised, that the Angel had been corrupted by this world. By Gere, perhaps.

Either way, the substitute High Priest thought, *it is a matter that must be dealt with – but not by us. Only the Voice of the Angels can judge if Sa-Kal is what he says he is, and whether he had been corrupted.* This Voice of the Angels was the highest authority of the priesthood, who lived in a secret temple several days' journey away, in a location only the High Priest knew of.

Sa-Kal had been dismissive when confronted, then defensive, then had acquiesced to their demand that he be questioned and judged. "I can't stop you taking me away from here," he'd told them. "Only know that I do not wish to go."

Rielle muttered a curse in her language, briefly musing that for once she was in a place where the words would be understood if anyone had overheard them. The only way she could find Qall was to seek him and the High Priest in the minds of people he might have passed along the journey to the secret temple. Tracking him this way was slow and would use a lot of the magic she carried. He was several days ahead of her and might arrive in the secret temple before she caught up.

She had no other choice, however. She must track him in whatever ways she could. If Qall died because she was a few days late, she would never forgive herself.

Or Baluka, for delaying me, she could not help thinking.

CHAPTER 8

R ielle had always been fascinated by the way that fog made objects appear larger and further away. The whiteness of the place between worlds had the same effect, enhancing the imposing size of the gates of Amete, the secret temple of the priesthood and home to the Voice of the Angels. They loomed over Rielle like the doors to a giant's world.

Each was four times the height of a man, carved deeply to depict a parade of Angels. The figures were ones she had learned about as a child, representing birth, death, drought, storm, wild, tame, fire, snow, justice and love. Valhan had claimed to be the Angel of Storms perhaps because it would be easier to convince followers that there were more angels than the eight they knew than to pretend to be one of those eight convincingly. Qall had been given the title of Angel of Justice, since he was to decide whether this world was worthy of restoration.

The priests had brought Qall all manner of local matters to settle, but he'd wisely refused to oblige, saying that the Angels trusted humans to deal with minor issues. He also avoided being drawn into conversations about theological matters, especially with those who held doubts that he was truly an Angel, to reduce his influence on the world. He had one job, and one alone, and as a result he asked the questions, but didn't have to answer any.

Several days of tedious tracking had led Rielle here. She drifted through the closest gate into its shadow on the other side. The road continued on, low houses edging either side. Everything was symmetrical: the road straight, houses identical to those opposite, central doors with the same number of windows either side. Even the rows of potted plants beside doorways were of identical size and shape. Only two elements were uneven: the many priests walking along the road, and the stance of the two guards standing either side of the gate. One had turned towards her. She glanced at him to see why.

He was staring at her, his mouth open in disbelief and shock.

She hid her dismay, turning away as if he didn't matter before propelling herself down the road. He might believe he had seen an Angel or a ghost, but more likely the latter since an Angel was not likely to be wearing travel-stained clothes and carrying a pack.

She moved quickly so that if anyone caught an impression of her transparent form she would be gone before they could question what they'd seen. Taking a side street, she sought an unoccupied place to arrive in. The openness and symmetry of the temple meant it was some time before she found somewhere suitable – a cellar under one of the buildings.

Once in the world again, she endured a savage wave of dizziness, as denying her body of air for so long caught up with her. When her sight cleared and she was no longer gasping for breath, she found herself kneeling on the floor of a liquor storeroom. Rising, she dusted herself off, then sat on a low stool next to a barrel topped with a couple of dirty glasses.

Concentrating on sensing magic, she was surprised to find it stronger here than anywhere she'd encountered so far in her world. It flowed from several points in the complex, suggesting that many forms of creativity were taking place. One of these was quite close, so she was able to release a little magic to strengthen the area even further without risking drawing notice.

Her caution was justified by what she found. The minds around her belonged to priests, and priests alone. Where a village of ordinary people might normally provide goods and services to a local temple, here priests undertook the same tasks in order to keep their home self-sufficient and secret.

This meant every person in the temple was male. If she emerged to mingle among them, she would stand out as an imposter immediately.

The fastest way to find Qall would be to appear before a priest and ask where Sa-Kal was, and read the answer from the priest's mind if he was unwilling to tell her. Then he would no doubt alert the temple there was an imposter present, however, and if Qall was in danger her questions about him might push the priests into harming or killing him.

Better to stay hidden and watch the minds around her. It would take longer, but eventually someone would think of Qall, and his location. Once she had it, she could skim to him and take him out of the world. Unless she bound and gagged him . . .

But what of testing him to see if Valhan has overtaken his mind? She drummed her fingers on the barrel as she considered. *I will take him somewhere else in this world to do so before we leave.*

She began to watch the minds around her. After some time, she reached the point where the magic she had released had thinned to the degree that she could not read thoughts any more. The only minds she'd encountered were of lower-ranked priests, who hadn't thought once about a man claiming to be an Angel in the temple. Most likely only a few priests knew Qall was here. If everyone knew a man who might be an Angel was incarcerated here, it would be sure to cause upheaval and possibly trouble.

She could release enough magic to strengthen a larger area, but that might be noticed. Instead, she decided to move to a location closer to higher-status priests. Rising above the temple, she headed towards a larger building near its centre. Entering one of the spires, she found a space within the conical peak just large enough for her to sit and scan the minds below.

No priests were thinking about Qall, but one among a group

of administrators did pause to wonder about a secret matter occupying the Voice of the Angels these last few days. The administrator didn't know about Qall, but Rielle did learn of the Voice's probable location.

Roaming through the rooms of justice even as a ghostly figure would be risky, so she searched for a place to spy from in the buildings that surrounded it. Near the kitchens she found a latrine she could pause in, lockable from the inside. Just as she located the temple's prison cells, a priestly cook came by and started to complain loudly that whoever was in there was taking too long. She was tempted to leave the door locked when she left, but didn't, instead letting him open it to an empty room and wonder if he was going a little mad in his old age.

Her hopes of finding Qall in the cells were soon dashed. They proved to be unsuitable as a place to hide, too. Open on one side, they were constantly watched by guards. These priests were attentive enough that the passing of her ghostly figure had them jump and stare in her direction, and she quickly retreated below the floor.

There she found another storeroom, this time full of cabinets. Establishing that she was alone, she emerged into the world and caught her breath as quietly as she could. Catching sight of a few oddly-worded labels, she gave in to curiosity and opened some of the cabinets. Inside were piles of documents and boxes full of personal items. None of the labels explained why the latter was here, with only a person's name written on the front of each box. Perhaps they were the earthly possessions of each priest, given up when they took their vows.

Bringing her attention back to her task, she released magic slowly and impatiently watched for thoughts to emerge from the silence. As her senses touched each mind, she listened and watched only long enough to establish if anything useful was passing through their conscious thoughts. Most were occupied with administrative tasks. Then, like a magical light sparking into existence, a mind bright with anxiety flared into her senses. This man was half afraid, half angry, and ached with exhaustion.

I travelled all this way to bring them this man pretending to be an Angel, he thought, *and now they're ignoring me. As if I was part of the deception.* Instead, the Voice of the Angel's attention had turned to a strange, scarred priest who he believed had been an Angel's human assistant many years ago, who was supposed to be able to tell if one had come to the human realm in mortal form.

Seeing the face of the strange priest in his memory, Rielle's heart skipped a beat. *But he's supposed to be dead!* Yet the scarred features were familiar, even if deepened by age. It *had* to be Sa-Mica. Who else could it be? She let out a sigh of relief. *If he sees Qall, he'll recognise him as Valhan. He'll confirm that this is the Angel he knew.*

Seeking more minds, she jumped from one to the next. After what seemed like an age, she suddenly found herself in Sa-Mica's mind. Though she had never read it before, she knew him immediately from his humourless manner and quiet intellect. Her delight at finding him was eclipsed by horror, however, as she witnessed him telling an important priest that Sa-Kal was not an Angel.

"How do you know?" the other man asked. This, Rielle saw, was the Voice of the Angels himself.

"He has the appearance of the Angel I knew," Sa-Mica said, his disappointment sour in his mind, "but his manner and way of speaking is quite different. The Angel I knew had a . . . a weight about him. You knew he had existed for thousands of years."

He was right: Qall had none of Valhan's presence. She cursed as she realised how wrong she had been. Sa-Mica would never have been fooled by Qall's disguise.

"Then we must deal to him the appropriate punishment," the Voice replied.

Sa-Mica flinched as he realised death was the likely sentence.

He had badly wanted the pretender to be the Angel, just so that he could be in the man's presence again. He had been so wrapped up in considering what he would say that he hadn't considered what would happen to the young man if he declared him a pretender. Knowing that he had taken part in the decision to execute Sa-Kal would sit uneasily with him for the rest of his days, despite knowing the youth's guilt.

Rielle moved to the Voice's mind to find out if Sa-Mica's guess was true. The man was watching Sa-Mica – noting the sadness and dismay in the old priest's face. *If Sa-Mica is unsure of his assessment, he had better tell me in the next few hours*, the Voice thought. He looked for a sign of doubt, but all he saw was sympathy for the young man, and that Sa-Mica missed the true Angel who had blessed him with his trust and favour.

Wait a moment, the Voice thought. *I am reading his mind! The magic around us has increased too much. I will have to have words with the artisan priests . . .*

Suddenly all the magic in and around the building rushed to one point. The minds within it vanished from Rielle's senses and an impression of darkness enveloped her. She stared at the cupboards around her, her awareness abruptly restricted to her physical senses.

What can I do now? she wondered. Since the Voice had stripped the area to protect his mind from being read, he would notice if she released more magic. She pushed aside panic and considered the situation carefully. She could not do anything until she located Qall. She could not read minds again in this location. Who outside this location might know where Qall was?

She was in an administrative temple building. As far as she could tell, nobody slept here. At some point, someone who knew where Qall was would leave the building. She needed to find a place from which to search their minds as they did.

That place turned out to be another wine cellar. The temple certainly had a lot of them. She released more magic and searched in vain for Qall between skimming the minds of the priests who left the building. Several areas of the city were devoid of magic, and she guessed Qall was in one of them.

Then Sa-Mica left. She watched him walk across the temple to his rooms. His thoughts lingered on Qall, but not on the pretender's location. Frustrated, Rielle wished she could ask him directly . . . then realised that, of all the priests, he was one she could approach. Surely he would remember her. If he didn't, she might still see Qall's location in his mind.

It was a risk worth taking. Pushing out of the world, she skimmed into his room and emerged. His back was to her as he leaned over a basin of water, washing his face and hands. She let out enough magic to imbue the room and waited until he had patted his face dry.

"Sa-Mica," she said.

He jumped and spun around, his eyes widening with recognition and shock as he saw her.

"Rielle Lazuli," he replied. He glanced at the door, thinking that he had locked it. "How did you get in here?"

She shrugged. "The same way I left this world, all those years ago."

He stared at her a little longer, noting there had been only a subtle change in her appearance. She looked older, but not as old as she ought to look.

"It is good to see you again."

"And you." She smiled. "I am happy to see you've not joined the Angels, as they believe in Fyre."

"As am I." He looked down at himself. "Though it will not be many more years before they will be right." He frowned and his gaze became sharp. "Are you here because I judged wrong?"

"Of Sa-Kal?" She grimaced. "No, you are right that he is not the Angel you knew. But . . ."

"But?"

"He is no pretender, either."

His face paled and he pressed his hands to his cheeks. "What have I done?"

"No more than anyone in your position would have done," she assured him. "And nothing you cannot rectify."

"You want me to speak to the Voice?"

She nodded. "But first, I must speak to Sa-Kal. And none but you must know I have."

He rubbed his palms together. "That will be difficult. He is guarded." He frowned. "If I distract the guard and you both disappear, they will believe I let Sa-Kal escape."

"I will ensure they know you acted only on my orders."

He drew in a deep breath, then let it out again. "Then we had best hurry. He is to be executed in the next hour."

Rielle caught her breath, then let it out slowly. "Tell me where he is."

CHAPTER 9

Hovering over the building where Qall was imprisoned, Rielle recalled Sa-Mica's description of the configuration of rooms and corridors inside. She got her bearings from a row of pipes projecting from the roof to ventilate the toilets below. They ran crosswise to the corridor Qall's room was located on, and the corridor stretched along the spine of the building.

She moved further out of the world so that her surroundings looked like a bad-quality painting left in the sun, then plunged downwards, passing through roof tiles and beams into an attic, then through a wooden floor into the second-level rooms. She saw a face in the shadows very close, eyes closed, and realised she was passing through a person napping in a large chair. Another sat staring out of a window, looking bored.

Hastening past, she dropped through the floor – this time of stone – and entered what ought to be Qall's cell. Uniform greyness surrounded her, but she made out a stirring of movement. She could not make out any detail, so she drew nearer to the world. It was a priest, pacing the room. As he turned, he faced in her direction. And stopped. And started walking towards her. She looked around and saw nobody else in the room.

Whoever he is, he's seen me. I may as well see who it is.

His face grew more distinct as she came even closer into the world, and at last she recognised it. She pushed herself the last distance back into the world in a rush.

"Qall," she gasped, then sucked in a deep breath as an urgency in her chest told her she'd spent a little too long in the place between worlds.

"Rielle," he said in a low murmur, catching her shoulders as she swayed. When she had caught her balance and her breath, he let her go. "Are you all right? You're a bit overdue."

She frowned at him. Why did it seem like everyone was pointing that out lately? "Yes," she replied as quietly. "Sorry about that. You did tell me last time that you would probably stay more than another cycle."

He nodded and shrugged. "I did but, well . . . circumstances changed. Things became a bit complicated."

"So it appears." It was always strange, seeing him in the priestly robes of her home world. But then, she felt stranger wearing the priest's underrobe Sa-Mica had given her, pointing out that her travel-stained clothes were hardly appropriate for an Angel. Though it did not look like priests' robes, especially as it was much too large for her and she hadn't belted it, she could not shake the feeling she was breaking some kind of taboo.

She thought of Gere then. Complications, indeed. "Are you ready to leave?"

"I am." He sighed and looked away. "Yes, it is time."

"What of the tests we talked of?"

He pursed his lips. "I'll leave that to your judgement. Either way, we can't leave here straight away. There are matters I should . . . settle . . ." He looked towards the doorway, from which voices could be heard. "Is there someone outside?"

She moved to the opening and peered out. Sa-Mica stood nearby, talking sternly to a younger priest. Drawing a little magic, she stilled the air in the doorway to help muffle her and Qall's conversation.

"Sa-Mica and the guard," she said, returning to Qall. "I've shielded us against sound. What matters do you need to settle?"

He smiled crookedly. "For a start, there's someone who will pay dearly if I don't leave this world on good terms with the priesthood."

"Gere?"

His eyebrows rose a fraction. "You met him?"

"No, I read his mind."

"So you understand why I can't just leave." His smile vanished. "We must convince the Voice that I am an Angel and Gere has done no wrong."

"I've already told Sa-Mica you are an Angel." But that wouldn't be enough, she realised. "But if he tells the Voice he has changed his mind, he'll need proof."

"If you restored this world, it would convince him."

Wrapping her arms around her body, she considered the idea. "Changing a world so dramatically usually causes chaos."

"Of course it does. I would be surprised if it didn't."

"We can't be sure that it will be for the better."

"No, but this world has been expecting the return of magic for centuries. The people here will accept the change. They may even adapt more easily than a world that wasn't expecting one." Qall's voice deepened. "Are you sure you aren't hesitating for personal reasons?"

She narrowed her eyes at him. "How do you mean?"

"This world was not kind to you. Do you still hold a grudge?" His expression did not hold any of the glint of curiosity or sympathy she had seen when they had discussed the possibility before. He was serious. His tone was urgent, and not just because Sa-Mica might lose the guard's attention at any moment. "Did you visit your parents, as I suggested?"

"No." The word came out flat and louder than she'd intended, and they both paused to look towards the doorway. When no guard appeared, she drew in a deep breath and let it out slowly. "I have no desire to, but I did wish to see my aunt again." She paused and managed a smile. "Thank you for sending her to Fyre to meet me."

His shoulders rose and fell, but his expression did not soften. She looked away again.

"I'd rather not see my parents, Qall. It would too easily influence whether I decided to restore this world or not."

"I am the one deciding, remember?"

She turned to find him smiling, a familiar amusement in his gaze. She resisted the urge to smile in reply and shook her head. "This is no game, Qall. Don't subject my world to a change that may ruin it for the sake of winning an argument."

He grew serious again. As they stared at each other, she took in his appearance properly. He was thinner, which made him resemble Valhan even more. Yet her mind no longer saw Valhan first then Qall second. He was the young man she had saved and who the Travellers had raised. *Is that test enough?* She frowned. *Probably not.*

"You don't have to restore the world much," Qall said. "Just enough to impress the priests."

She looked down as she considered it, then nodded. "That might work." Then she smiled. "It's a compromise, anyway."

"One you're willing to make?" he reminded her.

She nodded, and was surprised at the relief she felt. Sometimes when it was not clear which decision was right, any decision felt good. "What exactly are we going to say and do?"

"I've had plenty of time to think about that." Qall smiled. "What do you think of this . . .?"

A little while later, Rielle set the air around herself aglow with radiating lines of light, as the Angels were depicted in paintings. She pushed away a mild discomfort, reminding herself that the original Angels had probably been sorcerers, so what she was going to claim to be wasn't that great a lie, and stepped into the hall, followed by Qall. The guard spun around and froze, staring at her.

"Take Sa-Kal to the Voice of the Angels," she ordered. Then she turned to Qall. "I will see you there, brother." He bowed his head.

Pushing out of the world, she skimmed away, back to the administrative building where she had previously encountered the Voice's mind. She found the man pacing in a large room. The only furniture was several grandly carved chairs set in an arc, the largest at the apex. Several other priests milled about in groups of two to five. As she arrived in their midst, she set the air glowing again and let magic spill out into the room. Startled, the priests backed away a few steps, eyes wide with astonishment and fear.

The Voice had frozen, his upper body facing her and his lower caught midstep. She turned to face him.

"Arennel Vascine," she said, addressing him by name. "I am Rielle. I come to you on behalf of my brother, Qall, who you know as Sa-Kal."

He drew himself up with visible effort, then bowed. "We are honoured by your presence, Rielle Lazuli."

At once, the other priests dropped to their knees, their backs bending as they bowed to the floor.

"I am known only as Rielle now," she corrected him gently, then lifted her chin a little. "Rise, faithful servants." The priests hurried to obey. Rielle ignored all but the Voice. "Qall was sent to this world to judge whether it is time for us to restore it," she told him. He winced. She paused, examining the faces of the other priests in the room. All showed guilt and fear in some measure, and a grim acceptance. A good sign. They would accept Qall's holiness and judgement without question.

Not even the sound of breathing eased the silence. She set her gaze back upon the Voice.

"When he arrives, he will deliver his judgement."

He bowed again. "We will accept his judgement."

Lowering her eyes, she waited, motionless. The rest did not move, not even the Voice, who swayed a little towards the larger chair as if he longed for the reassurance of its sturdy majesty. Time lengthened and stretched, no doubt more agonising to them than her.

At last faint footsteps reached her ears. They grew louder, as did voices rising in argument. Rielle turned to face the doors, then sent them swinging open with magic. To her relief, Qall and Sa-Mica were striding towards the room, closely followed by several other priests.

Those priests now skidded to a halt as they saw Rielle. The first of them threw themselves onto their knees. The others quickly followed. She had to resist a smile as Sa-Mica and Qall strode with a grand dignity into the room. Sa-Mica stopped before her and knelt.

"I have brought him, as you requested, Rielle," he said.

Excellent. Now they know he was acting on my orders.

She walked towards them. "Thank you, my old friend," she said quietly, briefly placing a hand on his head, but keeping her gaze on Qall. "Well, brother. Are you sure of your decision?"

Qall nodded gravely. "I am." He stepped forward and turned to the Voice. "I have decided that this world must be restored," he said. "But . . ." – the collective sigh that followed the news was cut short by the word – ". . . only a small measure of magic will be restored. While I have seen an abhorrence of war in the hearts of humans, and I am reassured that the atrocities my predecessor found here are no longer tolerated, there is still much that disappointed me. I saw too much corruption, hate and harm and too little truth, love and healing. I hope that when one of us visits this world again it will be worthy of full restoration, not one in which the gift we bestowed has been used for ill deeds."

The standing priests and their Voice bowed.

"We accept your judgement," the Voice said. "We are humbled by it, and by your faith in us. We thank you, and all the Angels, for your gift, and promise to only do good and kind deeds with magic."

Good luck with that, Rielle thought, then reminded herself that good intentions that failed some of the time were always better than accepting and embracing the dark side of human nature. The priests of her world might have succumbed to corruption in the past, but at least most tried to benefit people and this world. *Am I actually softening up towards them? Enough to forgive them for what they did, and intended to do, to me?*

Qall had accepted the Voice's promise with a nod. He now turned to her. "That is my decision," he told her.

Which meant she must now generate magic. She had tucked a sheaf of paper and a drawing stick into a pocket of her dress, but drawing seemed too earthly an activity for an Angel in this moment. After hundreds of years waiting for the Angels to return and restore the world, something more dramatic was needed. Something visually spectacular. Something ethereal. But . . . what?

Light, she thought. *Movement.* An idea sprang into her mind, and she caught her breath. *Oh, I can do spectacular. I can do it very well.*

Drawing magic, she set a tiny point of air before her vibrating so fast it became a spark of light. She created another, and another, forming an arc. This she moved to form a crown about her head. With a push of her will, she sent the sparks flying outwards, and as they did so they left trails of light – in radiating lines like those in paintings of Angels. Letting them fade, she set another crown glowing and pulsing outwards, then another.

The priests backed away, spreading out so they formed an arc that reflected the arrangement of the chairs. The Voice drifted to his seat and dropped into it as if he'd lost all strength, his face caught in the same expression of rapt astonishment as had come over the others.

Now Rielle sent the sparks spiralling and twisting around her and Qall, creating increasingly beautiful and elaborate patterns. They were so bright they left ghostly after-images seared into her sight. She kept the sparks swirling around as she opened her senses to the magic of the world. Power infused the space around them and was flowing outwards in a great spherical wave. The minds of priests through the temple became readable as it spread, and she realised there were thousands of them here.

Yet, as always, she became aware of an absence where her eyes told her a person stood: Qall. He wore a look of wonder and amusement. The latter, strangely, reminded her of Valhan, and suddenly she realised her error.

He could now take all this magic and escape the world.

She hadn't tested him yet. There was no time to consider how. The only way she knew was the most obvious, least gentle one. However, if he opened his mind to her now, the priests might see into it and learn the truth.

Or would they? Seeking out their thoughts, she saw that they were drinking in the spectacle, entranced by her lights; knowing this opportunity to see the work of an Angel was rare, they felt they must see and memorise all of it. As long as nothing distracted them, none would notice that they could read Qall's mind, especially as they weren't used to reading minds. It might not even occur to them to try, if they did look away from the lights. She met Qall's gaze.

Open your mind to me, she commanded.

His smile vanished. For a second his eyes glinted with resistance, but it quickly faded. His chin dropped into a nod, his shoulders rose and fell in a sigh, and then he dropped his guard.

His presence appeared to her senses like the sound of a gong. His thoughts, in contrast, were high and melodic, like pipes. *What should I think about?* he asked himself. *Nothing too personal.* A memory flash of pale flesh in a candlelit room was quickly suppressed by a deliberate recollection of Vella. It was curious that the book was the first thing his mind grabbed when he wanted to think of something else. *But then, Vella also contains all my most personal memories*, he thought. *There's a strange kind of balance in that. I had to give all my secrets, such as they are, to Vella in order to take Valhan's knowledge in. Now I have to do the same to Rielle to prove I didn't absorb his consciousness as well.*

The thought that Valhan might still lurk within him frightened him, but it was an old fear. He'd never felt another mind within his own in the last five cycles. It was possible the Raen was lurking somewhere in it, waiting for the right moment to emerge. He'd tried to nudge it into waking, but nothing had happened. Perhaps only leaving Rielle's world would awaken it. Perhaps it was waiting for a particular trigger to surface.

Relief came to Rielle like the cool desert air of evening. It was not what he was thinking, but the sense of his personality that told her that this was not Valhan pretending to be Qall.

Is he not lurking somewhere I can't sense him? Qall asked. He paused, waiting for her to see something in his mind that he couldn't. *Sometimes it's like I hear him speak in my mind.* It only happened when he wondered what Valhan might have thought about something, as if Qall knew what the man would have said in response. He also heard Rielle's voice in the same circumstances, however.

Rielle frowned. The only way to be sure the Raen could not return to the world was to keep Qall trapped here, doomed to die of old age. He did not want that. He did not deserve that. If he was willing to risk having his personality overtaken when he left this world, it was his choice to make.

What do you think? she asked.

His shoulders rose and fell. *I believe I'm me. I don't want to stay here out of fear that I'm not.*

She nodded. *Then we will leave.*

His mind vanished as she turned her attention back to the magic around her. It had lessened as it had spread outwards. Though the sparks were still moving, she was not generating much magic now. She was not creating but repeating a motion. *Is it enough yet?* she asked Qall silently. His gaze became distracted as he examined the magic, and he nodded.

She extinguished the sparks. The room looked darker, now that they were gone. The Voice and his priests blinked at her and Qall or stared sightlessly as they sensed the magic surrounding them. Rielle searched their thoughts. They had not read anyone's minds.

Not even the Voice. She decided they need not be addressed again. She'd had enough of this world. Already. Again.

She held out a hand to Qall. "Are you ready?"

He nodded and enclosed her palm in his.

Drawing some of the newly generated magic, she pushed out of the world. The room faded to grey. She moved first to Sa-Mica's room, where she had left her pack. Gathering it and another few breaths, she pushed into the place between again.

"*Head north,*" Qall said. The words sounded to her like he had spoken them, but his mouth had not moved. Even after all these cycles, the disembodied voices of her companions in the place between worlds still disturbed her. She frowned at him.

"*Why?*"

"*We need to fetch Vella. She was taken from me in Dothu.*"

"*You didn't tell me that before!*"

"*I didn't get a chance. We were too busy working out how to convince the Voice that we are Angels. Nice light show, by the way.*"

She ignored the compliment and accompanying grin. If she'd been able to breathe, she'd have sighed. Instead she settled for rolling her eyes.

"*Tyen will never forgive you if anything has happened to her.*"

"*I know.*"

"*I trust you know where they took her?*"

He nodded. "*Head north.*"

Moving up through the building into the shadow of a night sky, she got her bearings and skimmed away.

CHAPTER 10

"So," Rielle said as they began walking up the steep mountain path. "Gere."

Qall laughed. "Shocked?"

"No, just surprised. The last person you were infatuated with was a rich young woman, and before that, a Traveller girl."

"Well, I was very young and having someone propose to you is very flattering."

"You're not interested in women, then."

He chuckled. "I'm not *not* interested in women. Or men. With Gere . . . I was curious." As she looked at him sideways, his smile widened. "I saw enough in Dahli's mind to know men might be just as appealing to me as women. By the time I met Gere I was ready to test that theory, and Gere was willing though he knew I wouldn't be around long." He paused. "My theory proved to be right."

Dahli's name had sent a chill down her back. "Dahli didn't do anything—?"

"No," Qall replied firmly. "You are right about him. His ruthlessness was entirely due to Valhan's influence, though I suspect he'd be so again if anyone he loved was threatened."

"That's not a comforting thought."

"No. Especially not for the one he loves. I wouldn't want to be his reason for killing so many people."

A dark shadow had appeared in the rock wall ahead. No carvings or signs of human habitation gave away the cave's purpose. Qall said no more until the whole opening yawned before them.

He stopped. "Have you ever . . .?" he began, but did not complete the sentence.

She frowned. "What?"

He looked down and away, avoiding her gaze. "With another woman."

Cheeky kid, she thought. *Hoping to see something "interesting" in my mind, are you?*

His cheeks reddened, confirming that he was reading her mind, but he met her gaze and lifted an eyebrow.

"No," she told him. "I have known women who have, and no, I didn't spy on their thoughts. It would have been an invasion of their privacy."

Qall looked sheepish. Perhaps too chagrined. She did not want him interpreting her words as disapproval of his choices. She softened her tone. "It doesn't bother me who other people love, as long as they don't hurt anyone," she told him.

He smiled, then as quickly became serious. Turning his attention to the dark void before them, he sighed. "I've stayed here before. The Head Protector, Sa-Olm, is a friend. That doesn't mean he'll cooperate, but I would rather try to persuade him than ruin our friendship and leave behind an unpleasant story about Angels who visited this world." He sighed. "If I'd known Vella would end up here I'd have never helped him modify the protections to deter powerful sorcerers from reaching the priesthood's treasures."

"Why did you?"

"In case I needed to hide." He grimaced. "Whether because the locals got sick of me, or someone outside this world worked out where I'd gone and decided to make sure Valhan could never return."

Rielle peered into the darkness. "What changes did you suggest?"

"Multiple vaults, all kept in darkness so a sorcerer can't find them by skimming just outside of the world. Plus several illusions, traps and decoy vaults. First an invader must get through the main gates. The mechanism for that changes each time it is opened, so a new key must be forged and the coding can only be deciphered by a priest with a rare skill in mathematics. If the gate is forced, heavy barriers fall into place, blocking off the vaults in several locations, allowing time for some treasures to be destroyed."

"Is Vella one of those treasures?"

"Probably. We'll know for certain when we talk to Sa-Olm."

Rielle sighed. "As Angels we ought to have no limitations to our powers. Sa-Olm will wonder why we are bothering to negotiate and persuade him to give us Vella." It was also likely that Vella had arrived with a letter explaining that Qall's claim to be an Angel was in doubt, and that the book should not be returned to him without first acquiring permission from the Voice.

"Perhaps we should have asked the Voice to write us a letter explaining everything," she said dryly. "That'd really convince him we're omnipotent beings."

Qall smiled. "Don't worry. I have a plan."

Rielle's eyes had adjusted to the low light, and she could now make out the interior of the cave. The ceiling curved down to the floor. She could see no door or gate. Scanning the minds of the priests deeper within the mountainside, Rielle saw that the guards had been watching them approach since they'd first arrived on the path. How the strangers had reached this part of the mountains without them noticing was a source of consternation and worry. Now, as she and Qall paused on the threshold of the cave, the Head Protector was able to see their faces and had recognised Qall.

Sa-Kal, the man thought, a shiver running down his spine. *An Angel made human, or not, if the High Priest of Dothu is correct.* He didn't think much of the man. *Sa-Wan may be a remarkably sceptical man for a priest, but he is smart enough to hold his cynicism in check until he has proof against whatever he disagrees with. Does Sa-Kal being here mean he failed?*

As Sa-Olm moved to the mouthpiece of the pipe that allowed

him to communicate with visitors, Qall stepped forward into the gloom.

"Sa-Olm," Qall said, returning to the local dialect. "I request entry for myself and my guardian, formerly Rielle Lazuli."

The Head Protector paused in shock as he recognised Rielle's name. He knew more about her than most priests. Unless he was specifically told not to, he always studied each new treasure to arrive here. Ten cycles ago, Sa-Mica's record of his encounters with Angels had arrived and had made for illuminating reading.

And yet, how do I know this truly is her*? If Sa-Wan is right about Sa-Kal, then this woman may be another pretender.*

Rielle smiled. "I am who and what he claims," she told him. "I respect your caution, as it protects the objects kept here. I will provide the proof you seek. Watch with your minds."

She stepped away from Qall, drew magic and once again created dancing sparks of light. Directing them into a swirl of patterns, she spent only a few moments creating magic before she stopped, as she did not want to strengthen the world much more than she already had.

Seeking the priests' minds, she was satisfied to see they were both amazed and confused by the sudden increase of magic. Sa-Olm gathered his thoughts with an effort and began to explain. One priest asked him if this proved she was an Angel; another asked if she was the source of the sudden strengthening of the world's magic the night before. Sa-Olm could not answer, only advise caution. His own nerves tingled with excitement. He'd had a feeling that great things were happening in the world since he had first met Sa-Kal. He turned to the Keeper of the Lock and nodded.

Rielle heard Qall let out a quiet sigh, and something relaxed within her. Perhaps retrieving Vella would not be as difficult as they feared. The sound of a dry scrape filled the space. Qall turned to her.

"Don't lie to him, even if it means not answering a question," he advised, returning to the Traveller tongue. He gestured towards a dark slash that had appeared in the dimness. "As my guardian, you should go first."

Remembering his description of traps beyond the gate, she created an invisible shield of stilled air close around herself as she stepped through. The priests weren't about to spring any without Sa-Olm's orders, but if something caused them to change their minds she'd rather be ready than not.

A short corridor followed, ending in a small hall. This was blocked by a heavy iron gate. A priest – she read that he was the Keeper of the Keys from his mind – was unlocking it from the other side. He stepped aside and kept his eyes lowered as she and Qall moved through. Once the priest had locked the gate behind them – the mechanism continuing to click even as he stepped away from it – he beckoned and led them down the hall.

A convoluted journey followed, ending when they stepped through a small, humble door and found themselves in a cosy room occupied by an elderly priest.

"Sa-Olm," Qall said, walking forward to the old man and embracing him. "I am so glad I am seeing you one more time before I go. I miss our conversations."

"As do I, Sa-Kal," the Head Protector replied, with equal warmth and wariness.

"Qall is my true name," Qall told him. "I took on a priest's name for my time in this world. This is Rielle, formerly Rielle Lazuli." Sa-Olm turned to her and bowed. He noted the travel stains on her clothing and the worn pack she carried, observing that she did not look much like an Angel.

Well, thought Rielle, *if Qall had warned me I'd be making this little side trip I'd have kept Sa-Mica's underrobe.*

She smiled. "We are not as glamorous as you imagined, Sa-Olm." Moving to one of the chairs, she sat down and sighed. "We must adopt physical form to visit a world. A body requires clothing, food and water."

His gaze brightened with interest, though he reminded himself that he must be wary of everything they told him. *Even so . . . she made more magic in a few moments than even the most gifted Maker can produce.* If he did not believe they were Angels, but they were, what then? Would they punish him for his caution and distrust? If they weren't Angels but powerful sorcerers, what would they do next?

Why were they here, anyway?

"I doubt you have come to this place merely to chat," Sa-Olm began.

"No," Qall replied. "We are here for the book Sa-Wan sent you."

The old man's face fell. "Ah."

"That puts you in an awkward position. I am sorry."

Sa-Olm shook his head. "Does it? Why do you not just take it, now that you are here?"

Qall looked at Rielle. "It is my last task as a mortal."

She resisted a smile. It was, technically, true. He would be ageless again once he had access to enough magic.

The old man nodded. "How much time do you have to complete this task?"

"Waiting for you to send a messenger to the Voice is, I'm afraid, a little too easy a resolution of my task. I must convince you to give it to me."

"And if I refuse to give it to you?"

Qall looked at Rielle. "It falls to Rielle to retrieve it."

She kept her expression serious as the old man looked at her and weighed what that might mean. What might an Angel do in order to regain one of their treasures? He suspected her search would be as subtle as her production of magic.

He also suspected he would lose his position here, if he relinquished a treasure of the Angels and this pair proved to be charlatans, and Rielle a powerful Maker but not an Angel. He did not want to leave. His greatest wish was to read as many of the books here as he could before he died. It would take a lifetime, and he had only gained this position in his middle years.

What to do? *Delay for now*, he decided. *Continue questioning them and look for a flaw in their disguise.*

"What of these accusations Sa-Wan made?" he asked of Rielle.

"That Qall is not an Angel?" she asked. "It is not my task to convince you either way," she reminded him.

He nodded. "My apology." He turned to Qall.

"Are you an Angel?"

Qall nodded slowly. "Though currently I am both Angel and not, having taken on physical form."

An evasive answer? Sa-Olm wondered. "But you were an Angel before then?"

"Yes."

"Can you make magic too?"

He nodded again. "But not to the degree that Rielle can. It is her particular gift."

Interesting. "Did Rielle create the magic that filled this world last night?"

"Yes."

The old man narrowed his eyes. "So you judged this world worthy of it?"

"I did."

Sa-Olm turned to Rielle.

"Would you have done so?"

She smiled, then made her expression serious. "No."

A chill ran down Sa-Olm's spine, then he remembered that her answers might simply be designed to intimidate him. He must stop hearing her replies as those of an Angel and consider what they meant coming from a pretender. "Why not?"

"You know my history in this world," she reminded him. "Which is why we sent Qall here. Someone needed to judge this world who did not hold a grudge against it."

The old man shivered. "I thank you for making that decision." It seemed even Angels must resist baser feelings. At once, he recalled the more troubling part of Sa-Wan's letter and turned back to Qall. "What of the claim you seduced a young priest at Dothu?"

Qall shook his head. "I did not. I did not force him to do anything he did not wish for. Nor he me."

Sa-Olm frowned. "Then it is true that you . . .?" He glanced at Rielle, his expression uncertain.

"Love is never a sin, when it is without intent to harm," she told the old man. "It can be powerful, and therefore the powerful fear it. It can be misused, so the cautious do not value it. But it is as precious as water, and as easily taken for granted."

He blinked, and she was disturbed to see he was committing the words to memory.

"It was not until Gere showed me pure, unselfish love that I realised this world was worthy of restoring," Qall added. "You said yourself, once, that love was the antidote to war."

The old man regarded Qall thoughtfully, then nodded. He drew in a deep breath and sighed. "If I give you the book, I risk sacrificing much that is dear to me. If I refuse, I fear I may be acting against an Angel — two Angels," he added, nodding to Rielle. "What will you do once you have the book?"

"We will leave this world."

"That is all?"

"Yes. I would ease your mind if I could," Qall said earnestly. "I regard you as a friend, and do not wish to place this difficult choice upon you, but great things *are* happening in this world. You must be a part of them. You have glimpsed the nature of the book."

Sa-Olm flushed and lowered his eyes. "Yes. I confess I gave in to curiosity and opened its pages, but when the text began to form, I closed it again. I did not read it."

"It contains the soul of a woman — one of our kind. She holds the wisdom and knowledge of all who have touched her. She cannot lie. She must answer all questions." Qall paused. "I want you to open her and ask two questions."

Rielle caught her breath and cast him a warning look. If Sa-Olm did so he could learn she and Qall were sorcerers, not Angels. Why would he risk this?

"The first is this," Qall continued. "'What are the Angels?' The second is: 'Why did Qall come to this world?' Will you do that?"

Rielle swallowed hard, resisting, with effort, expressing her alarm.

It took a moment for Sa-Olm to recover from his surprise and consider Qall's request. Questions crowded his mind. How could he know if it was true that this book could not lie? Why would Qall want him to ask about the nature of Angels if they were what the priesthood believed them to be? Why ask for Qall's reasons for coming to this world, if what Qall had told him was true?

It could be a ploy to help the pair locate which vault contained the book. They would be, no doubt, reading his mind as he descended to it. But a certain degree of disorientation was built into the route. Sa-Olm never knew exactly where he was under the mountain when he visited a vault. It was one of the many precautions Qall had suggested.

What proof did he have that they were Angels? *The extraordinary magic Rielle created. The fact that all minds here but theirs are open to me now. That nothing in our past and current meetings have given me reason to doubt him. That Qall clearly is free, not imprisoned by the Voice.*

What evidence did he have that they were not Angels? *Just a letter from a priest who is a known sceptic.*

He nodded. "I will do as you ask."

After the old man had left, Rielle turned and raised her eyebrows at Qall. He smiled. "Yes, I do know what I'm doing."

She shrugged and settled back in her chair to wait. Not long after, a priest arrived with food and a hot, bitter drink. She hadn't eaten a proper meal in days, so the humble meal tasted wonderful, and her attention drifted away from Sa-Olm's thoughts as he made his way past the traps and decoys to the vault containing Vella.

Qall ignored the food and sipped at his drink, seeming to enjoy the taste of it.

As the old man opened Vella, Rielle watched his mind more attentively. The inevitable truths astonished and dismayed Sa-Olm initially, but as he learned more and more, he realised that what was real and false was not entirely clear. Though Qall and Rielle had once been human, they were so powerful they might just as well be Angels, and the possibility that the Angels had originally been powerful sorcerers had been explored in some of the forbidden texts stored here. *Did it matter?* he wondered. *Whatever they were, they set down rules and laws designed to help this world recover.*

Which it had, a little, before Valhan stripped it in order to leave. He had ended the terrible shame at the Mountain Temple, but he had also been a ruthless ruler of worlds and had meant to destroy Qall's soul in order to cheat death.

Rielle had saved Qall, but a second attempt to resurrect Valhan had nearly succeeded, leaving Qall afraid that the man's mind had lodged within his soul and might overtake it. Qall had come to this world in order to trap himself somewhere with almost no magic while he worked out whether he would become a danger to the worlds.

A noble decision. He could not help asking more of the book. The questions flashed through his mind. Were Qall and Rielle good . . . whatever they were? The book confirmed it. Should he give her to them? If he thought it was the right thing to do, was the reply. The fact that she didn't say "yes" was interesting, and finally convinced him that he would.

So he had the answers Qall had told him to seek. Angels were most likely powerful sorcerers, and Qall had come to this world to protect all worlds. He could not help asking one more question: what would happen to this world now? Vella admitted she could not predict the future, but based on what she knew it was likely that more ordinary people would discover they could use magic, and if the priesthood set itself against them there would be trouble.

Though it was unlikely anyone would stumble upon the method of travelling between worlds for some time, if a powerful other-world sorcerer discovered that this was no longer a dead world they might come here seeking to rule it. The local sorcerers needed to be prepared for that possibility, whether it meant welcoming or fighting such an invader.

These revelations occupied his mind on the return journey. When he pushed through the door to their room, his brow was deeply furrowed. Qall rose and walked forward to meet him, so Rielle followed suit.

"She is yours," Sa-Olm said, holding out a worn leather bag to Qall.

Qall took the bag and smiled crookedly as he tucked it into a pocket of his robe. "Actually, she isn't. She was loaned to me. I will return her to the one she belongs to." Straightening, he fixed the old man with a direct stare. "You have my thanks, but I doubt you wish to thank me for what I have revealed."

Sa-Olm shook his head. "No, I do thank you. The truth is . . . necessary. It is not that great things have happened and will happen, but that you saving this world will have consequences, and not all of them will be good."

"You must awaken this world to that truth," Qall told him. "But do so with great care. Many will not like it. Begin slowly and in secret. Gather proof. I would not be surprised if there were books here that contained it. The great war that stripped this world was not so long ago that no records will have survived. Go abroad and seek out other sources of knowledge."

"But I am old. Even with help, it would take many years to search the library here."

Qall held out his hands. "*That* I can do something about."

The old man looked at them, then reluctantly extended his own. Taking them, Qall closed his eyes.

Dark, radiating lines flashed out from him as he took magic from the world. Sa-Olm gasped and swayed, but his body instinctively recovered its balance. The sagging skin of his face began to tighten, the wrinkles losing their depth, spots fading to leave a more uniform brown. His shoulders and back straightened. His eyes grew clearer, the dull brown deepening to almost black. When Qall released his hands, the priest looked down at them, then brought them to his face. He stared at Qall in astonishment.

"A few decades of life, at least," Qall told him. "More if you get out into the sunlight for a short while each day and eat a varied diet."

"You really are an Angel," Sa-Olm whispered.

"Perhaps we are," Qall said. "But this world needs to know there are thousands more of us than it believes, and some are dangerous. It will need its own Angels to defend it. Such a task will take years. I only ask that you begin it. Find others to help you. They will carry on when you are gone."

Sa-Olm nodded solemnly. "I will."

Qall smiled, then quickly embraced the man. "I wish I did not have to burden you so, friend, but I know no other better suited to this job." He stepped away, moving to Rielle's side. "I also wish that I could remain to help you, but I cannot. I bid you farewell, Sa-Olm. Thank you for your trust and understanding."

"Farewell, Sa . . . Qall. Thank you for restoring and caring for this world. And farewell, Rielle Lazuli. I hope when you next return you are willing to forgive it."

Rielle inclined her head. "I hope so too."

She felt Qall's hand wrap about her own. As she looked at him, he nodded, so she gathered magic and pushed them out of the world. The priest's eyes widened, then a wry smile creased his now-younger face as he faded from sight.

Once their surroundings had mostly disappeared, Rielle increased the speed of their journey. New shapes and patterns appeared as they passed the midpoint. Trees in a rocky landscape appeared and grew sharper. She moved so they would arrive a slight distance above a patch of bare, flat ground.

Cool air surrounded them. Qall let her hand go and looked around.

"Ah," he said. "Magic."

Examining this world with her senses, she detected an abundance of it. More than what her world contained. Part of her was relieved to be free, despite the fact that her world was no longer a potential trap for sorcerers.

"Did you plan that all along?" she asked.

Qall turned back to her. "What?"

"To tell him to start a new religion."

He frowned. "Not a religion. Just a group of people who might be able to lessen the problems that will come with the return of magic."

"They'll make it a religion. They know no other way."

His lower lip pushed out. "I suppose. I admit, I don't really know. They might make it an anti-religion. Whatever it becomes, it'll be based more on something closer to the truth than the old ways. Hopefully, in future, when women discover they have magical ability they won't have to hide the fact."

Rielle's annoyance and fear faded as he smiled tentatively. He only wanted to make things better. She knew he would eventually learn the hard way how sometimes people twisted your attempts to help into a way to harm, but maybe that was better than never trying to help at all.

At once, memories of Doum and Murai returned. She knew this was how she should regard her and Tyen's failed efforts in the two worlds, but until now she hadn't been able to feel more than anger and disappointment. It was why she'd resisted being drawn into local conflicts since. Perhaps she should not be so reluctant to help.

"You can only try," he told her.

She narrowed her eyes at him. "Stop reading my mind."

He grinned. "Okay."

"So . . ." She rubbed her hands together and looked around.

"What now?" She thought of Baluka and immediately wished she hadn't. "I guess we should find Tyen and give him Vella."

Qall reached into his pocket and brought out the pouch. "Why don't you do it for me?"

She took it and looked up at him in surprise. "You don't want to see him?"

"Yes, but I have other things to do first."

"Like what?"

He smiled. "Private matters."

"I see." Rielle pushed away her disappointment and a niggling worry. She had seen his mind. He hadn't become Valhan. Most likely he wanted to find his original world and family.

His gaze was low and distant now. Drawing in a deep breath, he closed his eyes. The magic around him stirred. He was taking it in, she guessed, but it was rich enough to smooth out instantly, so no radiating lines appeared around him as they had in her world. Then she realised his hair was lightening to a pale brown and his skin wasn't so white. His face had become squarer, too. When he opened his eyes, they were a dark blue.

"Qall," she said quietly. "Is this your original body?"

He shook his head. "Not exactly. The changes are superficial, and I'll have to maintain them. It's likely that the less of Valhan's pattern I have, the less of his strength I'll keep."

"Ah. But you can't travel around looking like him or people will try to kill you."

"Or become my followers." He shrugged. "Eventually they'll forget him."

She grimaced. "Not me. Or Tyen."

"No, and I'm sure you'd rather not be reminded of him whenever we meet."

He sounded grim and grown up. An unexpected lump formed in her throat. "Are you sure you want to do whatever you plan to do alone?"

He nodded. "For now."

She took his hands and squeezed them, then let them go again. "Take care of yourself, Qall."

His smile was sudden and bright. "I will. Don't worry. You'll see me again." Then he paused, and she saw the young man he truly was reflected in his face. "Thank you for coming to check on me, cycle after cycle. Thank you for believing that I'd still be me, but making sure I was. Say 'hello' to Tyen from me."

He bent forward and kissed her on the forehead. Reaching up to touch his face, she found her hand passing through it. His features were fading fast, but before he had moved too far from the world for her to see him, he winked.

And then he was gone.

She was alone.

Again.

She looked down at the pouch in her hands, fighting disappointment and sadness. This must be what it was like to see a son or daughter leave home to begin their own life. It wasn't so surprising, in that context, that he wanted to explore the worlds on his own. Who'd want a mother tagging along? The thought of her own mother following her about made her shudder, and she hoped she'd been a better guardian-figure for Qall.

She took a deep breath and stowed Vella in her pack. The thought of approaching Tyen made her hesitate, but strangely not as much as returning to Baluka. Should she let the Restorers know Qall had returned to the worlds? Qall hadn't said whether she should tell them or not. There was no danger of them seeing someone who looked like Valhan and trying to kill him now.

No, she decided. *They don't need to know. I will seek out Tyen first. Though that may not be easy, if he's trying to hide from Liftre. Still, there's an obvious place to start.*

Pushing out of the world, she headed for the only person who might know where her former lover might be.

PART TWO

TYEN

CHAPTER 1

The city of Turo stank, as only a metropolis without good plumbing could stink. The waste from each house was piped to an open drain in the centre of the closest street – if you could call the gaps of varying widths between buildings "streets". In some places these thoroughfares were so narrow that only a small ledge allowed pedestrians to hop along, from one side of the drain to the other, until they reached a wider part.

And yet, at night the city was breathtakingly beautiful. All walls were rendered with a pigment that retained light, and once darkness fell the city glowed a silvery blue. Turo needed no street lamps, and no dark corners existed for thugs and thieves to ambush their victims from. That didn't mean no crime existed, of course. Successfully tricking money out of others was a source of pride among the citizens. Many of the laws seemed to have been written by someone who regarded cheating as a game and challenge. Often only the ability to read minds kept Tyen and his friends and students from being parted from their limited savings.

Tonight he'd seen an even darker side of this city. He'd set out at dusk to the home of one of the Elders, having been hired to do the sort of menial magical tasks that paid the rent. On arriving, he'd discovered the Elder had been murdered.

Nobody in the household knew why or had seen anything, but from the minds of the servants Tyen learned that the body had been found in a locked room, with no obvious signs of the cause of death. Since sorcerers were known to be able to move through walls, the man's brother had been a little suspicious of Tyen until he'd questioned everyone and the timing of events had been established. The Elder had been alive and in company just before Tyen had arrived, and Tyen had been talking to a door guard at the time of the murder.

Everyone had been questioned, so Tyen was late returning home. When he finally pushed through the main door of the large house he rented, he found all was as quiet as he expected, and started towards his room. But as he glanced in the open doorway of the dining room, two students leapt from the chairs by the fire.

"Master Tyen!" one said. "We've been waiting for you."

"We're worried about Regur."

"He's locked himself in his room. We tried to talk to him, but he says nothing."

Tyen nodded and started down the corridor to Regur's room. The young man was a former student of Liftre. Many of Tyen's students were, but Regur was the one most traumatised by his time there. Liftre was a harsh place now. While the teachers were not yet refusing admission to those who didn't fit with their ideals and prejudices, they, and their approved students, made such entrants feel unwelcome and unsafe.

If these newcomers then left, they had few remaining choices for sorcerous training. Liftre's new founders had declared to the worlds that they would not tolerate the existence of other interworld schools of magic. Though the Restorers had refused to support Liftre's position, the tactics Liftre's sorcerers used to enforce their "law" had forced many smaller schools to close.

Some of the students driven to leave Liftre, or left teacherless when other schools had closed, sought out Tarren, but the old man could not take on many students and turned most away. He sent them to other teachers he knew of, and those students with a superior understanding of and skill with mechanical magic he sent to Tyen.

These were perhaps the bravest students of all. The machine makers at Liftre had decided they owned all knowledge of mechanical magic and were fiercely protective of it. They had formed a kind of guild and enforced their compulsory membership with threats and violence. This had not curbed the production of war machines, but instead promoted and boosted it.

Though Regur was undeniably brave and studious, the constant threat of the Liftre machine makers finding him meant his moods swung towards the bleak and paranoid on a regular basis. Thinking back over the last few days, Tyen considered what might have sparked this one. If anything, Regur had been in good spirits lately. Normally he started to get jumpy before succumbing to melancholy.

Reaching the young man's room, Tyen stopped at the door. It was the largest of the rooms and would normally be used by the head of the household, but Tyen had selected it for Regur because the young man wasn't always the best companion for other students, and Regur had noted that the route out of the building was the shortest from it. Some of the newer students had been a bit jealous at first, but if they did not understand Regur's fragility they soon decided his brilliant mind earned him the right to a little favouritism.

Tyen knocked on the door. The sound was odd, as if something heavy lay against the other side. No reply came, so Tyen called Regur's name, gently but loud enough to penetrate the door. A long silence followed. Tyen tried opening the door. The handle would not move. His heart skipped a beat.

Locked from within. No reply to knocks or calls. Just like the Elder. Had Regur been murdered, too?

Stop it, he told himself, but his concern did not fade. He didn't like to invade his students' privacy without a good reason, and had forbidden them from reaching each other's thoughts, but this was no time for scruples. Searching beyond the door, he soon found the young man's mind.

Immediately he regretted his rule of mental privacy. If the other students had known the true situation, they'd have sent someone to get him. Regur was sitting up in bed, trying to be as still as possible, staring at a lump under the blanket beside him – a war machine, set to explode if it sensed sound or movement.

A chill ran through Tyen's body. The young man looked at the far wall and resolutely thought about other things. Soothing memories, like the sound of his sister singing or the gentle landscape around the house he'd grown up in. This was keeping him calm, but was no good for Tyen. He needed to know everything about this bomb if he was going to save Regur.

The student would reveal what he knew if he realised Tyen was watching. Tyen called Regur's name again, but the young man didn't hear it. He hadn't heard Tyen knocking, either.

Quiet, quiet, Regur thought. *Keep quiet.*

Understanding came. Regur had created a shield around the room to prevent the sounds from the other students setting off the bomb. Tyen could smash down the door, but Regur wouldn't hear it.

But he would see it. And Tyen didn't need to smash down the entire door to get Regur to see him.

Drawing a deep breath and some magic, Tyen spread his hand over the wood in front of him. He created a small ring of heated air and pressed it into the surface. Smoke billowed out and the two students hovering behind him began to cough. The ring slowly penetrated, then reached the other side all at once. The circle of wood did not fall through, so Tyen quickly pulled it out. He leaned close to the hole, looking through and searching for the young student.

Regur stared back at him from the bed. Tyen looked down at the blanket and back to meet the student's eyes, then nodded.

At once, Regur's thoughts filled with recent memories. A stranger had appeared in the room not long after he had settled into bed to read. The man had said that no more warnings would be given, then placed the machine on the bed, explaining that it would explode if it detected movement, sound or the depletion of magic around it. Then the stranger had disappeared.

Tyen frowned as questions crowded his mind. *This happened some time ago. Was it before or after my customer was killed?* The Elder hadn't been blown up, however. Tyen didn't recognise the stranger in Regur's memory, but the man did not look like the local people. *No more warnings?* Tyen had received no warnings from the locals.

But he had from Liftre. He sighed. *It never seems to take long for them to find us these days.* He occasionally scanned his students' minds, but had found no evidence that any were spies. *That is a puzzle for another time. I need to get Regur or the bomb out of here.*

Gesturing for Regur to wait, Tyen turned to the two students hovering nearby, both on the edge of asking questions.

"Get everyone to shield themselves and leave the building as quickly as possible," Tyen instructed. "And do it quietly, making as little vibration as possible."

The two stared at him as they comprehended the threat, then hurried away. Tyen turned back to Regur and sought the young man's mind again.

I guessed the machine wouldn't start sensing anything until the sorcerer was gone, Regur explained. *Just after he began to fade, I threw a blanket over it.* Tyen nodded to show he understood. It had been a smart move, but it meant it was impossible for him to examine the object and seek a way to defuse it. *I'm nearly out of magic.* Regur swallowed hard. *Get everyone away and tell them to stop making noises.*

Tyen nodded again to show that it was being done. He could hear the shuffle of many feet and the occasional voice rise in question, only to be abruptly silenced. Ignoring the exodus, he concentrated on the dilemma posed by the lump under the blanket.

As far as he knew, no mechanism could sense magic beyond its physical structure, as humans could. Most likely the sensor worked by using some of the magic it encountered to keep the trigger disengaged. That meant that the bomb itself was depleting the magic around it. Fortunately, the magic here was plentiful and flowed in to replace what the mechanism used faster than it could take it.

The movement and sound detectors were more dangerous. Most likely simple disruption devices, they would be set off when a part was knocked out of place. They couldn't be too sensitive, or Regur's breathing would have set them off already.

A faint sound brought Tyen's attention back to the passageway. One of the students was approaching quietly.

"We're out," he mouthed. Tyen nodded, then waved to indicate the young man should leave.

Having guessed at how the bomb worked, he considered Regur's options. The student couldn't get off the bed without causing it to move. He had realised he couldn't hold the bomb still with magic without setting it off because when a sorcerer was in control of an area, he was also in control of the magic within it, which would stop its flow to the trigger. The young man had considered stilling everything around the bomb, but he was worried that Liftre had developed a way for a machine to detect the flow of magic around it. He could see how it might be done. Magic was nearly always moving, so for it to go still would be unusual.

Regur had contemplated surrounding the bomb with a shield and letting it explode, but he wasn't a strong sorcerer, didn't have much magic stored, and couldn't guess how powerful the bomb was. When he'd risked creating a noise-blocking shield around the room, he'd hoped it would also reduce the damage to others when the bomb exploded.

But he was running out of magic by keeping the shield in place.

Tyen considered releasing magic for Regur to take, but the young man's fear that the bomb could sense the flow of magic made him pause. Better that he shield Regur and himself, now that the building was unoccupied. But he wouldn't be able to until the student stopped shielding the room, as it prevented Tyen reaching the air inside.

Looking up at Regur, Tyen pointed to himself, then at the room, and mimed turning the handle. Regur blinked as he worked out Tyen's intention. The latch released and the door swung inwards.

Tyen leaned against the frame and unlaced his boots, slipping them off, then placing them gently on the floor. He stepped forward. An invisible wall stopped him, but the pressure immediately melted away. At once, Tyen placed a wall of stilled air between Regur and the bomb, dividing the room in half. This would not still the magic around the mechanism, since magic still existed on the other side of the room. He also stilled the bedframe in the hope that this would prevent vibrations.

Tyen beckoned. Moving very slowly, Regur unbent his legs, swivelled and placed his feet on the floor. A gradual lean forward shifted his weight enough that he could stand. Once upright, his movements were a little faster, and he padded on bare feet to Tyen, the fear in his eyes turning to relief and gratitude.

Go, Tyen mouthed. Regur nodded and slipped past into the corridor. Tyen listened to the faint sounds of his movements fade away, then drew in a deep breath and let it out again.

Alone with the bomb, Tyen considered what to do next.

He could leave and let it explode. That seemed unfair. The landlady might be an overbearing miser, but she didn't deserve having her property destroyed.

He could hold a shield around the bomb as it exploded. It was a risky option. Tyen could not guess how powerful the bomb was. It looked small, but he knew of powerful explosive compounds that could be packed into tiny capsules. The chance that his shield wouldn't be strong enough for the blast was small, but if it wasn't, he might be struck by some of the force. Tyen could heal himself . . . if he was still conscious.

However, he badly wanted to see what was under the blanket.

He needed to be certain that Liftre's sorcerers – if they were behind it – had meant for it to kill him. This was the room he would have occupied if Regur hadn't had his particular sensitivities. Also, since mechanical magic was least effective against sorcerers, particularly powerful sorcerers – and Tyen was one of the most powerful in the worlds – there must be something particularly clever about this machine.

Unless it was intended for Regur, or another student or teacher. Attack me by attacking others. Ensure no more students come to me for tutelage.

Examining the bomb could tell him how far Liftre's development of mechanical magic had progressed. Letting it explode would teach him nothing, not even how to defuse a bomb like it in future. He took a step towards it.

Perhaps I'm supposed to try to defuse it. Perhaps it is a trap.

Well, he couldn't just leave it there.

So how can I move it without setting it off, let alone examine it?

He smiled as the answer came to him.

Walking slowly and silently to the bed, he stopped before his invisible shield. Drawing on his store of magic, he enveloped himself in a thin, strong shield of stilled air. He let the wall of still air between himself and the bomb dissipate, reached down and took hold of the corner of the blanket covering the device. Then he stretched his conscious will out through the blanket to encompass the bed beneath . . .

. . . and pushed out of the world a little way.

Nothing happened. Nothing but the usual bleaching of his surroundings. The room didn't explode. The blanket remained draped over the bed and bomb, all caught in the place between worlds.

It was a strange sight.

Since learning how to travel between worlds, Tyen had been perplexed to find that nobody could explain exactly what was happening when he did. He could think, but the physical sensation of emotion was absent. He could move, in what seemed like a physical way, and before he'd learned pattern-shifting his body would have died of suffocation if he'd stayed there too long. He could take hold of other sorcerers and, since almost all were weaker than him, take them wherever he wanted. As long as he touched an object he could bring it into the place between, as well as the objects touching the one he touched if he concentrated on the space they took up.

Yet this, he suspected, was an illusion. He suspected that objects and living things didn't have a physical form outside of a world, and had formed a theory: though they were oriented with each other in a familiar way, their mass had been translated into some other state. He suspected that people only perceived them to be physical objects because the human mind had no other way to interpret what it was sensing.

For this he was grateful, in this moment, because it would allow him to examine the bomb safely. He pulled the blanket towards him and a dull metal disc appeared. It did not explode. Perhaps his theories about the place between worlds were wrong, and it was simply the lack of air that prevented whatever chemical reaction would cause an explosion, but he preferred his theory that it was no longer a physical object and so couldn't react like one.

He let go of the bed and blanket. They would slowly drift back into the world. Taking a couple of small tools out of a pocket, he soon had the machine's cover in two pieces. Within the body he found the motion-detecting mechanisms he'd expected, tiny and beautifully made. Two small squat bottles, one full of liquid, the other empty, filled most of the interior. A residue remained in the uppermost, empty bottle, telling him that two substances had been mixed. The trigger had been set off a moment before he'd brought it out of the world, but the chemical reaction hadn't had the time it needed to happen.

So, when this re-enters a world, it's going to blow up. He looked around the faded room. *Better do that somewhere it won't do any damage.*

Searching with his mind, he sensed a faint path leading away to the east. He guessed it had been made by the sorcerer who had left the bomb. There was no other path. The man had arrived and left along the same route.

Moving through the ceiling, he continued through the roof and shot up into the night sky. When the city below was a small glow, he stopped. Unscrewing the filled reservoir, he left it hovering while he checked to ensure no other explosives remained in the device. Then he put the empty bomb in his pocket and looked at the chemical mix. With a mental push, he propelled the bottle back towards the world.

He knew the moment it arrived when his surroundings went white. A muffled boom reached his ears. Just as quickly, all went dark and silent again.

Satisfied that no danger remained, he propelled himself downwards. By the time he arrived, the streets of Turo were dark with people, their faces turned up to the sky. Most expressions were of puzzlement and worry. Few would have been looking up at the time of the explosion. They'd have heard the boom and run outside to seek the source, only to find no clue about its origin.

Withdrawing further from the world so the onlookers wouldn't see him descending, Tyen dropped through the roof of his school and aimed for the hall inside the main entrance. Arriving, he paused as his body healed from the damage caused by lack of air, then walked to the door and pushed outside. At once, his students hurried towards him, most of them with expressions of worry.

No relief, he noted. He sought their minds and saw why. At the same moment, an old man in the uniform of the Elders strode up to Tyen and saluted in the local fashion.

"Teacher Tyen," he said, holding out a scroll. "I bring orders from the Elders for you to leave this world."

Tyen looked into the man's mind as he reached out to take the scroll. He saw guilt. The Elders had agreed to the demands of another otherworld sorcerer, who had threatened to destroy the city if Tyen and his school weren't sent away. The Elder who had been murdered had objected to the decision, and the others suspected he had been punished because he tried to warn Tyen.

Tyen realised his face was aching and relaxed his jaw. *Here we go again.*

"Will you go?" the Elder asked, his attempt to sound forceful foiled by the tremble in his voice.

"Of course," Tyen replied. "Unlike the man you encountered, we do not seek to harm the worlds, but to help them. We wish you only freedom and prosperity."

Turning away from the man's relief, Tyen considered his students and fellow teachers. All radiated anger and disappointment – and resignation. But also determination.

"We'll find somewhere else," one of them said, and the others nodded.

Tyen smiled grimly and straightened his back.

"You know what to do," he said in the Traveller tongue. At once, all hurried into the house to gather personal belongings and pack instruments and books. Tyen followed, forcing his mind away from the two disasters of the night to the challenge ahead. *Liftre knows where we are. They'll have scouts around this world waiting for us to leave. They may try to follow us, and if the bomb is an indication of their intentions, perhaps even attack us.*

But he had evaded them many times before and would do so again.

CHAPTER 2

The students' packing never happened quickly enough for Tyen, but he was impressed at how fast they managed it this time. He'd taken to keeping most of his belongings in his pack so he could be ready to leave in moments, as did the students who had stayed with him the longest. Some of the newer students still had a habit of strewing their belongings about their rooms, and they always held up the rest.

He hid his impatience as the last of his students joined the group. Jefit and Vate, who spent as much time teaching as learning, stood on either side of him, their attention snapping to every movement in the room. As the final and ninth student joined them, her pack making a heavy thump as it hit the floor, the pair looked at Tyen expectantly.

"Right. That's everyone," he said. "Yes, it's annoying that we have to seek a new home again, but remember this: a school is not a place. A school is a group of people dedicated to teaching and learning. *We* are this school, and as long as we work together Liftre cannot stop us sharing knowledge."

They nodded, shifting restlessly and wondering why he was wasting time making a speech. He held back a laugh. The students were the impatient ones now. But they needed a moment to collect their thoughts and be ready for the journey ahead.

"You all know what comes next," he told them. "We'll travel in the usual formation. If Liftre's sorcerers see us, they'll try to follow, but we'll outrun them. When I'm sure we've hidden our trail well, I'll start looking for a new place to settle."

Will they let us go? one of the students thought. *This time they tried to kill one of us.* He wasn't the only one worrying, but most were assuming that if Liftre had wanted them all dead, the bomb would have been set off in the midst of them, not left in Regur's room. They, too, thought Tyen had been the target.

It's strange to hope they're right, Tyen thought. As he swung his pack onto his back, the students followed suit. Behind him were the two large chests he'd bought a few cycles ago to hold books and tools for his lessons. He insisted they pack them away every night, and it was fortunate they were making an evening exodus, not a midday one.

Four students picked up the two chests by the handles, one at each end, and the rest formed a close circle around them. Everyone took hold of another person, two others if both hands were free. Tyen joined the circle and waited until they were still. "Anybody not ready?" Nobody replied. "Take a breath."

A collective inhalation followed. None of his students had learned pattern-shifting yet. It was always the last thing he taught, if at all, since few were capable of it and unpopulated worlds strong in magic were hard to find. He must keep in mind that they would need to stop in worlds to breathe. Doing so would slow them down, but his powerful magical ability meant he could also travel faster than most sorcerers, which would keep them ahead of pursuit.

They had gathered magic already, the weakest first, followed in turn up to the strongest, so that all had access to some. Tyen had boosted his store by collecting it from the most distant edges of the world, where the absence would not be noticeable. The strengthening of the students had left the city in a temporary void, which he doubted local sorcerers were happy about, but magic would flow in to fill it within a few hours.

They didn't say we couldn't take any magic, Tyen thought wryly.

And they won't get the opportunity to object before we go. Pushing away from the world, Tyen sent himself and his companions into the place between.

During their stay in Turo, the school had taken care to never travel directly away from their home so no path would be created that would lead back to it. With no advantage in following that rule now, he headed straight into the whiteness. Turo's official arrival place was a few streets away, close enough that a new path running parallel would take them near to the established path's destination in the next world.

Where he expected sorcerers would be waiting to ambush them. He angled away from the other path. Doing so increased the likeliness they would arrive in a different world. Many of Turo's neighbouring worlds were not hospitable to humans. One world in particular was volcanic, which made the atmosphere poisonous even in regions where there were no eruptions. Deadly air was invisible, so they could not trust the benign appearance of an emerging landscape. He always skimmed across a new world until he found signs of life, preferably human before arriving.

However, his students couldn't survive in the place between worlds long enough for such a search. That wasn't his only concern, too. As they travelled, he stretched his senses beyond the group, seeking shadows or sounds that might betray the presence of strangers.

He found them as soon as they passed the halfway point.

They came from three different directions, suggesting they had been patrolling the place between. Two men and a woman. As the trio rushed towards Tyen and his charges, the expressions of the students changed to dismay and fear. They looked at him expectantly.

Tyen did not bother trying to evade the sorcerers. The first slowed so that the others would arrive at the same time, then all three moved close to grab hold of arms and shoulders. One student, Temi, let go with one hand in an instinctive move to push a sorcerer away, then realised the danger and quickly grasped the next student again. If any of them let go, Tyen would no longer be in control of their progress. A stronger sorcerer could pull them away, and Tyen would have to choose between abandoning them or letting go of the group and risking that one of the strangers was stronger than all of the students.

Fortunately, the students were in no physical danger from the sorcerers holding them. In the place between worlds, no person was physically stronger than another. Nor could one object damage another. Tyen felt a light pull to one side as the trio tried to influence the schools' direction of travel. It was not hard to resist. None of these sorcerers were a match for him. However, once they arrived in the next world, the strangers could attack in physical ways.

New surroundings were rapidly emerging from the whiteness. A horizon line cut at a steep angle, so he orientated his group with it. The sky was a purple-blue. Below it was a white, featureless mass. White features were the hardest to discern in the paleness of the place between worlds. It could be snow, it could be a layer of mist with the ground just below or it could be clouds high above the landscape.

Faint texture emerged, swirling and bubbling, revealing that the whiteness was not snow or mist, but a pale liquid.

Tyen stopped. He could skim higher above this strange sea, then create a floor of stilled air for them to stand on as they arrived, but he did not trust the air over such a place. Looking back at the group, he saw that the strangers had let go and moved away a little.

Not wanting to be pulled into the world with us, he guessed. *But I can take advantage of this.* He sent the school skimming rapidly sideways, above the sea. At the same time, he drew them higher in relation to the sea so that he could see the landscape ahead. The strangers raced after them, but Tyen was faster and the trio shrank into the distance.

He could not travel this way for too long, however. His charges needed to breathe. Either he must return to Turo or hope that other parts of this world were hospitable. The sea soon changed, the whiteness fragmenting to reveal that it was only scum coating the surface. The liquid beneath reflected the colour of the sky. Land appeared on the horizon, coming rapidly closer then – in a flash – replacing the sea. At the sight of lines criss-crossing it, Tyen drew them to a sharp halt. Roads? He searched for signs of humans, still not willing to trust the air. As soon as he found them – a family travelling in a well-laden cart – he sent his students downwards, stopping when his feet were a hand span above the ground.

Their arrival in the world was followed by the sound of air being sucked into many throats.

"We can't stay long," Tyen told them, looking for signs that the trio of sorcerers was catching up. Nobody replied, too caught up in breathing. He slipped out of the world a little so he could sense other presences. By the time he detected minds coming their way, the students were no longer gasping, just breathing hard. He returned to the world and linked with them again.

"Take a breath."

They obeyed. He pushed out of the world again and skimmed away. Now he searched for a city, ruined or alive. Or a temple. Places where arrival locations were established. Places where he was more likely to find well-used paths. The chances were high there would be Liftre allies watching for him, ready to pursue, but he'd rather risk that than his students suffocating or dying in a toxic world. He could outrun pursuit. He could even heal away the damage of suffocation if he were quick and they hadn't already died in the place between, but not for all nine students.

They had to stop twice more before he found what he sought. A city appeared at the horizon and he sent them towards it. The arrival place was obvious from above: a circular space within a large city square. Vendors had set up stalls nearby, hoping to sell trinkets or food to visitors, which suggested a well-used path.

Tyen estimated he'd travelled a quarter of the way around the world. Pursuit was far behind, but he'd left a clear trail and the sorcerers would eventually catch up and know where the school had left this world from. Speedy travel down well-used paths would give him the time he needed to start hiding their traces.

He brought the group into the world high above the city, their feet resting on stilled air, so they could breathe. This time he waited until all were well recovered before pushing out of the world again and heading towards the arrival place. Once there, he did not stop, but pushed them deep into the place between.

Though their surroundings faded to white, dark shapes emerged and took on the shape of figures. Tyen cursed and increased his speed, dodging the strangers ahead of him so they could not attempt to catch hold of the group and be carried along.

The sorcerers followed. Passing the midpoint, Tyen searched the shadows of the next world for signs of danger. Low, plant-like shapes surrounded a cleared area, paved with stone slabs. Beyond that stood a group of large animals, only their round, furry backs visible until one looked up, vegetation hanging from the still-chewing maw of its massive head.

Plants. Living creatures. All good signs of a healthy world. He'd have preferred to see people too, just to be sure. Perhaps he would, if these sorcerers followed the group into the world.

"Hold your breath when we arrive," he instructed.

As air surrounded them, he created a strong shield of stilled air around them. A wry relief came as the first of the pursuing sorcerers emerged too. At least that proved this world was safe.

"Breathe."

They did. He let them exhale and draw in a second breath before he pushed out of the world again.

The strangers hadn't attacked, but they followed. In the next world, Tyen waited for them to arrive, then sought their minds.

They were waiting for other sorcerers to join them. They'd also been told that Tyen was a pacifist, and would avoid a fight.

Interesting.

In the next world he waited for them to arrive so he could read their minds again. Two more sorcerers had joined them, and they expected their leader to meet them soon. He learned that they were mercenaries hired by Liftre. It was tempting to wait until their leader arrived so he could read her mind, but the sorcerers intended to attack when she did and he did not intend to waste magic in defence.

"Inhale," he ordered, then pushed out of the world. The sorcerers pursued but quickly fell behind. The school arrived in the small empty space in the middle of a crowded market. Tyen did not stop, propelling the school along the only other path leading away. As the crowd vanished, many of the people that had been in it did not. Twenty figures had replaced the five Tyen had left behind.

He considered stopping to fight them. He was reasonably sure he was strong enough to defeat them all. But the mercenaries were right: he did not like fighting – not because he feared losing but because he feared winning. He had killed enough people in his life already, and indirectly caused many more deaths. It was unlikely he would avoid it again, but he was determined to delay doing so for as long as possible. He would not, however, sacrifice the people he was bound to protect. If the situation became dangerous, he would do whatever he must to defend his students.

As they neared the next world, he caught sight of more figures between it and his group. To his relief, they retreated. Perhaps they were only other travellers. The arrival place was a ruin, judging by the broken walls and fallen statues, but despite this, several people milled about among the rubble. Perhaps the destruction was recent, and some humans still occupied the area. As he drew closer, these people noticed and backed away to allow room for the arrivals.

When Tyen and the school arrived, he realised his error. They weren't locals, but more mercenaries. In the first moment, he created a shield to ward off the inevitable attacks. In the second, he muttered a curse as he heard the students haul in deep, tortured breaths. He couldn't leave. They'd never make it to the next world.

The air outside Tyen's shield vibrated and flashed with the energy of the mercenaries' attack. More were arriving, including those from the previous world. Tyen did not retaliate; instead he read minds. He confirmed that Liftre wanted him dead. They hadn't been hired to kill his students, but hadn't been told to avoid killing them either.

The sound of hard breathing around him slowly diminished.

"We can go now," Jefit said quietly, in a strained voice. "We've all recovered."

Tyen knew Jefit wasn't entirely correct, but he estimated all the students would survive the journey to the next world if he travelled fast. "Take a deep breath," Tyen ordered. They obeyed. "Anybody not ready?" No reply.

He pushed out of the world, seeking the next path away. Three choices met his searching senses, the path he'd arrived on and two more, equally well-used ways. His search of minds had helped him locate where he was in the local worlds and he picked the path that led towards an area of reliably habitable, magically strong worlds. Away from the fringes of the known worlds, where it was easier to hide, but the fringes were vast and he could always make his way back towards them.

The mercenaries followed but once again were unable to keep up with Tyen. *If I didn't need to stop, I could outrun them easily.* No shadows appeared as he neared the next world. No people awaited them at the arrival place. He did not pause, but pushed on, taking the only other route. When he stopped next, the students sagged, those carrying the boxes setting them down and sitting on them as they gasped for breath.

"We . . . could . . . split . . . up," Bilt said. He was one of the newer students, who hadn't bothered trying to join Liftre since he knew he wouldn't fit in. "Lead . . . them . . . away."

Tyen was tempted for a moment. Bilt's magical reach was impressive – he might be strong enough to learn pattern-shifting one day.

"But if they catch you . . ." Vate started, shaking her head.

"They won't kill us," Donyd finished. "It's Tyen they want. If Regur hadn't taken the best room . . ."

"You can't be sure of that," Jefit told them. "Besides, they might use you as bait."

Bilt shrugged. "Then don't try to rescue me. They won't kill me, and when it's clear you've abandoned me, they'll let me go."

Tyen shook his head. "We can't take the chance." Even as he said it, he knew it was true. "These mercenaries are different to those who have chased us before. If they're willing to kill me, they will not hesitate to harm or kill any of you to get at me. They have no reason not to."

"But—"

"Enough," Tyen said. If they'd recovered enough to hold a conversation, they were recovered enough to move on. "Take a breath."

They passed through three more worlds without mishap. Then Vate looked at Tyen and frowned.

"*Are you sensing what I'm sensing?*" she asked, her words sounding clear in Tyen's mind though her mouth had not moved. Vate tilted her head to the left, then turned to stare in that direction. Following her lead, Tyen focused his senses on the whiteness. An impression came of another presence, heading towards them.

Even after he arrived and left another world, it was still there. Someone tracking them. Tyen increased his speed.

"*No!*" Vate's voice jolted Tyen's attention back to the group. "*Bilt!*"

Too late, he saw that the student had separated from the group and was heading towards the tracker. Tyen drew the group to a halt, then started after the young man.

"*Come back now, Bilt,*" he ordered.

Bilt didn't look back. "*Take the rest to the next world. I'll deal with this one or lead them away.*"

Tyen increased his speed. "*Take hold of him,*" he ordered as the group caught up, but Bilt dodged and evaded the hands reaching for him. Navigating a large number of people took no more magic than one, but the student had moved to the other side of the group where it was hard for Tyen to see what he was doing.

"*Incoming!*" one of the other students said.

Tyen looked around and only saw the mercenary as she flashed past. He heard Bilt say "*Hey!*", then the student was gone.

"*She's taking him away!*" Jefit exclaimed.

"*What do we do?*" another student asked, as Tyen located the woman, rapidly shrinking into the distance. "*We can't just leave him.*"

Tyen had no time to weigh the risks. Once she dragged Bilt out of the range of his senses it would be extremely difficult to find him again. He pushed the group into pursuit.

Though they sped through the whiteness, time seemed to pass slowly. It felt like far too much time for the group to survive in the whiteness, yet he knew they had not been there long. The woman headed back to the previous world, entering it as soon as she was able so that her presence in the place between vanished. Tyen raced down the path she'd made, searching in the lessening whiteness for signs of her and Bilt.

He emerged in a muddy village overshadowed by looming mountains. As air surrounded the group, Tyen stilled it in a shield. Locals had stumbled to a halt, gaping at the visitors in confusion and wondering where they had come from.

Tyen and the other students searched for Bilt and the woman. A long, tense silence told of their lack of success. Then someone yelled the missing student's name. Tyen sought their mind and saw what they had found: two locals dragging a limp body between them. At once, the students broke ranks, half of them hurrying towards the men.

131

"Is he dead?" a student asked.

"No! He can't be!"

"Hey! Stop that!"

The two locals had begun searching Bilt's clothing, one pulling off the pack.

Tyen pushed out of the world, propelling the students still with him, and the chests, after the ones running towards Bilt's prone form. They all arrived together. The local men fled, one still carrying the pack.

As a student took a step to follow, Tyen grabbed their arm. "Have you forgotten we're sorcerers?" He reached out and stilled the pack. The thief's grip broke as he continued running, and when he glanced back to see the pack floating towards the strangers, he decided to keep running.

"Oh, Bilt," Vate said quietly.

Tyen looked down. Jefit had rolled the student onto his back. Blank eyes stared up at the sky. Tyen's heart sank, disbelief too quickly shifting to acceptance and pain. No blood mingled with the mud that smeared Bilt's clothing and face, but his mind was silent.

He sighed, then stilled the mud under Bilt and lifted him. The students stepped out of the way as he placed the limp form on top of one of the chests. One placed the pack on the other chest.

Tyen looked around, meeting gazes and reading minds. They were in shock. Horror was turning to anger for some, but fear had settled over them all. Returning to his previous position beside one of the chests, Tyen held out his hands. The woman would be long gone, he guessed, in case he sought revenge. Alone, she would have no hope against him. He could try to track her, but she would probably reach her allies before he caught up. That wouldn't have saved her, if he'd had the inclination for vengeance.

Even if he had – and he admitted he badly wanted it right now – he must keep the rest of his students together and alive.

The best way to do that was to travel far away, as quickly as possible.

So once the students were in formation and linked together, that's what he did. They did not encounter any more mercenaries. A long stretch of time and many worlds passed before they stopped for anything but air. They acquired food in one world and stopped to eat it in another, in an ice cave of a cold world, silent in shock and exhaustion.

As the students gave in to their weariness one by one, Tyen brought out Beetle, who now contained an intricate clock, and saw they had travelled for more than two Traveller days. Moving to the chests, he considered Bilt's body, which the students had laid out and cleaned. The broken end of a pole had been found protruding from his lower back, angled towards his heart. The sorcerer had forced Bilt to arrive within it, killing him near-instantly.

Tyen looked at the sleeping men and women and sighed. When they woke, there would be grief and anger, and talk of revenge. He would, as always, talk them out of the foolish plans they would begin to make, pointing out that there were too few of them to revolt against Liftre and none of them had finished their training. Bilt was proof of his inability to predict and forestall all their bad decisions, but in general they trusted and obeyed him. The loss of one of them hurt, and he felt responsible for it, but he'd rather feel bad than become numb or uncaring over time, as some ageless sorcerers seemed to.

I bet Tarren has a saying for that, he mused. Thinking of his former mentor made Tyen's heart constrict a little. He missed the old man. It had been too long since Tyen had visited him, but travelling to Tarren's world from the fringes was time-consuming and dangerous.

Tyen frowned. Tarren's school had been attacked before. Few knew its location now. He ought to warn the old man about the Liftre sorcerers' willingness to kill to stop other schools operating. Tarren's world was not close, but if Tyen travelled alone he could reach it and get back to his students within a Traveller's day or two, as long as he managed to avoid Liftre's spies. The students would be safe enough here for that long with the supplies they had.

Tyen nodded to himself. Once Bilt was buried or cremated, as was his custom, Tyen would seek out his old friend.

CHAPTER 3

Visiting Tarren's old home had always sparked nostalgia, wonder and regret in Tyen. He had never tired of the amazing view from the top of the spire, but it also reminded him of his many failures, the greatest of them losing Rielle's trust.

Tarren's new home was secretive and inward-looking, in particular the arrangement of the arrival place, encircled by study rooms. Before Tyen had fully emerged from the place between worlds, the students within those rooms had already seen him and alerted everyone, and by the time he breathed the air, the windows were lined with people watching him warily. As air surrounded him, he turned so that all could see his face and, having recognised him, they relaxed and returned to their studies.

Only one figure remained by a class window. Tarren waved to Tyen, then beckoned. Walking over to the door closest to the window, he opened it and waited for Tyen to reach him.

"Well, well. What excellent timing you have," the old man said, his smile wide and his eyes mischievously bright. He paused, and when Tyen made no comment, he shook his head. "Aren't you going to read my mind, young Tyen?"

"Only if you insist," Tyen replied.

"Go on then."

Seeking the old man's thoughts, Tyen saw a name and his heart skipped a beat.

Rielle was here. And she wanted to speak to him.

Tarren chuckled. "Ah, that was worth it for the look on your face. Come in – and steady yourself. It's business, not pleasure, that she wishes to raise with you."

"Of course," Tyen replied, smothering his disappointment.

He followed his former mentor out of the classroom and down a long, snaking corridor. He wanted to rebuke Tarren for teasing him, but in truth he wasn't sure he'd find the right words or tone. His heart *was* beating a little too quickly and his mind was full of questions. What would he say to her? *Has she forgiven me yet?* She had said so during their few brief meetings after Qall's self-imposed exile began, yet a distance still remained between them that hinted otherwise.

Tarren didn't know why Rielle wanted to see Tyen, and he was full of curiosity – and hope that she wouldn't insist on privacy when she did. It had been so long since he'd seen them together. Would the spark of attraction still fire between them?

"How are you?" Tyen asked.

"Good. My students are, on the whole, hard-working. I wish it didn't take corruption at Liftre to inspire such dedication."

Tyen nodded, his mood darkening. "Have you had any visitors from Liftre recently?"

Tarren shook his head. "I'm hoping, perhaps foolishly, that they don't know where we are."

"Perhaps they don't. Or perhaps they don't regard your school with the same murderous hatred as they do mine."

"Murderous?" Tarren's eyebrows rose. "What happened?"

Tyen told him, finishing as they reached the door to a small atrium filled with plants. Which was just as well, because the moment he saw who was waiting there he lost track of what he'd been saying.

Rielle smiled at him, the expression warm but also tired and still a little wary. She looked no different to how he remembered, despite losing her ability to halt ageing five cycles ago. Her brown skin glowed with health, and her dark eyes sparkled with vitality.

"Tyen," she said, getting out of one of the garden chairs. She was wearing an elegant, though crumpled, dress and her scarf was still draped over her head. "How are you?"

"Currently homeless," Tyen replied.

Tarren waved Tyen towards a chair. "Hungry? Thirsty?"

"A little of both," Tyen admitted.

Tarren reversed out of the door. "I'll find an idle student to attend to you."

"Idle? Weren't you just telling me how dedicated they all were?"

The old man shrugged. "I didn't say all of the time."

He left, and Rielle returned to her seat as Tyen sat down.

"So why are you homeless?" Rielle asked.

She listened patiently as he went through the story again.

"It is sad, the death of this student," she said when he was done. "Do you think the mercenaries acted beyond their orders?"

He spread his hands. "They weren't ordered to kill students, but they weren't ordered *not* to either." He shook his head. "However, they *were* told to kill me, if they could. That is new. In the past their task was simply to force my school to close or move."

"What will you do?"

He shrugged. "Look for a new home. Keep teaching."

"Why don't you join Tarren here?"

"Tarren doesn't teach mechanical magic. The Liftre inventors are particularly determined to ensure they are the only ones teaching it, so if I set up here Tarren would be in even more danger." He grimaced and shook his head. "But enough about me. How are you?"

"I've had an interesting time lately." She smiled. "Qall decided it was time to return to the worlds."

Tyen paused as he comprehended the implications of both. "Qall is free?"

"I read his mind and saw no sign that Valhan was in control."

"Where is he now?"

She frowned. "I don't know. He didn't say what he planned to do."

"What would I do if I were him?" Tyen wondered aloud. "Probably seek out loved ones."

"The Travellers. Yes." She smiled briefly, then became serious again. "Or maybe his original family. He saw his identity in Valhan's memories. Oh – and he has changed his appearance."

"Does Baluka know?"

Her left eye twitched. "I sent a message."

He looked at her closely. "Has something happened between you and Baluka?"

She looked away. "No . . . well . . . he asked me to do some things I wasn't happy about."

"Can you tell me?"

She sighed. "The first was to strip a world. I refused. Then he sent me to top up a world's magic, but he didn't tell me it wasn't fully depleted, or that there were political issues between it and a neighbouring world that I'd have to solve. Nothing too difficult, but I don't want to be put in that kind of situation. I visited Qall after that, and while Baluka doesn't know what I do when I take time off each cycle, he knows it will take several days. But I've been gone longer than usual now." She frowned and looked away. "I know I'm avoiding it. Maybe just to remind him that I only work for the Restorers because I want to."

"Sounds like he needs the reminder."

She tilted her head thoughtfully and met his gaze. "Trouble is, I don't want to go back. Not yet. It's not because of what he asked me to do but . . . I'm tired of it." She spread her hands. "I've barely spent a day doing anything else for, well, four or five cycles."

Though she looked perfectly healthy, she now did appear tired, her shoulders sagging and her expression weary and strained. As if her earlier vitality had been a coat hiding her true state, which she had relaxed enough now to shrug out of.

"Then take a break," he suggested. "Perhaps that's all you need."

"Perhaps," she agreed. She drew in a deep breath and straightened her back. "Do you know of any places where you could hide from Liftre?"

He shook his head. "I was hoping Tarren might know of some."

"If he did, it would be easy for Liftre spies to read it from his mind."

He sighed. "That's true. I guess we'll have to find somewhere ourselves. You know, I've wondered occasionally if we'd be better off hidden in a dead world, like Qall was."

Her eyebrows rose. "Would you be able to teach magic use without magic?"

"Perhaps if we used other forces to demonstrate principles of magic. Or if we found worlds like your home world, with very little magic, and scaled down the exercises."

"I just restored my world, so don't go there." Her fingers briefly rapped on the edge of the seat, then she looked up. "What about your world? Are you still wary of restoring it?"

Tyen's heart skipped a beat, then began to race, but he was not sure if it was from sudden excitement or dread. He had always hoped to go back to his home one day. In recent years he'd thought about it more, all too aware that his father was getting older and deserved to know his son was alive and well, but he'd been too occupied with keeping his school safe to visit.

"I was," he said, "back when I feared some other knowledge from my world would spread and cause even greater havoc in the worlds than mechanical magic has. But I've thought of nothing that hasn't already been invented and misused in some way elsewhere."

Her smile was grim. "Yes, it seems like there is little that humans can do that hasn't already been done, and abused. If you do wish to restore your world, I recommend you enter and look around first to judge whether having sudden access to plentiful magic will have a detrimental effect on the people."

He nodded. "Oh, it will. And yet it will have benefits, too. I'd have to provide some guidance." He rubbed his hands together slowly as he considered what would need to be done. "Some things must be sorted out first, however. How can I get in touch with you when, and if, my world is ready to be restored?"

"Would you mind if I came with you and looked around while you make preparations?"

He blinked in surprise. "What about Baluka and the Restorers?"

"It has occurred to me that if Baluka is sending me to strengthen rather than restore worlds, there probably aren't so many worlds needing help now. Maybe he wants those that do to wait a little." She shrugged. "I'll let Baluka know where to send a message if something requires urgent attention, and how long I will be absent for. How much time do you think you'll need?"

He paused to consider. "A quarter-cycle, at most."

"*That* much." Her eyebrows lifted again. "Sounds like you have quite a few things to sort out."

"Only an accusation of theft to have quashed, a fundamental misconception about magic to disprove, an ancient school run by hard-headed fossils to take over and an emperor's approval to gain."

"Sounds like fun." She smiled, but it quickly faded, and her worried expression sent a chill down his spine. "This feels familiar. In a bad way."

He nodded. "Yes. Last time we attempted to manipulate the situation in a world the result was disastrous."

"And this time it's your home world. I don't want you hating me for helping you if we get this wrong."

Tyen paused to consider that. "Well, if it's any assurance, the people of my world aren't at war with another," he said slowly. "Unless big changes have happened, nobody in my world is aware that sorcerers can read minds when there is enough magic about. We will have the advantage once magic is restored."

"We won't be able to read minds until it is," she warned. "Except where we release enough magic to make it possible."

"Then we will do that. I won't be making the same mistake I

made in Doum – not reading minds. And with you there, we won't have to worry about running out of magic and becoming stranded."

Her smile returned. "No." She stretched. "So, will you take your students with you, or wait until you're sure the locals are friendly?"

"I'll wait. I'll have to move them to a safe place while I'm gone."

She nodded. "Perhaps I can restore another dead world for them. One that's unoccupied and known to have been dead for a while, so nobody will risk visiting it. I know of one, but you'll have to bring food and water in for them. Would they be prepared to live independently and isolated?"

"As long as they are safe, my group will be willing to live just about anywhere."

The door to the atrium opened and Tarren walked in carrying glasses and a bottle, followed by a student carrying a tray laden with food.

"That took a while," Rielle told the old man teasingly. "Did you cook it all yourself?"

Tarren hooked the toe of his shoe around the leg of a nearby table and dragged it close to her seat. "Oh, I kept changing my mind about what to serve," he said, winking at the student. The young man smiled faintly and placed the tray on the table, then obligingly retreated when Tarren waved him away. "I'll take it from here."

"So," he said as he sat down bedside Tyen, then looked at Rielle. "Did you sort out what you came here for?"

"Oh!" she exclaimed, straightening. "Not yet. I'll go get something from my pack."

As she hurried away, Tarren raised an eyebrow at Tyen. "Well?"

"Well what?"

"Is the spark still there?"

Tyen chuckled. "It never left, for me, but I have no idea if she still feels anything for me. However, we have just made . . . I guess you'd call it a business arrangement." Except they hadn't discussed what Rielle would get in return. He had once offered to restore her youth, when she grew older. It seemed a bit soon to be doing so now. Close up, he had noted small signs of age and how they suited her, from the way her more prominent cheekbones caught the light and how the soft skin around her eyes creased a little when she smiled. It gave her a maturity and confidence that was very appealing.

"Don't tell me about it," Tarren said. "So that there's no risk of it being read from my mind."

"Hmm. Yes, we'd better not. Thank you," Tyen replied.

A look of disappointment crossed the old man's face, but it was quickly replaced by a mischievous smile. "Besides, it's more fun to guess."

"Guess what?" Rielle said as she pushed through the door to the atrium.

"What you two are going to be up to next," Tarren replied.

"Wouldn't you like to know," she teased. Then she grew serious. "I'm sorry, Tarren, but what we do next must be done in private."

"I'll make sure nobody interrupts," Tarren said, getting up.

"It's not what you're thinking."

"Not at all, I'm sure."

She sighed and crossed her arms disapprovingly. Grinning broadly, the old man left the atrium. Rielle waited a little longer after the door had closed, then unfolded her arms and dropped something into Tyen's lap. "With thanks from Qall," she told him.

Tyen stared at her, then picked up the object. It was a small package wrapped in cloth tied with string. The size and weight were about right. He tore the string off, grabbed the edge of the cloth and lifted. A well-worn satchel slipped out and landed in his lap.

Vella!

Suddenly he was overcome with hesitation and a lingering guilt at abandoning his promise to create a body for her. The repellent experience of trying to resurrect Valhan was part of that decision. Mostly it had been realising, thanks to Qall, that much of her personality was actually his own expectations reflected back at him. To make her whole again wouldn't put the person he thought she was into a body. Instead it would destroy most of what she was to make an almost entirely new human.

And then it had been so obvious that Qall needed her more than him.

Clearly that was no longer true. He felt a surge of gratitude to the young man for giving her back when he didn't have to. She had passed from carrier to carrier for thousands of years.

What would it be like to own her again? Would it be the same? Once he touched her, she would know everything he had done and learned in the last five cycles. *But I have fewer new secrets in my head now than all those from the past.* She, on the other hand, would have absorbed a great deal in that time. She had all of Qall's memories. *For him to trust me with all that . . .* He felt a wave of surprise and gratitude.

Qall's memories weren't the only new content within her. The Raen's were in there too now, transferred there by Qall. *Everything Valhan knew is available to anyone who reads her.* That thought was sobering, and he realised that it wasn't just his trust that Qall had given him. *He has given me the responsibility of ensuring that knowledge doesn't reach the wrong hands.*

Maybe that was why Liftre had sent sorcerers to kill Tyen. Maybe they knew that Vella was back in Tyen's hands and hoped to steal her. But how could they know that? They didn't even know she contained Valhan's memories. Only Rielle and Qall knew. Unless Qall had told someone . . .

"Does that change your plans?" Rielle asked.

"No," Tyen replied. "No, if anything it means I must find a

secure hiding place sooner rather than later." He looked up. "It means it is time I returned to my world, and I'd be honoured and very much in your debt if you would come with me to restore it."

CHAPTER 4

A sparse forest landscape surrounded Tyen and Rielle. When he'd first visited this world, he'd been surrounded by snow and bare trees, but now green predominated. Yet as they emerged, cold air prickled his skin. The air smelt familiar, which surprised him. He'd stayed with the local people for several days after arriving in their world, but not long enough, he'd have thought, to remember how this world smelt. Still, his first experience of a world other than his own had been both profound and frightening, so perhaps that was why the details had lingered in his mind.

To sense so much magic around him had been a shock, as was being able to read minds. What he'd already learned from Vella about other worlds had proved inadequate. He'd been asking the wrong kinds of questions. The people who had adopted him had very strong ideas about sharing personal possessions, so he'd kept Vella hidden, which gave him few opportunities to consult her. They treated him like a cross between a holy man and a child, feeding and protecting him, often laughing at him, but also encouraging him whenever he used magic.

During the time he'd stayed here, it had not occurred to him to wonder how the vegetation could be the same as that of his world. Now he knew that it was a sign that humans had travelled to his world more often in the past, distributing plants and animals either deliberately or unintentionally. *Did humans spread from, or to, Leratia?* he wondered. He doubted his home was the original source of humans. The history of Leratia didn't stretch back as far as that of some worlds. *Where did we originally come from?* Would it be possible to trace humankind back to one location if someone studied the histories of all worlds, digging deep into the past of those that had been inhabited the longest and looking for a pattern?

"Is this your home world?" Rielle asked.

She was watching him closely, no doubt noting his hesitation. He shook his head, at the same time bringing his thoughts back to the present. "The next," he told her.

She squeezed his hand lightly. Communicating reassurance, he guessed. It had been so long since he'd been unable to read anyone's mind, it was taking some time to get used to reading mannerisms again. She might mean that she was ready, or that he would be fine. Or both.

He ought to be easing *her* worries, not she easing *his*. She'd listened to all his warnings about Leratian prejudices against women and other races. He'd told her about Veroo and Sezee, the Princess and her niece who had travelled to Beltonia seeking schooling in magic only to be turned away by the Academy – and establishments such as hotels and the like – because of their gender and race. To her question whether he should change her skin colour to make their task easier, he'd said no. Leratians, indeed the whole world, would be in her debt once she restored magic, and it would help a great many people if their saviour was a brown-skinned woman.

Making sure that this fact could never be erased from history was part of his increasingly complicated plan.

Squeezing her hand back in thanks, he drew in a breath to signal that she should too, then when she had, he pushed into the place between worlds. He could feel their fresh track leading back the way they'd come. Ignoring it, he sought a faint sign of a fifteen-cycle-old one.

In vain, however. Nothing remained of his earlier path out of his world. The substance of the place between worlds, like magic within worlds, eventually evened out, smoothing over any signs of passage. It would have been reassuring to follow a trace of his former journey to where he'd left his world, but he shouldn't need one. As long as he left this world from near where he'd arrived in it, he should return to a place close to where he had exited his own.

Which was a prospect he'd been dreading. Knowing that he would see the remains of Spirecastle roused memories of its fall and a guilt he'd never completely shaken since that day. Though he knew with certainty that it had been Kilraker who had stripped the magic within the tower, causing its structure to fail, he still felt partly to blame. If he hadn't been at Spirecastle, Kilraker would never have been there either. Tyen had brought the source of destruction to its door. He should never have cooperated with the man.

He knew he and Rielle had reached the midpoint between worlds when all signs of the forest had disappeared, but as he travelled onwards no new features appeared. They ought to be seeing a cliff to one side, a flat plain to the other, and the ruins of Spirecastle surrounded by hills, roads and houses below. Rielle looked at him, questioning. He frowned and shook his head, but did not want to voice his worries.

Had something happened to his world? He'd heard about worlds vanishing after a cataclysmic natural disaster. Should he retreat, and try to re-enter from somewhere else?

Then cold, damp air surrounded them and they began to fall.

He laughed and quickly created a platform of stilled air under their feet to catch and support them. Warming the air about them to ward off the chill, he looked around.

Clouds, he thought. *Just clouds.*

He began to lower them – judging the direction only by the pull of gravity. The swirling mist darkened, then abruptly thinned and released them into clear, rain-filled, air. He extended the stilled air of the platform to form a sheltering sphere. The landscape he'd expected was now visible, or at least a diminished view of it. He could not see the top of the cliff as it was shrouded with cloud. Curtains of rain veiled the distant plains, but below . . .

"Ah," Rielle said. "The tower."

Below, Spirecastle still thrusted up from the plain below, but now half the height it had been before he'd left his world. It was clear by the texture of its stone that the tower's base had once been a rock spire, perhaps isolated from the cliffs by erosion. He recalled how the windows and walls had been shaped in a way that appeared natural, hiding where the spire ended and building began. All he could see now was the top, however. It was an uneven mound of rubble but for the centre, where a hole gaped. The darkness within revealed nothing but the faint first steps of a staircase.

Tyen moved them downwards. As they neared the ruins, he chose a relatively flat area to land on. Rielle caught her balance, then closed her eyes briefly.

"There's magic here, but not a great deal." She picked her way to the edge. "There's still a thriving city below."

He followed. The city at the base of the spire was larger than the one he remembered. Knowing that people still lived there made him feel a little better. At least Kilraker's actions hadn't destroyed the Sselt civilisation entirely. He'd seen the ruins of cities on other worlds that had died after smaller calamities than this.

But as he looked closer, he felt his heart lodge in his throat. Vast chunks of rock interrupted the pattern of streets and houses. When Spirecastle had fallen, the top half had rained down upon the city. More people had died then than those who hadn't escaped the tower's fall. He silently cursed Kilraker yet again.

He did not want to go closer, but they needed to be near people if they were to release magic and read minds. He took Rielle's hand again and pushed them out of the world so they could descend more easily. He chose the top of a large chunk of fallen rock to land on. Once they emerged into the world again, he released magic, feeling it spill out to gently embrace the area.

Seeking minds, he found plenty.

"Are you going to look for people you know?" Rielle asked.

"No. Most of those I met probably died in the fall." A memory of Mig and Ysser climbing into their flying contraption returned. They had made it out of the building before it fell. He still hoped they landed safely. "There's a chance that the survivors blame me for what happened or suspect I played some part in it." He sighed. "Look for officials. It will be useful to find out whether the south is in contact with the north and, if so, whether anything has changed in my homeland."

They both stood silently for some time, occasionally murmuring information they had discovered and thought the other might want to know. Eventually Rielle drew his attention to the mind of a general who, while watching the training of new recruits to the Sseltee army, wondered if his work was really necessary. If the threat from the north had truly diminished, as their spies claimed, the south had no need for a large army any more.

Tyen added that to what he had learned so far. The Leratian Empire had sent sorcerers to investigate the disappearance of the professors who had died during Spirecastle's fall, then a year later, to offer terms for trade. The latter sounded more like the instructions of an occupying force, and were rejected by the southerners. The departing Leratians had warned that a larger delegation would arrive to negotiate an agreement if the terms were not accepted.

The general had been hired to oversee the building of an army strong enough to defend the south. Another had been set the task of giving the creators who had not died in Spirecastle's fall new homes among those living at the base. All were given the resources they needed to train more apprentices and start collectives in order to generate more magic. Sorcerers were ordered to take and store magic so that as little as possible drifted towards the north for the enemy to use.

That larger delegation never came. Spies in the north had reported magic diminishing to almost nothing in the empire, but described sophisticated weaponry that did not require magic, so the southerners did not relax.

The recruits the general was now about to start training were fresh from the Sseltee School of Sorcery. They knew how to use magic, but not how to apply it in battle. Though they had been taught much about the north by the two foreigners who had joined the school years before, they had a lot to learn.

I'd wager those two are Sezee and Veroo, Tyen thought. Sure enough, two familiar faces flashed through the general's memory. Sselt spies had confirmed all the information the pair had given was true. He thought them trustworthy. They had grievances against the empire and did not want the south subjugated in the same way their own homeland had been.

"The school is to the west," Rielle said. "One of his students just traced the journey in his mind, as seen from a flying contraption."

"An aircart?" Tyen asked. "Does it have a large inflated capsule on top?"

"No. It has rigid boards on top. It flies fast and needs a long length of flat ground to land upon." She chuckled. "It was a memorable ride, at least to him."

Tyen wanted to seek out the young man and see his memories for himself, but Rielle was holding out her hand. "Wait. Vella contains a map of the south," he told her. Drawing the pouch from under his shirt, he slipped Vella out and opened her cover.

Hello again, Tyen.

Hello Vella. Could you draw the map Ysser showed you, with less detail so we can read it easily?

Lines formed on the open pages. Rielle's finger hovered over Vella as she traced the student's path back to the school.

"There," she said. "Where that river emerges from the cliffs and splits in three. I'll transport us if you like."

He nodded. Holding Vella open with one hand, he took Rielle's hand in the other. The world faded a little, then Spirecastle dropped below them and they glided away to the west.

Soon it was clear that Rielle was following the main road marked on the map. It wound through the hills, moving away from the cliffs and creeping ever westward. For a time it hugged the side of a river. All along it were towns of various sizes, some nearly as large as the one below Spirecastle. Rielle brought them back into the world twice so she could breathe. Not long after the second stop, their direction of travel turned abruptly and she headed back towards the cliff.

As it neared, Tyen examined it closely, wondering if Spirecastle hadn't been the only city carved into rock. He saw plenty of holes that might have been windows, and ledges that could have been part of trails if they had linked up with others, but no sign of people.

Then, when they were about twenty strides from the cliff face, it was suddenly apparent that it wasn't as flat as his eyes had first told him. One side of a crevasse overlapped the other, the gap between barely large enough for a person to squeeze through. The entrance was wider at the base of the cliff, allowing two carts to pass.

Rielle guided them into the shadows within. Here were the windows and ledges he'd expected, carved into elaborate designs. Numerous bridges crossed the gap, most made of rope, but some built of stone. It was to one of the highest of the latter that Rielle now took them, stopping at the apex and emerging into the world.

"*Thank you, Vella,*" Tyen thought. He closed her and slipped her back into her pouch, then as his feet touched firm ground he looked around. Two nervous guards stared at them from openings in the cliff at either side.

"We mean you no harm," Rielle assured them in the local language.

Tyen blinked in surprise, then realised that she had already released magic and the guards' minds were readable. One had sent word of the strangers' approach to their superiors. They watched the newcomers, frightened but determined to hold out as long as possible if they were attacked.

"Wait here or look for your friends?" Rielle asked Tyen.

"Both," he replied. She smiled in understanding. If they continued on into the crevasse, the Sselts might think they were invading, so it was better to search by mind. The magic Rielle had released hadn't spread far, so he released more. The minds of teachers and students bloomed before his senses. The news of the ghostly strangers who'd flown into the ravine had spread quickly, and procedures established for emergencies had been initiated. Tyen had to admire the Sselts' efficiency. They were as ready as they could be for a sorcerous invasion.

But they would not attack without provocation. They believed avoiding conflict was best. These visitors would be given a chance to show their intentions were benign.

Tyen glanced at Rielle, then walked to the end of the bridge, where another nervous guard regarded him.

"I wish to meet with the leaders of your school of sorcery," Tyen told him. "Tell them I am Tyen Ironsmelter, a friend of Sezee and Veroo. This is Rielle Lazuli, a sorcerer of another world. We intend no harm."

The man nodded briskly, then brought out a whistle and let out a piercing blast. Immediately a young guard appeared, the whites of his eyes flashing as he saw Tyen and Rielle. He memorised the message he was to deliver and raced away without comment.

It was not long before a woman arrived. She was uneasy, but not frightened. Veroo had been found and confirmed that the messenger's description matched her memory of Tyen, though she did not recognise his companion.

"Follow me," the woman instructed.

The corridor she led Tyen and Rielle down was surprisingly bright, a cool light illuminating it from glass discs set into the ceiling at regular intervals. The guard had taken up a position at their rear and, seeing Tyen look up at them, thought that the light holes, lined with mirrors to reflect sunlight downwards, must be a mystery to these strangers.

After several turns, they arrived at a room with an open door. The guide stopped on the other side of it and gestured to the room within. "Please make yourselves comfortable."

Tyen stepped through and found himself in a long, narrow space. On one side, windows looked into the crevasse, which allowed in so little light that the windows looked more like pieces of black glass set into the walls. Chairs had been arranged in circles, small tables set between. Tyen debated whether he should sit down now or wait. He looked over to Rielle, who was peering out of a window, shading her eyes in the hopes of seeing more detail.

Then a sound from the doorway drew their attention. A woman stepped into the room. For a moment he didn't recognise her. Her hair was grey and long, and the skin around her face and mouth wrinkled deeply as she smiled. Then he felt a jolt as he realised who it was.

"Veroo!"

"Tyen," she replied. Striding to him, she placed a hand on each of his shoulders. Her eyes roved over him, then she shook her head. "You've not changed at all. Except . . ." Her gaze bored into his own. "Your eyes are older."

He did not know what to say to that. "Because I *am* older?" he ventured.

She chuckled. "That must be it." Releasing him, she turned to Rielle. "Welcome to our world . . . Ree-el? I apologise if I have your name wrong. The message was rather garbled."

"I am Rielle Lazuli," Rielle replied. "It is a pleasure to meet you, Veroo."

The older woman smiled again. "Are you hungry? Thirsty?"

"Some small refreshments would be welcome," Rielle replied. Tyen doubted she was hungry since they'd eaten not long ago, ensuring that such necessities would not be a problem for some time after they arrived, but it was a common ritual in many worlds to offer food to guests and in many it was rude to refuse. Tyen hadn't realised on his earlier visit that this was also true here. He'd never refused any meals – so far as he could recall.

Veroo took a step towards the door. "I will send someone to fetch them. I have so many questions and I don't want to miss any of your answers, though I will have to wait for our leaders to ask theirs first." She paused. "That sounds like them now."

Sure enough, as Veroo opened the door several men and women entered. She made the introductions and ushered all to a ring of chairs, which grew larger as more were added to cater for everyone. Two of the Sselts were members of a small council that ran the school; the other was an expert in security and diplomacy. One of the last people to arrive was a younger man, who stared at Tyen intently, then nodded.

"It *is* you," he said.

"Forgive me, but did we know each other before?" Tyen asked.

"Briefly. I am Mig. I was Ysser's apprentice."

"Ah!" Tyen exclaimed as he remembered the boy. "Yes, I remember. You had made an air craft!"

"Which worked, thankfully." Mig grimaced. "I was able to save Ysser."

"I am relieved to hear that," Tyen said with feeling. "How is he?"

"He died two years go," Mig replied sadly. "He was very old."

Tyen sighed. "I am sorry to hear of his death. I would have enjoyed telling him what happened to me after that day."

"He would have liked that," Mig replied. "He did wonder what had become of you, and hoped you hadn't perished in the fall."

Tyen opened his mouth to assure Mig that he'd had nothing

to do with the tower's ruin, then paused and glanced at the others. "I expect you all wish to know what happened that day."

Mig's mouth twitched to one side. "Indeed we do."

And so Tyen joined the circle of sitters, of which there were now seven, and told his tale. "I could not return to this world, as there would be no magic for me to use to prevent my falling, so I had to push on to the next," he said as he finished. "Since then I have travelled the worlds, learning to use magic, and surviving in what proved to be a time of great upheaval."

"You have not returned home since then?" one of the council members asked.

"No."

"Why have you now?"

Tyen drew in a deep breath. "Many reasons. At the most personal, I wish to see my father. I also have a small group of young sorcerers I am teaching and thought I might be able to base myself here. In return," he glanced at Rielle, "my friend has the means to restore this world's magic. She is a Maker of great strength – perhaps the most powerful the worlds have ever produced."

Silence followed his answer, as the Sselts and Veroo exchanged glances and considered the implications of what this might mean.

"Do you wish to base yourself here?" Veroo asked.

Tyen shrugged. "If the Academy proves too much of an obstacle, I will return here and ask if you will allow us to join you."

"You will first offer power to our enemy, but not us," the adviser pointed out.

"No," Rielle replied. "I will fill the entire world with magic. If what Tyen told me is still true, the Leratians will put most of it to use running machines, so they will soon be magically weaker."

"And the magic will flow towards them," the other council member said.

Rielle merely nodded in reply.

The Sselts exchanged glances. Some looked excited; some worried. Veroo shrugged and looked at Tyen.

"You will do what you wish to," she told him. "We cannot stop you. However, the Tyen I knew would not willingly bring harm to others, and I trust that this has not changed."

"It has not," he assured her. Then he met each of the Sselts' gazes. "I am returning to my homeland seeking a safe and peaceful place to teach, not out of loyalty or obligation to Leratia. If I see that establishing a school and restoring this world will lead to warfare or conquest, I will abandon my plans and look elsewhere." He glanced at Veroo, then back to the adviser. "If it is not too much to ask, I would appreciate any information you have on the state of the Leratian Empire, so that I am as prepared as I can be when I arrive there and do not trigger any strife. Would you tell me what your spies have learned?"

More glances were exchanged. The first council member shook her head. "We need to discuss this with the King first."

"I understand," Tyen replied. "And I am relieved to learn he and many others escaped Spirecastle before it fell. I wish all had. I wish it had never fallen. I wish, too, that I had never visited, or come south. I'd rather have been imprisoned in Beltonia than bring such destruction and grief to you."

The first council member shook her head. "Those who met you did not believe you were the type to be so careless, whereas the men who pursued you did not give such a good impression. You could not know what they were going to do, or prevent it when they did, so do not blame yourself."

"Ah, but I always will in some part," Tyen replied quietly, bowing his head.

"Is there anything you wish to ask us?" Veroo asked.

Tyen nodded, then smiled. "How is Sezee?"

The woman chuckled. "Well and happy. Married, with six children."

"Six!"

"Yes." She shook her head. "Sometimes I'm glad to escape to the school for the day." Her gaze flickered towards Rielle, who smiled knowingly. "And you?"

"I've been . . . too busy," he said. "The worlds are full of endless distractions." Rielle chuckled in agreement but said nothing. "I could tell you some tales but," he continued, then nodded at the rest of the listeners, "it would take days so perhaps I should save them for another time."

Veroo turned back to the Sselts. "It will take a day for a message to reach the King and return, so we have plenty of time." The door opened and all turned to see two young men carrying trays laden with food and drink. "And here are your refreshments." Veroo raised an eyebrow at Tyen. "Would you accept our hospitality in exchange for your tales?"

Tyen replied. "With gratitude and pleasure."

CHAPTER 5

"Sorry," Tyen said as Rielle began to breathe deeply. "That was a long stretch without air. I should have stopped sooner."

She shrugged. "I remember how hard it was . . . to judge how long I was . . . between worlds. Especially when I was . . . intent on something." She paused to take a few deep breaths. "Do you want to meet your father alone?"

Tyen looked up and down the street. Few people were about, but all were staring at him and Rielle. As a carriage passed, he glimpsed a woman passenger glaring at Rielle suspiciously.

"No, you had better come inside."

He led the way across the road and to the gate of the third narrow house in the row. Pushing through, he approached the door, remembering how he liked to sit on the steps as a child. His mother used to keep the small garden tidy, but after her death it had become weedy and a constant subject of complaint from the neighbours. Now it was so neat it was almost barren.

A polished bronze plaque was affixed to the wall beside the door. The name on it was not his father's.

He hesitated, then rang the bell anyway. If his father had died, or moved, the current occupants might know.

A long silence followed. Tyen waited, reading the minds of the servants watching them through the curtains of the room beside the hall. The middle-aged housekeeper wanted to answer the door, but the elderly butler did not. Both eyed Rielle with a kind of dismayed curiosity. What was this woman wearing? She was practically naked in that simple sleeveless shift. And browner than a farmer.

Finally, the woman grew tired of waiting for them to give up and go away, and, ignoring the hiss of the butler, approached the door.

"The master is out," she snapped as she opened it.

"Would that be Deid Ironsmelter?" Tyen asked.

The woman's eyebrows rose. "No. He went to live with his sister. In Brokebridge."

"Thank you." Tyen nodded politely and stepped back.

"She can't go about wearing that," the woman blurted.

Tyen looked back. The woman was staring down her nose at Rielle.

"Can you recommend a dressmaker who would supply us with acceptable clothing? And a tailor," he added, glancing down at his own clothing.

The woman bit her lip and began to shake her head, then paused and frowned. "Hahten Beve might have something. Behind the hatter on the main street. Enter from the back alley."

Tyen nodded again. "I know the thoroughfare. My thanks."

The woman's eyes widened as he took Rielle's hand and pushed out of the worlds a little, then skimmed in the direction of the row of shops he'd visited countless times as a child. It was busier there, so he brought them back into the world in the alley the servant had described and started towards where he estimated the back of the hatter's was.

Sure enough, a tiny sign in a narrow door read: "Hahten Beve: Tailor". He and Rielle entered, setting a bell on the door ringing, and found themselves in a cramped shop barely larger than a closet. The proprietor's name wasn't typically Leratian, so Tyen was not surprised when a swarthy figure swaggered through a door to greet them. He *was* surprised, however, to learn from her mind that she was female. Most Beltonians assumed from her stature and male clothing that she was just an odd-looking foreign man, which was fine with her.

"How can I help such a handsome couple?" Hahten asked, beaming at them. As her gaze moved from Tyen to Rielle, she did not flinch or stare. Tyen silently thanked the housekeeper again, though she had sent the foreigners to a foreign clothier out of prejudice, not kindness. At least Hahten was not so quick to judge.

"A set of clothing for each of us," Tyen replied. He turned to Rielle. "Do you mind?" he asked in the Traveller tongue. "I'm afraid the local forms of dress are very restrictive."

She shook her head. "Not at all. I do try to adapt to the expectations of different worlds, when necessary. It can be fun to try new styles of dress, too."

"I'm not sure you'll find this fun for long," he warned, then turned back to Hahten and resumed speaking in Leratian. "Do you have anything already made up in our sizes?"

Hahten's gaze flitted over the both of them, and she nodded. "To what purpose?"

"Something suited to visiting family in Beltonia, but not inappropriate if we happened to encounter the Emperor. What do you recommend?"

Hahten's mouth spread into an incredulous smile. "The Emperor, eh? Well, I don't have much that would impress someone so lofty—"

"They don't need to impress, just not offend."

"Ah." She nodded. "I'll see what I can find." Turning with the ease of someone familiar with every part of the cramped space, she disappeared back through the door to the back of the shop.

A few hours later, Tyen drew himself and Rielle out of the place between worlds just outside the hamlet known as Brokebridge. It was two hours' carriage ride from Belton, set at the bottom of a modest valley fringed by young plantation forests. His aunt's husband had inherited part of that forest and a comfortable house around the time Tyen had joined the Academy. Fifteen cycles ago the couple had been raising four small children, who would be adults now, possibly married and beginning their own families.

The house had once impressed him, being a double-storey building with two small wings either side of the central section. What had seemed grand before he now admired for its simple, sturdy construction. He'd seen palaces the size of cities and mansions as large as villages, filled with countless treasure and luxuries, yet this place still stirred a little jealousy in him. He realised he still saw it as the ideal home, far from the city's noise and pollution, large enough for a family and a servant or two, but not so big that anyone would get lost inside it or the upkeep be too much for a successful middle-class man.

Taking a deep breath, Tyen walked up to the door and knocked.

It opened straight away to reveal a butler, who bowed stiffly. "Yes?"

"Tyen Ironsmelter, here to see my father, Deid Ironsmelter."

The man stilled, his eyebrows rising as he regarded Tyen with startled intensity. His mouth opened, closed, then he straightened. "I will enquire as to whether he is receiving visitors."

The man closed the door and retreated. Soon after, footsteps could be heard hurrying to the door, which was snatched open this time by a mature, robust woman. She stared at Tyen for a moment, her eyes widening with recognition.

"Tyen!" she exclaimed. "It really is you!"

"Hello, Aunt Moirie," he replied, smiling. As her gaze flickered to a point over Tyen's shoulder, he added: "This is Rielle Lazuli. A friend."

"I . . ." Moirie began as she considered how to respond to someone so obviously foreign, then she concluded that good manners were always the best beginning. "A pleasure to meet you, Rielle Lazuli." Her gaze snapped back to Tyen and she stepped aside. "Well, you two had better come through. Your father is in the garden, with my grandchildren."

"Grandchildren already!" Tyen exclaimed as he entered.

"Yes. Sovie married three years ago, to a local lad." Moirie chatted about her four offspring, two of which had joined the navy, as she led Tyen down the hall to the door leading out into the garden. As she opened it, the kitchen garden came into view, where two children so similar they must be twins raced around an old man sitting in a chair, a blanket wrapped about his shoulders.

All three looked up as Tyen followed his aunt out. The old man frowned as he saw Tyen, then his eyes went wide.

"Father," Tyen said, descending the stairs. At the bottom he paused. Deid was frozen, gazing at Tyen with what appeared to be incomprehension, then he blinked and life returned to his face. He pushed himself up out of the chair and walked unsteadily towards Tyen.

He seemed shorter. Smaller. So very much older. He did not stop a stride away but came up and threw his arms around Tyen. "Son."

Tyen paused. His father had never been a physically affectionate man. Public expressions of fondness were discouraged in Beltonian society. But Tyen's arms knew what to do, and without him really thinking about it, he returned the embrace, thankful that the man could not see that he was blinking away unexpected tears.

"I'm sorry," Tyen said. "I should have come home sooner."

"You would have if you could," Deid replied. He stepped back, and the glistening of moisture around the man's eyes made Tyen blink rapidly and look away.

"I'm afraid I could have," Tyen admitted. "I didn't have the courage."

His father nodded. "That's no surprise. The Academy would arrest you if they knew you were here. They think you're a thief, and possibly a murderer. A mass murderer."

Tyen frowned. "It was Kilraker who destroyed the tower." Then he grimaced. "Though I can't deny the rest. I did steal something from the Academy, and I'm afraid I have taken lives – though nobody in this world and not out of murderous intent."

Deid nodded. "You have some stories to tell, I see." He looked around, his gaze moving to Moirie, then noticed Rielle for the first time. His eyes widened, and a faint smile tweaked the corner of his mouth. "And who is this?"

"A friend. Rielle Lazuli."

His father stepped around him and bowed to Rielle. "Welcome to my sister's home. I don't think she will mind if I invite you two inside for warmth and refreshments."

"I would be honoured to accept," Rielle replied.

He looked at Moirie, who smiled and nodded. "I'll have Settie boil the kettle and bring it to the sitting room."

Soon after, Rielle, Tyen and his father settled into large, comfortable chairs arrayed around a freshly lit fire. Tyen began his tale, starting from his discovery of Vella in Mailand. His father listened intently, interrupting occasionally to ask only questions that clarified part of the story. Finally, Tyen finished by explaining how Liftre's sorcerers were trying to stop his efforts to start a school of sorcery, so he had come back to his home world to set one up in secret. Deid leaned back in his chair and let out a long breath.

"Amazing," he said. Then he bent forward a little and looked at Rielle. "Is it true that he is immortal now?"

Rielle hesitated. "I'm not sure the word you're using is the right one."

"We are called 'the ageless' by some," Tyen said. "We are not invulnerable. We can die."

"Are you ageless too?" Deid asked her.

She shook her head. "I am a Maker. We cannot be ageless."

"What is a Maker, if you don't mind me asking?"

"When people create, they generate magic," she told him. "Some more than others. I am able to create a great deal very quickly."

Deid stared at her, then turned to Tyen. "I did hear that right?"

"Yes."

"That is . . . controversial. Can you prove it?"

Tyen smiled. "Oh, very much. It is quite amazing to sense Rielle generating magic."

His father let out another long breath and closed his eyes. "Oh, the Academy is not going to like this."

"No," Tyen agreed.

Deid opened one eye. "You are planning a demonstration, then." Tyen nodded.

Both of the old man's eyes widened. "Is that wise? Even if you convince them, they still consider you a criminal."

"We will be fine. They are no threat to us."

"No threat? Not even the strongest and best sorcerers in the empire? You may have travelled the worlds, my son, but you can't defend yourself with confidence and stories alone. There is so little magic in the centre of Belton now that you will be as vulnerable as any ordinary man."

"I carry several times more power than this whole world contains," Tyen told him.

"And he is one of the three most powerful sorcerers in all the worlds," Rielle added.

Deid looked from her to Tyen and back again. "Really?"

She nodded. The man's eyes glowed, then he grinned as he looked at Tyen again. "One of the three most powerful! My son! Now that's something I can tell that judgemental bag of morni dung the locals elected as Brokebridge's Head next time he reminds me of my apparently criminal offspring."

Tyen winced. "I am sorry about that, Father."

Deid leaned forward and patted Tyen's arm. "I always knew you had a good reason for doing whatever you did. Imagine if the Academy had destroyed that book. You would never have left this world and become 'ageless'." He smiled, then it slowly slipped away. "But why are you bothering to prove the old myth is true? Why not set up your school elsewhere?"

"The Academy is a resource I'd like to have access to," Tyen replied.

"That old place?" His father shook his head. "They don't even know for certain that other worlds exist. Surely they are far behind the rest of the worlds?"

"You might be surprised. This world wasn't always isolated."

Deid wasn't convinced. "You should find yourself somewhere wonderful to spend eternity. You will be wasted here."

"Not at all," Tyen told him. "Once Rielle restores this world there will be plenty of magic to go around, and since this world is believed to be a dead one, my students and I will be able to work in peace and safety." He paused. "However, establishing myself here will have consequences for you, Father. What I plan to do will gain me enemies. Some may seek to retaliate or blackmail me by harming those I love. It would be safer if you moved to a secret location, temporarily."

"No!" Deid objected. "I don't want to be sent away to wait, alone, for news of you. I want to see what happens when you show them what fools they are!"

"But if they—"

"No!" Deid's expression was fierce and stubborn. "I am not leaving here unless I come with you."

"Can you hide him in the city?" Rielle asked. "They won't expect that."

Tyen looked from her to his father. "I'd rather not."

"If you take me far away, I'll immediately head home," Deid declared, "even if you put me on the other side of the world."

Tyen let out a long breath as he considered, then mused that it was the same mannerism he'd observed in his father.

"I'll watch over him," Rielle said. "You won't need me there most of the time."

Deid patted her hand. "I could not think of better company to have while my son shakes up that fusty old institution."

She smiled at him, then turned to Tyen. "I don't think you'll convince him otherwise, and you do have to make up for disappearing for fifteen cycles."

Tyen made a wordless sound of protest, to which both his father and former lover merely smirked. Rolling his eyes, he let his shoulders slump.

"Very well. But you had better do everything Rielle says, Father. We have a lot of catching up to do and that won't happen if you're kidnapped or murdered."

"That's enough of that talk, now the youngsters are here," Moirie said as she arrived, carrying a heavily laden tray, the children following. She set the tray down, then looked up at Tyen. "Have you still got that mechanical beetle you made? I've been telling the children about it, and they want to see it."

"Yes, I do!" Tyen replied and reached inside his jacket. "It's changed quite a bit, but it is still essentially a beetle shape, and it still does tricks to entertain the young." As he drew Beetle out and sent it flying around the room, he saw it through the eyes of his extended family – a slightly battered lump of metal that, as its wing covers flipped open and its legs extended, transformed into an intricate, beautiful object. He'd modified it constantly over the cycles, though mostly to give it abilities not needed here and now, where all it needed to do was fly in circles and crawl along children's arms to sit on their shoulder.

Beetle is a bit like me, he thought. *Older, with new abilities, but essentially still the same shape and form. While I can do so much more, I hope I'll never be above humble tasks like entertaining children and looking after my family.*

CHAPTER 6

Deid Ironsmelter rubbed his hands together eagerly as they left the hotel and set off in the direction of the Academy.

"Oh, this is going to be fun."

"We will be doing nothing more than talking to them," Tyen reminded his father.

"I know. I know." Deid's grin did not fade. He looked ten years younger than he had when Tyen first saw him, which made Tyen feel bad about seeing an old man when he'd first laid eyes on him. "But I can't wait to see their faces when you tell them what you want to do."

Tyen suppressed a sigh. Since he needed Rielle with him, and someone had to protect his father, he had no choice but to bring the man with him to his meeting with the Academy. It felt inadvisable to involve his father in his plans, but when he weighed up the risks they were no worse whether he had Deid with him or not. If Kilraker could track Tyen all the way to Spirecastle, then the Academy would find Deid eventually, no matter how carefully Tyen hid him. At least keeping Deid close meant that he was protected by two powerful sorcerers.

The streets of Belton were as busy as they had ever been. He and Rielle attracted curious glances, and not only because one of them looked so different to the locals. They had bought a second set of clothing, grander than the first ones. Even his father looked dignified and refined in his new suit. It had all been paid for with money Tyen had earned over several days by supplying magic to some of the local factories at the edge of the city. Many of Beltonia's industries had moved out of the centre of the metropolis, where magic was now completely depleted by mid-afternoon. Sorcerers once employed to drive the railsleds in the city had been laid off, as the lack of magic meant fewer engines could be run. Some had gained new jobs as watchmen, making sure nobody used more than their quota of magic.

Tyen had ensured no watchmen sensed the magic he released for the factories by making sure the sorcerers working there took it as quickly as he released it. It was part of his plan to have news of a powerful sorcerer selling magic precede his meeting with the Academy, but the last thing he needed was for them to suspect he was breaking laws in order to do so.

The grand front entrance of the Academy appeared as they turned a corner. Tall, elaborate gates stood open within a high wall. Three sets of broad stairs led up to rows of columns supporting a solid stone, half-circle porch. Deid fell silent as they walked towards it. Glancing at the old man, Tyen saw that his father's back was straight and he walked a little stiffly, his chin raised.

Tyen smiled. As a student, he had always entered the Academy through a side gate. Now he would use the same route the Emperor would when he was inclined to visit the school. Tyen doubted he'd be received as eagerly, however. Looking at the men standing around the Academy entrance and on the stairs, making a pretence of pausing to speak to a colleague or enjoy the view, Tyen didn't need to read their minds to know they were there to watch for him – and defend the institution if the need arose.

Tyen slowed so that Rielle and Deid were walking on either side of him as he reached the stairs. He met the gaze of each of the sorcerers waiting nearby, nodding respectfully. A few he recognised as either professors or former students. None returned his nod, but he thought that a few expressions may have softened a little.

They reached the top of the stairs. One of the great doors was open; the other closed. Both would have been open for important visitors, but that didn't bother Tyen. He hadn't expected a warm welcome, let alone a respectful one.

He stopped outside the door and bowed slightly as he gestured for Rielle, as a woman, to enter first. He then indicated that his father should enter next. Following, he saw several men standing in the Grand Hall, some clustered in twos or threes as if they had paused to converse. As if Tyen didn't know that members of the Academy did not usually loiter near the public entrance.

Nobody stepped forward to greet them. Tyen exchanged a glance with his father. They could wait here until someone came to guide them, but he figured the Academy needed reminding that he knew his way around. Ignoring the watching men, he led his companions down the hall and turned into the corridors beyond, starting the convoluted path to the Director's office. Their footsteps echoed in the narrow spaces, with a ghostly extra echo from those who followed at a discreet distance.

"Quite a labyrinth," Rielle murmured at one point, as Tyen ushered her through another doorway. "Are we still in the same building?"

"It depends if you consider the many wings as separate or part of the whole." He shrugged. "I've always suspected the first Director deliberately selected an office that took some time to get to so that anyone wanting to complain to him would have ample time to change their minds."

A staircase took them to the second level, then another long corridor finally delivered them to a closed door bearing a bronze plaque gleaming with the single word: "Director". Tyen paused to raise an eyebrow at Rielle and his father. The pair nodded to show they were ready. Turning back to the door, Tyen let out a little magic. As it flowed outwards he sensed the mind of the Director, alone in the room beyond. In rooms to the side were several sorcerers, tense and waiting in case the school's leader called for help.

Tyen knocked.

The door creaked open. Director Ophen stared at Tyen for a moment. *It really is him*, he thought. He'd sensed the magic that had abruptly flowed out from behind the door and guessed that Tyen had released it. *Why do that? Was it to get my attention? Impress me?* His eyes moved to Deid and Rielle briefly before returning to Tyen. He stepped aside and held the door open.

"Tyen Ironsmelter. Please come in and introduce your companions."

Once again, Tyen ushered Rielle and his father ahead of him before entering. Ophen closed the door and turned to face them.

"This is Rielle Lazuli," Tyen began, nodding to her. "Known throughout the worlds as the Maker."

Ophen nodded politely, noting that Tyen had used the plural of "worlds" and struggling to keep a sneer from his face. Though he knew references to other worlds existed in older texts, he didn't believe they existed.

"And you already know Deid Ironsmelter from your extensive investigation into my disappearance," Tyen added, gesturing to his father and noting both guilt and suspicion in the Director's mind as he nodded to Deid. Ophen pushed guilt aside. Many still thought Deid had helped his son disappear.

"Well, yes," Ophen said, avoiding Deid's gaze. "Our questions were necessary at the time."

Tyen turned to Rielle. "This is Director Ophen, Head of the Academy."

She nodded. Tyen turned back to Ophen as the Director moved behind his desk and sat down.

Ophen smoothed his jacket, then looked up at Tyen. "I don't think I need to explain that you are still regarded as a thief here. There are additional allegations that you were involved in the death of Professors Kilraker, Millen and Ragen and the adventurer, Tangor Gowel, as well as several thousand people of the Far South."

Tyen inclined his head. "My father has enlightened me about those charges."

"What do you have to say in response to them?"

Tyen held his gaze. "I am guilty of the theft, but not of the murders. Kilraker was ordered by the Sselt King not to take magic from within the structure of Spirecastle. He ignored that order and brought about the collapse of the building."

"You can prove this?"

"Yes. One of the survivors still lives." Tyen was not sure how good a witness Mig would be since he could not sense magic, but the young man could confirm that Spirecastle had fallen after Tyen had moved out of the world.

"One of the southerners?" Ophen made a dismissive gesture. "They were of little help to our investigation. Besides, they are hardly going to be able to travel here to speak at your trial."

Tyen smiled. "It can be arranged, if you are still determined to hold one after today."

Ophen frowned as if he'd tasted something disgusting. "Why on earth wouldn't I be?"

"I have something to offer the Academy, indeed this entire world, that may cast such matters in a different light."

"Which is?"

"Magic. More magic than this world has contained for hundreds of years. Enough magic to enable Academy sorcerers to travel out of this world and explore others."

Ridiculous, Ophen thought. "Oh, and where would you get this magic from? Other worlds?"

"No. It would be rather impolite to weaken neighbouring worlds in order to strengthen this one." Tyen looked at Rielle. "Would you please demonstrate, la' Lazuli?"

She smiled, opened her small drawstring bag and brought out a folded piece of paper and a slim black rod. "Might I use a corner of your desk as support?" she asked of the Director.

Ophen nodded. "Of course."

Unfolding the paper, she ran a hand over it and the creases disappeared. Then, looking up at Ophen with a sudden intense gaze, she began to draw. Tyen watched in fascination. He had seen her create magic only a few times before. Within confident strokes she captured the character of the Director's face. A few more and she had filled in eyes, nose and mouth. He was so impressed it took a moment for him to notice the burst of magic that had exploded from her.

The sound of doors slamming open made him jump. He instinctively strengthened the shield he'd been holding around himself and his father, and extended it to surround Rielle. It turned the air cold, so the breath of the four sorcerers now surrounding him misted.

They were casting about, wary and confused.

"Should I continue?" Rielle asked. She remained bent over the desk, the drawing stick hovering over the portrait.

The newcomers looked at Ophen, who scowled. "I said come in only if I called."

"But we sensed . . ."

"The magic . . ."

"We thought . . ."

Ophen flapped his hands. "Out!"

The four retreated to the adjoining rooms, closing the doors behind them. Ophen used the time to collect his thoughts. He'd sensed the outflow of magic. He'd guessed what Tyen would say next. *"See?" he'll say. "Creativity generates magic! Forgive all my sins and honour me with accolades for proving that old myth is true." It is a trick.*

"It is no trick," Rielle told him. "You will see, if you observe closely . . ." Her drawing stick lowered to the paper.

"No!" Ophen shook his head. "Apologies, la' Lazuli," he added in a gentler voice. "That will not be necessary." He looked at Tyen, his eyes bright with anger. "Is this your offer? Did you not learn anything while studying here? Do you really think we would be fooled by this?"

"Actually, this isn't my offer," Tyen replied. "Proving that creativity generates magic is a minor thing. More important is to ensure the Academy adapts to the benefits and dangers of the return of magic. Once this world is accessible, otherworld sorcerers are sure to visit. Not all of them will have good intentions. With my help they will not find an ignorant, vulnerable world but a strong one prepared for trade and defence. The Academy could become one of the largest and most powerful schools in all the worlds."

Ophen stared at Tyen, incredulous but also hating the spark of fear that had flared at the dangers the young upstart had hinted at.

Before he could speak, Tyen continued. "But you are right, Director; I did not think you would accept anything I told or offered you. I doubted the Academy had changed since I left. I expected your response. I had to at least offer you the chance to consider your position, and the Academy's. And this world's. Give yourself a few days to think. It is a lot to take in."

The Director's face flushed. "You won't frighten me with these lies." Ophen rose and pointed to the door. "Leave, before I call on my assistants to throw you out."

"I take it you don't need time to consider?"

"NO! LEAVE!"

Tyen looked at Rielle, who shrugged and dropped the drawing stick back into her bag. Deid was frowning, but as Tyen looked at him, the glint of smugness returned to his gaze. Tyen smiled, turned his back on the Director and opened the door. He ushered Rielle out.

"You're an old fool, Ophen," Deid said as he followed, pausing to look back from the corridor. "This world and the Academy have a rude awakening coming, and the only person interested in helping is my son."

"Come on, Father," Tyen said, pressing a hand gently on the old man's shoulder. He stepped out into the corridor and pulled the door closed. From within he heard a muffled voice speak.

"You know what to do."

The Director's meaning was clear in his mind. Tyen said nothing as he led his companions back through the maze of corridors to the entry hall. The number of sorcerers there had grown, and their pretence at nonchalance was spoilt by the hurried arrival of more. They moved to block the main entrance. From the side Tyen heard a raspy old voice speak, and he turned to see Professor Delly hobble in from a side room.

"You shouldn't have come back, Tyen Ironsmelter." The sorcery teacher looked around the room. "Arrest him!"

As the men closed in, Tyen wondered what they intended to do. They had no magic. Perhaps they meant to manhandle him into submission. He held a hand out to Rielle, then another to his father.

"Take a deep breath, Father," he instructed. Listening to the old man and Rielle, he waited until they had filled their lungs, then pushed a little way out of the world – just as the first of the men reached him. Hands passed through them. The Academy's best sorcerers stared and exchanged confused and wondering looks. Tyen paused for a few heartbeats to enjoy Delly gaping like a simpleton.

Then he skimmed away.

CHAPTER 7

It is a shame I never got to see the palace before I left this world, Tyen mused as he entered the building's Great Hall. *I've seen so many spectacular buildings out in the worlds that this seems . . . disappointing.*

And yet, he'd have preferred to be even less impressed by it. Or rather, he'd have been more impressed if the palace had been restrained in its display of wealth, as he knew many of these sumptuous fabrics, elaborate gilded furniture, wall decorations and artwork had been acquired with wealth gained from the conquest and colonisation of other lands.

As his armed escort guided him down the entry hall, he looked through doorways on either side to corridors running parallel to the hall. More doorways opened upon huge, highly decorated rooms beyond. The palace entrance followed the same plan as the Academy – though more likely the latter building had copied the palace – only at a grander scale. The greatest difference were the two enormous doors at the end of the hall that his escort was leading him towards, exactly where the Academy had a mural depicting the institution's founding.

He expected that one of the doormen would open one of the doors to begrudgingly allow an expelled Academy student entrance beyond. Instead, both men moved, hauling the doors open just in time for Tyen to reach them and pass through.

On the other side was a smaller hall, lined with tasteful sets of chairs for those awaiting an audience. Tyen let out a little magic as he saw that a quarter of these were occupied. The well-dressed men and women watching him were relieved to have a moment's distraction from their long wait to see the monarch. They examined Tyen closely, wondering who he was to be welcomed with full-door access and a guard of honour. A foreigner, some guessed, since they believed they knew all the important people of Belton on sight. Perhaps some dignitary of the colonies. Whoever he was, the doors to the audience chamber were opening, so he must be very important indeed as he was getting immediate access to the Emperor.

Tyen hid a smile and let out a gentle drift of magic as he passed. Though some were sorcerers, none of them took any of the magic he was releasing. None sought to read his mind. It simply did not occur to them to try.

Would they have been so passive if he'd come here with Rielle? He'd left her with Deid, guessing that coming alone would seem less threatening than arriving with someone not of the empire. While the Emperor's guards might not be as wary of a woman, and they did not know she was a powerful sorcerer, she would be regarded with more caution than Tyen due to her clearly being a foreigner.

His escort headed towards yet another pair of doors, but these did not open. The man stopped and tapped lightly on the right-hand door. It opened slightly and a thin face peered out. This was the Emperor's secretary, and as he saw Tyen he pushed the door open fully and stepped aside.

"You may enter, Tyen Ironsmelter."

Tyen nodded to the man and obeyed. The room beyond was small compared to the halls behind him, but large for an office. A long table stood at the far end of the room, behind which sat a fashionably attired and immaculately groomed middle-aged man. The Emperor watched him approach calmly. *Looks like moustaches are still in vogue*, Tyen mused. Several other men stood at either side of the room. Tyen judged where to stop by their thoughts, then bowed and remained bent, keeping his eyes on the floor.

A silent pause followed, then Emperor Omniten spoke.

"Tyen Ironsmelter. Welcome back to Leratia."

"Thank you, Imperial Majesty."

"You may rise."

Tyen straightened and met the man's gaze directly, noting curiosity as well as wariness before he looked down again.

"I received your gifts." A rustle of paper came from the table. "Fascinating. Are you claiming that these places are real?"

Tyen glanced at the table to confirm the man was referring to the maps he'd sent. "They are, your Majesty."

"Do you have proof of this?"

"The only way I could convince you beyond doubt would be to take you out of this world and visit them."

The Emperor paused. "Or you could take someone else. Someone I trust to tell me the truth of the matter."

Tyen nodded.

"I may do that . . . but I would like to know more about you before I risked such a man. Why should I trust someone who admitted to Director Ophen that he stole an item belonging to the Academy?"

"Because the Academy had no right to own her."

A pause. "*Her?*"

"The item he refers to is a woman. She was transformed into a book thousands of years ago. I believe owning a person is considered slavery and outlawed here."

"It is, indeed. Do you still have her?"

"Yes."

"Does this not make you her owner?"

"I am her carrier and protector."

"I see. You can prove all this?"

"I can only try. There is always the possibility that you will think it a trick."

"Let me be the one to decide that."

Tyen loosened his shirt and brought out Vella's pouch. Opening it, he drew her out. "She absorbs all the memories of the people who touch her," he warned. "And she has no choice but to answer questions. I recommend that you let me hold her while you communicate with her."

"Very well."

Opening Vella, Tyen looked down at her pages. Words formed.

Hello, Tyen.

Hello, Vella. Let me introduce you to the Imperial Majesty Emperor Omniten of the Leratian Empire.

"Your Imperial Majesty, Emperor Omniten, meet Vella," he said aloud.

He turned her outwards so the Emperor could see her reply. The man leaned forward and squinted, then beckoned Tyen closer. Moving to the other side of the table, Tyen extended his arms. The man's eyes moved back and forth as he read.

"Greetings, Vella," he said. "Tyen tells me you were once a woman. Is this true?"

Since Tyen could not see Vella's reply, he read it from the Emperor's mind.

Greetings, Emperor Omniten. Yes, it is true.

"And how did you become a book?"

The sorcerer, Roporien the Clever, transformed me.

The man's eyebrows lowered. "Roporien. I see. So, if you absorb all the memories of those who touch you, you must contain all of his knowledge, too. Is that right?"

Yes. But when he realised this made him vulnerable, he avoided touching me, instead having others hold me when he wanted to make use of me.

The Emperor's eyes narrowed. "Well, I should not be surprised that he took such precautions. How do I know that what you are telling me is the truth?"

Having not read your memories, I cannot tell you how you may be convinced of this.

178

"I see. How could you be destroyed?"

Take me to a world with no magic. I can store a little, but it would soon be depleted — all the faster if I had to use it to actively defend against attempts to destroy me. Eventually the materials I am made from would deteriorate beyond the point of revival.

"Are you saying you can't be destroyed in this world, because there is magic here?"

That is correct.

"So . . . am I right in guessing a sorcerer would have to surround you in Soot?" he asked, using the Leratian term for the darkness where there was no magic.

Yes.

"Are there other ways you might be destroyed?"

Yes.

The Emperor smiled. "But you're going to make me ask specifically what they are, aren't you?"

I am hardly going to make it easy to reveal the means to my destruction.

He laughed. "No, you would not, and it is not polite for me to ask." He looked thoughtful. His gaze flickered up to Tyen and back again. "Well, then tell me something Tyen does not know, that I do."

When Director Ophen handled me fifteen cycles ago, I learned that he gained his position through bribes and threats, not in a fair election, and had since sold off some of the Academy's treasures to help buy properties.

Tyen hid his surprise. *I thought Ophen ignorant and stubborn, but not dishonourable!* He looked up to find the Emperor watching him.

"How is it that he does not know this?" the ruler asked.

He never asked me to tell him the Director's secrets.

"Well, that seems unbelievable. Is he really not that curious?"

He has not had the time or need to wonder about the lives of people he did not think he would meet again.

The Emperor glanced at Tyen. "Didn't he?" He did not wait for an answer. "I suppose if you contain several lifetimes' worth of memories it will take several more to access it, and he hasn't owned – no, carried – you for more than a small part of one lifetime. Is it true that he is immortal?"

No.

"Was Director Ophen lying when he told me Tyen claimed to be?"

He was in error.

"In what way?"

Tyen will not age unless he wills it. However, it is more likely that he will die than he will not. Ageless sorcerers rarely live for more than a thousand years. Many do not last more than a few hundred.

"Can anyone be immortal?"

I cannot say. I would have to live for ever in order to know that someone had lived for ever, and since for ever in your mind is a continuous, never-ending concept—

"I see what you're saying." The Emperor waved a hand. "So how is it that Tyen does not age?"

Very powerful sorcerers can, with enough magic, alter the pattern of their bodies so that they constantly heal and renew themselves.

Omniten glanced up at Tyen. "Can he make others the same?"

Only if they are sorcerers of adequate strength.

The man's shoulders slumped. "Sorcerers," he muttered, as if the word was a curse. He sighed and lifted his chin. "Are there truly many worlds beyond this one?"

Yes.

"Is it true that creativity generates magic, and Tyen's companion, Rielle Lazuli, can restore the magic of this world?"

Yes and yes.

He nodded. "Thank you, Vella. It was a pleasure talking to you." He looked at Tyen. "Please close the book without reading it."

Tyen obeyed.

"I am convinced," the ruler said, "that you are not putting the words on the page. I have seen no proof that a woman was transformed into this book, rather than it simply being a book that appears to think and speak. However, I would prefer to give any such sentient being all the rights of a person anyway. So, open her to me again."

Tyen did as he was bid.

"Are you a slave, Vella? Are you free to do what you want and go where you wish?" the Emperor asked.

No and no.

"Why are you not free to do and go where you wish?"

I am, as you can see, in the form of a book. That somewhat restricts my ability to move. I rely on whoever carries me for transport and protection.

"Are you happy to rely on Tyen Ironsmelter for this?"

Yes. He is an honourable man who has never even asked how he might destroy me.

The Emperor chuckled. "Then I will not seek to remove you from his protection." He looked up, scanning the faces of those in the room. "Let it be known that Tyen Ironsmelter is not guilty of theft. The Academy does not have the right to possess Vella. Tyen is her guardian and protector."

Blinking in surprise, Tyen looked down at Vella in wonder. He'd not thought that introducing her to the Emperor would lead to this. It made him nervous. If he had not anticipated this, could he have also not anticipated something that would go wrong for him?

Or was this a trick, to make him relax his guard and think the Emperor was on his side until some other ploy to apprehend him was found? The Emperor was not thinking of such an intention. He was watching Tyen closely, though, noting his hesitation to express gratitude.

"Thank you, your Imperial Majesty," Tyen said hastily.

The man shrugged. "It is a small matter. According to Director Ophen, you have other, greater reasons for returning to Belton. Tell me what they are."

Tyen drew in a deep breath. "I am seeking a place to settle and teach a small group of young sorcerers. This world is familiar to me, without the problems associated with a local language to adopt and customs to understand. It is also my home, and I do still feel some sentimental attachment to it. It would benefit from my school's presence here. In order for this world to be suitable as a school's location, it needs to be rich in magic. Rielle is the greatest Maker ever known. She can generate in minutes more magic than this world has contained in hundreds of years. With what she produces, not only would my school have enough to use in training, but sorcerers of this world will be able to use it again without any machines coming to a halt."

The Emperor's eyes narrowed. "And what price would she ask for such a restoration?"

"None, from this world." Tyen shook his head, then shrugged. "I, however, will owe her a favour."

"What would that favour be?"

"That is . . . private. It is for her to reveal if she wishes to, not me."

"I see. And will she be a part of this school of yours?"

"No. Her task is restoring worlds, not teaching. Though I would welcome her help if she ever wished to join my school."

The Emperor drummed his fingers on the table. "Then what is the price *you* ask of *us* for arranging to have our world restored?"

Tyen paused, considering again whether his request – or demand – was too much to ask. Then he reminded himself that he did not actually need the Emperor's permission to do anything. Nothing could stop him from seizing control.

He did not, however, wish to. Not just because he had no desire to run an empire but because it was so much easier and more convenient to make use of what was established here in Beltonia. If the Emperor did not accept Tyen's offer, there was the Sselt option. Or Tyen could set up in one of the distant lands where the empire's control was weak, or help one of the colonised territories rise up and drive out their conquerors.

With so many options, he may as well ask for what he'd come for.

He smiled crookedly. And what Vella had revealed would only improve his chances of getting it.

"Why start a new school when there's one here already? I want the Academy."

CHAPTER 8

A few days later, as the walls of the Emperor's audience chamber resolved around them, Tyen was amused to see that Ividian, the Emperor's close friend, was still grinning broadly. The man's euphoric expression only wavered as air surrounded him and the urge to gasp for breath returned. But he recovered his composure quickly, straightening and striding towards the monarch.

"That was . . . amazing!" he panted. "The things . . . I saw! And this . . . method of . . . transportation is . . . most efficient!"

Omniten rose from behind his desk to meet him, his relief obvious as he took his friend's arm. "Are you well, my friend?"

"Yes, yes! Just . . . out of breath . . . no air between worlds. Must hold your breath."

The Emperor glanced at Tyen. "And why are you not short of breath?"

"An advantage of agelessness, your Majesty."

The man's eyebrows rose. "Well then, you have provided the proof I requested." He glanced at Ividian, who nodded enthusiastically. "The rest is up to you, Ironsmelter. While you were gone I ordered the Academy to immediately arrange a meeting between yourself and the Board of Governors. It shall commence as soon as you arrive. Two of my people will accompany you, to make it known that I am in favour of you replacing Ophen as Director, once the Academy has ousted him." A pair of sorcerers stepped forward, bowing to the Emperor and favouring Tyen with a respectful nod. "As I said earlier, it would be unwise to overrule the agreement between the palace and the Academy that they may elect their administrators. You must persuade them."

Tyen nodded. "I will do my best." He bowed. "Thank you, your Imperial Majesty."

The man smiled. "Good luck, Tyen Ironsmelter."

As Tyen left, the two sorcerers fell into step beside him. He turned to the one on the left. "What is your name?"

"Berre Capster."

He turned to the other. "And you?"

"Xarol Gilden."

Tyen nodded. Gilden was the name of an old and powerful family. Berre was a foreign first name but Capster was a local surname, and the man's mannerisms and an edge to his speech hinted at a middle-class upbringing. Both men were young enough that they would have finished their education only a few years before Tyen had become a student.

He had let loose magic as he had arrived, but it had thinned as it drifted outwards and he could now barely sense their minds. As he released more, Berre checked his stride.

"You let magic out constantly," he said. "Do you mean for us to take it?"

Tyen hid his dismay at the idea. If they did, he would have very little chance to read their minds. Fortunately, they had asked because they were not sure if it would be bad-mannered – or a trick. "Why do you think I do it?"

"To remind us of what we'll have if we cooperate," Xarol replied, his voice low but full of amusement.

Tyen chuckled and turned to him. "Perhaps. Are you in favour of the return of magic?"

The man nodded once.

"Of course," Berre replied. "What is the point of being a sorcerer in a world with no magic?"

"Can you see no benefit in it other than to sorcerers?" Tyen asked.

Berre frowned. "Of course I can. It benefits everyone." A note of disapproval in his voice spurred Tyen to look closer. The suggestion had stirred a strong belief in fairness and strengthened his dislike of sorcerers who used their ability for selfish reasons.

Interesting, Tyen thought. Perhaps the Emperor had chosen Berre as one of his representatives, knowing the man's values would see any attempt to bribe him or the professors fail, but he had inadvertently chosen the perfect assistant for Tyen.

They had reached the palace entrance now. Tyen did not slow, conscious that any hesitation might be seen as weakness. A carriage waited. Tyen was going to ignore it, but he caught the vehicle's purpose from Berre's mind just in time. Still, it would look arrogant if he assumed . . .

"For us?" he asked.

"Yes," Xarol replied.

The journey from there might have been faster on foot, as the streets were busy with traffic of all kinds. Tyen noted a lamplighter cleaning one of the street lamps. They had been converted to oil since magic had diminished. That explained why the city air was smokier than he recalled. Deid had said that the rich were having fireplaces installed for their hydraulic heating systems, and the city administrators were investigating alternatives to magically pumped sewerage. They passed a long carriage drawn by a team of four mergels – normally seen only in the countryside, bred for meat or milk – hauling passengers destined for the outer railsled stations, since there was not enough magic in the centre to run a reliable service.

All this would change soon. Tyen had told the Emperor he would have Rielle restore the world whether he became the Director of the Academy or not. He was relying on the threat of another country hosting Tyen's school and gaining the knowledge of other worlds, rather than on the lure of plentiful magic, to persuade the Emperor and Academy to give him what he wanted. Now he worried that he had given up a stronger lure.

The carriage turned off the street into the one that soon passed the Academy gates. It gave Tyen little forewarning before they pulled to a halt and the door opened. The two sorcerers did not move to alight, politely giving Tyen precedence. He nodded to them in gratitude and climbed down to the ground.

No guard stood watch at the Academy gates or main entry. No professors stood waiting either. Tyen waited until his companions had exited the carriage, then straightened, stepped through the gates and started up the stairs.

Though flanked by the Emperor's men, he suddenly felt very alone. His father had wanted to come, but Tyen had insisted Deid stay in the hotel with Rielle. Tyen wanted nothing distracting the professors from the proposal – and revelations – he was about to present to them.

Once at the top of the stairs, a graduate so young he must have only recently finished his studies stepped forward.

"The Board of Governors awaits you in the meeting hall."

Tyen nodded. "Lead the way."

The journey was considerably shorter than the one to Director Ophen's office. After leading them down two wide corridors, the young graduate stopped before a pair of carved, wooden doors. A deep, low hum reached Tyen's ears. As the guide pushed open the doors with magic, the sound magnified into the cacophony of many voices.

But the chatter was already diminishing as the doors swung open, and heads had turned to face Tyen. He paused for a moment before entering; then, as he did, he let forth more magic than he had released so far since entering the world. It spilled out and filled the meeting hall, allowing him to seek who, of the twenty-seven men sitting in the V-shaped arrangement of chairs, was paying enough attention to magic to detect it.

Five of them had. Not Professor Delly, the Head of Magical

Studies, he noted. The old man was concentrating on examining Tyen, noting how the disgraced student did indeed appear well preserved for his age. Which would not work in Tyen's favour, he believed, since youth reduced a man's air of authority.

Half of the twenty-seven Governors were sorcerers; half were not. Like the late Professor Kilraker, many of the sorcerers did not necessarily specialise in magical subjects – particularly if their ability was small. The Academy had remained strong despite the diminishing of magic because it was an institution of learning, not sorcery. This, Tyen reminded himself, was why he'd decided not to use the return of magic as the reward for their cooperation, but the lure of knowledge.

The young graduate stopped at the opening of the V-shaped seating. "Tyen Ironsmelter," he announced, then walked back to the entrance. As Tyen stepped forward, followed by the Emperor's sorcerers, the doors closed firmly behind him.

Director Ophen rose. "Tyen Ironsmelter. You have persuaded the Emperor to ask us to meet with you. Please explain why."

"With pleasure. Good afternoon, all," Tyen said, inclining his head towards either side of the seats. "I am here to persuade you to not just allow me to join your ranks, but to elect me as Director of the Academy, so that I may protect and guide you during the changes that are about to overtake this world."

Gasps, curses and quiet laughter followed, but all were subdued. Tyen met the gaze of several of the men and found them unsteady. Some had seen him, Rielle and Deid disappear from the Grand Hall, and had considered that everything Tyen had claimed was true. Some had heard rumours about Tyen's conversation with the Emperor. All emanated worry and fear, and a little admiration for his boldness and honesty.

"Will you listen?" Tyen asked. He had meant it as a rhetorical question, so he was surprised when a murmur of assent came. Not from all. Director Ophen's growl cut across the sound.

"Why should we listen to you, a thief and a liar?"

Tyen smiled sadly. "Because I am neither. Because I intend to run a school of magic in this world that will be respected in all the worlds, whether that school is the Academy or I join another or begin a new one. Because that school will gain the knowledge I've gathered travelling many, many worlds, and that of the teachers I bring here. Because to run that school effectively I'll need a world full of magic, and when I have arranged for this world's restoration, the Academy will discover it is not prepared for such a change, and I can guide and protect it as it adapts."

"You can do all this?" one of the professors asked, but before Tyen could answer, Ophen spoke over him.

"The Academy already has a Director." The man stared at Tyen, his stony face hiding the doubts and fear that shivered beneath.

Tyen shrugged. "Not for long." He turned to the Emperor's man, Berre. "Look at Ophen. Look at him with your mind. Reach out and listen." The man frowned as he stared at the Director. "Can you hear anything?" Tyen asked.

Berre blinked, his eyebrows rising. "I can. It's . . . more than words. It's . . ."

Tyen turned back to the Director. "Tell me, Director Ophen, how many Academy treasures did you sell to pay for your houses? What else have you sold them to pay for?"

As Berre sucked in a breath, the Director went pale. He glanced at the other professors, who were watching him closely. "Lies," he said. "It is a trick."

"It certainly is not!" Berre declared angrily. "Ironsmelter has not done anything but show me how to see your thoughts. I see your guilt, as plain as if you confessed it. And more so, for I can *feel* it!"

"I, too," a quiet voice added. Heads turned to the speaker, the quiet professor of Biology. Tyen saw that the man's shock at being able to see Ophen's thoughts was greater than at the man's guilt. *It is so easy*, the man thought. *What can be seen in* my *mind?*

In the corner of Tyen's eye he saw Berre lean forward and begin to focus on other professors' minds. At once, Tyen reached out and stripped the room of magic.

All the sorcerers winced.

"I apologise. That was abrupt but necessary." Tyen took a step forward. "In a world where minds can be read, strict rules of privacy need to be established. There are also ways to block one's mind from examination. This is one of the many reasons you will need my guidance, once magic is restored." Tyen looked at Ophen, whose gaze now slid away. "Shall I elaborate on the other reasons?"

The Director remained silent. After a moment, another of the professors replied:

"Yes. Please do."

Tyen bowed his head for a moment as he considered where to start. He so wanted to tell them of what happened at Spirecastle, but Kilraker's crime would make Ophen's seem diminished and the story would not drive home the point he needed to make.

"When I left this world, I was as ignorant and vulnerable as you are," Tyen told them. He looked up and saw how they bridled. "Yes, ignorant. It has been far too long since this world was in contact with those beyond it. The Academy has forgotten not just that other worlds exist, but the benefits and dangers of links to the outside.

"It became immediately apparent that I had a lot to learn about magic, so I joined a school well respected in the worlds. I paid for my tuition with the one kind of knowledge this school lacked: mechanical magic. You see, in our isolation, the sorcerers here developed something unique to the worlds: the unification of magic and machinery. As our invention slowly depleted this world of magic, we made our machines ever more efficient and clever. When I brought that knowledge to the worlds, it was the first new field of knowledge seen in thousands of years.

"Many sorcerers out in the worlds would be eager to visit the place in which mechanical magic was invented, if they knew where it was." Tyen paused, noting the pride they could not help feeling even as they struggled to believe him. "Those I taught it to passed the knowledge on to others, and as the concept spread it developed further and, as so often is the case, was turned to uses both good and terrible. The latter includes war machines of brutal efficiency and horror." He shook his head. "I do not doubt that many peoples of the worlds would try to destroy the place in which mechanical magic was invented, and the people who created it, if they knew where it was."

A murmur of anger and fear began to rise, but Tyen raised his hands to forestall it. "You might be tempted to hide from such a threat, choosing to give up all magic for the safety of isolation. But you already suspect that Leratian society will go backwards, diminishing to a primitive state, without magic. You know many will starve, as food production slows. I am here to warn you: a dead world can still be found and entered, if a sorcerer is powerful enough. Letting this world's magic run low will not save it, if it is discovered." He let his arms fall. "If this world is restored, we will have enough magic to protect it from such visitors . . . as long as sufficient sorcerers within it know how to defend against sorcerers capable of wielding large amounts of magic."

He shrugged. "I have told you this world will be renewed whatever you decide. I do not need your permission to start a school of magic. However, I do need your support if I am to run it here, as part of the Academy. If you elect me as your new Director, I promise to help the Academy adapt to the return of magic, teach sorcerers how to defend this world and, in future, give advice on matters of trade and alliances with the outside. The decision is yours." He took a step back, noting the Governors' varied expressions, from doubt to dismissal. "Do you have any questions?"

Nobody spoke. As the silence stretched, Tyen watched the Governors exchanging glances and felt doubts rising. Finally, he let out a little magic, ignoring Berre's chuckle as minds became readable. He learned that all were hesitating not because they had nothing to say, or were reluctant to speak, but because most wanted to do so without Tyen there. Some feared what he would do if they spoke against him, others did not want to admit they had been persuaded by him while he was there, in case they looked like they were grovelling, or seeking to ally themselves with him. And then there was the matter of Ophen, who many thought should be dealt with first.

"I will leave you to discuss it," he said, then glanced at Berre and Xarol, "and also to consult with these two fine men, who the Emperor has sent to make his wishes clear on the matter. I will return to my hotel room and await your response."

With that, Tyen bent in a shallow bow, then turned away. He walked to the doors, opening them with a small push of magic from the other side, then closing them behind him once he was through.

Then he allowed himself a small, brief smile before heading back to the hotel, Rielle and his father.

CHAPTER 9

The expressions on the faces of Tyen's father and Rielle could not be more opposite. Deid was beaming with pride as he looked around at the polished wood cabinets filled with old books and treasures. Rielle's eyebrows were raised as she considered the small, dingy room with ill-concealed dismay.

"This is really what you want?" she asked in a low voice.

Tyen smiled. "Yes, though I'm planning to move the Director's office to somewhere more easily accessible to visitors as soon as possible."

"And a little more impressive, I hope."

Deid regarded her loftily. "The Academy is foremost a place of learning and knowledge, not of displays of wealth or power."

She turned to face him, nodding respectfully. "If I believed Tyen cared more about the latter I would not be helping him. However, his work will be easier if he is respected, and it will help him to earn that respect if his office conveys authority as well as responsibility."

Tyen's father pursed his lips. "I suppose I agree with that, but there is also the philosophy of the Academy to maintain."

"The one that allowed it to help the Emperor conquer other lands and grow rich by taking their resources?" she asked.

Deid winced. "Some Academy members did protest during that time, but they dared not speak too loudly against the Emperor."

She smiled and touched his shoulder gently. "That is all too often the case. I'm glad to hear someone tried, at least."

Tyen looked from his father to Rielle. His heart had lifted at her first words. *She believes my motives are good.* Did that mean she trusted him again? *It's not the same thing.* He was all too aware that he was relying on her a great deal. If she changed her mind about helping him, he'd have to abandon his plan to establish a safe place here for his students. He'd be laughed at for his grand unfulfilled promises. It would likely lose him respect, his new position, and he'd probably have to leave his world out of shame.

Respect. Yes, it was important. As the pair turned to regard him, he glanced around the office. "The plainness of this room does seem like false humility now, considering Ophen's theft from the Academy. I have seen similar guilt in the minds of more than a few professors since he was arrested. He was not the only one selling treasures."

"Kilraker was doing the same," his father reminded him. "Sometimes people only join in a minor criminal activity because everyone else seems to be doing it."

"And yet they made such a fuss about Tyen taking Vella," Rielle mused.

"I'd wager she is more valuable and dangerous than anything the professors sold," Tyen pointed out. "They would have sold items that wouldn't be missed."

Deid nodded. "But were there pieces more valuable than they realised? Something they didn't understand. I wonder if there are any records of what was bought by whom."

"I doubt it, but I could order an investigation."

"Make it official and all traces of evidence may disappear," Rielle warned.

A chime brought their attention to a small, ornate clock on the desk; then they looked up and exchanged glances. Tyen's heart had quickened at the sound, and his father's eyes were suddenly bright.

"I still can't believe you convinced almost everyone to make you Director," Deid said. "Especially the Emperor."

"He seems like a smart man," Rielle replied, "who has foreseen all the ways this could go, and chosen the path of least conflict. Perhaps he is also excited by the prospect of a revived and changed world – and not just because he may benefit from it. He does care about his people."

"That is good to know." Deid frowned. "Though maybe not for Tyen. I will worry even more that he will try to get rid of you, my son. You hold too much power."

Tyen nodded. "He has no plans to at the moment, but that doesn't mean he wouldn't in future, if the threat I pose outweighs the benefits of having me around."

"He'll be looking for signs of weakness that he can exploit should you come into conflict," Deid warned.

"As we inevitably will, I expect." Tyen sighed.

"You should let him find one," Rielle advised. "Something that appears to be a weakness but isn't."

They paused as a knock interrupted them. With a small application of magic, Tyen opened the door. One of the Academy message-carriers hovered nervously in the opening.

"They've left the palace, Director Tyen," the young man said.

"Thank you, Simel," Tyen replied. A look of surprise and puzzlement crossed the messenger's face, as he wondered how Tyen had learned his name when he was new to the job. "You may go."

As the boy hurried away, Tyen stood up and straightened his clothing. "Well, we had best make our way to the Grand Hall."

"Can't keep the Emperor waiting," Deid agreed.

Once they were in the corridor, they remained silent. The details of the coming ceremony had been decided already, as well as how they would act if something did not go to plan. As they neared the Grand Hall the hum of hundreds of voices reached them, growing louder as they arrived at a side entrance. When the side doors to the ornate room opened, the sound rolled out over them, but not for long. As their arrival was announced, it became a hushed murmur.

Tyen paused. Even after everything that had happened to him these last fifteen cycles, he still found being the object of such attention disquieting. He looked at Rielle. She appeared elegant and otherworldly, clad in a silvery grey dress in the cut of Belton fashion, and with no ornament but the familiar silver lozenge pendant at her throat and a plain silver clip holding her long dark hair up in a neat arrangement upon her head. More eyes would be following her than him, he decided. As he glanced at Deid, his father smiled and stepped aside.

Ignoring the crowd, Tyen entered the hall and walked, with Rielle at his side, down the length of it towards the main doors. The interior was utterly empty of magic, to ensure the Emperor's mind could not be read, and Tyen had agreed not to release any more during the ceremony unless magical defence was needed. The Emperor's requirements were to be expected. It would not have surprised Tyen if Omniten had decided the world must not be restored in order to keep his thoughts private, but the ruler believed that it was a sacrifice he must make, and he would be able to find other ways to protect his privacy and secrets.

The main doors were open. As Tyen and Rielle stepped outside, two lines of royal guards in the palace's elaborate formal uniform, bordering the stairs to the main street, came into sight. Beyond the open Academy gates, the street was crowded with onlookers hoping to see the Emperor, kept to either side of the road by city guards.

A roar of cheers rose from this audience, but as far as Tyen could see, nothing had changed. The faces of the crowd were turned towards the Academy, not the direction the royal carriage would arrive from. He glanced behind, looking for the source of their excitement.

"It's you, Tyen," Rielle murmured.

He looked at her in disbelief, only to catch a brief, amused smile.

"You haven't skimmed the minds of your people lately, have you?" she said. "You've become quite the hero – a poor commoner with a rare gift who explored the worlds and has come back to save everyone, rich and poor alike."

He snorted. "I wasn't poor."

"No, but you weren't rich and powerful either. Wave to them. See what they do."

Though it seemed a little silly, he lifted a hand, turning to include all in the gesture. At once, a cheer rose, louder than the last.

Rielle chuckled. "See?"

He gave her a sidelong look. "Your turn."

Her smirk faded. One eye narrowed. Then she straightened and raised a hand. Another, though quieter, cheer broke from the audience. She smiled. "They don't really know much about me, other than that I am a sorcerer from another world, who looks very different to them."

He nodded. "We should address that. They need to know they will have you to thank for restoring their world, not me."

He had wanted her to generate magic in a public place, so that as many people as possible would see they owed the return of magic to a dark-skinned woman, and perhaps would not be so prejudiced towards women or people of other races in future. The Emperor's advisers and protectors had firmly disagreed with the plan. Their priority was to ensure that everyone understood that the Academy was the place for matters of magic. It was easier to see to the Emperor's safety between walls than in the open, too. Tyen would have to be content with a few hundred people from the most powerful families, as well as diplomats from around the empire, witnessing Rielle's miraculous act.

She shrugged. "I don't mind if they don't. You are the one who arranged for it to be done, after all."

"But—"

"Here comes the Emperor," she said.

Sure enough, a large carriage had turned into the street. It was entirely gilded, glinting in the sunlight like a ridiculously large but somehow still grand and imposing sweets jar. This was Tyen and Rielle's cue to descend the stairs. He turned and bowed to Rielle before offering his arm. As he'd instructed, she did not dip in reply before hooking her hand under his elbow. The newssheet writers who wrote about etiquette would note this, as would those dedicated to women's interests. Those concerned with matters of immigration and the purity of Leratian blood-lines would too, and would express their indignation. He knew change wouldn't happen without resistance, even change for the betterment of all.

The carriage reached the gate just as they did. When it had come to a stop, the stepman jumped down and placed a small set of stairs before the door. Emperor Omniten emerged, accompanied by more cheers. The ruler – or perhaps his advisers on ceremony – had chosen a suit of old-fashioned style and cut, and Tyen had to admit the modern clothing the man usually wore suited him better. A walking cane was tucked under one arm. Once on the ground, the man turned and extended his hand to assist a woman out. She wore a dress with an old-fashioned skirt and a contemporary bodice, both in a fabric dyed a rich red only achievable with one of the modern dyes.

Tyen and Rielle emerged to meet them at the base of the stairs. There, after bows and long and formal greetings, he and Rielle parted so that she walked beside the Empress and he beside the Emperor, as they climbed the stairs to the Academy doors.

"Ividian cannot stop talking about what he saw in our neigh-bouring worlds," Omniten told Tyen. "He is most impressed."

"I am fortunate that the worlds next to this contain some unusual landscapes and animals, and cities of a size and sophistication that they could not possibly be mistaken for those of this world. If we did not have such interesting neighbours it would have been difficult to convince him we'd left this world at all."

"I would like to visit these places one day."

Tyen glanced at the Emperor. "I imagine such a tour would be far more complicated to arrange and involve many more assistants than Ividian's short trip."

The Emperor chuckled. "Indeed, it would, as well as much research. I would not like to give the wrong impression to those who rule these cities and lands."

"Could such an adventure wait until matters in the Academy are somewhat more settled?"

"It can and should. Don't worry; I am not going to risk the stability of one of the empire's greatest institutions out of desire for a holiday."

"For that I am immensely grateful."

"Yes, I imagine your hands are rather full at the moment." Omniten looked up at the open doors of the Grand Hall. "How are you settling in? Have the professors given you any trouble?"

"Better than expected, but not without upheaval, your Imperial Majesty. As you can imagine, my appointment has not been received without objections. Some have left; some have stayed. A few are a little too eager to gain my favour, others are waiting to see if I survive for long before making any moves."

"No surprises then."

"Little will change in the studies of non-magical fields, of course, so those Heads only required reassurance. As for the Heads of magical studies . . . I have warned them to brace for change. Their new magical abilities will require new laws and etiquette, and they had best curb their enthusiasm for using them until they understand their new vulnerabilities as well as their strengths. I also warned them I will not allow disorder and selfish opportunism to ruin this ancient institution."

"A much-needed assurance, considering your predecessor's crimes."

"Yes. Which were more of a popular hobby, I'm afraid."

The Emperor glanced at him. "Will you root out all who partook in it?"

"Not unless you insist I do. I fear charging everyone guilty of it would leave the Academy rather depleted of staff and produce too many angry professors with nothing to do but plot against me."

Omniten chuckled. "So you will pretend not to know."

"Until it proves advantageous. However, if you need to know who can be trusted . . ."

"I will ask." The Emperor inclined his head slightly, then smiled. "My advisers warned against allowing you to restore the magic of this world. They said it would place power into my enemies' hands and render some allies less useful."

"So, why are you allowing it?"

"I will gain power as well." His gaze was hard as he regarded Tyen. "I doubt this empire would continue much longer in its current state without the magic that enabled its formation. It may not crumble without it, but it will be much easier to maintain with it." Then his face relaxed. "Also, aside from scandal, there is nothing better than great enterprises to occupy the people's minds, and who knows what I may achieve in a world rich with magic? I may even add new worlds to the empire."

A chill ran down Tyen's spine. "I would advise against that."

"Oh? Why so?"

"Without my advice, you would likely lose." They had reached the top of the stairs.

"So you would refuse to give it?"

"Yes. I do not kill or enable others to do so, unless not doing so would cause more harm."

They reached the top of the stairs. Omniten stopped, then turned to look out at the crowd to hide his need to catch his breath, earning another cheer. When he had recovered, he turned to face Tyen. "But I am your Emperor. As a subject of the empire, you must obey me."

"The Emperor's rule is not absolute." Tyen met the man's eyes. "The right of refusal on the grounds of conscience may be a weak defence for most, but it still exists in law and I think would have greater effect coming from a stronger defendant."

The Emperor regarded Tyen thoughtfully. "It is hard to disapprove of your stance against violence when it ensures, in theory, that you will not rise against me."

"Unless, in theory, not doing so would cause greater harm." Tyen shrugged. "But since we are talking philosophically . . . What gives you the right to take, through violence, what is not yours?"

The Empress gave a small hiss of anger. "We have brought civilisation and progress to the furthest parts of this world."

Tyen turned to her and bowed. "That is the perspective of a conqueror, Empress. Civilisation and progress aren't usually offered as part of a fair negotiation of trade between equals."

Omniten frowned. "Nevertheless, the empire had brought order and peace to the world. War has not threatened us in years. As my father said, if you do not rule them they will seek to rule you." He spread his hands. "Either the strongest rules or disorder and chaos reign."

Hearing a growing murmur from beyond the Academy doors, Tyen turned to see people leaning forward to see why the ruler and his companions were not entering. "I disagree, but perhaps this is not the time for such a debate."

The Emperor's eyebrows rose, but he turned back to the doors and resumed walking. "No, it is the right time," he said, entering the hall. "Who has the right to rule, Tyen Ironsmelter?"

"Whoever is best suited to it. My mentor once said, 'bloodlines and strength do not guarantee a good leader'. He also said that while wisdom and intelligence is essential, a desire to do good is more important – but it also helps to have a realistic expectation of failure."

Omniten's eyebrows rose in amusement. "Was he describing yourself?"

"No. I have never sought to rule. My talents lie in invention and teaching." He shrugged. "Who do you believe has the right to rule, your Imperial Majesty?"

"The strongest."

"Not the one with the noblest blood? The birthright?"

"No."

Tyen regarded Omniten with surprise. "So if the people of Leratia believe the strongest man here has authority over them then—"

"Then Tyen would have authority over you, and all emperors of all worlds," Rielle said. "As would I. But would the people shift their allegiance to Tyen or me without question, without us trying to win them over? No. So the strongest is not always the one who rules."

The Emperor, his wife and Tyen turned to regard her. Which reminded Tyen that he wanted to, at every opportunity, ensure all understood her value.

"You would have greater authority than I, Rielle, since you are the Maker," Tyen reminded her.

Her lips curled in a small smile. "And, like you, my talents lie elsewhere. In Making." She looked at the Emperor and Empress. "Rest assured, Tyen spoke the truth when he said he would not seek to supplant you, but he will not be persuaded to do anything he does not consider right."

"An honourable man," the Empress said, narrowing her eyes at Tyen. "Sometimes the most difficult to deal with, but not nearly so distasteful as some."

Tyen smiled. "I can live with 'less distasteful'."

The woman's expression softened and her mouth quirked to one side.

They had nearly reached the end of the hall, where two ornate chairs had been placed for the monarch and his wife. Tyen's skin prickled with anticipation and nervousness.

"Well, your Imperial Majesty," he said in a low voice. "Do you still wish to go ahead?"

Omniten glanced at him, then looked at his wife. "I do," he murmured. "If nothing else, I acknowledge that this will happen anyway. I'd rather be in control of it. Or as much in control as I can be." He stopped – the signal that Tyen and Rielle should remain where they were – then took his wife's hand and led her to the chairs. When they had settled into place, the Emperor rapped his cane on the floor. The quietness in the room deepened into an expectant silence, and the ruler began to speak.

It was a long speech, which had been prepared for him, and he had spent days memorising it and the inevitable late amendments. Tyen admired the man for this skill, born out of a lifetime of practice. *Will I have to do this? I suppose I might. Until I have the skill of it, I will have to have someone read my speeches, so I can see it in their mind.* It seemed a bit like cheating, but he didn't have the lifetime of training a born ruler had to call upon.

The audience listened quietly and attentively, many shifting their weight from one leg to the other to counter fatigue. Tyen admired this, too. No suggestion had been made to supply chairs. The endurance test of speeches was an accepted part of Leratian ceremonies, and was never questioned.

Tyen looked around the room, picking out faces in the audience that he recognised from his time as a student. Some fellow students had changed a great deal, the years stripping away youthful round-ness, or an indulgent life adding it. A small chill ran down his back when he recognised Neel. His former friend met his gaze and nodded once. Of Miko there was no sign. Was he unable to come, or did he fear Tyen held a grudge against him for revealing that Tyen had "stolen" Vella all those years ago?

When, at last, the Emperor came to the end, Tyen breathed a sigh of relief. It was followed by a new anxiety as his own part in the proceedings resumed. Omniten gestured to Tyen to begin it. "And so, I bid Tyen Ironsmelter, Director of the Academy of Leratia, to begin the restoration."

Tyen bowed low. "As you command, your Imperial Majesty."

He straightened and turned to Rielle. "Rielle Lazuli, the Maker, will you do me the favour of restoring this world?"

All eyes moved to her. She nodded once. "I will."

Turning towards one of the side entrances, she beckoned. Two Academy servants hurried out, one carrying a small easel with a sheet of paper clamped in place in readiness, the other holding a box. The three legs of the easel clunked firmly on the floor before her, the sound echoing in the expectant quiet.

Rielle looked to the Emperor. "With your permission, your Majesty, I will draw you."

He inclined his head.

Her eyes returned to the paper, then up at the Emperor and narrowed. She inhaled. Exhaled slowly. The sound was wistful. Her hand dropped to the box, fingers selecting a piece of charcoal, then lifted it to the surface of the paper. The soft scrape of it against the sheet seemed loud.

Then Tyen heard no more as his senses were overwhelmed by magic. It poured from her, a burst of energy that, had it produced light, would have blinded everyone in the room. Instead, most of the occupants looked bemused, first at why the foreign woman was drawing the Emperor's portrait rather than doing what he'd asked, then at the gasps and exclamations from the sorcerers scattered through the audience.

Finally, understanding spread among those with no magical ability as these sorcerers explained what they were sensing. Tyen glanced at the Emperor. Instead of wonder, the man was watching the audience carefully. From his mind Tyen caught an old jealousy: the man had wished to be a sorcerer all his life. Not just in order to strengthen his position, but because magic had always fascinated and thrilled him.

Tyen was about to look around the room when his eyes were caught by the Empress's expression. She was leaning forward, staring at Rielle intently. Now that the room was full of magic, Tyen could see that she had magical ability, a gift that had passed to her two sons. She had played down the strength of it to her husband, knowing how much he regretted not having any. Recently he'd spoken of it, asking if she would be able to tell him if Tyen released magic into the Grand Hall prematurely, or warn him of intentions of treachery once magic was restored.

Interesting, Tyen mused. *Would she help me persuade people that it's worth teaching women how to use magic?*

He turned away to seek the source of the murmurs in the hall, and saw that people close enough to see Rielle's work were exchanging glances and nodding. They were noting her talent and thought it novel that a woman of her colouring might be so skilled. Some were even debating how much it would cost to have their own portrait done.

Tyen sighed. They could not see that Rielle was doing something much more extraordinary. The sorcerers in the room might tell them, but would they truly understand? Was watching Rielle draw enough to undo centuries of prejudice?

I can't hope to win over everyone, or even most people straight away. But the fact that a foreign woman restored the magic of this world will help me combat objections when I allow women and foreigners to enter the Academy to learn magic.

Rielle's gestures were smaller now, moving about the drawing as she made final touches. She paused between them, her gaze shifting to the distance. Taking her cue, Tyen stretched his senses out. Magic was still billowing outwards, but it had left her in waves, and at the extremes of his reach he could feel the earliest of them meeting at the far side of the world. This richness of magic was more familiar than the feeling of a near-empty world, he realised.

From this moment, this world had effectively rejoined the rest of the worlds. Nobody outside it yet knew, but eventually someone would discover or reveal the change. Not too soon, he hoped. Sorcerers from other worlds would have to find his path and follow it in order to discover the "new" world. Sorcerers from within his world would have to work out how to travel through the place between on their own, and successfully, for them to make a path outwards. A sorcerer might find this world out of curiosity or chance, but it was much less likely.

"I am done," Rielle announced. She unclamped the sheet of paper from the easel, then bowed slightly to the Emperor. "Your world is restored, your Imperial Majesty, Emperor Omniten of Leratia. And your portrait is finished."

He looked around the room as she approached. "Is the world full of magic?" he asked.

A unified assent rose from the sorcerers around the room.

"More than I have ever sensed, for as far as I can sense, your Majesty," one added.

"It is . . . miraculous," another added.

"Then I thank you, Rielle Lazuli," the Emperor said, rising from his chair and coming to meet her. She held the portrait out to him, but he ignored it, instead dropping to one knee. Quiet gasps filled the hall. "I thank you, on behalf of this world and all the people within it. You will be known here as Rielle the Restorer, and your great gift written of in all the histories. It will be made law that, should you ever return to this world, you will be received with the greatest honours that can be bestowed upon a visitor, whether you come here in my time or during the times of my descendants." Rising, he bowed, then reached out to take the sheaf of paper. Looking at it, he smiled, then held it out so all could see. "And you are also a gifted artist!" he added. "Thank you again! This will be treasured by myself and my Empress, and copies made to be displayed throughout the empire so that all may admire it."

Rielle bowed her head. "Long may it bring you pleasure," she replied.

The Emperor reached out and took her hand, drew her towards Tyen, then, standing between them, spread his arms.

"Thanks to these two, the world has been restored. No longer is the use of magic forbidden within Belton, or any other city. Go forth in gratitude. Go forth and enjoy the abundance!" Cheers filled the hall. Men stamped their boots on the wooden floor. Women clapped, their gloved hands making a soft patter. Then, noting the tone of finality in the Emperor's words, they turned to each other, beginning excited and inquisitive conversations.

The Emperor beamed at Tyen and Rielle. "What a day!" he said quietly. "I do like being part of a momentous occasion! Perhaps this one may be the most historic of my reign. Not a victory, but perhaps more significant in the long term." He turned to Rielle. "Is there any way I can convince you to stay in my world, Rielle Lazuli?"

She smiled and shook her head. "I am flattered by your request, but the answer must be 'no'. Other worlds need my help, not to mention other friends." She glanced at Tyen, her expression telling him that she wanted to communicate something, but he was not sure if it was regret or apology.

"We will miss you," the Emperor said.

"As will I," Tyen added.

She lowered her eyes. "It is kind of you to say so," she replied to the Emperor, "especially as you barely know me."

"But if you stayed, I would have the chance to." He smiled as she shook her head again. "Well, at least promise me you will visit."

"I will certainly try to." She looked at Tyen again. "After all, I want to keep in touch with my dear friend Tyen."

Omniten looked at Tyen, an easy smile in place but his gaze sharp. Tyen silently thanked her yet again. The possibility that his world would need restoring again in future would be another reason for the Emperor to treat Tyen carefully.

"I will return to the palace now." Omniten informed them. "Let me know if you need any assistance reshaping the Academy."

Tyen bowed. "I will."

The Emperor bowed to Rielle, then returned to the Empress,

who rose and took his arm. Rielle and Tyen stepped aside, joining the crowd in bowing as the royal couple started their dignified exit from the Academy. As the doors closed behind the Emperor and his Empress, the room's occupants exploded into chatter.

"That seemed to go well," Rielle said in the Traveller tongue, one eyebrow raised as she turned to look at Tyen. "Do you think?"

He nodded. "Yes. Yes, it did."

"What now?"

He looked around at the people. A couple nearby eyed Rielle and Tyen with interest, but before they could approach, three sorcerers passed them with intentions to question Tyen. "I think some are already discovering the limitations and consequences of their new ability to read minds."

"To which you have an unfair advantage."

Tyen turned to her, giving himself a small respite as it would be rude for the sorcerers to interrupt a conversation. "Do you want to go? You don't have to stay, if you'd rather not answer any questions."

She shrugged. "I won't be answering any I don't want to. Would you rather we worked together, or separately?"

"How about you talk to the couple, while I tackle these two sorcerers?" Tyen suggested.

Rielle pulled her hand out from under his arm. "Be gentle with them. Remember what it was like when you first left this world."

He nodded. "I will. And I do."

She smiled, then turned to greet the couple, and for the next few hours he did not see her again.

CHAPTER 10

As Tyen skimmed through the wall of the Grand Hall, a few days later, he was surprised to see a small crowd waiting. The Emperor's official envoy was there, as well as a handful of men and women of means who had taken an interest in all things otherworldly. Some of the Academy members were present, including and not surprisingly, a few of the ruler's unofficial spies. Omniten knew that Tyen must be aware of the latter. Tyen guessed they were there to observe Tyen's students and the Academy's reaction to them.

Tyen had ensured they would be difficult to track by taking a roundabout route and travelling by non-magical means within worlds several times. It had been tempting to try leaving and returning to his world from somewhere closer to Beltonia, but it was safer to have only one arrival place – the one high above Spirecastle.

As he and his students arrived, he heard deep inhalations, then sighs of relief as they set down their packs and Tyen's chests. They had already been taking in their surroundings as they'd neared the world, noting those watching them arrive. The onlookers were examining them closely. Reaching out to the professors' minds, Tyen saw dismay in many as they took in the variety of skin colouring and body shape of these foreigners. A few were even female. What did they expect? Tyen wondered. That all people outside their world looked like them?

Women sorcerers and foreigners, one thought with disgust. *That's where our Academy is heading. Next we'll have mixed-race babies being raised in the school.* Three of the students turned to glare at the man and he belatedly realised that they had read his thought. Though having his prejudices read so easily made him flush with embarrassment, it did not occur to him to feel guilty about them. He believed that Tyen's decision to allow foreigners and women to join the Academy and learn magic would only confirm his belief that both were inferior, and he pitied these people who were about to discover they were unequal to the new Director's expectations.

Tyen resisted a sigh and turned his attention elsewhere as the man glanced his way. At least this doubter was here, willing to be introduced to the newcomers. Many of the professors were determined to have as little to do with Tyen's students as they could manage.

They would change their minds eventually, Tyen told himself. He began introductions. After he had spoken the last name, a gasp drew his attention. Two of the students were gazing towards a side entrance, mouths open. Following their gaze, he saw that Rielle had entered the room, dressed in an even simpler gown than that which she had worn during the Restoration Ceremony.

As she neared, more of the students noticed her and fell silent. Then, as she reached them, Regur dropped to his knees, as was the customary gesture of respect of his people.

"Rielle Lazuli, the Maker and saver of worlds," he said with a tremble in his voice. "It is an honour to meet you."

"Stand, Regur of Mahee," she said in his language. "I am no greater than you."

He did so, but then could not speak, only watch as each of the other students honoured her with their customary gestures of respect. Though she accepted all with serenity, a small twitch in her cheek told Tyen that the attention discomforted her. He did not stop them, however. Instead he sought the minds of the locals, watching with satisfaction how they weighed the students' reaction to her. They understood the awe: they had seen for themselves the miraculous gift she had. But why did all these students feel such intense gratitude towards her? Had she restored all of their worlds? How many worlds out there needed restoring? A few sought the students' minds in the hope of learning more, but could not see past the newcomers' mind-reading blocks.

Many of the local sorcerers were still getting used to the complexities of their new ability. Tyen had explained the basics: that they should learn to block mind-reads, but the skill would only be effective against weaker sorcerers. A few had already requested lessons, but Tyen had found no time yet to oblige them. Some had instinctively learned to block their minds and were assisting others to do the same.

As the last student finished stammering out his admiration, Rielle looked around the group.

"Welcome to the Academy of Leratia," she said. "Accommodation has been arranged for you, and these guides . . ." She turned to beckon and three Leratian students nervously emerged from the same opening she'd entered through. ". . . will take you there and then show you the rest of the school, including the dining hall. Though I advise you to eat lightly, because we have a welcoming feast arranged for tonight."

The newcomers lifted their packs and moved to join the guides. Tyen thanked the observers and professors for coming to welcome his students. As they departed, he turned to Rielle and gestured to the chests.

"Let's take these to my new office."

She nodded. As he lifted one of the chests with magic, the other rose as well. He took the lead, moving the chest before him. The new Director's office was a short, direct journey from the Grand Hall. To Rielle's disappointment, the interior was much like the old one and it was only four times the size. Though it was lined with bookshelves, they contained as many objects as books, all on the theme of mechanical magic. Tyen's desk was in the centre. A large table and chairs for meetings stood at one side of the room, and a workbench and tool cabinet occupied the other.

"If I couldn't read their minds I'd suspect you'd set your students up to do that," Rielle murmured as they entered.

"Their respect for you is genuine."

She moved to the chair sitting opposite his desk. "As is their respect for you, but they didn't bow and kneel in your direction."

"No, I'm afraid the source of my fame is somewhat less glamorous than yours," he reminded her as he moved around the desk to take his seat. "More something to overcome. I have had to earn the respect and trust of each and every one of them."

She paused, then nodded. "Yes. It doesn't seem fair, though."

"Of course it's fair. Your actions were always open and made with integrity. I dealt with secrets and lies." He shrugged. "Our goals may have been similar, but we took a different path towards them."

"It's strange, but those differences seemed a lot greater then than they do now." She shook her head. "And now we do not share a goal at all."

"No," he agreed. "This is my goal, not yours. You are merely helping me." He regarded her thoughtfully. Her gaze was fixed far beyond the room, and her expression was melancholy. *Her task here is done*, he thought, not for the first time since the Restoration ceremony. *Soon she will leave . . .*

"So . . . what is your goal?" he asked.

Her shoulders rose and fell as her focus returned to him. "I have none, now that Qall is free of my world."

"And you've done all I asked of you here."

She nodded. "It is time I left."

Tyen's stomach sank. Though he had known she eventually would go, hearing her state it was harder than he'd expected.

"Will you return to the Restorers?"

She hesitated, a thoughtful frown creasing her brow. He

wondered if she was tempted to stay. Did the idea of teaching magic appeal? *But that is not her skill, as she pointed out during the ceremony. She is the Maker, and there would always be worlds needing her help.*

Her frown deepened. "Probably. I did make a promise to Baluka that I would."

"But . . .?"

She pursed her lips, then sighed. "Before I freed Qall, during a restoration, I met a young sorcerer who is seeking a lost library containing information about Maker's Curse. He is not a powerful sorcerer, so it will take him some time to travel through the worlds. If I join him, he can travel faster, and we might learn what is so dangerous about a Maker becoming ageless." She looked at Tyen. "Clearly it's possible, otherwise there'd be no warning against it."

Tyen straightened, hiding his disappointment that she wasn't tempted to stay here with him. "That makes sense. Finding answers may be important to the worlds – perhaps more important than restoring worlds. After all, if you can be ageless and a Maker at the same time, you can help far more worlds – and it won't be so dangerous for you to enter them."

Rielle nodded. "That's true." Then she smiled. "Though I am tempted to stay and watch you build your school, too. I'm always leaving worlds after I help them. I rarely find out what happens next."

His heart skipped. "You're welcome to stay. The Emperor said so."

She chuckled. "Yes, but I won't be attending to my responsibilities or learning more about Maker's Curse if I do. I'm afraid I can't indulge my curiosity this time."

He nodded and looked away. He would miss her company, and more. She understood the pleasures and dilemmas of being both powerful and famous. They had lived through great moments in the history of the worlds. Since she had joined him here, he'd got to know her in ways he'd never had the chance to before. *I think I'd rather we never became lovers again, if it meant spoiling our friendship.*

"I'll look forward to your next visit, then."

"Thank you. But can I visit? I'd risk leading your enemies here."

His heart sank. "Hmm. I'm afraid it would better if you did not take that risk. But this world won't be isolated for ever. Probably no more than a few years. When we are strong enough to defend ourselves, I will send word to you via Baluka."

She sighed and pushed up out of the chair. "Well . . . you've got lots of paperwork to do and I should stop distracting you."

"Actually, I was going to visit the Librarian. I haven't seen him since I got back." His heart skipped a beat. Could he delay her just a little longer? "Would you like to come?"

Her eyes brightened. "I'd love to. From what I've seen in minds, he's quite a character."

Tyen stood up. "Come on then. I'm sure he'd like to meet you."

She rose to follow him out of the room and through the Academy. "I barely knew such things as libraries existed until I left my world," she told him. "There wasn't one in my home city, but one was mentioned in a tale in the Book of the Angels."

Tyen glanced at her. "There wasn't even a private library?"

"If there was, I was never told about it. My family was rich, but not through inheritance, and the luxuries my parents purchased were bought for status."

"Still, you were taught to read?"

"Yes. By the temple." She paused. "I am perhaps as amazed that you have no large temple in Belton as you are that we had no library."

He smiled. "We have lots of modest ones. The Emperor's great-grandfather came into conflict with the Lorekeepers and stripped them of their assets last century. He declared worship should be private, local and modest, and it has been ever since. Not without the occasional effort to revive the old glory days, though."

"Do you believe in these gods?"

"No. Nor does my father. For the last hundred years reason has been valued over superstition in Leratia. Unfortunately, that led to the dismissal of the idea that creativity generated magic. I'm amazed how quickly that is being accepted now. I hope it doesn't swing public ideas in the other direction, so that more people start believing in gods and all sorts of nonsense." He looked at her and saw she was frowning and realised his mistake. "I hope I haven't offended you. Do you believe in the gods of your world?"

"Not really. It wasn't Valhan pretending to be an Angel that convinced me they probably didn't exist. I have seen some strange things in the worlds, but the more I learned and was able to sense, the more I saw they could be explained by natural forces rather than supernatural beings. I've read the minds of those who believe they've seen proof of their god's existence, but their reasoning is as common across the worlds as naïve beliefs regarding fertility and longevity and countless other matters people have to guess about." She shrugged. "I'd rather live with integrity and wait until I die to find out the truth, than risk harming others by blindly following what dogma says it is."

They were nearing the Academy library door now. Tyen slowed. "I can't help thinking any god who expected otherwise of a person is no god worth worshipping."

"Isn't it odd that we two, who both abhor killing and conquest and enslavement, are non-believers? Aren't people like us supposed to be without morals or kindness, as so many religions claim?" She nodded at a pair of open doors ahead. "Is this it?"

"Yes." He led her through the door and into the Library. They moved around the reading tables in the centre of the ground floor, currently occupied by several students who had paused in their study to stare. Above the tables, a wide space in the ceiling revealed four more levels, all lined with bookcases.

"Tyen Ironsmelter." The voice came from the direction of the tiny office the Librarian occupied. "Or rather, *Director* Ironsmelter."

A silver-haired man strode into sight. He looked different to

215

the man Tyen remembered, though he could not say why. *But of course he does. He's fifteen years older.* Even as he thought it, he realised the changes in the old man were not those of age. The slight hunch to the man's shoulders was gone, and he walked with energy. For a second, Tyen wondered how this could be the same person, and if the man had somehow aged backwards.

"Librarian . . ." Tyen replied. "I apologise. Nobody ever told me your name."

"Kep," the man replied. "Rytan Kep."

"This is Rielle Lazuli," Tyen said. "Rielle, meet Librarian Kep."

Rielle looked from the Librarian to Tyen and back again, her eyebrows raised and a small smile curving her mouth. "So, Librarian Kep, how long have you been in this world?"

Tyen blinked, then sought out the man's mind. At once, the answer to the man's vigour was plain to see.

Rytan Kep was ageless.

"A little over three hundred years," the Librarian replied. "I had assumed for not much longer, but then you arrived and restored this world, so I offer my thanks, Rielle Lazuli, for saving my life."

"But . . . you are Leratian," Tyen spluttered.

"Yes, though the Belton I grew up in was considerably different to the one of today. I left this world when there was magic enough left to do so, then returned when I was tired of exploring the worlds. I have been here ever since."

"But . . . how did . . . does anybody . . .?"

The man laughed. "A few people have worked it out over the years. Most don't pay enough attention. I kept my appearance of age ambiguous, so if anyone ever thought about it they'd conclude I was as old or young as they expected."

"So you've been trapped here all this time?" Rielle said.

"Is a willing prisoner truly a prisoner?" the Librarian asked her. He shrugged. "It has been a peaceful existence. Though I expect it won't be for much longer." He raised one eyebrow and regarded Tyen. "You don't expect to keep this world a secret, do you?"

"No, but I will be keeping it hidden for as long as possible."

"Do you have enemies?"

Tyen hesitated, then nodded. "Who doesn't?"

"I hope they are not many, or powerful, or the favour you did this world will be outweighed by the disservice."

Tyen met the man's eyes. "I'm afraid I did all the worlds a far greater disservice when I released knowledge of mechanical magic. One of my aims here is for the Academy to help solve that problem."

The Librarian's eyebrows rose. "Ah."

"There is always harm as well as benefit in progress," Tyen told him. "Or so a wise friend once told me."

The man nodded. "Yes, unfortunately that is true."

"Do you wish I had not brought magic back to our world?" Tyen asked.

The Librarian paused, then shook his head. "Not yet, at least. This society is used to rapid change. Look what it has achieved in a few hundred years. It will adapt and grow stronger."

Tyen nodded. "I hope so. In fact, I am depending on it. Once this world is strong enough, I want young sorcerers to come here seeking the best magical training in the worlds. When my enemies find me, they will find a strong Academy ready to defend itself and this world."

For the first time, the Librarian smiled. "Now that's something worth sticking around to see."

Tyen smiled. "Will you help me?"

The man nodded. "If it means I can continue on here, as Librarian."

"If that's what you want, then I would be a fool to remove you." Tyen smiled. "But is there much here that will be of use?"

"Oh, plenty." The man smirked. "Whenever ideas about magic changed and it looked like the professors might start a cull, I removed the offending books to protect them. Is there anything in particular you would like to see?"

"Not specifically, but . . ." Tyen looked at Rielle. "My friend may wish to do some research."

The Librarian turned to Rielle. "What do you seek?"

She looked around the room. "Have you read all these books?"

The man laughed. "Not even half of them. I'd need far more than three hundred years to get through everything here."

"Have you heard of something called 'Maker's Curse'?"

His silvery grey brows lowered. "It is not a familiar term. What is it in relation to?"

"The versions that I've encountered say that a Maker cannot be ageless, or something terrible will happen to the worlds. They don't specify how or why."

He shook his head. "I've never encountered anything like that, but I can look for it. Do you know how old this idea is?"

"Many thousands of cycles," she replied.

His mouth pressed into a grim line. "Probably older than any book would survive. Still, old books are often referred to in younger ones. I will have a look."

She nodded. "Thank you, Rytan Kep."

He smiled, suddenly looking far younger than his aged appearance suggested. "It is the least I can do for the woman who restored this world and my life."

As the Librarian moved away, Rielle turn to Tyen. "I guess I could stay a little longer, but only for a few days."

He glanced around the library. "A search like this could take a lot longer than that."

Her smile became sad. "Then I'll have to rely on you to get a message to me if Kep finds anything."

"I understand," he replied. "The worlds need you more than I do right now. Just promise me you'll take care of yourself, and visit us from time to time."

She reached out to squeeze his hand. "I will."

PART THREE

RIELLE

CHAPTER 11

The whiteness around Rielle changed subtly as she pushed out of Tyen's world. The cloud above Spirecastle was almost featureless, but the pale mist had enough faint colour that she noticed the change as she moved into the place between worlds.

Finding the beginning of the path out of Tyen's world had not been easy. With the area above the broken tower swathed in cloud, it had been hard to get her bearings. She had blindly skimmed back and forth for quite some time before she found it, then had to return to the world to catch her breath before leaving it again.

If the path had been more regularly used it would have been easy to sense, but it had been traversed only five times since she and Tyen had first arrived: once for their arrival, twice when Tyen had taken the Emperor's friend, Ividian, out to prove the existence of other worlds, and twice more when Tyen had left to fetch his students and bring them in. If all went well, nobody would be leaving or arriving in Tyen's world again until the Academy was well able to defend it. Once out of his world she must do her best to avoid leaving a trail leading back to it, in case someone saw and recognised her, and decided to see where she had been recently.

She had promised Tyen that she would not tell anybody where he was, not even Tarren or Baluka. His world might be amazingly well developed in technology, but the knowledge of magic had faded along with the source of power. The sorcerers there would not easily defend themselves against even a small group of other-world invaders.

The sparse forest of the next world began to appear. The sky was a pale blue, and the air that surrounded her as she arrived was brisk. She paused, remembering Tyen saying this world was populated only by tribes living a simple existence. Searching for minds, she was relieved to find nobody nearby. That made this an ideal place to create a break in the trail she would make through the worlds.

She stilled the air before her in a disc, stepped up onto it, then extended the edges up until it almost surrounded her. Propelling herself high into the air, she stopped when the trees were tiny dots beneath her and it was unlikely anyone below would see her. Shaping the stilled air into a cone shape, with the point aimed in front of her, she set off across the world, protected from the rush of chill air. A beautiful landscape passed below, with only the occasional cluster of small buildings near a stream or lake to indicate it was populated.

She could not travel too far, however, as the further she went the greater the chance the next world would not be the one she and Tyen had passed through on the way here. When the landscape became more mountainous, she stopped, took a deep breath, and pushed out of the world.

She arrived above a storm-tossed ocean. A flash of light immediately blinded her, and a simultaneous explosion vibrated the shield of stilled air she'd instinctively created around herself. Gulping in a fresh breath of air, she pushed out of this world and headed in another direction, hoping she would arrive in a more hospitable world next.

Darkness greeted her. It had a familiar uniformity, like what she sensed when skimming underground. She had no idea which way was up, and it could easily take too long to skim around randomly hoping to find the surface of this world, so she back-tracked to the last world. Once over the ocean again, she stopped short of arriving and propelled herself across the water until she had outrun the storm. Land appeared, on which roads were clear lines. She followed those to a large city. A circular paved area lay at the centre – the typical shape of an arrival place. It was clear of obstacles, hinting that it was regularly used. That probably meant the next world was hospitable. She pushed out of the world and sought the next.

Continuing onwards, she picked her paths mostly in order to confuse trackers, which meant she travelled somewhat aimlessly. Eventually she was far enough away from Tyen's world that she did not need to hide her tracks any more. But, being in no hurry to set herself a destination, she wandered through worlds, enjoying a sense of freedom she hadn't felt in a long time. She grew hungry and sought food when she encountered a market. She stopped in a particularly lovely arrival place to rest and admire a bay filled with delicate arches of rock. She joined the crowd in an enormous city celebrating a night festival.

It wasn't that she had no place to go, but that she had so many choices.

I'd like to help Annad seek the library, she thought as she rose after a night sleeping on a floating island. It wouldn't be easy to find him after all this time. His trail would be cold, but she might be able to track him by finding people he had met on his journey.

Yet she also wanted to check on Qall and learn what he had done since leaving her world. He had probably visited Lejikh and his family. The group of Travellers had established a new circuit of worlds to trade along, so she had only to find part of it, then follow the route until she encountered them.

She wanted to see Tarren, too, and not just to catch up and reassure him that Tyen was safe. The old man and his students were always at risk of another attack by Liftre's sorcerers, and Tyen's experience had left her worried that attackers would use deadly force against Tarren if they found him again.

She also wanted to ask Baluka what he was doing about these attacks. Would he be more firm with Liftre, once he heard what they'd done to Tyen and his students? Of course, he would want her to resume working for him. She had neglected her duties for many, many days – nearly a quarter-cycle. There would be a backlog of worlds requesting help. More than enough time had passed to have made her point: that she would not restore worlds that didn't need it to resolve political disputes for the Restorers.

Which of these choices will benefit Tyen's world the most? she asked herself. Seeking Annad's secret library, Qall, Lejikh or Tarren wouldn't help Tyen at all. Raising the issue of Liftre with Baluka, on the other hand, might. He might not be willing to do anything, but she would lose nothing by trying to persuade him to.

So the Restorers it is.

Though she had come to a decision, she did not set out for the base straight away. She stopped to eat again, all the time acknowledging she was delaying returning to the Restorer base because she was not looking forward to meeting with Baluka. He would be angry with her for all but disappearing. Though she'd sent a message via the Restorers saying she would be helping a friend for a while, she hadn't said for how long.

Finally she grew tired of imagining the argument they might have and decided to get the real one over and done with. Setting off for the base, she stopped trying to hide her tracks.

Not long after she resumed travelling, she sensed someone in the place between. They remained in the distance, behind her, but they were still there three worlds later. Following her.

She quickened her pace and soon outran them. The incident didn't worry her too much. Whoever they were, alone they were not a threat to her. But three worlds later she sensed another presence in the place between, travelling along her path. Once again, she sped up and lost them. She journeyed within a world for some time to ensure they couldn't track her, then continued on towards the base.

When a third stranger appeared behind her, in the place between worlds, she stopped. Even if they had not recognised her, sorcerers were following sorcerers and there must be a reason for it. The sooner she knew why the better. Reversing her journey, she shot backwards.

A figure resolved out of the place between. Her pursuer was a young man, and he came to a halt, startled, as she rushed towards him. But he did not flee, remaining in place when she stopped a short distance away.

"*Rielle Lazuli?*" he asked.

She did not answer. "*Why were you following me?*"

He placed a hand on his chest and lowered his eyes. "*I have a message for you from the leader of the Restorers. He requests that you meet with him on an urgent matter.*"

She stared at him, feeling a little foolish. She'd been fleeing from messengers, not spies. "*How old is this message?*"

He paused, his brows creasing with thought. "*Perhaps eight Traveller days.*"

"*Thank you.*"

The young man backed away, then faded as he emerged in the previous world. Rielle considered following him and reading his mind to make sure what he'd told her was the truth, but if messengers had been told to look out for her in all the worlds, she would confirm his words at the next arrival place.

Sure enough, a Restorer was waiting and watching in the next world. As he recognised her and stepped forward, she waved him back. He took the gesture to mean she had already received the request and said nothing.

She continued on. Every few worlds, when she stopped to catch her breath, a messenger began to approach her and she shooed them away.

What is this urgent matter? she wondered. *Has Baluka made arrangements that relied too heavily on me? Is his control of worlds failing?* The prospect of an argument on her arrival seemed more and more certain, but she did not slow or hesitate. *If he wants my ongoing help, he will have to hold to our agreement about what my help entails.*

Another shadow appeared in the place between. She paused only long enough to say, "*Yes. I know. I'm heading there directly.*" The messenger retreated and vanished again. This happened several more times, which only had the effect of delaying her. By the time she emerged in Affen she was exasperated, and a little disturbed at the thought of how many people were able to recognise her.

The watchers guarding the arrival place eyed her, then relaxed. Striding past them, she set off for the strange squat building that served as the Restorers' base. The people she passed on the street all smiled and nodded to her. Reaching the door of the base, she was greeted by a young woman and told that Baluka had heard of her arrival and was waiting in the meeting room.

"He says go right in," the woman said, gesturing towards the stairs.

Rielle thanked her, then descended several floors. Reaching the door of the meeting room, she paused to take a deep breath before reaching out to push the door open. But it swivelled inwards before her palm had a chance to touch it . . .

. . . and revealed a taller, younger man than Baluka. Something about him was familiar, yet she was sure she had never seen him before. Then she drew in a quick breath as she realised she could not read his mind. Which meant this was . . .

"Qall!" she exclaimed.

"Rielle," he replied, his smile more than a little smug. "Come in."

She examined him closely as he led her to the chairs. He looked nothing like Valhan now. Did people here know who he was? She looked around the room as he led her to the chairs. Nobody else was present.

"Where's Baluka?"

"On his way." Qall gestured to the chairs. "Sit. Relax."

She lowered herself into a seat with a view of the door. "How long have you been here?"

"Forty or so days, I think. About an eighth of a cycle." Qall sat down facing her. "The time has gone so fast. There is so much to learn."

"About?" She heard a sound beyond the door, but it didn't open. The mind of a messenger flashed in and out of her senses.

"Leading the Restorers."

She tore her gaze from the door and stared at him. He laughed. "Not what you were expecting?"

"No." *But he's so young!* she thought. *How can he lead when . . .?*

"Baluka was not much older when Tyen passed the leadership to him," he pointed out.

"Yes, but they were the Rebels then, and a much smaller and simpler responsibility."

One of his eyebrows rose. "And yet the idea doesn't displease you."

"No." She shrugged as she realised this was true. "It's your life. Your choice."

"You don't want me to suffer the hurt of failure."

"Of course not." She examined his expression. His eyes were bright and his mouth curled in a smug smile. "Something that might help is avoiding making it obvious you're reading someone's mind by telling that person what they're thinking and feeling. It's undiplomatic. And irritating."

He looked down, his confidence suddenly gone. "Sorry. It's a bad habit, I know."

She sighed. She hadn't meant to dent his self-assurance, but if he was going to deal with leaders of the worlds he would need to learn quickly, and she doubted Baluka was sparing his feelings either. Still, she made her voice gentler as she asked, "What led you to make this decision, then?"

Qall leaned back in the chair. "After I left you I visited Lejikh and my family. That was nice, but I can't live with them and I found I didn't really want to. It's too quiet a life after everything I've done and seen. So I went to the world I was born in and had a look around. Then . . ."

She straightened. "Did you find your parents?"

His shoulders lifted. "In a way. They had died before Valhan took me. I did find the school where I was being taught magic before he found me. The principal used to search orphanages for children with magical ability, adopt and train them, then sell them to wealthy clients. He sold me to Valhan for a rather large sum." He made a face. "I didn't particularly want to seek out the principal and I knew I didn't have any friends at the school because the other students were jealous of my strength." He shrugged. "So there was nothing to keep me there, either. That's when I decided to see what the Restorers were up to. I met with Baluka and we had a long chat. He has wanted to resign for many cycles, but hadn't found the right replacement. He suggested I take over as leader, and I agreed."

"Just like that."

"Well, I did think about it for a few days." Qall met her gaze, his expression serious. "He won't be abandoning the Restorers straight away. There's my training to finish, and finding a safe, secret place for him to live out the rest of his life."

Rielle's heart skipped a beat. Suddenly her annoyance with Baluka felt trite and foolish. When he did leave the Restorers, he would make very sure he would not be easily found, even by her. If she had stayed with Tyen much longer she might never have seen him again. They had been close enough in the past that she'd like to at least have the chance to say goodbye.

"So you've been helping Tyen," Qall observed.

Realising he would have read Tyen's location and intentions from her mind, she felt a chill run down her spine.

"I won't tell anyone where he is and why," he assured her.

She nodded. *You had better not*, she thought. *Or thousands of deaths could be on your hands.* Which reminded her of why she had decided to meet with Baluka.

"Liftre's sorcerers tried to kill him," she told him. "They succeeded in murdering one of his students while the group was fleeing their previous home. You no doubt know of other attacks on schools. Baluka was reluctant to punish them after the attack on Tarren, saying that nobody was hurt. Now it's clear they are willing to kill to ensure no other schools compete with them. Is he . . . are you going to do anything about them?"

His expression grew serious. "I mean to, though it has become a far more complicated issue . . . which I will explain in a moment." Rising, he walked towards the door.

Guessing that Baluka had arrived, Rielle reached out to his mind, then quickly pulled back, remembering their agreement that she would not read it. Though now he was no longer leader of the Restorers, perhaps she was no longer required to avoid doing so.

Qall looked back and smiled. "You may read his mind. In fact, I think you should have been doing so all along. You would have found his instructions more easy to understand and sympathise with."

Without waiting for her to reply, Qall opened the door. Baluka stepped into the room, his face brightening as he saw Rielle. Another man followed. His face was unfamiliar, but as Rielle read his mind and learned his identity all concerns about Baluka left her. She shot to her feet.

"What are *you* doing here?" she demanded.

Dahli smiled wryly, his gaze unwavering as he met her stare. "No 'how are you?' or 'are you well?'," he asked drily. Then his smile dropped away, and his mouth formed a grim line. "I came here to request the assistance of the Restorers," he told her. "And to warn them of a new threat to the worlds."

CHAPTER 12

Rielle jumped as she felt a hand touch her shoulder. She turned to find Qall standing close behind her.

"Relax, Rielle," he told her. "You are safe, and Dahli truly isn't here to cause trouble. Sit. The news he brought us is serious and needs discussing."

She looked from Dahli to Qall, then to Baluka. The former Traveller nodded to her in reassurance, then he frowned at Qall.

"You should have warned her Dahli was here."

Qall nodded. "I was working my way up to it."

She considered Dahli again. Was he still trying to resurrect Valhan? Or was he meddling in some other way in the Restorers' affairs? Had she spent so many cycles restoring worlds only for him to start another war that would deplete them again? "You promised to undo the damage you did in the service of the Raen," she reminded him. "Are you honouring that promise?"

He met her stare levelly even as his thoughts betrayed him. "Not exactly. I have been helping Zeke find a way to stop war machines. I would not have . . . delayed keeping that promise if I did not know the machines were a greater danger."

She also caught glimpses of Zeke in his mind, all imbued with a feeling of deep concern. Something had happened to the young inventor, but Dahli feared more than that. He believed he had discovered the first sign of a danger that might threaten all the worlds. He needed their help, and he was worried that nobody would take his warnings seriously.

Quelling the anger that had boiled up from within, Rielle forced herself to sit down again. As the others settled into chairs, she did not look away from her former teacher and enemy. Dahli could not have appeared more different to his former self. He was shorter and thinner, his hair straight and now so pale it was almost white. His skin was darker and a short beard bristled from angular jowls. Despite all this, his eyes did not appear to have changed. Rielle found she was no longer glaring at him, just wondering what it was about them that remained so familiar.

Baluka and Qall were also looking at Dahli.

"Tell her what you told us, Dahli," Qall said.

Dahli nodded but his eyes did not leave Rielle's. "As I said, Zeke and I have been looking for ways to neutralise war machines. He insisted it was more important than anything else. We had come up with several ideas, and had just begun producing our solutions in quantities ready to sell or distribute, when, nearly a half-cycle ago, Zeke left to pick up supplies and never came back." Dahli sighed, his breath shivering slightly. "I could never impress upon him the risk of making such trips alone, even short ones. Of course, I looked for him. Whoever took him knew how to hide their trail, and I soon lost it. So I sought out and questioned everyone I could think of who might identify the kidnappers and where they'd taken Zeke."

His gaze slid away as he recalled what he'd learned. "I heard rumours of a world where machines outnumbered people, and where new kinds were being invented. If Zeke was alive, then the most likely reason was so that his captors could use his mind to refine their weapons, so this machine world sounded like the place they would have taken him. I sought out sellers of war machines and through them found a world where whole cities were dedicated to making them. Zeke wasn't there, but I learned of more worlds like it. In these worlds people still outnumbered machines, so I

231

figured the description of the place I'd been told of was exaggerated. That was, until I tracked one of the men in charge of these factory cities to a world that did match the description I'd been given."

Dahli shook his head slowly, his eyes wide and fixed on nothing but his memories. "I've never seen anything like it. I doubt Valhan did, or any of his Predecessors. It was entirely filled with machines, the former human occupants long gone or dead. I suspect it was a huge store of weapons waiting to be used. Most of it was as still and silent as death. When I did finally see movement, it was other kinds of machines working on these machines. Some were pulling apart machines and carrying away the pieces. I followed those to huge scrapyards. There I found a small group of humans overseeing the recycling of parts. I hoped to learn something from them, so I arrived and tried to get near them without being seen, but the closest of the machines came to life and attacked me . . ." He looked up and met Rielle's eyes again. "They attacked with magic. Not much individually, but in such numbers that they forced me to leave the world, or be trapped there."

Rielle frowned. "Trapped? So this world is a dead one?"

Dahli nodded. "No magic. Except where the people were, and then not very much. There must be a great deal of magic held in all those machines, though." He grimaced. "Perhaps that is why it is dead. All the magic has been taken by them. I tried several times to return to the world and search for Zeke, but on each visit I was detected sooner, until on the last I was attacked immediately. I did not detect the minds of any people again. Those I'd read on the first visit were subordinates, but from them I learned a little about the group in charge of the whole enterprise. They are former students of Liftre."

"Liftre," Rielle growled, then looked at Baluka. "I told you when they attacked Tarren that you needed to do something about the school."

Baluka spread his hands. "I sent them a warning, and they

replied with an apology and a promise to keep the inventors in check."

"Which they've broken many times since."

"I know, but I cannot shut down the entire school. I am not Valhan."

Dahli winced. "As I said, these were former students. Ones who had been expelled. Shutting down the school would not have prevented this situation, but instead given more students reason to join these war-machine makers."

"And it wouldn't be fair on students studying other subjects," Rielle agreed. "I do not mean to suggest shutting down the school, but that the Restorers should be doing something to combat the corruption within it. Many of the students Tyen has taken on were driven out of Liftre because they did not agree with making war machines, or were from races the teachers did not like, or were treated as lesser people because they are women."

Baluka shook his head. "The machine makers are now the most powerful teachers in the school. They've bullied and bribed their way into the top positions. I'm afraid they're the ones in control."

"Even if you could fix or shut down the school, it would make no difference to the danger these machines pose." Dahli turned to Rielle. "Do you know where Tyen is, Rielle?"

She glanced at Qall. "Yes."

"He would want to know about this. He will understand the dangers and limitations of these machines better than any of us."

"Tyen is in hiding," Qall told Dahli. "Liftre's sorcerers attempted to kill him, and when they failed they killed one of his students instead. Now that he has found a place of safety, I will not risk revealing his location just to get his advice on this."

Dahli frowned and opened his hands in appeal. "But he may be the only one who can do something about—"

"He may turn out to be, but there are other inventors who will help us. Until we've explored the alternatives, I won't risk making an enemy of Tyen by putting him and his people in danger." Qall looked at Rielle.

She nodded. "Give him time to gather his strength and he will return to the worlds far better prepared to help us."

"I agree," Baluka said. He turned to Rielle. "Are you able to help us, Rielle?"

"Of course."

He frowned. "You seemed to want more independence lately and—"

"This is different," she interrupted. "Clearly." The surge of desperation she picked up from Dahli made her look closer. *I am no closer to saving Zeke*, he was thinking. She softened her voice. "Are you sure Zeke is alive?"

A tormented look entered his eyes. "No, but I doubt they would kill him if they knew of his talents. Even if he refuses to help them, they have only to read his mind to learn what he knows, and if they present him with mechanical problems he will find it hard not to think of solutions."

She nodded to show she understood. *Poor Zeke.* She could feel how badly Dahli feared for his lover and his guilt for not taking better care of him. But feeling sympathetic also sparked a warning. *This is how it is with Dahli*, she reminded herself. *I see his pain and feel for him, and next thing he's at war with and killing those I love.* He could have other plans, hidden behind memory blocks. He might not even know he'd buried them until some pre-arranged reminder told him, and then he would release the memories and suddenly they'd be at war again.

Qall glanced at her, frowning, then he turned back to Dahli. "Do you have anything else to tell us, Dahli?"

The man paused, then shook his head.

"I'd like to discuss this with Rielle and Baluka alone now," Qall told him. "Thank you for retelling your story."

Dahli nodded, then met Rielle's gaze briefly before rising and leaving the room. Rielle considered his look and the thought behind it. He believed she cared enough about Zeke to try to save him. He'd only come here, knowing it meant breaking the condition Qall had made on him remaining alive, because he'd run out of options.

Or so he wants us to believe. She looked from Qall to Baluka. "What have you done so far?"

The current and former leaders of the Restorers exchanged glances. "Nothing," Qall admitted.

"We wanted Tyen's advice first."

"You're not going to get it," she told them. "I suggest you investigate this world of machines Dahli found, as well as find experts in mechanical magic to help us – if any are still alive." A memory of the burned houses in Telemna-vo and Woperi came to her. Had they been the hiding places of inventors, or of the expelled students? Or where Zeke and Dahli had worked? That gave her an idea. "Dahli said he and Zeke had found a way to combat the machines. See if he will tell us about it. We may need it."

Baluka's eyebrows rose. "He said these machine armies were to be sold to worlds in conflict, not that they were designed to attack us."

"Do the Restorers have no enemies?"

"Plenty."

"Then what is to stop them using machines against you?"

Baluka shrugged. "Dahli said they do not use much magic, individually. That is as it has always been. They are more of a danger to non-sorcerers – though I am not dismissing that as a less important problem."

"Dahli said that they were a threat when in large numbers."

"To one sorcerer." He shrugged. "We can call upon thousands. No, Dahli just wants to frighten us into investigating in the hope we'll save his lover in the process."

Rielle looked at Qall. "What do you think? Could he be hiding memories to conceal a different motive and plan?"

Baluka turned to the young man. "You said he has no memory of blocking any."

"No, but as Rielle reminded me, he could have blocked his memory of blocking the memories, and arranged for something to remind him at the right moment."

"That would be a great risk. What if something upset that arrangement?"

"Valhan took an even greater risk, relying on me to resurrect him," Rielle pointed out.

"Valhan knew he was flirting with oblivion," Qall told her. "A part of him welcomed the idea."

She stared at him, first in surprise, then in amazement at the revelation – and then she looked away, disturbed by the reminder that he held so many of Valhan's memories.

Qall shrugged. "We shouldn't ignore the possibility that Dahli is hiding something, but it would be foolish to ignore his warnings, too. Zeke is particularly clever, and if they are stealing ideas from his mind, we should be worried." He spread his hands. "We know machines are growing more sophisticated. Waiting around to see if they become a threat does not seem wise. We should prepare ourselves, even if only with knowledge for the moment."

He turned to Baluka. "Organise a search for inventors we can seek advice from."

Baluka nodded. "I'll begin straight away."

Qall looked at Rielle. "Seek out this machine world to learn if it is as dangerous as Dahli fears, and to see if Zeke is there and we can rescue him."

"No, no." Baluka shook his head quickly. "Send someone else to the machine world. Rielle is unique, as the Maker, and much as I doubt Dahli is right about the severity of this threat, she is too valuable to risk losing."

Qall frowned. "Her ability to generate magic may be invaluable to an investigation, if the machines are drawing in all the magic."

"She can't easily whip up a drawing when under attack."

"Oh, she has a new way of making magic that won't be so inconvenient."

Rielle looked at Qall. "I do?"

He waved his hands around in graceful curves, and like a bolt of light she recalled the dance of lights she'd made in her own world. *Of course, it would be easier to do that than drawing if I was under attack. I could even make it part of my defence . . .*

Baluka's eyes had lit with curiosity, but he did not ask what Qall meant, knowing that it would be all too easy for someone to read the answer from his mind. *The sooner I leave here the sooner my average magical strength will stop being a vulnerability of the Restorers,* he thought. *But I must make sure Qall isn't going to make any foolish decisions. He is so young and sometimes unwilling to listen . . .* He paused, and cast a guilty glance at Qall.

The young man smiled sympathetically. "I *am* young, Baluka, but I'm not your average youth. And I do value your advice and help."

Drawing in a deep breath, Baluka straightened his shoulders. "Then my advice is, don't send Rielle. She is not ageless. She can't heal herself. If war is coming, we need to ensure we have powerful allies. We need to ensure that those who would rather avoid assisting in battle will have no choice, if they're indebted to us for strengthening their world."

"I was going to send ageless sorcerers with her, but . . ." Qall began. He grimaced apologetically at Rielle. "I know how you feel about restoring worlds purely for political reasons, and I had intended to find another way to satisfy these allies, but I am going to have to ask you to put aside your qualms for the sake of preparing for the worst."

Rielle quelled a sigh. So Baluka *had* made arrangements for her to strengthen worlds that weren't dead. Annoyance and rebellion rose, but they both faded as she read a plea in Qall's eyes. She was conscious of Baluka watching her. Turning to him, she narrowed her eyes to communicate her displeasure. He looked away, but his jaw tightened.

"Will you do it?" Qall asked. "Strengthen worlds, that is."

She sighed. "Very well, but I want some say in which worlds I restore."

"That's reasonable." Qall nodded, then he grimaced in sympathy. "I'm afraid there are quite a few worlds, so you're going to be occupied for some time. Maybe even a whole quarter."

Rielle sagged in resignation. "Where should I start?"

CHAPTER 13

The arrival place was unlike any Rielle had seen before. As the world grew visible she found herself standing on the ghostly palm of an enormous statue. Lying on its stomach, the androgynous figure held its arm outstretched, eyes fixed just above its hand, smiling in welcome.

It was such a strange and disturbing sight, it was an effort to turn her attention away and take in the rest of the surroundings. The prone figure filled a large courtyard, much longer than it was wide. Two humans lingered nearby, wearing shaggy fur capes that reached the ground, watching her arriving. The stone of both walls and statue began to sparkle. The reason became apparent as cold, brittle air surrounded her. Light reflected off frost all around her. Her breath misted in the air as she exhaled.

The two humans were men. They stepped forward to meet her, stopping before the giant stone palm and smiling up at her.

"Welcome to Po-Gni," they said in unison, their accent so guttural it took a moment for her to realise they'd spoken in Traveller tongue.

"Thank you," Rielle replied. "Is there a Restorer outpost nearby?"

"Not in this world," the pair replied together. "The next. Tiloppa – the grass world." They both pointed at the statue's other hand, behind her, also held out to receive visitors.

She nodded. "Thank you again."

Pushing out of the world, she turned to gaze at the statue again. Was it simply a fancy place for visitors to arrive or was there a greater significance? She did not have the time to linger and find out. Skimming to the other hand, she sensed another path leading away and sent herself along it.

The statue faded. Long vertical lines formed around her. Their smooth uniformity reminded her of the poles that had descended just as the Restorers and their allies had arrived at the beginning of the battle with Dahli, piercing their bodies. She slowed, examining them cautiously. As detail formed, she realised they were blades of grass about the width of her hand and at least twice her height.

Another giant thing, she mused. *Only this time something living.*

A stone circle about six paces wide lay beneath her feet, the edges worn smooth. No humans were visible. Air surrounded her as she arrived, and a sound both soft and loud. This was the shifting of the grass above her, stirred by a wind she was well sheltered from. She moved to the edge of the circle and looked down, but the grass was so dense she could not see the ground.

Casting her senses out, she found a large world of average magical strength. Though her ability to sense thought did not reach nearly as far as that for magic, she encountered plenty of minds to read, particularly in one direction. Guessing this indicated a nearby city, she pushed out of the world a little and skimmed upwards. She burst from the grass into bright sunlight. The vegetation stretched to the horizon in all directions. No city broke through it. Puzzled, she started in the direction in which she'd sensed all the minds.

She found it entirely by accident. One small stone tower poked out above the endless leaves. Arriving on its roof, she stretched out her senses and, finding minds, learned she was in the middle of a multitude of people. They were not far below her, in homes and walking along thoroughfares within the grass.

A hatch in the tower roof beckoned, but she did not want to

trespass. Instead she travelled slightly outside the world again, sinking down through the grass slowly. The leaves all curved away from her, bound in place by plaited foliage to make room for worn stone slabs, laid end to end to form a road.

The people she'd sensed nearby saw her, and stopped to stare. They were pale and bald, and covered in tiny spots. She emerged in the world and bowed, as they expected a respectful visitor to do.

"Which way to the Restorers?" she asked in the local language, which was as much whistles as words.

The people approved of her speaking their tongue. One came forward and offered to guide her there. She accepted and was led along the path, passing gaps in the grass walls on either side. She saw no doors anywhere, so was able to glimpse all manner of groups of people in rooms beyond these gaps, from families and couples to larger gatherings. At one point they passed a market of sorts, and later an enclosure that appeared to be full of green elongated sacks, cinched at regular intervals to form ribs. At the last moment, she glimpsed the end of one and had to hide a shudder. A round mouth lined with teeth revealed that these were giant creatures of some kind.

Not long after, her guide stopped at another wide opening, the space beyond occupied by humans whose difference to the locals was clear from their varied colouring and stature. Her guide bowed and left, not requiring more than a nod in thanks. The locals did not speak much, she had noted on the journey.

Stepping through the door, Rielle met the gaze of the other-worlders. They rose to meet her.

"Rielle Lazuli, the Maker?" one asked.

"Yes," Rielle replied.

"We have two messages here for you."

"Two?" she repeated in surprise.

The woman smiled. "I will fetch them."

The other three sorcerers moved forward, introducing themselves.

241

One in particular was overcome with awe, and she could not help trying to reassure him that she was just an ordinary person. The others disagreed, one starting to list her deeds, so Rielle was relieved when the woman returned with her messages.

The first was from Qall, as she'd expected. He'd chosen the next few worlds to be strengthened, and assured her that he'd checked to ensure no intention to conquer or oppress lay behind the requests. He had planned out a rough path for her to reduce the amount of backtracking, and so she would not have to keep returning to the Restorer base.

She had been travelling for many days – almost a quarter-cycle – but had visited almost sixty worlds in that time. As a result, her drawing skills were improving again. She had been getting out of practice, what with only being able to make art when she generated magic. She was also accumulating quite a collection of drawings.

The second message was a little tattered, written on low-quality paper. She unfolded it and read the awkward scrawl of someone not especially familiar with the written version of Traveller tongue. The writer's name was written at the top of the page: Annad of Infae.

To Rielle the Maker. I have opened three clues my mentor gave me. This gives me large hope I find the place we spoke of. If you want the answers go to the temple at home. I leave messages at Restorer outpost also. I hope you are well. Annad.

She smiled. Her visit to Infae had only been half a cycle ago, but it seemed longer. Learning that Annad had interpreted three out of seven of the clues to the secret library made her wish she was free to join him in the search.

Scanning the message again, she frowned. Annad hadn't mentioned what he was looking for. If anyone had intercepted the message, they'd only have learned he was looking for answers she

242

might want to hear. But was that enough to draw attention to him? Would someone who resented the Restorers seek Annad to find out more, perhaps hoping to find a way to strike against her or those she worked for? Thinking of poor Zeke, kidnapped by the machine makers, she realised that every message Annad sent her might put him in danger.

She sighed. It would be safer if he didn't send her messages at all. She considered how to tell him not to. If she asked him outright, and *that* message was intercepted, an enemy would know that Annad and his search was important to her.

What was she to do, then? She considered the problem, then opened her pack and brought out pen and paper.

To Annad of Infae, I enjoyed reading of your progress in decoding the puzzle your mentor gave you. You have done well. I would very much like to hear of the answers you found but my time is now occupied attending to matters for the Restorers. I am travelling a great deal and may not receive future messages, so do not risk that your efforts will be wasted. I am sure we will meet again one day and you can tell me everything. Good luck and take care. Rielle.

Rereading it, she nodded. It had the tone she had aimed for, of someone powerful indulging but also distancing an enthusiastic follower. Annad would not believe she cared so little about his search, since he knew the importance of Maker's Curse to her. At least, she hoped he would see through the message to the warnings within.

Leaving it with the Restorers with instructions for its delivery, she pushed out of the world and set off for the next to be strengthened. Qall's message had said only that it was a cold place. She was dressed in her usual simple dress and shawl, so she would have to generate heat with magic when she arrived – unless the locals provided her with warmer clothes during her stay.

Several worlds later she emerged in an interior arrival place. The room was circular and the walls were made of a dark, glossy substance. The stone floor did not meet the walls, and flames flickered in the gap between them, except where the floor continued out into a corridor through two doorways.

She chose a doorway. As she stepped through, two exceptionally short, brown-skinned men leapt to their feet from low chairs made from what looked like hide stretched over a frame. She sought their minds and learned they were sorcerers and guards of the arrival place.

"I am Rielle the Maker," she told them. "The Restorers sent me. I am to meet with your leader, Mimpu du Purmeme."

The pair made a polite gesture that mimicked removing head coverings – in the outside world, baring heads to the elements in greeting was a great honour. One sang a word in the local language, and a woman with long dark hair in a braid that fell to the floor stepped out of a nearby doorway. A guard made a quick sign, and the woman turned and made the same welcoming gesture. She took one of the long ends of a rope tied around her waist and offered it to Rielle. This, too, was a polite gesture mimicking a custom rooted in the harsh environment outside. When storms could reduce visibility to nothing, holding the waist rope of a guide was the only way to know you were following them.

Rielle stepped forward and took the end of the rope, then followed as the woman shuffled out of the room. They entered a great maze of corridors. None were straight, and many of the rooms Rielle glimpsed were round. As she walked she skimmed the minds around her, seeing multitudes of them involved in domestic tasks, many different forms of employment, learning or playing. Stretching out further, she found a group of men moving furniture from one side of the city to the other, a constant task as the glacier the metropolis was built upon moved and fragmented at the leading edge. In a local year or two, the arrival place would have to be relocated, too, and none were looking forward to shifting the heavy otherworld stone floor. They preferred the bone paving and walls, which were lighter.

Bone? Rielle took a closer look at the walls, noting how few seams were visible. What manner of creature did these bones belong to? Some of the pieces were wider than she could have stepped across. She looked further, seeking a memory or image to explain the mystery, but only caught vague thoughts about the hunting season. One woman worried how long the city would last, if magic continued to be created too slowly for the hunters to gather enough meat, skin and bones for the city.

By that time the corridors had grown wider and the walls were carved and decorated. Rielle examined artworks quickly as she passed. The skill of their makers was impressive. Her guide noticed her looking and began to talk about the subjects, memories of the icy landscapes and iceberg-riddled oceans enhancing her stories. She pointed out the creatures from which the bones had come: huge animals that swam in the ocean's depths but must come to the surface to breathe.

Music reached her ears from the direction they were heading. It was unstructured and gentle. The source was revealed as she was led into a large room. Sculptures were spaced evenly across the floor. One was a machine, and from it emanated the tune. In the centre of the room, several low chairs surrounded a circular table. A woman and two men had risen and were walking towards Rielle.

"Welcome, Rielle the Maker," the woman said, using the Traveller tongue. "I am Queen Purmeme, and these are my most trusted advisers."

A ritual containing many formal phrases and gestures followed. When all were done, Purmeme ushered Rielle to a chair.

"We are so happy that you have come," she said. "Especially considering the news about the machine armies."

A chill ran down Rielle's spine as she read that machines had been used in attacks on nearby worlds. Was this local strife, or something worse?

The sorcerers that Qall had sent to investigate the world Dahli had seen had found only an empty, dead place. All signs of the machines had been removed, and the investigators found no clue to where they had been taken. Baluka had located only a few inventors who had not died or disappeared. All had given up their trade under pressure from Liftre. All refused to help.

Rielle hoped her concern did not show as she asked, "What news is this?"

"You do not already know?"

"No. I have been travelling for a long time, so the news I hear is often old."

"Worlds not far from here have been destroyed by armies of machines," the Queen told her. "Their cities were levelled and all magic was stripped away. Sorcerers fled with as many people as they had time to transport, but those who were stranded suffered the same fate as their homes."

"How long ago did this occur?"

"Ten of our local days."

Rielle shifted in her chair. It was uncomfortable – made for a smaller build. "It is possible that the Restorers do not know this. Did any of those who escaped come here?"

Purmeme shook her head. "No. We heard this from traders."

"I had better meet with these traders and learn as much as I can, then send that information to the Restorers."

"You will not seek out the attackers?"

"No, not alone."

Purmeme smiled. "I would invite you to stay here a while and see more of my world, but I expect you will want to deliver this news as soon as possible."

"Yes. As much as I would like to see more of your world and receive your hospitality, I cannot stay – not just because of these attacks, but because I have many more worlds awaiting my help."

"It will be our loss." The Queen smiled. "Let us meet with the city's sorcerers." Purmeme rose, and the advisers followed suit. "I must warn you: they have many questions for you regarding how we may maintain the balance of magic generation and use."

Rielle stood, glad to be out of the chair. "I will be happy to give them advice. It is wise of them to seek such information."

Purmeme led the way to the door. As they left the room, the Queen looked at Rielle and her nose wrinkled. "You may not find our sorcerers wise, when you learn how we came to find ourselves in this situation," she said in a conspiratorial whisper. "They have looked down upon and separated themselves from our artisans and makers for many years now."

Rielle sighed. "This is not the only world to weaken for such reasons. Sorcerers too easily come to think themselves superior to all others. They tend not to like my advice."

"Here, magic is vital to survival." The Queen's smile was hard with determination. "And our survival is my primary responsibility. I will not let them destroy this world out of pride."

"That is good to hear. I will not always be around to strengthen worlds, since I am not ageless."

Purmeme's expression became serious. She nodded. "I will ensure they understand this." She took one end of her rope belt and offered it to Rielle. "Let me take you to them."

Rielle took the rope, pushing aside a feeling of foolishness. It was like being a child, clinging to its mother's clothes so it would not get lost, and yet here it was a great honour to be led by the Queen. Straightening her shoulders, she followed with as much dignity as she could muster.

CHAPTER 14

R ielle hadn't noticed on her first visit to the grass city that the binding that shaped the leaves formed patterns inside the buildings so intricate and complex that only skilled artisans could have made them. It never ceased to amaze her how humans found ways to create beauty even in the oddest and harshest of places. She was still admiring the patterns when the leader of the Restorer outpost, who had greeted her on her return, came back. Tearing her eyes away from the walls, Rielle saw that a man and a woman had also entered the room.

"This is Adene and Liroc," the leader told her, then turned to the pair. "This is Rielle the Maker." Introductions done, she smiled at all of them, then left the room so they could talk privately.

"An honour to meet you, Rielle," Liroc said in a startlingly deep voice. He gestured to Adene and then himself. "Qall has sent us to assist your investigation into the rumours of a machine army."

Rielle blinked in surprise. She had assumed that the pair were meeting her only to hear what she had learned in detail. Qall's instructions and their purpose were foremost in their minds: to use their pattern-shifting ability to heal her if she was harmed. They were both from worlds nearby, and were worried about the rumours.

"Thank you for volunteering," she replied. "Hopefully you'll be useful to me only as a second and third pair of eyes and ears, not as healers. Are you newly arrived, or rested and ready to go?"

Liroc looked at his companion, who nodded. "We are ready to leave."

Rielle extended her hands. The pair took one each. For a brief moment she expected them to breathe in, but then she remembered that if they could heal her they must be ageless and did not have to worry about suffocating between worlds. She filled her lungs and pushed into the place between.

The traders she had questioned had described the route to the ruined worlds in detail, so she had only to retrace her steps to the place in which she'd interviewed them, then continue onwards following their instructions. Before long she and her companions neared the first machine world. The path between worlds had not been used recently, but it had the feeling of deep indentation that a previously well-travelled route gained. As they passed the midway point, she slowed and scanned the whiteness, anxious to make out the landscape she was approaching before arriving fully.

A dark band of irregular shapes below a blue-green sky appeared. As details emerged, she made out the foundations of buildings surrounded by the remnants of their former walls. A large ruined city lay before them, every surface blackened with soot. She positioned herself and her helpers in the centre of the arrival place, where the rubble was thinnest, and waited while her companions moved their feet into clear spaces. As air surrounded them, the stink of smoke and burned meat filled Rielle's nose. She took a reluctant breath and grimaced.

"No magic here," Adene said.

Rielle extended her senses and encountered a dizzying, endless darkness. She had been in many dead worlds since becoming a Maker, and all were disturbing places to be in, but none had been so utterly depleted of magic at this one. A sorcerer's reach limited the size of the area they could extract from, so if they took all the magic they could reach, they left a spherical void. An army of them could strip a world, but it tended to leave overlapping voids with little gaps between, the remnant magic slowly spreading outwards. The largest gap was always beneath the earth. Magic would eventually leach upwards into the voids, but it took time. An inhabited world that had been empty for a longer time usually contained clouds of magic around places of habitation where it was being generated by human creativity.

This world felt like a place sucked dry of life, from the interior to the furthest reach of the atmosphere.

How is that possible? Do the machines have a reach as great as the strongest sorcerers? Or do they dig their way underground to get at the world's interior magic? The only other alternative she could see was that a powerful sorcerer able to reach the far reaches of the entire world had assisted in the attack. The thought that another sorcerer that powerful might exist who was commanding machine armies turned her blood cold. *But why would someone that powerful need war machines?*

Since there was no magic, she could not sense even her companions' minds, let alone discover if the attacker or survivors were here. She could restore the world, but if there were machines here, or invading sorcerers, she would be giving them more power. Was it worth the risk, just so she could search for minds?

"Let's levitate up and get a broader view," she said, letting go of her helpers' hands.

The pair stepped up onto invisible platforms of stilled air. Doing the same, Rielle lifted herself up, her companions following. Streets and a city wall were revealed as they rose, as were the blackened shapes of burned corpses. To her right was a high mound, the only variation in their surroundings, so she headed towards it. As they drew closer it became apparent that it was no natural hill, but a larger pile of rubble. Gold-painted decoration glinted here and there, suggesting it had been a palace. She caught a glimpse of an arm clothed in a bloodstained, finely stitched sleeve. Was this person still alive? Was anybody?

She decided she had to check. Taking a deep breath, she let it out slowly, then began to create patterns of light in the air.

Adene and Liroc drifted away to give her more room, their grim expressions brightening to smiles and astonishment as they sensed magic spilling outwards. Their pleasure cheered Rielle and helped her push away the gloom that had settled over her. She made the patterns more intricate, drawing upon shapes she could now see within the two sorcerers' minds. But she could also sense that they, too, feared she was strengthening this world's attackers, so she let the lights blink out.

"Search for minds," she instructed.

Several heartbeats passed with them silently staring into the distance, scanning the area for thoughts.

"Nothing," Adene murmured in a soft voice.

"Empty," Liroc agreed.

"Let's look further afield," Rielle said.

Taking the lead, she propelled herself through the air. Eventually they found small groups of people living in isolated, wild areas, but wherever there had been cities and towns, all was in ruin. Areas occupied by humans were not the only ones devastated, however. They encountered large holes with fresh mounds of soil and rock around them.

"Mines?" Liroc asked.

Adene pointed. "Yes, there's a slag heap."

"There are no roads," Liroc observed. "Sorcerers must have brought in materials and took away whatever they were made into via the place between world."

Rielle descended to the top of a tailings heap. "Skim around the area," she told them. "Look for a path leading into the place between worlds."

For a moment she watched the two ageless sorcerers' ghostly images flashing back and forth, debating if she should join them or investigate the mine from the ground, but Liroc soon returned.

"There are several paths," he told her, "but they converge before leaving this world."

"Take me there."

He took her hand and pulled her out of the world and to a place at the centre of one of the craters.

"*Adene!*" Rielle called. The woman stopped, turned and zoomed straight towards Rielle, coming to an abrupt stop. Rielle held out her hand and the woman took it. Taking over the directing of their journey, Rielle propelled them along the path. The ruined world faded. Rielle approached the next cautiously.

The world they arrived in was in the same state as the last. Ruined cities, few survivors and the remnants of mines from which paths led out of the world. This time Rielle gathered all the magic she had created as they were about to leave.

"You don't want to leave the magic for the remaining people?" Adene asked.

Rielle shook her head. "I fear if I do, I will be fuelling the machines and their makers if they come back."

The next world was also stripped and devastated. However, as the one after grew visible they found themselves surrounded by motion. As details emerged, the source was revealed: endless rows of machines marching – if their smooth, multi-legged movements could be called that – past.

Rielle skimmed upwards so they would arrive somewhere not compromised by machine forms. They found themselves above another ruined city, many of the buildings still belching smoke. Columns of machines flowed over all, countless legs moving. Remembering Dahli's story of being attacked by a horde of them, Rielle rose higher, hoping to stay out of range of the machines' senses. She stilled the air in a sphere around herself and her companions as they arrived, so they had both support and shield.

All surface magic had been stripped from the world, but it remained within the interior. Though they were far above the city, the stink of smoke still reached her nose. She glanced at her companions. Both were staring down at the machines, eyes wide with horror.

"It's like they're alive," Adene said in a voice hushed for fear of attracting the attention of thousands of inhuman sensors.

"They're not," Liroc replied firmly, but with a slight quaver in his voice. He turned to Rielle. "Where now?"

She considered. Following the machines was the most obvious next step. The relentless flow was hard to ignore. Slowly at first, then with increasing speed, she carried them in the direction they were travelling, shaping her shield so it created less resistance to wind. Not long after, another river of marching machines joined the flow, then another. The width of the line widened until it was like a flood. They moved over a hilly landscape that had once been rural, with small towns linked by unsealed roads. The machines ignored these landmarks, surging over everything.

"What is *that?*" Liroc asked, pointing towards the horizon.

The machines ahead were turning a different shade of grey. As Rielle drew closer, and she was able to make out individual machines, it became clear the change was merely a shift in the reflected light off metallic bodies, as the moving machines joined the mass of still ones, the boundary between still and moving machines appearing to slowly ripple outwards.

Passing over the area of still machines, Rielle shivered as she saw how they had formed neat lines, stretching to the horizon. They were of different sizes and shapes, from the size of a lap pet to larger than a small house. The sight of so many was chilling. What world could resist such an army? And if each of those machines held enough magic to form one reasonable blast of heat or force, it was easy to imagine them defeating a sorcerer as powerful as Dahli.

But were they a danger to an *army* of sorcerers?

"So many. Will they continue making them until the entire world is covered?" Adene wondered.

"Maybe we should ask their guardians," Liroc replied. He pointed towards the horizon. "There's a citadel over there. I had to refine my sight to see it."

Rielle sought his mind, and saw what he was looking at through eyes enhanced by pattern-shifting. At times like these she sorely missed being ageless. A cluster of towers rose above the ruins of another city. Pinpoints of light suggested life behind the windows. Yet she sensed no magic in that direction.

"Will we go there?" he asked.

She considered. Zeke might be there, but she would never know unless she created or released enough magic to read minds. Which would not just strengthen the machines, but also alert any sorcerers to her presence. If Dahli was right, that would put her and her companions in great danger.

"No." She turned away. "I don't want to risk a confrontation until we learn as much as we can about the machines. The mines and forges we saw could not produce this many of them. Let's discover where they are coming from."

She propelled them back the way they had come. They passed their arrival place and continued on, picking ever smaller branches of the converging machines to follow. After an even longer journey, they found the end of a column in the middle of an empty plain.

"Can you see their tracks?" she asked Liroc.

He narrowed his enhanced eyes. "Yes." He pointed. "They go that way."

She carried them onwards. Now that they were not following machines, the danger of being sensed and attacked had diminished, so she descended enough that she could see the tracks for herself. After a short time, a motionless machine came into sight. It appeared to be missing several legs. They passed more of these broken machines, some still, some moving.

Finally they reached a place where the tracks fanned out over a large area, and continued no further. An arrival place? Rielle brought them down and, when they were just above the ground, pushed out of the world. As she expected, a path led away into the place between worlds.

"Follow the path?" Adene asked as Rielle returned them to the world.

"Not yet," Rielle replied. "I suspect it is one of many arrival places and I am wondering if I should look for more." She turned to Liroc. "What can you see?"

He scanned the horizon, then pointed. "Another line of them over there. And . . . that's interesting. There's a broken machine a few hundred strides away, and it has smaller machines fixing it."

"Tell me where."

She took them in the direction he indicated, and stopped when she was close enough to see what he had described. Two small machines were scurrying over the broken one's form. As she watched, they removed a leg and replaced it. She didn't see where the other leg had come from, but it became apparent when she took them up into the air again. Nearby, another machine was being dismantled by the small ones. She turned to Liroc.

"Let's investigate the other line you saw."

He directed her to it. The machines were a larger, slow-moving kind. The legs were short and thick, the bodies bulbous with a nozzle at the front.

"I don't think I want to know what is inside those," Adene muttered.

Rielle shook her head. "Nor do I. Let's see where they came from."

She followed the machines back towards their source. This line, too, simply ended, and a path led away.

"Where does this go?" Rielle murmured. She followed it to the next world, which was also a ruin. They arrived in a marshy area. The machines had left deep tracks in the ground. These led to a mountain ridge, to a dark opening in the rock.

Adene glanced at Rielle. "Another mine?"

"Possibly."

"Do you want to look inside?"

"Yes, but . . . before we go inside, we should look for minds.

I doubt there are any sorcerers left. They're probably with their machines, but we should check."

She set them down on a ridge overlooking the possible mine entrance. Taking a deep breath, she let it out and calmed her mind. Then she began creating patterns of light. It did not take long to fill the area around them with magic. The two ageless sorcerers did not watch her this time, but stared down at the cave entrance.

"There! There's one!" Liroc exclaimed. "Four of them, actually."

Rielle stopped and sought the minds he'd found. Four men waited in a small room carved out of the rock. None had noticed the return of magic, their thoughts full of expectation and impatience. Almost instantly she understood that they were in a mine and machine factory, and were awaiting the return of several companions before they all joined their general and continued on to conquer another world and strip it of raw materials for machines. As she roamed from mind to mind seeking more information, a name caught her attention and she returned to the one who'd thought it.

I hope Perren will be okay. Tarren's supposed to be smart. He'll have no hope against all the sorcerers Kettin sent, though.

Rielle sucked in a quick breath. This Kettin was their leader, she read from their minds. He had sent several sorcerers to attack Tarren some days ago. She quickly scanned the minds again, hoping to find out exactly how long ago the attackers had left, but all she found was a general sense that about half of the time they were expected to be absent had passed.

Half to get there, half to return. Which meant the attack could be happening right now!

She grasped Adene and Liroc's hands tightly, then pushed out of the world.

CHAPTER 15

"*This is not what Qall ordered*," Liroc said in the mild tone Rielle had so often heard used by the servants of feared leaders. He might have been making an observation about a small shift in weather, not her rush through the worlds. It broke through her focus, and filled her with apprehension at how she was coming across to these two people. She should be explaining her actions.

"*No*," Rielle replied. "*But if I had the time to seek his opinion, I believe he would agree with me that letting Tarren and his students die would be unwise. We need teachers like Tarren. We'll lose Tyen's support if we don't attempt to save him.*"

Adene's brow was deeply lined. She shrugged as Rielle met her gaze. Liroc nodded, but his posture still spoke of his discomfort at abandoning their mission.

Rielle paused before arriving in the next world so that she could speak without gasping for air. "*Someone ought to report to Qall, to tell him what we have learned so far and where I am going. Are you able to separate? I may need one of you in Tarren's world if I am injured.*"

The pair nodded, then turned to look at each other. Rielle brought them into the world, then bent over and braced her hands on her knees as dizziness from a lack of air overwhelmed her. Pain blossomed in her head and lungs. She felt a hand press against her arm and the pain faded. As her sight cleared, she looked up to see Adene's eyes fixed somewhere within her.

"You'll be of no use to Tarren if you arrive like this," the young woman said. She looked up at Liroc. "I'll go with the Maker. You return to Qall."

He paused, looking as if he wanted to argue, then pressed his lips together and nodded.

"Do you know where you are?" Rielle asked him.

He looked around, then shook his head.

"Stay with me for now. I will need to head towards the base first to get my bearings before starting towards Tarren's world. Let me know when you recognise a world."

Rielle took a deep breath, let it out, then sucked in another and pushed out of the world again.

They had passed through another twenty or so worlds when Liroc spoke in the place between.

"This. I know this place. We passed through it on the way to meet you, but on a different path than the one we're following now." As they arrived on a raised stone platform in the middle of a spectacular fountain, he pulled out of Rielle's grasp. "Be careful," he said, looking from Rielle to Adene. He smiled. "You still owe me," he told the young woman.

Adene rolled her eyes and made a "tsk" noise. "We'll see."

Liroc faded from sight. Rielle regarded Adene grimly. "Thanks for volunteering to come with me. I'm afraid you'll have to go blindfold from here."

The woman's smile faded. She nodded, and as Rielle took off her scarf and tied it around her head she did not protest.

Taking the woman's hand and a few more deep breaths, Rielle pushed on.

Tarren's world lay beyond the Restorer base, but not directly in line with it. She could have headed straight towards it, but that meant taking an unfamiliar path, requiring a slower pace to ensure the worlds she passed through were safe. It would be faster to travel familiar routes for as long as possible before striking out towards Tarren's world.

Quickening her pace, she rushed through worlds, managing

to pass through several between each breath. Eventually she had to slow, as her speed demanded so much concentration she'd had no time to consider how to approach Tarren's world.

She was all too conscious that she was creating a path leading right to Tarren's school. If it was under attack that would not matter – the ex-Liftre inventors and their leader, Kettin, already knew where it was. But if the four men had been wrong or misled, and those seeking Tarren only knew of his vague whereabouts, she might lead Tarren's enemies to him.

She couldn't afford taking the time to hide her tracks, however. If the men were right, by the time Rielle arrived the battle could be well underway. Or over.

She would not know the true situation until she reached his world. But then . . . she didn't have to be at Tarren's school to confirm it was under attack. As long as there was still magic in his world, she could seek out minds and see what was happening from far enough away that the attackers wouldn't sense Adene's mind. Then, if the school was not under attack, she could continue to the next world, and lead anyone on her trail away.

Still, it would mean leading them uncomfortably close to Tarren's school. Was there another way she could learn if Tarren was under attack without approaching it?

As the answer came she smiled: her ability to sense magic. She could sense all of the magic in most worlds. If she arrived on the other side of Tarren's, she could search for fresh voids of magic and new ones being formed, and that would tell her a battle was taking place. Tarren's lessons at the school never involved such easily detectable shifts in magic. He took his students away from its location if he needed to teach something that would have that great an effect.

By the time Rielle stopped to breathe again, she had a plan. She began pausing for shorter breaks and travelling for longer, but was forced to slow again when dizziness started to plague her whenever she stopped. Finally, Adene placed her free hand on her shoulder.

"Here," the young woman said. "Let me help."

Strength and steadiness returned with sudden rapidity. Rielle thanked Adene. "Can you do that whenever we stop, so we get there faster?"

Adene nodded. Pushing out of the world again, Rielle sped onwards, her pauses to recover shortening as Adene healed her. Even so, time seemed to slow, and the number of worlds between them and Tarren's world seemed infinite. But they weren't, and at last the number shrank to zero. They arrived in Tarren's world in a night-shrouded ruined city half a world away from the school. As Adene healed away dizziness, a heavy feeling of dread settled on Rielle. She closed her eyes and stretched her senses down through the ground. On the other side of the world she found several globes of darkness, sharply defined at the edges.

Her stomach sank.

Several sorcerers had taken magic, or one had taken magic several times. She could ascertain nothing more than that, but it was enough to convince her to risk skimming directly to the school. Taking her scarf off Adene's head, she met the woman's eyes.

"Are you prepared for a battle?"

The woman nodded once. "Yes."

"Then let's hope that's what we find, rather than the aftermath."

Rielle took them through the earth. If Adene was discomforted by this, Rielle could not see, since there was no light to show the woman's expression. They emerged at the other side in a rush, shooting up into bright sunlight.

Immediately it was clear that the best of the worst scenarios she had imagined was taking place. Tarren's school was under attack, but the battle had not yet been won or lost.

The ground exploded far below, rocks flying high and wide. A moment later, another patch erupted. The booms were muffled, muted by the place between but loud enough to hint at the true volume. Rielle entered the world cautiously, instantly creating a sphere of stilled air around herself and Adene. She searched for minds, and found them. Several sorcerers hovered in the sky a distance away, some of them smashing the ground below randomly in the hopes they would kill those they'd been sent to eliminate. They'd already destroyed the school and killed a few of the students, but they knew Tarren and the rest were in the maze of tunnels around and below it. They did not know where: their targets' minds had vanished when they'd taken a sleeping drug.

Tarren's alive! Rielle's relief was brief, as she realised any of the random attacks could have killed him and his attackers wouldn't know.

She caught a flash of thought. Focusing on it, she learned that some of the students were still conscious. Five of the strongest had volunteered to flee in different directions to lead the attackers' attention away. One thought of Tarren, asleep and rolling away in an old mining cart down into the lower levels. Tarren wouldn't know where he was when he woke. She hoped the Liftre sorcerers would give up and leave before then.

Turning back to the minds of the attackers, Rielle saw that their leader had ordered them to wait until Tarren awoke. Some were considering descending to the ground to search the passages. Whoever killed the teacher would be well rewarded. Few of them held much respect for the group's leader and some were contemplating acting against his orders.

Looking down, Rielle considered her options. She could see only three. Like the attackers, the only way she would find Tarren was to wait for him to wake up, or start searching the passages. It was likely the students were scattered, too. To rescue all of them would be easier if they were awake and in one place, which they couldn't safely be while under attack.

She turned her attention to the attackers, counting twenty-four of them. They hadn't noticed her or Adene yet. She didn't doubt she could kill them, but she pushed that option aside. Their minds churned with the fears and reasoning of men who had become caught up in something terrible. Regret and guilt warred with ambition and fear. Given the chance, some of them would flee the mysterious new leader of the ex-Liftre inventors. Kettin was willing to destroy whole worlds, and some worried that his gaze would fall upon their home worlds. A few did not care, however. They relished the power they had over others, and freedom from the restraints of civilised societies.

She sighed. Not killing wasn't easy. Though she had always believed it was wrong, Tyen's pacifism had given strength to her determination to never kill unless it would do more harm to avoid it than good. It was fortunate that these sorcerers didn't know that, or her third and last choice of strategy would not have been effective.

"I'm going to scare them off," she told Adene. "Brace yourself."

The woman nodded. Rielle moved her shield and support to take them swooping down under the men. She stilled the air between them and herself, forming a shield that also protected the school below. As one of the sorcerers sent a ball of rigid air downwards, it struck her shield, the force rippling outwards to be dispersed in the air.

The attacker's surprise at the lack of an explosion turned to confusion, then realisation as he saw her. Rielle set her personal shield aglow, drawing the attention of the rest of the sorcerers.

At once, all attacked. She deflected their strikes easily, and began to move towards the group. Her curiosity grew as the distance between them shrank. Would any recognise her? If any did, what would the leader decide to do?

She drew close enough to see the leader's face. She did not think she knew him. But he knew her. He'd seen images of her, created so that all the followers of Kettin would know her – and know to avoid a confrontation with her.

And then he was gone.

Where the sorcerers had been hovering was empty air. Looking around, Rielle sensed no minds but those of two conscious students. She took Adene's hand and pushed out of the world so she could reach the ground quickly.

"Let's find the two students who are awake." Rielle decided. "We'll have to wait until Tarren and the rest wake up before we can find them."

"And then?" Adene asked.

Rielle grimaced. "Tarren's not going to like it, but I think the only safe place for him now is with the Restorers."

PART FOUR

TYEN

CHAPTER 11

As Tyen walked past the classrooms, the teachers within noted his passing. Most ignored him, since he had walked this way at least once a day in the last several weeks, but he knew from their thoughts that they'd seen him. A few looked up and met his eyes, some wary, others anxious to please. He nodded to all who did, relieved that none needed anything from him, since he didn't have time to stop and help them.

Running the school now dominated Tyen's waking hours. Though he had arranged fine rooms in a nearby hotel for himself, most of his time there he spent asleep. When he had time to sleep.

Teaching seemed like a luxurious dream of the past. Studying the war machines he'd brought was impossible. When he asked himself how he had wound up in such a position, he had to admit it was entirely his own fault. He paid attention to matters his predecessor had never bothered with, which pleased or annoyed those in charge of them, depending on whether they wanted or resisted change. Even if he had ignored those matters, his workload would still be greater than Ophen's had ever been thanks to the introduction of new subjects of study, the expansion of others and the disputes that arose as a consequence of opening the Academy to entrants who had traditionally been barred from it.

Women and foreign sorcerers had begun applying to attend the school within weeks of Tyen advertising the new entry requirements in the main Leratian periodicals. At first only a few came, believing they would be rejected, then as the news spread that some of these had been admitted, enquiries increased dramatically.

Along with abolishing the ban on women learning magic in the Academy, Tyen had examined and then changed the written entry tests and standardised the practical ones to ensure fairness. Some of the old requirements had been deliberate obstructions to ensure failure due to race and gender. It had been a lot of work, but thankfully not ongoing. Once he was satisfied with the new system, he'd delegated, reluctantly, responsibility for overseeing it to people he barely knew but who appeared adequate for the task, and had created a new role called the Student Overseer, who ensured all new entrants to the Academy were treated well and equally.

As he entered another corridor, he looked out along the windows on one side and his gaze fell upon the roof of the meeting hall. Every week the professors had raised or relayed objections to the relaxing of the entrant rules. Every week Tyen reminded them that a foreign woman had restored the world and that if the Academy was to be equal to the best schools in the worlds, it needed to put aside its backward rules and prejudices and see the strength and potential it had been ignoring and wasting within its own world.

He lost a few teachers but gained three times their number as those who had distanced themselves from the institution, repelled by corruption or stifled by inflexible rules, had returned to see if their enthusiasm for it might be rekindled under this new Director. A smattering of foreign sorcerers applying to be students, both men and women, had proven to be so proficient in magic that Tyen immediately installed them as teachers.

But in the completely unfamiliar context of a renewed world bursting with magic, all were scrambling to adjust.

As Tyen left the corridor and entered the next, he smiled. *They're adapting faster than I expected, though. And they're turning out to be stronger than I expected, too.* Living in a world with little magic, both Academy and foreign sorcerers had been forced to be economical and smart in their handling of it. Since the Emperor had lifted the ban on using magic in the city, plenty of sorcerers were discovering that they were able to do much more than they had ever imagined. Even those who were cautious in testing their abilities had found ignorance could lead to unintended harm to property and, in a few cases, themselves and others. That had led some who had left the Academy, and many more graduates, to return and seek guidance.

In order to instruct them, he had made teachers of his own students, promising that their role would be temporary and he would resume their training soon. They weren't happy at first, but the smartest realised that they had plenty to learn from the locals, from their efficiency with magic to their grasp of technology, and once they pointed this out to the rest, along with the fact that they were in the "home" of mechanical magic, all accepted their unexpected promotions with grace.

Mechanical magic had always been a subject within the Academy's curriculum of general sorcery, but Tyen had elevated it to a department in its own right. He'd handed over his chests of war machines for study, though not without a measure of anxiety that he might trigger an arms race here in his own world. To alleviate some of that worry, he'd made sure that all those who applied to study mechanical magic undertook an ethical test as well as a skill and knowledge one, and he read their minds as they completed it to ensure they were honest and had no ill intentions.

Reaching the end of the corridor, Tyen pushed through twin doors into one of the many courtyards that lay between wings of the Academy buildings. He walked down a gravel path between manicured lawns and entered a part of the institution he generally kept clear of. The faint tang of preserving chemicals lingered in the air. Some of the classrooms here had plumbed sinks to help students clean up after their lessons. He glimpsed skeletons of both humans and animals in one room, and a wall covered in all manner of insects in another. It all reminded him of his failed studies in the world of healers, and he wondered what his teachers there would have thought of the Academy – and the Academy of them.

He'd reassured the professors of non-magical studies that nothing would change in their departments, but he'd realised belatedly that he'd told an unintentional lie. Learning that they would have to teach the new entrants, they'd immediately begun causing trouble. Tyen had blocked a proposal to bar women and foreigners from studying mathematics, engineering, history, chemistry and biology at the last meeting. Since then, complaints against the new students had multiplied as the teachers tried to make their point, or waste Tyen's time as retaliation.

I'm not surprised that women of my world would apply to study engineering and pure mathematics, he thought. *I just assumed they would take longer to shake off the expectations this society has trained them to have of themselves, and what their gender should be interested in.*

If the Academy's members had encountered the extraordinary people Tyen had met, and seen what they had achieved, they might not be so determined to hang on to their prejudices. But they hadn't – yet – so Tyen could only explain over and over why change was necessary and stick to his principles.

Which was more challenging some days than others. Today's complainant was Praimore, a teacher of history whose mind was as stiff and slow as his aged body. The man was waiting in the small meeting room at the far end of the wing. As Tyen entered he saw a small, yellow-brown-skinned man with short, spiky hair seated at the table. A native of Veyem, a small nation next to Mailand, Tyen guessed.

Both rose from their seats as he entered.

"Director Tyen," Praimore said. "Thank you for coming so quickly."

"Praimore," Tyen replied. He turned to the student. "Young Esp Galiana."

"Director," the student replied.

Tyen looked at the teacher again. "How can I help you both?"

"Well . . ." The teacher faltered at Tyen's deliberate use of "both", then straightened and remembered the speech he'd been constructing as he'd waited. "I knew there would be trouble when you insisted we teach the new entrants, and today I am proven right." He gestured to Esp.

"Trouble in regards to what?" Tyen prompted.

"Young Esp here continues to dispute the accuracy of our texts. He has shown no respect for the great historians of our empire and seems to have a particular hatred of the great Lahgina."

"I see," Tyen said. "In what way has he shown disrespect?"

"Interrupting in class," Praimore replied. "Disputing my marking and methods. Destruction of Academy property."

Esp made a faint noise of protest.

Tyen frowned. "Destroying property? In what way?"

Praimore bent and grabbed a book on the table, sliding it to the edge before picking it up. He opened it and fanned through the pages, then stopped and turned the book so Tyen could see. A faint curling script ran along the margin next to a sentence that had been underlined. Seeing what Esp had highlighted, Tyen had to resist a grim smile.

He turned to Esp, holding out the book. "What does this say?"

The young man glanced at the book, then scowled down at his hands. "This has never been true," he read.

Looking deeper, Tyen saw that Esp had deliberately chosen to study history alongside sorcery in order to address the lies and inaccuracies that persisted about his people. He hoped it would mollify those who felt he'd betrayed them for joining the very Academy that had helped conquer and suppress them.

Tyen looked at the book's cover. "Lahgina's stories have always sounded far-fetched to me, and as the biographer of General

Druvers he had a motive to make the peoples his subjects conquered seem more primitive than they truly were. I wouldn't be surprised if he had lied about their encounters with the Veyem."

"What! You support this vandalism of Academy property and, and, and questioning our superior knowledge!"

"No," Tyen replied, meeting Praimore's outraged gaze. "Writing on books you do not own is bad behaviour that should be discouraged." He turned to Esp. "If you feel the need to, buy a copy of the book."

Esp looked up at Tyen, his frown fading and a gleam of confidence entering his eyes. "I will."

Tyen held the young man's gaze, making his expression serious and tone firm. "I understand you wish to correct the errors of history, Esp, but that is a task that will only succeed through study and collection of proof – something that would normally take several highly qualified historians many years to achieve. If you want that sort of backing, writing denials in the margins of a book and antagonising history teachers who are teaching those you must convince will not help you attain it."

"Indeed!" Praimore interjected heartily.

"Might I suggest you break this task down into smaller ones that you can manage alongside your sorcerous studies?" Tyen continued. "Collect instances of inaccuracy that you encounter. Study the system the Academy uses for checking facts. Consider how you might prove both truth and lies, and how you may present that proof to have the greatest likelihood of acceptance." Tyen smiled and turned to Praimore. "It would be a worthy task, I think. Ultimately, truth and reason is what the Academy stands for, is it not?"

"Well . . . yes," the old man replied. A crease had appeared between his eyebrows as he realised that Tyen was not going to say that Esp was wrong.

Tyen looked back at the student. "I hope that, many years from now, I will have the chance to read your own book on the history of Veyem, and that it becomes the respected, *well-researched* text with which Academy lessons on the country will be taught. In the meantime, I'm afraid you will have to study what the rest of the students study" – he handed the book back to Praimore – "with the inevitable flaws that a constantly changing subject like history contains."

Praimore closed his mouth and nodded. "Yes, well, no book is perfect."

"Indeed. Are we done?" Tyen asked.

"Well, there's the issue of punishment," the teacher muttered.

"Erasing the marks in the book?" Tyen suggested. "Perhaps a written apology to the Librarian."

Praimore and Esp's eyes widened, and the pair avoided Tyen's gaze as he looked from one to the other. Peeking into their minds, Tyen saw that both found the Librarian a little unsettling, especially now they knew how old he was. *It's been a while since I visited Rytan Kep*, Tyen mused. *I must make time in my schedule.*

"Anything else?" Tyen asked.

"No." Praimore raised an eyebrow at Esp, who shook his head.

To Tyen's relief, the journey back to his office was uneventful. He settled behind his desk and began reading the reports the field heads sent him at the end of each week. Finishing a dry summary from the archaeology head – it took a perverse talent to make what had been Tyen's favourite subject so boring – he was happy to find the next was from the head of linguistics. The professor had a rare gift for making every report a fascinating read. He had persuaded the young men and women Tyen had brought into this world to spend a few minutes each day translating phrases into their native tongues, and his resulting theories about the similarities of language and causes of variance were fascinating.

A knock came at the door and Tyen muttered a curse in a language nobody at the Academy would understand. Looking up, he extended his senses to see who waited behind it. Vael Romtolin, the Student Overseer, hovered there, a little worried that the faint vocalisation he'd heard from within indicated Tyen was in a bad mood. *People might not understand the words of a curse, but they know the sound of one*, Tyen mused.

"Come in," he called, setting down the linguist's report.

Vael slipped through the door, closing it quietly behind him.

"Director," he said. He walked to Tyen's desk and glanced at the chair, looking uncertain.

Tyen gestured to the seat. "Sit." He resisted reading the man's mind. He'd caught enough of the man's thoughts to know he was here on an important school matter but not an impending disaster. "What is it?"

Vael grimaced, sighed, then sat down. "There has been an . . . unfortunate encounter between one of the new female students and three of the older male ones."

Again, the man paused, uncertain how to proceed. Tyen made an encouraging gesture.

"As you know," Vael continued, "the young women staying within the Academy are being housed in what had been quarters for the servants and must walk to what is now the women's bathing house. It seems . . . no, not seems, it happened that three of the male students encountered one of the female students returning from the baths." He paused, then added, "I suspect they were waiting for her, actually, but I have no proof as they are stronger sorcerers than I."

Tyen's stomach sank. "Which of the female entrants was it?"

"Flaim Purveil."

A strong-willed young woman, Tyen recalled. With exceptional magical ability.

"And the young men?"

"Alam Warden, Esteme Keeper and Darimon Starwriter."

"What did this encounter entail?"

"Well, they claim she taunted them. Showing her bare legs. That sort of thing." Vael shook his head. "She denies it, and says she was fully dressed, with her wet hair wrapped up in a towel."

"And . . .?"

Vael's arms were wrapped about his chest. He was clearly uncomfortable and distressed. Tyen had chosen a young graduate to be the Student Overseer because he hoped Vael would be more likely to recall what it was like to be a student, and the students might find him easy to confide in. But Vael did not command the same respect a man of greater seniority might, and some of the older students were testing his authority.

Vael drew in a deep breath. "They stripped her of her clothes and forced her to walk naked back to her quarters. Some of them even . . . manhandled her in the process."

Tyen's heart froze, then the heat of anger flashed through him. "Are there witnesses?"

"A handful who saw her towards the end of the ordeal. All of them students. Both male and female."

"How is Flaim?"

"Upset. Frightened."

Tyen nodded. "As would be expected."

"Except that she is normally very bold." Vael shook his head. "I've never seen her bothered by anything, and she is always quick to retort to a taunt."

"Taunts and threats are one thing," Tyen reminded him. "This is very different."

Vael frowned. "I know. But the boys point out that they've played this prank on other boys before, and nobody did anything but laugh. They say if the girls are to be treated equally, then they must go through everything the boys do."

"Better that no pranks of this sort happen at all," Tyen replied. He grimaced at Vael's pained look. "Yes, I know it is a battle to stop students coming up with ridiculous ideas about initiation rites, and I won't burden you with orders to stop them completely." He ran his fingers over the edge of the table as he considered the boys' excuse for their actions. "But we must prevent this happening again. Most of the time, for men, being stripped is simply humiliating. For women it is different. It is a mere step from a far worse crime."

Vael nodded. "Perhaps you will be better able to explain that to them."

"I will see Flaim first. While I am gone, gather the boys and bring them here."

Tyen watched the overseer rise and move to the door. A knot had formed in his stomach. He had feared something like this might happen, as the male students reacted to the presence of the females. Plenty of them held the same prejudiced views as the teachers and professors, but unlike the older men, very few had left in protest. Instead they either complained that the women and foreigners were taking up resources they had a better right to, or nursed plans to take advantage of the newcomers at every opportunity. Tyen's orders that the new students be treated with respect were never going to stop some young men testing how far they could push their luck.

Too far this time. Tyen would have to make an example of them. He grimaced at the inevitability of it, and the unavoidable consequences. When the rest of the school found out, the protests would be loud and angry.

Unless there was another way. He could consult Vella. *No, she may be an incredible store of knowledge, but Qall was right: in matters outside her experience she relies on the mind of the reader, and that would be like discussing this with myself.* Rielle came to mind. *She might have been able to give me a woman's perspective, but she isn't here.* And she didn't know the ins and outs of the Academy like . . .

Vael. Who better to consult than the Student Overseer?

"Wait."

The overseer paused with his hand on the door and looked over his shoulder.

"How would you punish the three young men?" Tyen asked.

Vael winced as he turned around. "Are you sure we have to?"

"You would let them off? What's to discourage them doing it again? Or worse?"

"You could threaten them with expulsion instead."

"Do you think that would deter them?"

"Yes."

"What about Flaim? And the other women. Why would they believe that we can protect them if we don't punish the boys?"

"You could insist that the boys apologise to her publicly."

Tyen nodded, then waved to indicate Vael could go. "I'll ask her if that would be enough."

As the door closed behind the overseer, Tyen rose and quickly tidied his desk. *How is it that I was expelled for half of a year for keeping an artefact found on an archaeological dig, but these boys assault a young woman and only have to apologise?* He considered that question all the way to the women's quarters.

Flaim answered his questions reluctantly. She did not want to show weakness, knowing that it would be taken advantage of. To his surprise, she also did not want a public apology from the boys. In her mind she was imagining the sniggers from the rest of the Academy as what had been done to her was discussed openly in front of all.

She didn't want the boys getting away with it either. Since she didn't expect the Academy to punish them in any meaningful way, she had been thinking about means to get revenge. Tyen realised that if he did not punish the boys, Flaim would seek to by other means.

He returned to his office more troubled than when he'd left.

The boys were waiting in the corridor outside when he arrived. None met his gaze as he passed them and entered the room. He made them wait a while before calling them in.

They filed in, then stood in a line before the desk, gazes lowered. Tyen looked at each in turn. They shifted from confident to fearful. Every time worries about punishment rose, they reminded themselves that they were the sons of important, rich Beltonians. This new, young Director would not dare do anything to anger their fathers, who were graduates of the Academy and did not agree with the changes in the institution. Who thought the return of magic was not worth the corruption of Leratian society.

"Vael Romtolin tells me you assaulted one of our new students," Tyen began. "Is this true?"

The boys exchanged looks. Normally they'd have denied it, but they were all too aware that Tyen could read their minds.

"If she wants to call it that, then yes," the one named Alam replied, his eyes flickering up, his expression briefly full of defiance.

"I wouldn't call it an assault," Darimon added. "We didn't touch her. Well, not intentionally."

"Perhaps you did not," Tyen told him. "But your companions did."

Darimon glanced at his friends, his eyes wide. Alam made a noise of protest. "We did nothing to her we don't do to any new student. If—"

"No, you were not treating her the same as any new boy," Tyen cut him off. "Even if you were women and she male, the consequence of your actions would not be the same." Hearing anger creeping into his tone, Tyen paused and drew in a slow breath. "I ordered that all new entrants be treated equally – *and with respect*. What you did is assault under Leratian law, which applies to everyone be they male or female, rich or poor. That your crime occurred within the Academy does not make it less so. Why should I not punish you as if you'd attacked a member of the Emperor's household?"

The three turned pale, but Alam was quick to recover. "You won't. You know what would happen if you did."

A bluff. A fairly good one, Tyen had to admit. One he wanted to call. *One I have to call, though it's going to lose me more than a few teachers.* These boys, and others like them were going to challenge the new rules and changes regardless of whether Tyen was ready or not.

Perhaps if the boys had been repentant, he'd have tried harder to find an alternative. But they expected to be ordered to apologise, and that was all. Tyen knew the punishment had to be more than that, or they *would* do worse.

"You are expelled," Tyen told them. "For sixty days. You will not be readmitted to the Academy unless you swear on your family name to uphold the Academy rules."

Three faces rose, three mouths hanging open. Then two turned to glare at Alam. The friends were blaming him for pushing the new Director into making a stronger decision than he might have if Alam hadn't spoken.

Behind them, Vael, too, was agape.

"Leave," Tyen ordered. "Collect your belongings and be gone by evening. And if I hear that any of you have approached Flaim, or any other new student, before you leave, the expulsion will be permanent."

Alam's mouth closed with a snap. He straightened and met Tyen's gaze. "You'll regret this," he muttered.

"Nowhere near as much as you think," Tyen replied, looking the boy up and down with undisguised disgust.

Vael ushered them out. He cast a worried glance at Tyen before he closed the door. Tyen smiled grimly, keeping an expression of confidence in place to reassure the overseer. Vael nodded in respect and closed the door.

CHAPTER 12

"What did you think would happen?" Emperor Omniten asked.

Tyen shrugged. "Objections. Posturing. Maybe a few more teachers leaving in protest."

"The families of those boys are very powerful. Did you really not anticipate that they would use their influence against you?"

"No, but I didn't expect they'd act so soon or so extensively." Tyen ran a thumb down the stem of his glass. "They did not expect their sons to do what they did. Many of the teachers and professors who have left are appalled and think that the boys deserve their punishment, but they are too afraid of the fathers' influence to express such sentiments."

"You think they will come back when the fuss dies down?"

"Perhaps. At the moment they want a gesture from me. Something to show I'm backing down."

"Will they get it?"

"No."

"Good. You cannot afford to look weak. Giving in will be akin to giving permission for male students to harass female. Perhaps even women in general. We can't have the sons of our great families behaving so dishonourably."

To Tyen's amusement, Omniten was reciting the words his wife had uttered. He nodded, glad that the Emperor understood, thanks to the Empress.

"What will you do about the deficit of teachers in the mean-time?" Omniten asked. "Will you recruit more from outside this world?"

Tyen shook his head. "I won't risk attracting attention from outside until the Academy is well able to defend this world."

"It would increase the number of your allies here."

"Yes, but at the expense of this world's safety."

Omniten nodded, pleased. He wondered if this was proof of Tyen's loyalty, if not to him then to his home world. As always, he was aware that Tyen was probably reading his mind. He'd considered making reading minds a crime – indeed many powerful men and women had requested he do so – but his most trusted sorcerers had told him it was often hard to avoid it.

The easiest way to prove that a mind-read had occurred was to allow the accused's mind to be read. The Emperor was all too aware that this placed power in the hands of the mind-readers, which meant even more authority given to the strongest sorcerers of the empire, so he had decided not to outlaw mind reading. And so far, having the minds of the empire's powerful open to him, via his wife and their most trusted sorcerers, had been both amusing and advantageous.

The disadvantage of his own mind being readable hadn't proven to be as problematic as he'd initially feared. It was refreshing, he mused, to no longer have to pretend that he liked everyone. Or to find subtle ways to convey his respect, whether fond or wary, without appearing weak. When you were the most powerful man in the empire, you had little to hide. It was only those who felt the need to scheme and make unpleasant alliances who had secrets to keep.

Nobody could betray him, he believed, at least not until they found a way to stop their minds being read . . . which was why he had a few trusted sorcerers searching for one, despite Tyen claiming that it wasn't possible. Whoever found a way first would gain a great advantage, so he intended to be that person.

The Emperor noted that Tyen was looking amused, as he always did when the subject of blocking a mind-read came up, silently or openly. Omniten brought his thoughts back to the subject.

"So, what will you do about your deficit of teachers?"

Tyen frowned. "I'm thinking a restructure of staff might be needed."

"The absentees won't like that."

"They're not around to complain, so I may as well take advantage of the situation."

The Emperor laughed. "I don't see the fuss dying down for some time then."

"Of course, it would die down much faster if you order them to return." Tyen took a sip of wine and looked over his glass at the Emperor. "They're more afraid of you than of the three fathers."

Omniten smiled. "It would and they are. But I won't, and you know why. The Emperor does not involve himself in the petty squabbles of the Academy, only matters of national importance."

Tyen chuckled. "The same answer you've given to those who have objected to me becoming Director. Which told them that favouring me was a matter of national importance."

"Exactly."

After taking another sip of wine, Tyen looked into the fire. The relationship that was building between himself and Omniten was unexpectedly pleasant. He was not sure he could call it a friendship. Maintaining his rule and welfare of his empire was the Emperor's first concern, and Tyen was not fool enough to expect otherwise. Nor did the Emperor expect Tyen's companionability to be unconditional. But they both silently acknowledged that they liked and respected each other, and that was as close enough to friendship between two people of power as could ever be expected.

The Emperor liked how smart, interesting and seemingly honest Tyen was, and that he was free to be truthful in return, knowing that Tyen would read the truth in his mind anyway. Tyen had found the Emperor to be smart, forthright and practical, and surprisingly open to having his opinions and beliefs challenged. Possibly the latter was because the last century had been full of discoveries that challenged accepted beliefs, forcing the royal family to embrace and support technical and cultural development – though not unwillingly. They were both enthusiastic supporters of progress, be it industrial, academic or social.

"The Empress raised the idea of creating a society or some other structure to support the young women embarking on an academic life," Omniten said. "It would be a body to take their complaints to outside of the Academy. Currently such matters are handled by men who never anticipated having to accommodate them or who are openly against their presence. Those from humble birth can attend lessons on the etiquette of the social class in which they will no doubt find themselves on graduation." The Emperor set down his glass. "Do you support such a proposition?"

"I think it is an excellent idea," Tyen said. "Please pass on my compliments to the Empress. I will offer as much help as I can give, though I fear it won't be much while we are so short-staffed."

Omniten chuckled. "Knowing the Empress and the women she will likely recruit, that will not be an issue." His expression grew more serious. "I have another proposal concerning the Empress."

He paused. Tyen waited, not reading Omniten's mind. Something about the way the man was hesitating suggested the matter was more personal than anything he'd raised so far.

"You no doubt know that Elaise has magical ability," the Emperor began. "It is not a great gift but does give her some advantages at court. I would like her to learn to use magic."

Tyen nodded. "That would make sense, since she is to mentor the female entrants."

"Yes. However, she does not seek this tutelage. In fact, she resisted the idea when I first proposed it." He smiled a little – a rare outward sign of his fondness for her. "She does not want to seem the stronger of us."

"Magic alone does not make a good leader," Tyen quoted.

Omniten nodded and sighed. "Unfortunately, plenty of people of influence are not wise or clever enough to have realised this. Still, there are no secrets now, and to some her gift makes her stronger, which makes me appear weaker to them. As so often is the case, I win as I lose, so I may as well choose the most advantageous outcome. I choose for my wife to learn magic." He picked up his glass of wine and sipped, then smiled wryly at Tyen. "Though I don't envy you the task."

Tyen's heart skipped. "You want me to teach her personally?"

The Emperor inclined his head. "Only the best for the Empress. I should warn you . . ." He paused, and in the sudden silence a faint bell became audible. Omniten turned to the door and raised his voice. "Come in."

A man in a plain dark suit slipped inside the room and handed the Emperor a small piece of paper. Omniten read it, then looked up at Tyen.

"A message for you. Visitors have arrived at the Academy requesting an audience with the Director."

Tyen set down his wine glass reluctantly. "I request permission to leave."

"Granted. Who do you think these visitors are?"

"Not my missing professors and teachers. More likely a group of foreign sorcerers seeking admission have found that Beltonian hotels have no empty rooms whenever strange-looking people arrive on their doorstep."

Omniten smiled crookedly. "You can push for change in the Academy, but the world outside it is not in your control."

"Nor do I wish it to be." Tyen shrugged and rose. "Maybe prejudice will fade naturally, once foreign graduates find employment in the city and the world doesn't end." He bowed. "Goodnight, your Imperial Majesty."

"Goodnight, Director."

Following the messenger out of the palace, Tyen tried to imagine the world he had hinted at. It was difficult. Travelling with Sezee and Veroo years before had shown him how ingrained Leratian prejudice was. He suspected that most foreign graduates would return to their countries rather than stay and work in Leratia, as much because they wanted to escape the unfriendliness and suspicion here as to use their skills for the benefit of their homeland.

That would be a pity. The Academy would lose good sorcerers, who also might have proven how valuable women and foreign sorcerers could be, and helped to allay the general animosity and prejudice between the empire and its colonies. For the rest of the journey back to the Academy he considered how he might persuade graduates to stay and locals to accept them, coming up with regrettably few ideas.

I wish Rielle were here. Maybe she would have some useful suggestions. When the familiar weight of Vella in her bag shifted against his chest as he got out of the carriage, he was reminded of another person he could ask. *But later, when I've dealt with these visitors.* It occurred to him then that Rielle had been the first person he wanted to ask, not Vella. *Maybe because she, being a foreigner and woman, has more relevant experience, whereas Vella can only tell me what people who have held her understood.*

As he climbed the Academy steps, a familiar weariness dragged at his legs, so he called on a little healing magic to revive himself. He entered the Grand Hall with a straight back, hoping his apparent confidence would reassure the visitors. Two people stood at the far end of the hall facing an Academy staff member. All turned as they heard his footsteps, and his heart lightened with delight and hope.

"Tyen Ironsmelter," Rielle said. "Do you have a position free for another teacher, and room for a few more students?"

Tyen looked from her to her companion. Tarren grinned in greeting. Tyen felt his heart lift even further, then freeze as he realised something bad must have happened for Tarren to leave his school.

"Of course," he said, and quickened his stride to reach them sooner. He embraced Tarren, but as he stepped back he found a weary frown had replaced the old man's smile, and he caught a dark thought. His stomach sank. "Your school?"

"Destroyed."

"Your students?"

"We lost a couple. The rest are with the Restorers."

"I am sorry to hear that." Tyen frowned. *With the Restorers? And the old man wants to join the Academy?* "It's more than that, isn't it?"

Tarren nodded. "Yes, but Rielle will explain it better."

"And I had best do so in private," Rielle added, her voice low and grim.

Tyen gestured to the side entrance of the Grand Hall. "Then may I invite you to my office?"

Tarren's eyebrows rose. "You have an office, do you?"

Rielle chuckled. "Oh, didn't I tell you he was Director?"

"Yes." The old man sighed with mock annoyance. "Many times." He took a step in the direction Tyen had indicated. "Well then. Lead the way, Director."

Rielle was silent as they walked, allowing Tarren to observe his surroundings. Empty but for a skeleton staff, the Academy wasn't presenting itself in its best light, but the stillness of the place at night had always inspired Tyen. It seemed full of potential, waiting to be discovered. All it took to free the knowledge within it was the presence of people.

Vella was much the same, he realised. When not held and read, she was like the empty corridors of the Academy, waiting for the moment someone brought her to life. *Vella is an Academy of sorts,* he thought. *One that can only be visited by a few people at a time at most – but with an information delivery service that presents answers as fast as you can ask questions.*

Was it possible to combine the two somehow? If someone, or several someones, read everything in the library and attended all the lectures by all the teachers and professors while touching Vella, they could add the entire Academy's knowledge to her. And if he, and probably many scribes to follow, wrote down everything she contained, then a great deal of knowledge could be added to the Academy.

The idea that Vella might benefit the Academy had once excited him greatly, but during the brief time she had been in the institution's possession its members had only wanted to destroy her. *Well, except for Kilraker. He wanted her for himself.* Kilraker was dead and the Academy was different now. Though he could not say if his reforms would become permanent. Perhaps they would only remain as long as he stayed in charge. *If they do stick, I might bequeath Vella to the school on my death.* Though being ageless meant that this might not happen for a long time yet, he'd survived too many battles to think his death couldn't possibly happen any time soon.

As he ushered his visitors into his office, Rielle caught his gaze.

"I hope you do not mind me bringing Tarren here," she said. "I was very careful to ensure nobody followed us through the worlds, and Tarren was blindfolded for the entire journey."

The old man was observing the room's décor approvingly.

"Of course I don't mind." Tyen directed the pair to the set of chairs in the corner, away from his desk. "Thank you for taking the precaution."

Tarren shrugged. "It was nothing. You'd have done the same for me."

Tyen turned to Rielle as she settled into a chair. "It is good to have you back," he said with feeling. "I've missed having someone to talk to who knows about the worlds."

She smiled. "What of your students, or the Librarian?"

Tyen sat down. "My students are very busy, and . . . well, I can't imagine having a chitchat with the Librarian. He was always so intimidating when I was a student here and I can't quite shake off my nervousness around him."

She chuckled. "You should talk to him more. He's very interesting."

He nodded. "I will when I have time. I barely get a chance to sleep even when things are going smoothly – which is not often." He looked from her to Tarren. They looked as tired as he ought to feel, and he realised he was being a bad host.

"Are you in need of refreshments?"

Rielle looked at Tarren, who had frowned. "He means food and drink," she told him in a low voice. "Not a bath."

"I guessed as much," the old man replied. "Have you noticed that Tyen slips into that odd formal way of speaking whenever he's nervous or wants to impress someone?"

Her eyebrows rose. "Now that you mention it . . ."

Tyen crossed his arms. Tarren had not even explained what had brought him here and already he was teasing. "Are either of you thirsty? Or hungry? Or both?"

"No," Tarren replied, shaking his head. Rielle shrugged in agreement. "We ate just before we left."

"Unlike Baluka, Qall insists that all Restorer meetings are well catered," Rielle added.

Qall? Unlike Baluka? Tyen lifted his eyebrows as he comprehended her meaning. "*Qall* has replaced Baluka as the leader of the Restorers?"

She smiled fondly. "Yes."

"When did this happen?"

"About midway during my stay here," she told him. "I was surprised, too. It makes sense, though. He *is* the most powerful sorcerer in the worlds."

"And contains Valhan's memories. Does Baluka know this?"

She nodded. "Yes."

"And he was willing to risk that the Raen might return through Qall? Or that he already has, and this is part of Valhan's plan to regain control of the worlds?"

"Amazingly . . . yes. In fact, it was his idea that Qall take his place. As he said, if either of those things happen, he can't prevent it, but the benefits of Qall replacing him outweigh the risks. Qall

288

is powerful, smart and, thanks to Valhan's memories, knows more about the worlds than anyone."

Tyen shook his head and leaned back in his chair, his skin prickling with cold as he realised what this meant. "So Qall has become the Successor after all. Valhan's plan succeeded, just not quite the way he wanted it to."

"A better way than any of us could have planned." Her mouth twitched into a crooked smile. "I thought you didn't believe in Millennium's Rule."

"I don't," Tyen assured her. "But if anyone becomes the sole ruler of most worlds, they are the Raen's successor. That's terminology, not prophecy."

Tarren chuckled. "That is true. But Qall becoming the Restorers' leader is not what we came to tell you." He looked at Rielle. "Go on. He's clearly not reading my mind, and the tension is unbearable."

She glanced at him, her smile fading, then turned back to Tyen. "This will be particularly distressing news for you, Tyen," she warned.

He nodded to show he understood, and braced himself.

"The mechanical magic inventors from Liftre have banded together under a leader called Kettin," she told him. "Between them and the forced assistance of imprisoned inventors, possibly including Zeke, they're creating a vast machine army. It has destroyed numerous whole worlds, killing most of the people, taking all of the magic and stripping resources to make more machines."

The chill Tyen had felt before was nothing to the ice that spread though his body now. *A vast machine army. Whole worlds destroyed. All partly my fault, because I released knowledge of mechanical magic into the worlds.*

"*How?*" he managed to say. "Machines hold and use very little magic, so how can they take all the magic of a world?"

"Through sheer numbers," Rielle explained. "And with thousands upon thousands attacking at once, they are a danger to lone or small groups of sorcerers, too."

Tyen thought of the bomb the Liftre sorcerers had left in his previous school. High numbers weren't the only way a machine could be deadly. His gut clenched. *Why?* "Why are they doing this?"

Rielle sighed. "We don't know. Other than killing off inventors who refuse to join them, they don't appear to have a particular target. Qall thinks their aim is to sell or lease the army, or parts of it. Unfortunately, our scouts have had no success finding out more. I learned most of what we know while investigating a ruined world, but I had to cut my visit short when I discovered that Kettin had learned the location of Tarren's school and sent sorcerers to destroy him and his students."

"Fortunately, she arrived in time to save us," Tarren injected, his expression becoming sad. "Well, most of us."

She glanced at him. "It wasn't all me. You wouldn't have survived long enough to be rescued if you hadn't thought of a clever way to hide yourselves."

"It wasn't that clever," he retorted. "The moment the drug wore off they'd have found us."

Tyen barely heard them. Anger and disgust filled him as he thought of what the Liftre inventors had done. "Who is Kettin?"

Rielle and Tarren exchanged glances. "We hoped you could tell us," Rielle said.

"I've never heard of him – or her."

"The sorcerers whose minds I've read believe Kettin is a man." Rielle frowned down at the table. Her gaze held a particular intensity Tyen had only seen once or twice before. His most vivid memory of it had been at the battle with Dahli. She had burned with determination, even at the end when the Restorers had lost. *She keeps saying "we" and "us". Sounds like she has chosen to support the Restorers again.* And no doubt wanted him to as well.

"You want my help," he stated.

She nodded. "And the Academy's."

"The Academy is not ready." He sighed. "The sorcerers here are neither trained nor united enough to protect this world, even from a minor threat."

"We don't need them to fight," Tarren told him. "We need them to help us find ways to hamper or stop the machines. This is the world in which magic-driven machines were invented. Therefore, the chances are good that a way to destroy them will emerge from here, too. Dahli says Zeke had discovered one before he was abducted, so it must be possible."

"And they may have abducted Z . . ." Tyen blinked, then looked from the old man to Rielle. *"Dahli?"*

Her lips pressed together in grim amusement. "Yes. He only emerged from hiding to warn us of the machine army and to ask for help in rescuing Zeke." She paused. "There's no sign of deception in his mind but . . ."

There wouldn't be. He could have blocked his memories of his true intentions. "Do you trust him?"

"Yes. No." She grimaced. "We're being careful – watching for deception and never assuming he's telling the truth. He doesn't recall blocking any memories, but he could have done it, then blocked his memory of doing so, setting up some kind of reliable way to instruct himself to unblock it in future."

"Hmm." Tyen considered the possibility. Dahli had always tried to avoid thinking about how he blocked memories when he was around Tyen, but in a few unguarded moments he'd given away some information. He had never blocked a memory of blocking memories because it was perilously close to losing the knowledge of how to block memories . . . or unblock them.

Would Dahli ever take that risk? He might have for Valhan, once. Would he do so for Zeke, now? Possibly. The man could be ruthlessly loyal. A trait that made Tyen simultaneously admire and distrust him.

"He is not to come here," Tyen said. "Ever."

Rielle nodded. She and Tarren remained still and silent, watching him. Waiting for an answer. He drew in a deep breath. Should he help them?

How could I refuse? It's my fault the worlds are full of machines.

Would helping them endanger his world?

Yes, but no greater danger than me being here anyway. The risks can be minimised.

"Nobody else is to know the way to this world," he said. "If you can find more inventors willing to help, that you are sure can be trusted to keep this world a secret, bring them to me. But they must be blindfolded when you do."

Rielle nodded again.

"We'll need more machines to study. Are you sure Zeke is their prisoner? If he is designing them, they'll be growing ever more sophisticated."

A third nod. "Dahli inspected some of the broken machines scouts brought back and says a few of Zeke's ideas have been incorporated into them."

Tyen winced as he considered what Kettin's people might be doing to force Zeke into working for them. He couldn't help thinking that Zeke would be living peacefully as a minor sorcerer in his home world if Tyen hadn't released knowledge of mechanical magic from his. *Of course I'm going to help . . . but I shouldn't be too quick to jump when the Restorers call either. That might not benefit my world in the long term.*

"I want to meet with Qall, Baluka and Dahli first."

She smiled. "They want to meet with you, if you can do so without compromising the safety of this world."

"I will need to choose someone to stand in my place while I'm away – and I should seek the permission of the Emperor to leave." Tyen said it more as an afterthought, but the eyebrows of his friends rose. "A gesture of respect," he explained. "It will lessen the chance of trouble later. Omniten has become a valuable ally and something of a friend."

Rielle looked impressed. "That's . . . unexpected, but not unwelcome."

"For both of us." Tyen shrugged. "Well . . . When does Qall expect me to meet him?"

She grimaced. "As soon as possible."

"But not immediately."

"You have time to make arrangements."

"Could they wait until the morning? My request of the Emperor will be received far more warmly if it doesn't arrive in the middle of the night."

"I think it can," she replied. "Is there somewhere we can wait?"

"Do you need to sleep?"

"No."

Tyen nodded, pushed back his chair and rose. "I have a rather nice set of rooms near the Academy, in a good hotel. The food is excellent, so order a meal when you get hungry." He grimaced. "At least someone will get to enjoy the benefits of my new position. You'll probably spend more waking hours there than I have since I signed the rent contract."

CHAPTER 13

A moment after the flash of lightning dazzled Tyen's eyes, a deafening peal of thunder roared overhead. He felt the vibration of it despite the shield of stilled air he'd created around himself. After the enormous rocks that ringed the arrival place of this world had been struck the first time, he'd retreated down the hill, below where a slight bulge in the slope directed rainwater runoff to either side. With nowhere to shelter, he simply crouched there, all too aware that he had no idea if his shield, or his body, could survive a direct lightning strike.

He could only guess how long it had been since he'd arrived in this world. It had been a calm, rural site then – a pleasant place in which to wait for Rielle to return from arranging his meeting with the Restorers. Clouds had blown in with frightening speed, and soon it was raining. And now hail was pounding his shield, obliterating all sign of the arrival place above. He hoped Rielle would be able to find him when she returned. He hoped she wouldn't be struck by lightning.

"Tyen," a voice said not far from his ear.

He jumped and spun around to find Rielle standing behind him, smiling with amusement. She must have skimmed into his shield before arriving. *Just as well she isn't an enemy, or I'd be dead now*, he thought. *I should be creating an inner shield too. Has living in my world made me relax too much already? I must be more careful.*

"Let's go somewhere more comfortable," she said, holding out her hand.

He grasped it and nodded.

The storm faded to white, then a different landscape emerged – this time a flat, pale expanse under a featureless sky, the only variation a circle of mounds around them. As they neared this new world the sky coloured blue, and the ground gained a pink tinge and the texture of cracked mud.

The pink substance crunched under their shoes as they arrived. A familiar tang hung in the air. Salt.

He turned to Rielle. "What did Qall say?"

She shook her head. "He wants you to come to the base."

Tyen's heart sank. He had been dismayed when Rielle said the meeting would take place in Affen and had asked her to go on ahead and request a different location. Too many people in the Restorers had reason to hate him. Surely Qall understood that.

"Qall promises you won't be harmed," Rielle added.

Tyen grimaced. "He can only promise so much."

"Do you doubt he can protect you?"

"No." Tyen sighed. "I doubt he can stop people thinking what they think of me."

Her eyes narrowed as she considered him. "So, this is only about facing their anger."

"Yes," he admitted, and looked away.

"You might feel better once you've explained why you did what you did," she told him. "And apologise."

"But everything I did, I did to help them. Or Vella." He paused, then sighed again. "Well, some of my actions were to save my life, but I never sacrificed another's life for my own sake."

Her lips stretched in a thin, humourless smile. "That may be true, but people were hurt. And killed. Are you sorry for that? Sorry for how things turned out?"

"Of course."

"Then that's what they need to hear from you." She paused, waiting until he looked up again. "Just as I needed to hear it."

He nodded. "I know. I just . . . I wouldn't blame them if they weren't willing to listen."

"You don't really expect to help the Restorers from afar, do you? Or without having to work to regain their trust?"

"No, I suppose not."

Damn you, Qall, Tyen thought. *I was hoping I could just outlive my reputation.*

But would he have, really? From the start he'd known establishing a respected school of sorcery would be difficult with the bad reputation he had. He had lain awake too many times thinking about ways he might restore his good name and he'd always come to the same conclusion: no matter what he did, the fact that he'd spied on the Rebels for the Raen, and then later appeared to be helping Dahli attempt to resurrect the Raen, would always overshadow everything good he'd done. He'd accepted that it was more likely that his crimes would be amplified and exaggerated and his good deeds forgotten over time. The future would not be easy, and he could do nothing to change that.

Five cycles ago he'd decided that he would never deny the truth. Whenever his students had gathered the courage to ask about his past and the accusations against him, Tyen had told them everything. The good and the bad. His regrets as well as his successes.

He'd expected to never work with Baluka again, or any of the Restorers' future leaders. They would make sure his betrayals would be remembered. But he hadn't anticipated that Qall would take over. *Or that someone would create a machine army capable of killing entire worlds, giving them reason to give me another chance.*

Because he'd done it entirely out of ignorance and self-interest, having brought mechanical magic into the worlds bothered his conscience more than his past lies and betrayals. If he could do anything to stop Kettin, he would, even if it meant facing the anger of the people he'd deceived. If all it took to solve the machine problem was an apology, he would ask their forgiveness over and over for centuries to come.

Taking a deep breath, he let it out slowly. He would approach this with the same policy of honesty he had with his students, though it wouldn't be as simple as answering questions whenever they arose. He'd need to clear the air before any discussions of the machine army began.

But I will not accept censure for anything I did not do, he told himself. *If they don't believe me . . . well, Qall can see my mind. He can correct them.* In fact, with Qall there he might even have a chance at establishing the truth. It was worth trying, anyway.

He reached out and took Rielle's hand. "Let's go."

She smiled, squeezed his hand, then pushed out of the world.

Despite his determination, in every world that Rielle took him through, the tension and dread in Tyen increased. Even the touch of her hand grasping his could not distract or comfort him. While the physical manifestations of these feelings disappeared whenever they were between worlds, each time Rielle stopped in a world to breathe, his stomach twisted and sank a little more. This wasn't helped when guards began to note their passing at arrival places. Most only recognised Rielle, but now and then one looked at her companion and thought they knew him despite Tyen having changed his hair and skin colour for the journey. He and Rielle did not stay long enough to know if they worked out who he was, and he wondered what would happen if someone did.

He began to consider changing his appearance more. It was a trick he was not well practised at, despite his former role as a spy. Doing so had always disturbed him, so he'd always relied on his ability to travel quickly to outrun anyone who recognised him and was bold enough to follow. His instinct to avoid it had been validated when Rielle had warned that ageless sorcerers could slowly lose track of what they originally looked like as the years passed.

"We're here," Rielle said.

Tyen looked around, immediately noting how closely the guards were inspecting him, having been forewarned that the Spy would be with her when she returned. Rielle nodded at them to indicate all was well, and they relaxed. She led Tyen out of the arrival place and down the wide streets of a serene city, its buildings surrounded by well-tended gardens. As they walked, Tyen shifted his appearance back to what he hoped was its normal state.

"This is it," Rielle told him, waving towards a squat, non-descript building.

He stretched out his senses and confirmed what he had been told about the building: most of it lay underground. His senses also bumped up against minds alerted to their impending arrival. Baluka waited near the entrance with Hapre, former general of the rebel army, and through their minds he saw that Qall had just emerged from below to join them.

It was possible this meeting was a trap that only Qall knew of. Though Tyen believed it unlikely, he couldn't help scanning all the minds he could read. He found none thinking about traps and most were immersed in whatever tasks they were doing, or avoiding in some cases.

"Are you ready?" Rielle asked when they reached the threshold, regarding him with one eyebrow raised.

He nodded. "As ready as I'll ever be."

She led the way through the open door. As Tyen followed, three figures stepped forward to greet him. Baluka was in the middle, a man he did not know walked to his right, and Hapre shadowed his left.

"Welcome, Tyen," the stranger said. "Do you really not know me?"

Tyen blinked in surprise. The voice was familiar, and now that he looked closer he realised this was no stranger.

"Qall?"

Qall grinned. "Rielle knew me straight away. But then, she is an artist, so pays more attention to details."

Tyen glanced at her. She wore a small smile. "I should have warned you," she admitted. "But I'd forgotten he'd changed his appearance."

Looking back at Qall, Tyen nodded. "I guess you can't go around looking like . . ." Tyen paused as he realised Hapre did not know who the young man had once resembled.

"Valhan?" Qall finished. "No."

"Well . . ." Tyen groped for an appropriate response. "The change looks very well on you."

"Thank you," Qall replied. He looked at his companions. "I don't think I need to introduce Baluka and Hapre."

"No." Tyen turned to Hapre. "I have long wished for an opportunity to speak to you, Hapre, to explain, and apologise, in person."

Her eyes widened a little. It wasn't the greeting she had expected. Baluka had told her all he knew of Tyen's motives for betraying the rebels and working with Dahli, but her anger towards him had never faded. Now it did, to her dismay.

"I look forward to it," she replied.

As he turned to Baluka the man stepped closer and, to Tyen's surprise, embraced him.

"You should have come back and told us," Baluka said.

"I didn't think you'd believe me," Tyen replied, returning the embrace awkwardly.

"You switched to our side at the end of the battle with Dahli," Baluka said. "Then left to rescue Rielle despite not knowing if Qall was Valhan or not."

"I . . . guess."

"Qall confirmed it later," Baluka said, releasing Tyen. He squeezed Tyen's arm. "I've missed you, old friend."

"And I you," Tyen mumbled, his throat suddenly tight. "And . . . well, I am sorry anyway. For everything I put you through."

Qall placed one hand on Baluka's shoulder and the other on Tyen's. "Let's continue to the meeting room."

It was hard, for a moment, to comprehend that this confident man in charge of the situation had been the awkward teenager Tyen had tried to help five cycles ago. Living in Rielle's world had matured him. Though from what Rielle had told him, her world would force any young outsider to grow up quickly.

Qall led the way towards a set of stairs, Baluka and Tyen either side of him, and Rielle and Hapre following behind. Rielle said something quietly, but Tyen couldn't make out the words. Hapre murmured an assent, sounding amused, and he read from her mind that Rielle had asked if Tarren's students were behaving.

They descended underground and arrived in a room furnished with several chairs surrounding a low table. The latter was covered with plates of food and a cluster of glasses beside a large pitcher. Everyone sat down, Qall indicating that Tyen should sit beside him.

"We should fill you in on everything we know," Qall said. "But for that we'll need something to wet our throats." He looked at the pitcher and glasses, which were closest to Baluka, so the former Traveller began to measure out a portion of a dark green liquid for each of them. After these were handed around, Qall drew in a deep breath. "Where to begin?"

"Dahli," Rielle replied.

"Yes. We should go over what we know. Dahli came to us more than a quarter-cycle ago asking for help," Qall said. "His lover, Zeke, had disappeared, captured by machine makers. During Dahli's search for Zeke he discovered worlds stripped of magic and life, and they led to a world filled with machines. While the machines did not wield great power individually, in the numbers he encountered they were powerful enough to drive him away.

"We sent scouts to confirm if what he claimed was true. Some did not return." He grimaced. "Those who did described worlds that had been emptied of people and magic, and evidence of mining for materials and the forging of parts for machines. They did not find the makers or the army. Then Rielle heard of a world only recently invaded. I sent her and two ageless sorcerers to investigate. She found a world still full of machines. A handful of inventors also remained, and from them she learned that their leader is known as Kettin. She also learned that Tarren's school was under attack, so she hurried back to defend it."

The young man glanced at Baluka. "We have also sought out mechanical magic inventors and learned that most have been killed or have disappeared. The few still alive have refused to help us." He turned to face Tyen. "You are the only one who has agreed to."

Tyen nodded. "I imagine they're too frightened of Kettin and his followers."

"Despite our offer to protect them," Qall agreed. "Though they may change their minds when they hear you have joined us."

"Or they may be more determined to stay away," Tyen added wryly. "The machine makers of Liftre have threatened or punished every world I've tried to settle in."

"And now you've settled in your own world," Qall pointed out. "Are you confident of its safety?"

Tyen frowned. "Not completely. It was, until recently, so depleted of magic it was effectively a dead world. Rielle restored it at my request. The local sorcerers have much to learn. Only Tarren and the students I brought to it know how to travel between worlds." *And the Librarian,* Tyen added silently. *He mentioned that he returned to my world after travelling the worlds for a few hundred years or so. I must find time to talk to him and find out what he's capable of.* "The local sorcerers are proving to be unexpectedly strong, which I suspect is a result of being born in and training in a weak world."

"I've noticed this effect too," Rielle injected. "If the world I restore has been weak – but not dead – for a long time, the sorcerers tend to have a greater reach." She shrugged. "I've not restored many worlds of that kind, though."

Qall nodded. "This may prove relevant," he said. "We gained some information about Kettin when one of our scouts returned a few days ago. She was born in one of these near-dead worlds you restored, Rielle."

Her eyes widened. "So I released her from her world." Then she frowned. "Kettin is a woman? That's not what the inventors I found believed. Are you sure?"

"The scout was certain of it." Qall glanced at Tyen. "It goes against what we know of these Liftre inventors. They tended to drive away women seeking to learn mechanical magic. She may be pretending to be a man whenever she is among the inventors or hiding the truth from all but a core group of followers, or she may even have learned pattern-shifting and changed to male. Either way, she would have to be powerful to hide the truth – and persuade them to teach her."

"She may have already learned mechanical magic when she joined the Liftre sorcerers," Tyen pointed out.

Hapre clicked her tongue. "Then the world she came from must have been restored early in the last five cycles, before the Liftre began discouraging schools from teaching mechanical magic."

Tyen shook his head. "We can't assume that. She may have learned outside a school. One of the recently killed teachers may have taught her. Or someone in hiding."

"What matters more is why Kettin is destroying worlds and making so many machines," Baluka told them. "Is she a conqueror? Is it revenge? Or is she only interested in selling or hiring machines in order to become wealthy?"

"We've not heard of anyone hiring the army or part of it," Qall said. "I fear it is for her own use."

"She may not be ready to sell or hire yet," Rielle said. "Or start her conquest. She may be waiting until her army is larger, so she can keep control of wherever she invades."

"Conquest is not the only reason to conquer worlds," Baluka added. "She may only be interested in stealing a world's riches."

"Then why kill everyone?" Hapre asked.

"To ensure nobody tries to take them back, or seeks retribution."

"Or to make room to transplant your own people there," Qall said. "She does not stop the locals leaving, only slaughters those who remain. One of the many sorcerers who escaped and came to tell us what they'd witnessed told me that the killing was entirely impersonal, as if humans were a mere nuisance to be swept away. Another wondered if it was done to ensure nobody would interfere with the making of more machines. And one said he thought the killing was a trial run or test of mettle for her underlings."

The room was briefly silent as all absorbed the horror behind these refugees' ponderings. Baluka was the first to stir.

"We need to find out more about Kettin."

Rielle nodded. "Not just her motives, but her strengths and weaknesses."

"So, we send more scouts?" Hapre sighed. "We need to do more than that. We need information from inside her ranks. To get into the worlds where the machines are being stored."

"If we're going to attempt that, we may as well try to rescue Zeke," Tyen said.

All turned to him. He smiled grimly. "He can tell us about Kettin and her followers, as well as what the newest machines are capable of. Perhaps how to disable them, too."

Qall nodded. "If Kettin needs Zeke in order to invent new kinds of machines, she can't be capable of doing it herself. Taking him away will weaken her."

"She won't be unaware of his importance," Baluka warned. "He'll be well guarded."

"Of course he will be." Rielle shrugged. "I didn't say it would be easy." She looked at Qall. "Dahli should be a part of the rescue."

Qall nodded.

"Dahli." Hapre scowled. "Must we? I don't trust him."

"I do when it comes to Zeke," Qall said.

Rielle grimaced. "Much as I'd rather have nothing to do with him, he will resent us if we don't include him in the rescue — especially if we fail and Zeke is harmed. Is he still here?"

"No," Qall replied. "For obvious reasons, he is keeping out of sight. Only I have a way to contact him." He looked at the others. "Who else will go?

"I will," Rielle replied without hesitation.

Qall paused, then nodded.

"No," Baluka protested. "I see the sense in Dahli going, but not you," he said, turning to her. "You're too important to risk."

"I am vital to any rescue," she countered. "Who is going to provide more magic when the machines take it all? It could be that the scouts who didn't return simply ran out of magic." She smiled humourlessly. "Remember, Kettin has told her people to avoid a confrontation with me."

"You don't know why," Qall pointed out. "What if she wants to kill you herself?"

"I'll go too," Tyen said. "I can protect Rielle – against machines or Dahli, if he turns out to be bluffing."

This time it was Qall who shook his head. "You are also important, Tyen. You are the expert on mechanical magic."

"Not the only one," Tyen replied. "I've taught most of what I know to my students. My world is full of sorcerers who understand it." He chuckled. "I am realising even as I say this that I am far more expendable than I'd like to believe."

"Not expendable to us," Rielle told him. "I doubt we outsiders would have much success gaining the help of the Academy without you there."

"Nevertheless, I ought to see these machine armies for myself." Tyen met and held Qall's gaze.

The young man didn't look away. "If I order you to stay or go, will you?"

Tyen paused. A small shiver ran down his back. Qall was asking for Tyen to acknowledge and accept his leadership. A part of Tyen resisted. He had been independent for so long. Though he obeyed the Emperor of his world, he did so only because the alternative was much worse. Even if he wanted to conquer and rule his world – even if there was a bloodless way to do it – it was easier to work with the existing system. What Qall asked for was different. This meant serving not just Qall, but the Restorers.

"I will," Tyen replied. "But only while this threat exists."

Qall nodded. "I understand. Will you trust me to hold and protect Vella until you return?"

A stronger chill went through Tyen, but he ignored it, and the possessiveness that had risen faded away. Qall had looked after Vella before. He understood her value. And it was reasonable that he did not want to lose all of his assets at once if Tyen and Rielle failed.

"Yes, that would be wise. If I don't return, would you protect my home until it is strong enough to interact with the worlds?"

"I will."

Tyen nodded in thanks. Qall smiled and looked at each of them. "Then it is decided. You take care of each other."

"We will," Tyen assured him. "Even Dahli."

Rielle lips pressed together. "Yes. I might not like him, but I have a feeling we'll need him."

"Then I'll send for him," Qall said, "and hope that with his help we can come up with a plan or three for how to snatch Zeke out from under Kettin's nose without losing two of the people I value most in the worlds."

CHAPTER 14

"How long has it been since you were here?" Rielle asked as she took in the neat green patchwork of crops, dotted with the burned skeletons of houses and ramshackle temporary new huts.

"Nearly half a cycle," Dahli replied.

"How did the people here get home? We've passed through several worlds containing no magic. They'd need a particularly strong sorcerer to transport them this far."

Dahli shrugged. "There may be an undepleted world next to this one, reached from a different direction."

"I'm surprised anyone dared to come back," Tyen remarked, looking down at the people working the fields and thinking of the devastated worlds they'd passed through. Kettin and her followers had been chillingly thorough at killing off all human life – in some cases all life, including domestic and wild animals.

"It is home for them," Dahli replied. "Too often it is safer to return home to a known danger than be a stranger seeking help in an unfamiliar land or world. These people may not have returned willingly. The people of the neighbouring worlds may have forced them to. Or they have become the servants or slaves of someone willing to risk the return of the machine army for the promise of owning good land."

"Is that Kettin's plan?" Tyen wondered. "Clearing land to give as rewards for her followers?"

Rielle sighed. "Land for food, perhaps, but not the resources her people took." She shook her head. "Was it really necessary to kill every person who couldn't escape, just for the materials to make machines?"

Dahli shrugged. "No, but it does eliminate the chance of rebellion. Refugee and scout reports tell us the invasion of each world, the mining of resources and the building of war machines is controlled by just a few sorcerers. When you consider that weaker sorcerers are attracted to mechanical magic because it doesn't require much, a large mob of locals could pose a threat to them. Or a strong local sorcerer."

"If Kettin's sorcerers are that weak, how do they leave the world they invaded once all the magic is gone?" Tyen asked.

"Stronger sorcerers may be transporting them out," Dahli replied. "Or gathering magic to give to them before they set out to attack a world."

Rielle shuddered. "How do they live with themselves after all the killing?"

"By passing on the blame, I'd say," Dahli guessed. "It isn't them doing it, it's the machines. They are just following orders." His lips thinned. "In some of the worlds I visited while looking for Zeke, I found that inventors had worked with local people to run the mines and machine factories. But then I found worlds in which the locals had rebelled as they realised all their resources were being taken and they weren't getting paid. After that I only found devastated worlds."

"So the inventors decided the best way to avoid trouble was to kill everyone," Rielle said.

"Or their strategy changed when Kettin joined them," Tyen added.

Dahli looked at him and nodded. "We're only guessing. If we are to learn why, we must find worlds occupied by Kettin's followers and question them."

"Reading their minds will do." Tyen held out his hands, but

Rielle's attention lingered on the people below, her expression hidden by the scarf draped over her head.

"Should I restore this world?"

"Perhaps later?" Tyen suggested, while at the same time Dahli firmly said, "No."

Rielle turned to Dahli. "Why not?"

"Only you can do it. If there are any inventors still here, or they return in the next few hours, they will know you've been here very recently and will alert Zeke's captors to a possible rescue attempt."

She nodded and took Tyen's hand. "I will come back, when I can."

As Dahli took Tyen's other hand, Tyen pushed out of the world. Skimming rapidly across the world, he took them down into the fresh ruins of a city to a circular area surrounded by a wall – a common formation for an arrival place. Sure enough, a path in the place between led away.

The next world was as empty and devastated as the last, but the one after had not been conquered. It was covered in a vast ocean, with countless jagged islands – many of them active volcanoes – emerging from the water. A thin spread of magic surrounded it, but none of them detected any minds.

"Either she didn't bother with this one because there are too few accessible resources to steal, or we're off course," Dahli muttered.

Tyen decided to continue rather than backtrack. The next world had been conquered, as had the one after. The following world had not been attacked. It was as dry as the ocean world was wet, with small communities clustered around the few reliable water sources. A moderate amount of magic remained, so they stopped to scan minds outside a small city.

"They call the conquest the Scourge here," Rielle said. "Look to the garden. It's the city's main gathering place. The Scourge, and why it didn't reach this world, is a favourite topic of conversation."

Tyen did as she suggested, finding two old women musing over their world's good fortune. They were surprisingly well informed about which worlds in the area had been devastated and in what order. To their understanding, the attacks had come in simultaneous invasions spreading like a wave across several worlds rather than one after another in a line.

"Interesting," Tyen murmured. "It's as if several armies advanced side by side. That means the trail is wide. It will be easier to follow."

Rielle nodded. "I wonder how wide."

Dahli grasped one of her hands and one of Tyen's. "Let's find out."

He waited until Tyen had nodded and Rielle had drawn in a deep breath, then took them through more worlds, heading at an angle across the sweep of worlds the city dwellers knew had been conquered. In most of the defeated worlds they didn't need to seek signs of devastation, since arrival places were usually in cities or other types of populated areas – places always targeted by the invaders. When their path took them to an arrival place away from civilisation – or the remains of it – they had to skim up and over the landscape to search for signs that Kettin's machines had been there.

The further they travelled, the deeper the hollow in Tyen's gut grew. Each conquered world suggested that Kettin's front line was larger, suggesting a bigger and bigger army. Whenever Dahli found a world that had been spared, he continued on to check the next, to see if they had reached the extent of the army's reach. Each time they found the following world had been invaded.

After thirty conquered worlds, Dahli stopped and looked at Tyen and Rielle thoughtfully. "I can see by your faces you are as disturbed as I am by how many worlds Kettin's forces can invade at the same time."

Rielle's expression did reflect Tyen's dismay. "Let's find the front line rather than try to discover its size," she suggested. "The closer we get to her army, the better chance we can read the mind of one of her followers. Then we'll learn its true size, and perhaps where Zeke might be, too."

"Wherever Kettin's followers are, the worlds will be dead," Tyen reminded her.

She grimaced in frustration. They had discussed this problem before they'd left. If they released magic in order to read minds and one of Kettin's sorcerers was close enough to sense them doing it, they would reveal their presence.

"We won't learn anything if we never take any risks," Dahli pointed out.

"I'll take us." Rielle dragged in a couple of deep breaths, then pushed out of the world. It faded to white rapidly, then another emerged. They found some survivors and returnees in a few worlds. It was tempting to approach and ask questions, but without the ability to read minds it was unlikely they'd understand the language the people spoke.

Gradually the signs of invasion and destruction grew fresher, until they were finding still-smoking ruins and newly arrived refugees. Many hours had passed since they'd arrived in the world in which Dahli had been attacked a half-cycle ago. They stopped to eat and rest. While Tyen and Dahli could have continued on, using pattern-shifting to erase weariness and hunger, Rielle was clearly exhausted. She accepted gratefully when Tyen offered to heal away her weariness.

When they set out again, with Tyen moving them, it was not long before they found a world the machines had invaded a handful of days before. He skimmed higher and created a platform of still air for them to stand upon above the highest walls of the city they'd arrived in. It was cold and windy, so he extended his shield around them and heated the air within.

A now-familiar scene of devastation lay below. Dahli pointed towards the horizon.

"There is something too consistent about the smoke coming up over there," he said. "It could be a foundry for making machine parts."

Rielle nodded. "Let's check it out."

Dahli took them back into the place between worlds and skimmed towards the column of smoke. It rose from the outskirts of a ruined city. Most of the metropolis had been smashed and burned, but the smoke was coming from an enormous chimney built into an intact building that reminded Tyen of the Grand Market in Doum. Machines marched out of a wide entrance to form rows in nearby fields.

Dahli brought them into the world high above.

"Can we get closer, do you think?" Rielle asked.

Dahli glanced at Tyen and raised an eyebrow.

Tyen shrugged and nodded. "As you said, we won't learn anything if we don't take any risks," he replied.

"Let's wait until dark," Dahli said, looking around. "It'll be night soon. I don't know if the machines would be less likely to detect us, but it improves our chances that humans won't."

As they waited, they watched the machines emerging from the foundry. It was not a steady stream, but an irregular regurgitation of metal and movement. Each machine joined others of its kind in the area around the foundry, forming orderly lines. All appeared to be behaving without instruction. Tyen altered his eyesight so he could see them better, trying to guess what purpose each machine had.

"Tyen," Rielle said after a while. He looked up to find he could see every pore and hair of her face.

"The sun has set," she told him.

He looked around, surprised, only to wince at the painful brightness of the sky at the horizon. Concentrating, he changed his eyesight nearer to normal vision, not so sharply focused but retaining an ability to see well in the dark.

"Take us down, Dahli," Rielle said.

The stilled air supporting them began to drop, slowly lowering them towards the foundry. They landed softly on a roof formed of long planks laid horizontally. Tyen lay down and placed his eye to the crack between two of them. He could not see much, but a little careful application of magic allowed him to carve a wider gap.

He heard Rielle and Dahli stretching out beside him as he took in the scene below. Machines filled the floor of the foundry, ranging in size from huge smelting contraptions to tiny constructors. All worked tirelessly at their different tasks, making parts, then assembling them into new machines.

A lone man watched over it all. He paced slowly through the foundry, occasionally stopping one process or starting a new one.

He yawned several times as he did this.

"He's not ageless," Dahli said. "Or he'd not be sleepy."

"There is a little magic here," Rielle said.

Tyen extended his senses and confirmed her words.

"Generated by creativity?" Dahli asked. He turned to Tyen. "Can machines be Makers?"

"I doubt it," Tyen replied. "But I can't say it's not possible." He bent to look below again. "It might be the overseer."

"Hmm," Rielle disagreed. "What he is doing is not that creative."

"Machines need magic to operate," Tyen said, thinking aloud. "Perhaps the overseer is releasing some for them to use." The man was approaching the area where new machines were nearing completion. He checked each, dark radiating lines springing from him as he did. Rielle sucked in a breath.

"Stain," she whispered.

Tyen was puzzled by the word until he recalled that the dark void where magic was absent was called "stain" in her world. "Soot," he murmured. She met his gaze and smiled grimly.

Tyen focused on the overseer. The man's name was Pelli. He was reflecting that he was good at his job now. He'd had enough practice at organising machine replication that, if the information scouts gave him was correct, he could extract a world's resources and convert it to new machines in as short a time as was physically possible. The trouble was, unlike in the early days, the machine makers now worked separately. Nobody was here to appreciate his efficiency, and he couldn't compare his progress with the others'. He hadn't even laid eyes on Kettin for maybe a sixth of a cycle. A masked face rose in his memory. Only when Kettin's messengers checked to see if he was ready to leave a world did he see another colleague, and they understood too little of mechanical magic to appreciate the work Pelli did.

As the man's thoughts turned back to the process of making machines, Dahli hissed. "We won't learn much from him."

Tyen frowned. "I could learn something about how these machines work," he said. "And he seems like a man who would like to boast about his achievements."

"You want to talk to him?" Rielle asked, a crease of worry between her brows.

Dahli nodded.

"He seems the type who would be easily persuaded to divulge details about Kettin's army."

Rielle met Tyen's gaze briefly, communicating a different kind of worry. "And if he proves harder to persuade than you expect? I won't have you treat him too cruelly, Dahli."

"This is war, Rielle," Dahli replied gently – more a warning than a rebuke. "I won't torture him, just nudge him into thinking about what he wants to conceal."

She looked at Tyen again, one eyebrow rising. Tyen searched Dahli's mind and saw no intention to harm Pelli. He nodded. "It's worth the risk, if we can learn more about how Kettin's armies work."

"And when we're done with him?"

"We'll put him somewhere his colleagues won't find him for a while," Dahli replied.

"How do we get close to him without the machines detecting us?" Rielle asked.

"We wait until he goes somewhere free of machines, then enter it from the place between worlds," Dahli said. "Since he's not ageless he needs sleep, and for that he'll want somewhere quiet. Or at least quieter than this building."

The wait was long, but not tedious, since Tyen could watch Pelli working through his thoughts. In the overseer's mind there were three main kinds of war machines: machines to attack with, machines to defend with and machines that could repair or construct more machines. In the early days some inventors had competed to find new and more horrible ways in which a machine could kill, but Kettin was not interested in their sadistic games. Neither did she particularly care about avoiding deaths. People were a nuisance and best removed. He suspected if machines could travel between worlds by themselves, and didn't need supervision now and then, she would eliminate the inventors and captains too. All that mattered to Kettin was conquering worlds as quickly and efficiently as possible.

What she wanted to do then, Pelli could not guess. He hoped this was all leading to something better for the worlds, because he doubted he'd have the courage to leave Kettin's service if it wasn't. Most of those who had tried to leave had been hunted down and killed. He assumed the rest were in hiding. He had no idea where he'd hide, if he had no choice but to flee.

Pelli continued his supervision until he could no longer keep his eyes open, then slipped away to a small, miraculously intact house a few blocks away and collapsed onto a bed. Dahli took Rielle and Tyen's hand and skimmed down to the city, through the roof and into Pelli's bedroom.

As they emerged, Tyen stilled the air around them. Someone like Pelli was bound to have rigged up a defence of some sort. Nothing happened until they stepped away from each other. Then a piercing alarm filled the air. It was silenced a moment later as Dahli smashed the machine making it.

Pelli groaned, decided that some small vermin animal had set it off, and rolled over, intending to go back to sleep. Then it occurred to him that vermin couldn't have turned the alarm off, and he forced himself into a sitting position. Perhaps it had run out of magic. He opened his eyes and created a light.

And blinked stupidly at Dahli, Tyen and Rielle.

"Where's Kettin?" Dahli asked.

No specific location entered Pelli's mind. *The captains would know*, he thought. *That's who I'd ask if I wanted to find her.*

"Where are the captains?"

Patrolling the conquered worlds.

Dahli took a step closer. "Where are the inventors she imprisoned?"

Pelli flinched away from him, tugging at the bedclothes to free his legs. "I don't know." But he thought it likely they were in Kettin's base world, at the centre of the worlds she had conquered. Which was about thirty or forty worlds away.

A sense of the arrangement of worlds and armies unfolded in his mind. The front line was a ring, moving steadily outwards from Kettin's world. Tyen looked at Rielle, whose expression of horror reflected his own. If the outer edge of it had moved outwards by thirty or forty worlds in the last half-cycle, how big was the circumference? How many worlds lay ruined within that ring?

"Please don't hurt me," Pelli said, his voice a whimper.

"We won't," Rielle promised. She sat on the edge of the bed and managed a small, sympathetic smile. "We can see you wouldn't be here if you thought you had an alternative."

"No, I wouldn't," Pelli replied. A voice in his mind disagreed. He did like being part of something big. Something remarkable, if deadly. Like many of Kettin's followers, he didn't think much of the Restorers. Then he realised these sorcerers could read his mind, and he hung his head in defeat.

"So, what are we going to do with you?" Dahli asked.

Pelli slumped even further. He did not want to fight them. He barely held enough magic to leave this world. Even if he won, he'd be trapped here.

"You're right," Tyen said. "You would lose a fight. So why bother fighting? Join us. We'll take you somewhere you won't be quickly found. Then we'll come back here when our business is finished and set you free."

Pelli looked up at Tyen as he considered.

"We can protect you," Rielle assured him.

The sorcerer turned to frown at her. "Who do you work for?"

She opened her mouth but paused as Dahli shook his head. "For peace," she said.

Pelli's eyes narrowed. "You're Restorers, aren't you?" He looked at each of them in turn.

"Yes," Rielle replied.

"No," Dahli said firmly.

"Yes and no." Tyen sighed. "I am working with them, but I am not a Restorer."

"Who are you?" Pelli asked. "Why should I trust you?"

"I am Tyen Ironsmelter."

Pelli's eyes widened. "The first . . . but you want to destroy all machines. And all machine makers, so nobody can replace them."

Tyen opened his mouth to deny it, but Dahli spoke before he could.

"Make up your mind, Pelli. Give up your magic or fight us. Stay here or come with us. What will it be?"

Pelli looked down. "I'll stay here."

"Then let all your magic go, so we know you won't follow us."

The sorcerer's shoulders hunched. He said nothing, resentment spilling from him as he released all the magic he had been holding. It spilled outwards, then vanished as Rielle and Dahli drew it in. When the man was powerless, Dahli placed a hand on his shoulder. He looked up at Rielle and Tyen.

"Wait here. I'll be back in a moment."

"Where . . .?" Rielle said, but Dahli and Pelli's figures faded and flashed away. She looked at Tyen. "I don't like the beginning of the thought Dahli was having as he left."

"I didn't catch it, but I think we should follow. We must stay together."

Rielle took Tyen's hand, pushed out of the world and skimmed in pursuit. They did not have to travel far. Dahli had returned to the world within the city, in the ruins of a house. He was crouched over a prone Pelli, and as they arrived he straightened and frowned.

"I told you to wait," he said.

"You can't hide your thoughts from us," Rielle reminded him. She knelt beside Pelli and placed a hand on the man's forehead. "Dead." She shook her head. "You didn't have to kill him, Dahli."

Tyen's stomach sank. He looked at Dahli. "Why did you?"

"He was a risk," Dahli said. "Someone might check on him. If he was alive they'd learn who we are and what we're looking for."

"Only when they found him." Rielle sighed and stood up. "We could have hidden him halfway around the world."

"He'd have found a way to signal to searchers," Dahli argued. "Maybe rig a machine to do it."

Anger flared within Tyen. "Or we'd have found a way to ensure he didn't. Could you not have given us the opportunity to try?"

"And if you did not find a way?" Dahli's voice was strained. "We can't risk it. We can't."

Rielle winced, then glanced at Tyen. Shaking his head, Tyen moved forward to stand by her side. "And what if it was Rielle or I who lowered your chances of rescuing him? How are we to trust you, Dahli?"

Dahli looked up, his gaze hard as they met Tyen's. "You can't. You can only trust that I will do whatever is necessary to free and protect Zeke."

"And when you have him, what then?" Rielle asked. "Will you tell him you killed another person? For him?"

Dahli's gaze slid away. Looking into the man's mind, Tyen saw that Dahli was remembering a promise he'd made Zeke. Not to never kill again, but to at least try not to.

"Will you abandon the worlds to the machines?" Rielle asked.

"I don't know," Dahli admitted in a low voice, lowering his gaze. "I'd rather take Zeke far away, to somewhere safe. But it is likely he will insist on joining the Restorers." He smiled grimly. "You probably haven't seen the last of me yet."

Rielle looked down at Pelli, then glanced at Tyen and extended a hand to him. "Let's get this rescue over with."

Dahli took her other hand without looking up.

Taking a deep breath, Rielle took them into the place between worlds. She headed back the way they had come, as quickly as she could travel without suffocating, passing through worlds defeated longer and longer ago. When they had reached the world in which they had started their journey, she did not pause, but continued on. Tyen silently counted. They passed through another ten worlds. Rielle stopped for a short time to catch her breath. They said nothing to each other. Rielle did not even look at Dahli. Dahli showed no sign of discomfort at this.

By now all the worlds they passed through were in ruins. A few had been recolonised, and contained a little magic. They had not paused long when Rielle indicated she was ready to move on.

"I'll move us from here," Dahli said.

He drew them back into the place between worlds. They had not travelled far when Tyen sensed the presence of another person.

"We have company," Tyen warned, nodding in the direction of the stranger.

Dahli stopped and looked the way Tyen had indicated, then shook his head. "I can't sense them."

"Further along the path, but coming this way."

Dahli moved them off the path, his brow creased in concentration. Looking back the way they'd come, Tyen sensed the substance of the place between worlds smoothing. He raised an eyebrow at Dahli.

"You're hiding our tracks," Tyen said.

"What if they detect the traces?" Rielle asked. "That's as good as telling them someone is sneaking around."

"They won't detect anything," Dahli said. He began moving them faster, no longer hiding their path. When they were far enough away that they could no longer sense the other traveller, he turned to Rielle. "Your attempts at concealing your path back when you were hiding from me were crude and unskilled. Did you think that something only Valhan and his most loyal servants knew how to do was so easy that anyone could learn to do it perfectly in a few cycles?"

Her eyes narrowed, but she said nothing. As she looked at Tyen, he shrugged. It was good to know, at least, that they might one day be able to hide their tracks effectively.

Rielle looked back in the direction of the stranger. "There. He is gone. We can return to the path."

As Dahli drew them through the area he had smoothed, Tyen concentrated and found no tell-tale sign of the man's work. Dahli hurried them along the established path. To Tyen's relief, they arrived in the next world without having to detour again, as he suspected Rielle would have run out of breath if they had. When they did arrive, he began healing her and she recovered quickly.

They moved on. Traffic between worlds was definitely heavier here. As they passed through three more worlds, they had to evade several more strangers. Dahli began travelling in parallel to the established path, using the other presences to orientate them. This meant they were going to arrive high in the sky in the fourth world.

"Machines in the air!" Rielle warned.

Tyen looked around. Dark shapes hovered, forming lines that curved in all directions, to the horizon. All were the same – a disc about the size of a human head with a propeller spinning above. The closest machines were revolving, a dark elliptical space in their shell coming to face Rielle, Tyen and Dahli. Guessing that this was where an attack would come from, Tyen quickly stilled a layer of air to form a spherical shield as soon as he felt them enter the world.

An instant later, the machines began to attack.

CHAPTER 15

The impacts set Tyen's shield vibrating, but he was well able to resist them. None of the blasts were particularly strong. The closest of the machines soon stopped their assault and dove downwards through the hovering network, most likely having used up their small store of magic. He enjoyed a brief respite, then the world appeared to twist and shift as the next rows of machines moved to fill the empty positions and the closest turned to attack.

"Tyen, keep focused on the machines in case their strategy changes," Dahli ordered. He turned to Rielle. "Search for minds."

That means there's magic here, Tyen realised. He didn't bother to look, keeping his attention on the machines. Row after row of them were replacing their fellows, spending their stored magic and falling away.

"Has anyone noticed us?" Tyen asked.

"Yes," Rielle replied. "People in a town below have noticed the spent machines arriving."

"Should we leave?"

"They don't seem too concerned—"

"No, because they believe Kettin's defences will deal with us quickly," Dahli injected. "We've reached her base world."

Rielle hummed in interest. "People are restoring the fallen machines, which are coming back up to rejoin the attack."

Tyen frowned. "They weren't smashed by the fall?"

"It appears they retain enough magic to land safely."

"I could break the machines so they can't be recharged," Tyen said, "but that will use up more magic than simply shielding." He glanced at Dahli. "I can see how this would quickly deplete a sorcerer's strength, if he or she was alone and hadn't prepared for it. It's like being attacked by an army of weak sorcerers."

"Who are wasting your magic," Rielle said. "We should find somewhere not guarded by machines so we can read minds without growing weaker."

"I suspect there isn't anywhere," Tyen told her. He squinted into the distance, then adjusted his sight again. The network stretched in every direction, all the way to the horizon. He shuddered, both chilled and amazed at the defensive strategy. "Considering the numbers of machines Kettin is capable of producing, I wouldn't be surprised if these cover the entire world."

"Then we stay put," Dahli decided. "Moving, only to emerge among machines again, will waste time we should be spending reading minds."

He and Rielle fell silent, their attention elsewhere. Restored machines began to swarm upwards to rejoin the attack on Tyen's shield. A thick, constantly shifting sphere of them had begun to form, holes appearing whenever one fell, only to be plugged with a freshly powered machine.

"The people below are growing concerned," Dahli said. "They didn't expect us to last this long. A few people have thought about warning Kettin but they don't know where she is. The town's leader is sending a messenger to report the presence of strangers to his superior in another city." He took Tyen and Rielle's hands. "I suggest we follow the messenger."

Tyen and Rielle nodded in agreement. The machine sphere faded as Dahli took them out of the world a little. They flashed out of it and through the network of machines, more of the metallic forms detecting them and beginning to follow. Quickening his pace, Dahli left the swarm behind. Wondering how the man knew where to go, Tyen searched the place between worlds and felt the presence of another sorcerer, positioned closer to the ground and following a road. Likely to be a weaker magician, the messenger did not appear to detect them. He stopped a few times to breathe, allowing time for Rielle to also do so.

Eventually the messenger reached a small city. Dahli stopped and brought them into the world. Tyen immediately created a shield again as air surrounded them and the closest machines in the network began to attack.

Breathing heavily, Rielle stared down. "These machines detect our movement, but they don't attack the people below. Would they ignore us if we, too, were on the ground?"

Dahli shook his head. "When we descend the machines will follow us. The people will know where we land."

"Yes, but not where we emerge again, if we skim beneath the ground for a distance," Rielle pointed out. "Of course, we'll have to hope we're lucky enough to emerge somewhere nobody sees us, and they'll be looking everywhere for us."

"Not if they think there's only one of us occupied up here." Dahli looked at Tyen. "If they're paying attention to one of us, they may pay none to the other two."

"You want me to stay here," Tyen guessed.

"Yes. Or move if that proves a better distraction."

"Or you could stay here and Rielle and I could go."

Dahli's eyebrows rose. "Rielle can read my mind, so we can communicate silently at least in one direction. She also has the greater store of magic now. And Zeke . . . I don't know what state his mind is in. He may see you or Rielle as an enemy, but perhaps he will know me. If not, I am better able to change my appearance to one he will trust, or at least obey."

Rielle looked at Tyen, then back at Dahli. "But if we part, how will we find each other again?"

"Return to the last world," Dahli suggested. "Remember the lake with the crescent-shaped island? Wait there, or nearby."

Rielle nodded. Tyen met her gaze. "Are you sure about this?"
She shrugged. "It does seem the best plan."
He looked from her to Dahli, quashing his misgivings. "Be careful. Both of you."

"You, too," Rielle replied. She let go of his hand and turned to Dahli. "I'll take us down."

The pair faded until he could barely make them out, then blurred and vanished. He looked down, but a swarm of black metal obscured his view of the ground. Once again, the machines had encircled him, battering his shield with blasts of power.

Seeking minds below, he found some people watching the machines above them swarming around and obscuring a target that was too distant to see anyway. The rest continued their daily tasks, confident that Kettin's defences would deal with any threat from outside. He stayed still, keeping his shield strong. Machines crowded ever closer. It was hard to resist the urge to push them away, or strike at them, but he did not want to use magic any faster than necessary. Though he, Rielle and Dahli had strengthened themselves far beyond what they expected to need in a battle, he was not about to forget that Dahli had barely escaped last time he'd faced a machine army, and Dahli was not a weak sorcerer by any means.

As time passed, most of the watchers below grew bored and turned back to whatever task they'd paused in the middle of. Catching the mind of a sorcerer wondering if any other invaders had arrived, Tyen realised his error. He was supposed to be a distraction. He had to keep their attention.

As long as the machines encircled him and hid him from view, he could move a little without revealing that he was alone. He began to push forward. The swarm followed like a malignant black cloud. He turned and moved in another direction. The locals began to watch again, wondering if this was a last desperate act before the stranger fell out of the sky. When he didn't fall, some began to wonder if this latest invader might be stronger and more dangerous than the usual Restorer scout. Surely the investigators would arrive soon.

Uh-oh! Tyen thought. *Dumb machines can't follow me into the place between, but sorcerers can.*

And yet as soon as he left, he would no longer be the distraction Rielle and Dahli needed. Moving in a wide circle, he searched more minds below. All too soon he found the thoughts of a sorcerer receiving orders to find out what or who the machines were targeting, and deal with it.

Time to go.

Tyen pushed out of the world. At once, he sensed something new in the place between. Focusing on it, he detected numerous other presences coming towards him. He pushed directly away from the world, realising as he did so that he could not be sure the next world was the one he, Rielle and Dahli had left, as they had travelled quite a distance from their place of arrival. He was also not sure how much magic he had left. For a brief moment he regretted that he hadn't thought to take all the magic from Kettin's world, but then that would have left Dahli and Rielle unable to read minds, and alerted all sorcerers that someone of his strength had attacked their world.

He remembered Tarren once warning him about the danger of using magic quickly. *"It is like pumping water through a hose. If the flow is slow, you have time to detect when you're about to run out. If it is fast, you can come to the end of your store so quickly that your mind is unable to sense the end of it before it has arrived."* Thanks to the vast number of machines attacking him, Tyen knew he had been draining his store of magic as fast as if he'd faced an army of sorcerers. He should make sure he was on the ground and safe, not levitating and in the middle of a battle with several sorcerers, when he came to the end.

At least he could move faster than most between worlds. The strangers fell behind as he travelled past the midpoint between Kettin's world and the next. Which meant he was drawing these sorcerers' attention away from Rielle and Dahli. Unless he was heading for the world of the meeting place. For all that he knew, Rielle and Dahli were already waiting there, and he was bringing trouble straight to them.

To his relief, the landscape that emerged was very different. At first, he thought he was arriving above a sprawl of dead tree trunks, but as details emerged he realised they were columns of stone. Their angular surfaces suggested immense crystalline forms, softened by an age of weathering. While many of the columns had fallen, creating a jumble of them propped up against or lying on each other, others still stood in clusters, projecting towards the sky.

He arrived and created a sphere of stilled air to support and protect himself, and immediately sent himself flying across the sky. The world was empty of magic. Nothing below looked like an arrival place. If he pushed out of this world again, would he find a way to the next world, or reverse back into his pursuer's path? He had to hope it would be the former. At least he knew that, in the place between worlds, he was still the stronger sorcerer. They could not stop him moving there.

Hearing a shout, he glanced back to see the figures had materialised in the world. More than twenty of them.

He stopped, drew upon his store of magic to push out of the world . . . and realised he did not have enough.

Fear lanced through him. He pushed himself back into motion, hoping to keep enough distance between himself and his pursuers that he would be a difficult target. The air around him sizzled and hissed as the sorcerers missed him. Then an impact struck his shield. He glanced back at his pursuers. One was much closer. As he watched, another suddenly streaked closer, then abruptly slowed, again.

They were pushing out of the worlds and skimming to get closer to him, since there was no air resistance in the place between. He cursed. They would all catch up soon. Defending himself would take up more magic. So would levitating. How long before he ran out and fell from the sky?

Better to be closer to the ground when it happened. Another strike shook his shield. He descended into the jumble of columns, ducking and weaving through the maze in the hopes that the stones would take the attacks aimed at him. He caught glimpses of his pursuers from the corners of his eyes. A few followed him from above, tracking him.

The columns did not provide consistent cover. His shield wavered under another attack and he had too little magic left to strengthen it. The realisation came, with a rush of fear, that he was not going to escape his pursuers, and if he did not descend to the ground soon, he would run out of magic in the sky, and fall, perhaps to his death.

That thought gave him one last desperate idea.

Pretend I am done. Pretend to fall. Catch myself at the last moment and disappear into the maze. It will buy me time, if nothing else.

He was doing it even as he thought it. He let his shield go and fell. The crystalline jumble of columns rushed up towards him. He altered his descent slightly to avoid one protruding spire, then dove towards the darkness of a hole. Then, just before he entered, he drew the last of his magic to shield his body.

Darkness surrounded him. He landed on a hard surface, barely softened by his hasty shield. Then he was sliding down a steep slope, unable to catch something to stop himself before he slipped off the edge. He fell. Not far, but with a bone-crunching end and an agony of pain.

He clenched his teeth and looked up, barely able to see the crazy jumble of stone surfaces surrounding him in the thin light, and wondered how long he had before the sorcerers found him.

And if they didn't, how in all the worlds was Rielle going to?

PART FIVE

RIELLE

CHAPTER 16

Rielle had lost count of the number of shadowed alleys and empty rooms she and Dahli had emerged in to spend long, tense moments searching minds. By a stroke of good luck, the third time they had done so they'd found the mind of a city's Head Sorcerer briefing messengers on whom to report the invader's – or invaders' – disappearance. That told them about the chain of command, as well as that Tyen had already moved on.

Rielle doubted he'd run out of magic already. More likely he had left to draw attention away from them. Even so, she couldn't help feeling a twinge of anxiety. *Be careful, Tyen. Your world needs you. All the worlds need you. And I would miss your friendship.*

The Head Sorcerer turned to other pressing tasks once the messengers had left, so she and Dahli set off after the man who would report to Kettin's assistants. He skimmed across the world, heading for another city. When he paused to catch his breath, Rielle and Dahli stopped nearby. Reading his mind, they saw him ponder the chances that Kettin would be there and he might report to her directly. The thought filled him with fear. He'd seen her kill another messenger, though nobody knew why.

An image appeared in his mind of a rigid, emotionless face, the colour of gold. A glint of reflected light was all he'd been able to make out of Kettin's eyes.

"She wears a mask," Rielle noted.

Dahli grunted softly. "Maybe she is scarred, or ugly."

The messenger sucked in several quick breaths in preparation for the second half of his journey. He could not afford to stop again, as Kettin did not approve of unnecessary delays. *I doubt she'll be there anyway. She spends most of her time with the inventors.*

Rielle and Dahli exchanged a glance, then followed as the man continued on his way. The world was a small one, so his path quickly took them around to the night side of the world, to a small city, where the matter of the invader was delegated to sorcerers, not Kettin. Rielle and Dahli arrived in yet another cellar. While it was easier for them to remain undetected at night, the people who might have had useful information were either asleep or thinking about friends and family, not where imprisoned inventors might be located.

Dahli's frustration grew more obvious the longer their search of minds proved fruitless.

"They'd think about it if we woke them up and asked them," he muttered, as yet another official's thoughts lingered on irrelevant domestic matters.

"Yes, and then you'd have to make sure they couldn't report the conversation," Rielle replied. "And that will limit our time here to what it takes for their body to be discovered."

"I can make sure it won't be discovered."

She met his gaze levelly. "No."

"Aren't you worried how long Tyen will last?"

She sent him a dark look rather than replying, afraid that her voice might betray how much she was. To her surprise his eyes lowered, and he nodded.

"Yes, that was low of me. I just . . . I don't know any other way. It's seems so naïve, what I promised to Zeke."

The note of desperation was back in his voice. "If there is another way, we'll find it," she assured him. "But we won't if we don't try."

He nodded and took her hand. "Let's try another city."

They followed a well-used path, only having to evade other travellers twice before they arrived at the second city. Here their luck changed. Though it was early in the morning, they caught the thoughts of a tired guard returning home after his shift. He reflected on how his income might have been different if he'd accepted the offer of a job in one of Kettin's laboratories. He'd declined because he'd heard the inventors were sorcerers held against their will, and he figured that, as a non-sorcerer, he would be one of the first to die if an escape was attempted. Now a friend claimed the prisoners were only weak sorcerers, held for their cleverness with machines. Perhaps it wouldn't have been so risky. Perhaps if he let them know he was interested in the job after all . . . Though it did mean a long journey to the Wechen Plains.

He didn't know the precise location of the prison, but at least Rielle and Dahli now knew the general whereabouts – but also that there was more than one laboratory. She took Dahli out of the world and skimmed in the direction the guard knew the plains lay. Passing a mountain range, they reached a stretch of flat lands etched with a pattern of fields divided by a winding river with many tributaries. They had travelled northward and away from the rising sun, so it was still early morning. A short pause to read minds in a village confirmed they were in the right location, and more stops brought them closer to a particular town where large buildings had been erected recently, from which odd noises and smells sometimes emanated.

"Look for Zeke's mind," Dahli asked, when they stopped in the outskirts.

Rielle searched. She found guards watching over storerooms containing both materials for making machines as well as finished and unfinished machines. No prisoners, however. Only the night watch was present, and they expected to be relieved by the day watch soon.

"There's a void around that house over there," Dahli said, his voice quiet but intense.

Rielle looked in the direction he indicated. Of all the buildings in the town, this house was the most brightly lit. She stretched out her senses and found a globe of darkness surrounding the house, like a more intense patch of the night. Looking within, she sensed magic inside it.

"There's magic within the void," she said, turning to meet his gaze. "I can sense minds within, but they are too vague to understand."

His grip on her hand tightened. "Shall we investigate?"

She nodded.

He took them further out of the world, so they could barely see their surroundings as they skimmed closer to the building. The bright lights around it had been placed to eliminate shadowed corners. The faint shapes of guards paced around the exterior.

Dahli gave her a questioning look. She nodded again. Then, when the guards' attention was elsewhere briefly, they plunged through a wall.

On the other side was a uniform greyness. As Dahli brought them closer to the world, the grey darkened and Rielle began to worry that he was going to emerge within something solid. Then shapes materialised. She could make out a bed. A man lay under the covers. Eyes closed. Chest rising and falling slowly

To Rielle's surprise Dahli brought them fully into the world. She tried to refresh her lungs quietly by slowly sucking in and releasing a deep breath, but the rush of air seemed loud in the space. Dahli didn't make a sound. His expression was distracted. Following his lead, she searched for minds, but they were in the void still and she found nothing.

Still holding her hand, Dahli led her to the door. He moved out of the world slightly and pushed his head through it, then moved forward and drew Rielle through.

They were in a corridor. Dahli returned to the world again. He crept forward, Rielle following. The corridor ended in a staircase, so they started to descend. At the bottom they reached a door, and simultaneously passed the edge of an inner area of magic. Suddenly Rielle could sense clearly that a guard was standing on the other side of the door. The man was full of anticipation as his shift was about to end and he longed for a meal and sleep.

Dahli's breath caught. Rielle looked at him.

"He's here."

The words were more mouthed than spoken. Rielle searched beyond the nearby guard for other minds and found a few more weary guards, and then the befuddled thoughts of a handful of sleepers.

Were these the inventors? From the guards' minds she found the answer: yes. They regarded their prisoners with wary respect. Many did not cause trouble because Kettin had blackmailed them. A few had no loved ones to protect but were easily cowed with threats. One had tried to escape once, setting his machines on the guards, but had been found and tortured to dissuade the others from making similar attempts.

Rielle guessed that Dahli had caught Zeke's name in the mind of a guard slowly pacing a room full of beds, mentally accounting for each prisoner as he passed them. She searched for the captives' minds. All were asleep. One was dreaming. Rielle had always found watching dreams simultaneously disconcerting and fascinating. Unexpectedly clear thoughts could appear among the strange disjointed imaginings within dreams. Sometimes the dreamer knew they were dreaming. Sometimes they could change the dream.

While she had grown used to spying on the thoughts of others, looking at other people's dreams always felt like prying. The young man was dreaming about machines, however. A nightmare of sorts. He was trying to disable a dangerous error, but everything he did made it worse.

Then a bell rang out, and suddenly he was lying in bed, staring at the ceiling of a room, hearing groans from the other beds.

I'm awake, he thought. *Still living. Another day survived. Another day to get through.* It was Zeke, but a different Zeke than the one she had known. Not just older, but changed. Both wounded and scarred. He waited for the guilt and horror to sweep over him, as it did every morning, and pass. Thoughts of ideas he'd had to modify and improve machines, which the stronger sorcerers had seen in his mind and then forced him to develop. *But at least I don't have to do that now. Though what Kettin wants me to do feels wrong, too.* He did not want to think about it until he had to, so he concentrated only on the present.

Dahli's hand pressed on Rielle's shoulder, bringing her attention back to her surroundings. Noises were coming from all around, and she understood that the bell had indicated the start of the day and change of shift. The house was full of people waking up and starting to move about.

She could feel the tension in Dahli from the pressure of his hand. He did not move or retreat into the place between worlds, however. Then footsteps sounded at the top of the stairs. They had to move or be discovered. The darkened staircase faded slightly and they slipped through a wall as Dahli took them sideways. On the other side was a storeroom, rows of shelving dividing the shadowy space. The air that surrounded them again was laced with a mix of pungent, tangy and metallic smells.

Again, Dahli remained still, only his breathing quickening as he watched and waited. Rielle sent her senses out again. Footsteps and minds told her the person who had descended the stairs was the closest guard's replacement. Others came down to take their shifts, or leave, but a few remained. Whoever had organised their schedule had sensibly made sure that guard changes didn't all happen at the same time.

Zeke followed his roommates to the dining table. She looked into the minds of the other inventors. Some were jealous. He had Kettin's favour, such as it was. His work gained him special privileges. They didn't know what it was, and assumed it was some even more deadly machine.

The inventors ate. None of them spoke to Zeke, who did not seem to mind. When they were done, they headed to one of three laboratories, the closest one next to the storeroom she and Dahli were hiding in. In each waited a sorcerer – one of Kettin's followers. They scanned their charges' minds looking for awareness of new ideas for machines, or plans to escape. Rielle turned her attention to Zeke, who was alone but for the sorcerer in charge of him. Through Zeke's eyes she watched him scan the room, taking in the parts and tools still in the places he'd left them, his thoughts tracing their purpose. His attention finally landed upon the machine he was developing . . . and Rielle's heart stopped.

It was Tyen's humanoid. The one he'd made in an abandoned attempt to provide Vella with a body.

No, it isn't, she realised a moment later. *It's different.* Though she did not clearly recall the details of the machine she'd smashed, it hadn't been as sleek and strangely beautiful as this one. Zeke could not help admiring it, even as it filled him with loathing. Kettin wanted it to be magnificent, to enchant as well as terrify.

And Rielle understood that Kettin wanted to *be* the machine. Tyen had never found a way to create a mind for his humanoid. Kettin wasn't interested in developing one for hers. She wanted, instead, to replace her body with a mechanical one. Finding a way was Zeke's task. He felt sick as he thought of the young man who had died the previous day during his tests, and Rielle shuddered in sympathy. How many people had he killed in his experiments now? *Even one is too many.*

Nausea rose, and he hastily turned towards the door. The sorcerer watching him rolled her eyes.

"Again?"

"Yes," he choked.

"Go on then."

She followed him as he hurried towards the bathroom, his stomach's insistence that it needed to reject his breakfast growing ever more powerful.

Rielle looked at Dahli. His eyes were bright.

"Ready?" he murmured.

"What about the sorcerer?"

"I'll handle her. You grab Zeke."

She swallowed. "What about the other inventors?"

He shook his head. "Zeke's best chance is for you to get him away as quickly as possible. They must have a defence in place for rescue attempts. The best we can do is strike quickly and travel fast. Trying to save the others will only slow us down. Unless you have any better ideas?"

"No," she admitted. She narrowed her eyes at him. "What are you going to do to his guard?"

He stared back at her. "She is not going to leave his side, and she'll report his rescue as soon as she is able to. We kill her and we get a head start out of here."

"Or you could simply knock her unconscious."

He opened his mouth to reply, but hurried footsteps sounded from outside the room, growing rapidly louder. Dahli moved them into the toilet, then stepped into the space next to the closed door. No walls for privacy hid the seats on which the users perched when relieving themselves, so there was no other place to hide. Rielle slipped behind Dahli just in time.

The door opened. Zeke rushed over to one of the toilets and threw up. A woman followed, her attention on the inventor.

Dahli simply reached out and took hold of her wrist.

And the pair disappeared.

A moment later a different bell rang out. Seeking minds, Rielle found a guard's and read that it was an alarm warning about an intruder. Searching further, she found the mind of a sorcerer who had just warned the rest that he had found a fresh path into the house on his rounds.

Zeke turned around, wiping his mouth, and stopped as he saw Rielle standing where he thought the sorcerer had been. He sucked in a breath.

"Ri—" he began.

She dashed forward, grabbed his arm and pushed out of the world before any sorcerers had a chance to read his mind.

The path Dahli had taken out of the world was easy to find and follow. Even as she sped along it, she sensed other minds in the place between worlds. She was only half aware of Zeke's expression changing from surprise to joy, then to worry. He looked away, searching the whiteness of the place between worlds.

Dahli's path ended abruptly. Retreating, she found that it simply stopped. He'd hidden his tracks. She could roam around looking for where it started again, but it would take too much time. Even if their pursuers did not manage to catch up before then, she and Zeke could only survive so long between worlds. Perhaps it would be better if she and Dahli stayed apart, splitting the attention of pursuers. She moved on, increasing her speed and heading towards the next world.

An ocean began to emerge from the whiteness. She skimmed to a place high above and created a sphere of stilled air to support them when they arrived.

"You found me!" Zeke exclaimed, throwing his arms tightly around her. "Thank you!"

"Don't thank me yet," she told him. "We still have to get you safely away from here."

"We?" he repeated.

"Dahli. Tyen."

Zeke pulled away a little. "Where are they?"

"I don't know. But we agreed on a meeting place." She adjusted the shape of her shield of air. If she travelled a distance within this world before she left it, it would be harder to follow her. "We will go there, but first I need to hide our tracks. Get a good grip on me. I'm going to move us – fast."

Zeke nodded and grasped both of her arms. She did the same to him. Altering the sphere of stilled air around them to a lozenge shape, she sent them toward the horizon, accelerating quickly. A trail of white began to form behind them. She wasn't sure why, and it stopped as she slowed again. She gritted her teeth. They would have to continue at a moderate speed or create a trail as effective as a path between worlds.

After she had put a good distance between herself and their entry point into the world, she pushed out of the world again. Sensing no other presences in the place between, she began to skim rapidly across the surface. The ocean continued unbroken. They passed through a storm and, blinded by the thick black cloud and flashes of lightning, emerged far higher above the water than before. When it was behind them, she slowed to a stop.

"I'm beginning to wonder if this world has no land."

"It has magic," Zeke pointed out. "Not much, but enough to supply sorcerers heading to and from Kettin's base."

She looked at him. "Is that why she didn't destroy some worlds?"

"Yes. None of her sorcerers are powerful enough to travel through a few dead worlds in a row. These worlds form stepping stones in and out of Kettin's territory."

"I see." Rielle looked around. "Do you know the paths? Do you know where we are?"

"I've been memorising fragments of what I've overheard or seen in the minds of the guards. There is only one world containing magic next to Kettin's, so it must be this one. There will be dead worlds beside this."

Rielle nodded. "That is good. They'll expect me to head along the stepping stones. We'll go sideways instead. I need to travel around the worlds surrounding Kettin's world to find the one we reached it from. Then we can find the meeting place."

As she drew in a deep breath, he did the same. Pushing out of the world, she headed into the whiteness. They hadn't travelled far when she sensed something – someone – in the far distance. They were so far away that it was probable they couldn't sense her. Passing the midpoint, she watched a new landscape appear, as alert for signs of people in it as in the retreating whiteness.

The landscape glistened below them, waterlogged and patched

with vegetation of several muted colours. She stretched her senses. "No magic."

Searching downwards, she found traces of magic deep below the earth. "There's magic far below. That suggests the world was once imbued with it – therefore occupied. Let's go look for an arrival place."

They stopped twice to catch their breath before they found a ruined city clinging to the sides of a rocky spire emerging from the bog. At the top of the spire was an arrival place, moss already starting to fur the stone surface now nobody was scrubbing it clean. Rielle pushed into the place between worlds and started down a path that was easily sensed from possibly centuries of use, despite not being used in some months.

The next world had been destroyed, but the traces of human life reminded Rielle of the survivors and returned refugees she'd seen earlier. In the next she recognised a distinctly shaped tree of the kind that had grown around the lake with the crescent island. Rising as high as she could without the air growing too thin, she criss-crossed the land until a water body caught her attention. Sure enough, a small crescent-shaped island lay at its heart. She descended. The island was unoccupied but she arrived there anyway, creating a strong shield in case the enemy had followed Dahli and now lay in wait for her.

A moment later, a blur in the place between warned her of a figure approaching rapidly from across the lake. She braced herself, then relaxed as the ghostly man stopped several paces away and rapidly grew solid.

"Zeke," Dahli exclaimed as he arrived.

"Dahli!" Zeke's face lit up with joy.

Rielle let her shield dissipate as the pair hurried towards each other. They embraced tightly, Dahli's relief so plain that Rielle felt her heart lighten. She reminded herself that Dahli had killed a man since they'd left the Restorers, but her disappointment and anger in him remained muted as Dahli searched Zeke's gaze.

"Are you all right?"

Zeke shrugged. "I am now. I hoped you'd come and get me – but I didn't want you to, in case they killed you."

"They didn't . . . obviously," Dahli replied, releasing Zeke reluctantly and turning to Rielle. "We can't stay here. I lost them only a world away, and it'll only be a matter of time before they look here."

"No sign of Tyen?" Rielle asked.

His expression was grim as he shook his head. Rielle's heart skipped a beat. She looked around at the forest fringing the lake. Even if the world had been full of magic, she wouldn't have been able to sense Tyen's mind if he was hiding. She started searching the ground for an etched stone like the one he'd left for her, long ago, when he'd been forced to leave the world he was learning to become ageless in.

"He wouldn't have left without leaving a sign he'd been here," she said.

"I know," Dahli said. "I've looked."

Her stomach was growing heavier as she tried not to imagine what had happened to him. "He left before us. Something must have delayed him. You go on. I'll look for him."

Dahli shook his head. "We might need you if they catch up with us."

"I'll make more magic for you now."

He paused, then slowly nodded. "If you are sure."

"I am." She looked at him, weighing up all the options she had and the possible consequences. Could she trust Dahli to take Zeke to the Restorers? If she put herself in Dahli's place, she would take her lover and flee to a safe place. *I ought to stay with them to make sure he doesn't do that.* The Restorers needed Zeke to tell them what Kettin was capable of.

But they also needed Tyen. He was too powerful to lose. He was smart. He was in charge of an entire school of sorcerers who understood mechanical magic. *And I can't abandon him.* It would

340

be too great a betrayal of their friendship. And she couldn't bear to lose yet another person she loved.

Love? Do I love him? She frowned. Was she willing to be in love with Tyen? Part of her resisted the idea. Part of her didn't. Another screamed at her to stop dithering and find him. *Do I love him romantically or as a friend?*

"Go get Tyen," Zeke told her. "I'll make sure Dahli takes me wherever you need me to be. Which would be to join the Restorers, right?"

She nodded and smiled. "Thank you, Zeke."

"So, make us some magic – and quickly."

She did, by filling the air with an intricate pattern of light, but not so bright it would be visible from a distance. The magic that poured out from her immediately flowed towards Dahli and Zeke as they took it.

"Is that enough?" Zeke eventually asked Dahli. The man shrugged and nodded. As Rielle stopped, Zeke wrapped an arm around Dahli's waist. "I hope you find Tyen, and we see you soon. Let's go, lover."

"We will wait for a while in Orgajika," Dahli added. "In case you are able to catch up." He glanced at his companion and a faint, fond smile curled his lips, then his expression returned to the grim one he had worn for the entire expedition and the pair vanished.

Taking a deep breath, Rielle pushed out of the world and found the older path she, Dahli and Tyen had taken when approaching Kettin's world. She sought presences in the place between. Before she had passed the midpoint, she heard voices. They were too faint to make out, so she cautiously approached the speakers, hoping she would get close enough to make out the words before the strangers detected her.

". . . *if he's still alive, he might ambush us if we get closer.*"

"*If he has enough magic left for that he'd have left the world already.*"

"*We found no path. We couldn't see much underground, and while there are cavities, they are too small to risk arriving in.*"

"*Then he's still there. Either he's dead from the fall or he's too weak to leave.*" A pause. "*Stay and watch, but be careful – there are more of them about.*"

The presences parted. One continued towards the midpoint between worlds, then moved away from Rielle. She followed, conscious that she must return to a world soon or she would suffocate. Fortunately, the sorcerer travelled at a steady pace, and when he or she suddenly became undetectable Rielle guessed they had entered the world.

By now Rielle could make out a bizarre landscape. Long, narrow pieces of stone were piled up on top of each other, some standing vertically. She skimmed higher and entered the world far above, creating a supporting shield as her lungs sucked air in and out and her head slowly stopped spinning. As soon as the dizziness retreated, she searched for magic and found none. Below, flying creatures were circling an area of fallen stones.

She looked closer. Not creatures, people.

Based on what she'd heard, she guessed they were hovering over the place they'd last seen the man they sought. Was it Tyen? *Who else could it be?* Was he dead? The sorcerers between worlds had spoken of him falling. They hadn't found any sign of a path leading out of the world.

She could try skimming through the piled-up columns in the hopes of finding the cavity Tyen was within, but if it was dark in there, she would never see him. And even if she found some way to let Tyen know she was nearby, how could he signal to her in a way that wouldn't attract the enemy's attention? She considered that for a while, finding no answer. Remembering Tarren's lessons, she thought of one of his sayings: "When the obstruction can't be removed, accept and go around it."

If I can't find him or contact him without attracting attention, then I must plan to attract attention.

Having decided that, she considered how to proceed. She doubted she could lift the stones without others slipping. It would be all too easy to crush Tyen, if he didn't have enough magic left to shield himself, or was unconscious.

If he's conscious . . . Rielle drew in a quick breath. *If he's conscious, all I have to do is create magic and he will get himself out of there.* Then she sobered. *If I create magic Kettin will know I was here and probably took part in Zeke's rescue. Nobody else in the worlds can do what I do, as far as I know.*

Did that matter?

Not as much as Tyen's life.

She smiled. Drawing upon her magic, Rielle heated the air and started a light show that the sorcerers below her would never forget.

CHAPTER 17

To her surprise, Kettin's sorcerers didn't attack. Instead they hovered between her and the ground and drew in magic. She assumed this was in order to prevent magic reaching Tyen, but when she looked into their minds she only saw a guilty greed. Kettin did not like her sorcerers collecting too much magic. They weren't sure how much was too much, but each had decided they would not stop until one of their fellows did.

So distracted were they, that none saw the ghostly figure skim past them. It shot towards Rielle and she froze in alarm, but as it slowed down to meet her, she recognised it, and her heart lifted. Tyen.

He smiled, and she grinned in reply. Taking what remained of the magic she had created, she pushed into the place between worlds, grabbed his outstretched hand and propelled them away.

If the sorcerers followed, they did so too slowly, as she sensed nothing of them. Not a presence between the worlds or a mind within one. She decided to avoid the trail she, Tyen and Dahli had created on their approach to Kettin's worlds, in case they led the sorcerers to Dahli and Zeke. Knowing, now, that the machine army was a great ring, expanding as fast as worlds could be conquered and machines made, she simply headed outwards, figuring they would pass through the front line eventually.

As before, they travelled near enough to arrival places that they could be sure they were heading for habitable worlds, but far enough away that no other travellers would detect them. The same pattern of dead worlds broken by the occasional untouched but weak one continued. The only change was that the dead worlds grew slowly more freshly devastated. But on this route, perhaps because the journey inwards hadn't been through worlds so badly damaged, or because she had been too distracted by the challenge of rescuing Zeke, the ruination and suffering were harder to ignore.

In one world, they glimpsed a vast, fresh graveyard. Graves at the edges were still being dug by people who had returned to their home world to give the dead a proper funeral. The air was tainted with the sickly scent of rot, even high above the ground.

In another, they entered a silent, smoking city of broken walls. Bodies filled the streets, a thick ring of them around the arrival place. The stench made them both gag and she quickly pushed on.

In the next, they found an idyllic agricultural landscape dotted with still-twitching bodies of domestic animals and a colourfully garbed people.

In the following, machines cluttered the sky. The unearthly sound of countless voices, mingled in terror, pain or plea, rose from a large town.

"Wait," Tyen said. She looked at him in surprise.

"Do you want to help them?" she asked, hoping that he would agree but seeing many reasons why they couldn't stop here.

He blinked, then his expression was grim as he met her eyes. "I didn't even think of that. What is wrong with me? Have I become too used to the carnage already? All I thought was that I could learn something about their strategy."

"Which would be good, too, but you also know we risk too much by lingering," she told him. "We have to find Dahli and help him get Zeke back to the Restorers as quickly as possible, so you and he can find a way to stop this happening, or it will be the fate of all worlds."

345

He seemed to not hear her. His mouth had slackened into an expression of shock, then hardened into disgust and he looked away.

"These people are preying upon each other even as they die. Let's go."

She pushed out of the world, bearing him away from the scene, thankful for the emotion-damping effect of the place between. The next world was occupied by only a few small tribes, clinging to life in a savage ice world weak in magic. The one after was more populated, with three small cities within a day's walk of the arrival place. Once again, Tyen spoke.

"Let's warn them. I will feel better about not helping the other world if we give these people a chance to evacuate."

Rielle nodded. "You skim from here."

His grip on her hand tightened, and their surroundings faded a little, then blurred past. Tyen brought them down into the closest city, in front of a large building that finely dressed people were entering and leaving. Their arrival attracted some interest and, from the minds of those who paused to look at them, Rielle learned that otherworld visitors had become more common recently, and that this was where the leader of the land resided.

Walking inside, they requested an audience and were granted one immediately. The local ruler, a middle-aged woman, greeted them warmly.

"What the people of Pwain can do for you?" she asked in halting Traveller tongue.

"We ask and need nothing of you," Tyen replied. "We only come to warn you that an army greater and crueller than any the worlds has faced is coming this way."

"If you begin organising now, you may be able to evacuate all of the people of this world in time," Rielle added.

The Queen shook her head, her expression sad and resigned. "We thank you for your warning, but we know of this threat. Many have warned us. We have sought refuge in other worlds further from the threat until the army has passed and we can return and rebuild, but all have refused us."

Tyen scowled. "That is shameful."

The Queen nodded. "We ask nothing more than what we did for the people of Yoomtk. But all worlds know they face the same fate, and do not wish to squander their stores of food and water on feeding refugees when it could be stockpiled to sustain those of their own people who survive." She sighed. "Have you any advice on how we might endure this invasion?"

Tyen shook his head. "Only to not be here when the machines arrive. They cannot be bargained with or bribed."

"I have heard that they leave some worlds untouched," the woman said. "The only common feature of these worlds is that they contain little magic. Do you think the machines would ignore our world if it was stripped of magic?"

Tyen's eyebrows rose as he considered. He looked at Rielle. "What do you think?"

She considered the idea carefully. The last world they had passed through was a natural candidate for Kettin's sorcerers to use as a stepping-stone world, and if this one contained any resources, she doubted the lack of magic would save it. But who was she to rob these people of hope, or a slim chance of saving themselves?

"It is worth trying," she replied. "Do you speak for all of the people of this world?"

The Queen spread her hands. "I did when we sought a safe haven. If it works, they will not mind me making the decision. If it doesn't, there will be nobody left to resent it."

Rielle sighed. "I fear you are right." She looked at Tyen. "I see no wrong in trying."

He nodded.

"Then I ask that you take all the magic of our world," the Queen said, a glint of hope igniting in her eyes as her back straightened. "And whatever payment you ask for in return we will give."

"No payment . . ." Rielle and Tyen both said simultaneously.

Then Tyen smiled and glanced at Rielle. "We will consider the magic more than enough exchange."

"And I will return one day, when I know it is safe to do so, and restore your world," Rielle added.

The Queen's eyes widened. "You are her?" she said in a hushed voice. "The Restorer?"

Rielle inclined her head.

"I am honoured to meet you."

"Thank you." As an old, familiar discomfort returned, Rielle turned to Tyen. "We cannot delay much longer, Tyen."

He nodded. "This will not take long." He bowed to the Queen. "I hope, for the sake of all your people, that this does dissuade Kettin's army from destroying your world." He bowed. "Good luck, your Majesty."

The Queen inclined her head, her eyes still wide as she regarded Tyen, thinking that maybe he was another legendary figure of the worlds. The name was familiar . . .

Then everything went black to Rielle's senses. After a few heartbeats, her mind adjusted to the lack of magic. Tyen let out a long breath.

"It is done."

The Queen straightened. "Thank you."

Tyen nodded to acknowledge the thanks, then took Rielle's hand. The world and its Queen quickly faded from sight.

Several worlds later they reached one they recognised. They stopped to rest and eat, buying food in one of the many huge inter-world trading markets and skimming to the outskirts to get away from the bustle of traders and buyers. At first, they ate in appreciative silence, as the food was good and, at least to Rielle, a bittersweet pleasure after all the death and ruin they had seen. But Tyen did not seem to be enjoying his. A haunted look had crept into his eyes.

"What is it?" she asked.

He blinked and looked up. "Nothing."

She raised her eyebrows in disbelief, and he winced.

"Nothing more than the usual shock at what people are willing to do to each other." He sighed. "When you asked if we should try to save those people . . . I looked into their minds, then wished I hadn't done so." He frowned, and shook his head. "There is always that question: do you look or not? It is wrong to ignore the suffering of others, but what we see may be so . . . so awful that it changes us. Perhaps for the worse."

"What did you see?"

He glanced at her, then away. "I will spare you the details . . . but they had turned on each other. For distraction, and a savage kind of pleasure. The certainty of their death was the excuse they gave themselves, as well as the knowledge that nobody would be left to punish them, and they wouldn't survive to feel guilt."

She reached out to take his hand and squeezed it. "And yet in some of the conquered worlds we saw it was clear the people behaved bravely and honourably to the end, some sacrificing themselves to protect others, despite the hopelessness of their situation."

He nodded. Swallowed. Drew in a deep breath and let it out. "What is it, I wonder, that makes some groups of people behave better than others?"

"I don't know." Rielle shrugged. "But perhaps what is valued and what is discouraged in that society has a part in it. In my world, everyone's sense of value relied upon feeling superior to others in some way. They would not think twice to harm another for their own benefit, or that of their family. I would not be surprised if they turned on each other if faced with a threat such as Kettin's armies. I've seen worlds where every person is seen to have a value, even if it is not obvious, or there is a philosophy that if the weak are made stronger then all are stronger. I think those people would protect each other to the end."

Tyen nodded. "Leratia is a strange combination of both. The empire is seen to be benefiting all, so most would fight to defend it, but it is also a society divided by class, in which the powerful have used the idea of improving and modernising the world to excuse doing terrible things to those they've conquered – as well as the weak and poor, who they believe have squandered their chances even while they exploit them." He let out a soft, bitter laugh. "Machines were supposed to benefit all, partly by taking over simple, low-paid jobs, partly by enabling an accuracy that humans can't provide. It will come as a shock to those who believe such things to learn what the worlds have done with mechanical magic."

A chill ran down Rielle's spine as she remembered the machine Zeke had been working on. Tyen was not going to be happy to know what that invention was being moulded into.

"What is it?" Tyen asked.

She looked up to find him watching her intently. The word "nothing" came to her lips, but he was as likely to believe that as she had been when Tyen had said it. Instead, she sighed.

"Bad news. Kettin is developing a humanoid like the one you made and I destroyed. Zeke was working on it. She had him experimenting with melding machines and people, and from what I saw of Zeke's memories, the results haven't been pleasant."

Tyen's expression flattened, and his gaze fixed on the ground. "I made another, but it disappeared. Did she take it, I wonder? Or did one of Liftre's inventors take it, and she discovered it among them later?"

These were not questions for her, so Rielle remained silent.

"I doubt it's possible," he added, his voice low. He said no more, brooding as he finished his meal, eating with no sign of awareness that he was. When he was done, Rielle rose and extended a hand.

"Dahli said they would wait a while in Orgajika."

Tyen nodded and climbed to his feet. "Let's go then."

As he took her hand, she pushed out of the world and sent them into the whiteness. Though they were still some distance from their destination, she found her way easily, as most of the route was familiar. When, at last, they approached the world of Orgajika, she skimmed a little way from the arrival place, taking them high above and to the wide horizontal bough of one of the jungle trees. Tyen regarded her knowingly.

"Wary?" he asked.

She nodded. "I want to find them first – if they're even here. See what they're planning."

"And be sure Dahli hasn't set an ambush for us?"

She frowned. "I don't think he'd do that."

"No? What if it would save Zeke?" He held her gaze. "What was he like when he found Zeke?"

"Relieved, mostly. I had to talk him out of killing a guard."

"Is he as obsessed with Zeke as he was with Valhan?"

Rielle considered. "Not in the same way. Valhan never loved him in return."

"So he's potentially even more ruthlessly devoted."

"Potentially. But . . . he does seem changed. I *was* able to talk him out of killing that guard. At least I hope I did." She shook her head. "It's more that he respects Zeke's sense of right and wrong. As if he relies on Zeke to set the rules. I'd be more worried about him if Zeke died or left him."

Tyen nodded as he considered that. "I was worried he'd grab Zeke and abandon you."

"Me too. But instead he decided to deal with Zeke's guard while I took Zeke away."

"He trusted you. Interesting."

She shrugged. "He knows I would not easily harm any person."

"Nor I." Tyen frowned, then shook his head. "I don't think we should trust him fully, though."

"No."

"But we need Zeke." He looked down at the complex of interconnecting walkways below. Following the direction of his gaze, Rielle noted the high-water mark below the boards. This world was subject to great tides, but the life native to it was well adapted to the surges. She extended her senses towards the arrival place, then in a spiral outwards, searching for familiar minds among the locals.

"Found them," Tyen said, then directed her to Dahli and Zeke's location. The pair were sitting together in a drinking establishment. Zeke's mind swum with memories and emotions, both of which obviously pained him. Dahli watched him, tense with concern.

"I can mute those memories," Dahli offered.

"No," Zeke said firmly. "Not until I'm sure the Restorers know everything. We can't risk that you erase an important detail."

Dahli nodded in acceptance, but the knots of worry in him did not loosen. "Then we should leave."

"It's not that I doubt you." Zeke looked up at his lover and sighed. "But I'd feel safer travelling with Tyen and Rielle. If Kettin's spies saw us with those two, they wouldn't dare to attack."

"I can defend you. You can defend me. Rielle made sure we carry plenty of magic. And if Kettin's followers track us here before Tyen and Rielle arrive, we will face the same threat as if they encountered us travelling."

"But travelling means passing through arrival places, where the spies will be watching." Zeke argued. "Kettin's network of spies is more extensive than the Restorers know."

Dahli nodded in reluctant agreement. He placed a hand on Zeke's shoulder. "I did try to get you out of there, after they first took you."

"I believe you," Zeke replied. "I'm glad that you tried, but I'm even gladder that you failed and lived than failed and died."

"I'd have tried again sooner, but I could not convince the Restorers to help."

Zeke shrugged, pretending not to care despite knowing Dahli could see how it hurt. "Why would they? We tried to bring Valhan back. We were their enemy. As far as they know, we still are."

"*I* was their enemy," Dahli corrected. "Not you."

"I chose to be with you. That is the same."

Dahli winced at the guilt that rose in him. Guilt that had once been more powerful, until Zeke had asked if Dahli's memories could be muted instead of erased. Dahli had tried, and found it was possible. "You chose not to be, before then, and you were right to. I was a monster. If it weren't for you—"

"Don't." Zeke scowled. "We've been down that path too often."

Dahli hung his head.

"Everyone will need to put aside their old hatreds and arguments soon," Zeke said, more as a statement to the worlds than to Dahli. "Something far worse is coming. The longer we wait, the stronger it gets."

"How long do we have?"

Zeke shook his head. "I don't know. Kettin said she believed that machines will, one day, be able to do everything that sorcerers can do."

"Travel between worlds?"

Zeke nodded. "Read minds. Pattern-shifting. Everything." He swallowed, his mouth suddenly dry as his memories took him back to the laboratory. "She wants to be part machine. She believes humans are too flawed. We are just animals, acting on instinct and emotion. She will become something better."

"She sounds quite mad."

Zeke let out a bitter laugh. "Yes. She has a cold, merciless kind of madness." He shuddered, then shifted to look at Dahli. "Oh, I wish Tyen and Rielle would hurry up. There is so much to tell, and the sooner the better."

Rielle looked up at Tyen. He nodded. Taking her hand, he stepped forward off the limb, but did not fall. She joined him, and her stomach swooped as they dropped down towards the drinking establishment, landing in front of the entrance. A customer about to leave yelped in surprise, attracting the attention of those still inside, including Dahli and Zeke. The pair rose and strode over to meet Rielle and Tyen.

Dahli smiled. "Perfect timing," he said, holding out a hand and taking Zeke's with the other. "Let's not keep Qall waiting any longer."

"Qall?" Zeke echoed. "Qall is with the Restorers now?"

Rielle smiled. "Qall is leader of the Restorers now."

Zeke's mouth lifted in a lopsided smile. "Well, he must have grown up these last five and a half cycles."

Tyen chuckled. "He certainly has." As he took Zeke's other hand, Rielle felt the jungle world slip away, and all faded to white as they plunged into the place between worlds.

CHAPTER 18

None of the sulking boy Rielle had protected more than five cycles ago was evident in Qall as he greeted the men and women arriving for the Restorers' war council. Rielle could not help looking for something of Valhan, but nothing in his manner reminded her of the dead ruler either. This was the man Qall had grown into in her world, adapting easily to yet another demanding situation.

She felt pride and wondered if she would ever have children of her own and feel this way about them. *Well, apart from occasionally fearing they'll be taken over by a dead sorcerer's mind.*

Looking around, she scanned the thoughts of the ambassadors, rulers, generals and military advisers, as Qall had suggested. It was not a pleasant experience. Several were representatives of worlds that had been destroyed by Kettin, and had seen mass slaughter. Memories of it weren't far from their thoughts. The sorcerers from worlds under threat who were powerful enough to read their counterparts' minds were growing ever more anxious and afraid.

Drawn together by mutual interest and profession, the generals and martial experts of the Restorers and allies were sizing each other up, their conversation designed to reveal the limits of knowledge and influence of each other, and the potential hierarchy of the army they expected would form under Qall.

A pitifully small group hovered nervously around Tyen. The few inventors who had avoided Kettin's abductions and assassinations were all too aware that they would be dead without the Restorers' protection. Some were a little in awe of the man who had brought mechanical magic into the worlds, though they knew he hadn't invented it. They were all excited by the prospect of going to the world where it had originated, even if some were worried that if they found a way to destroy all machines, their main source of income in future would also be eliminated.

Rielle could not help thinking there ought to be another group to examine. Baluka had left to meet with the Travellers and hadn't returned in time for the meeting. Earlier appeals for their help had resulted in polite refusals. She couldn't blame them. They had lost many powerful sorcerers in the fight with Dahli, including Ulma, their only ageless sorcerer. They did not fear the machines in the same way they had feared Valhan's return, so they had returned to their former policy of avoiding involvement in the conflicts of the worlds.

The door to the meeting room opened again, and as each pair of eyes fell upon the two men entering the room, a shocked silence spread.

Dahli had changed his appearance back to what it had been when she had first met him. Rielle sought the reason in his mind and learned that Qall did not want to lie about him. Qall had suggested that, if Dahli did not hide his identity and took a major part in saving the worlds from Kettin, it was possible some would forgive him. Not all, and probably not enough that they would ever consider him trustworthy, but it was better that Dahli earn a little forgiveness than none at all.

Zeke didn't like it, but he trusted Qall. He was impressed by the man Qall had become in the last five cycles.

"Zeke. Dahli," Qall said, striding forward to meet the pair. "Thank you for coming. Please join us." He stepped between the pair, turned and placed a hand on each man's shoulder, then raised his voice so all could hear. "I have called everybody here today to discuss the advance of Kettin's army, and what we can do about

356

it. Vital to this meeting will be the information provided by these two men. You all know of Dahli, formerly the Raen's most loyal servant. Many of you do not know Zeke, former inventor of Liftre. They joined together more than five cycles ago to secretly search for a means to disable war machines, and came close to success. Their efforts were ruined when Kettin abducted Zeke and forced him to work in her machine-inventing laboratories. Dahli, Rielle and Tyen recently rescued him from Kettin's base world. What he has to tell you of Kettin's abilities and intentions will be invaluable to us all in the coming days." Qall paused to look around the room, meeting all gazes, his expression serious. "The threat we face is immense and frightening. We will not survive it if we do not unite, even if that means joining with old enemies. Dahli once meant to do great harm to me. I have put aside all feelings against him. I trust that he will help us." Qall's mouth twitched up into a smile. "I *know* that he will. He doesn't want the worlds ruled by machines any more than you do. So please, sit down and listen to what he and Zeke have to tell you."

The silence had turned tense and a little sullen. Now it was broken by the shuffle of feet as everyone moved to the tables, which had been set in a large square. Qall sat at the centre on one side, Zeke to his left and Dahli to his right. Tyen moved to the place beside Zeke and Rielle to Dahli's right, as had been decided earlier. It was no surprise to Rielle that the inventors hurriedly took the places next to Tyen, but she was intrigued to find the generals and military strategists moving to her side. As Hapre took the seat beside Rielle, their eyes met, and the general inclined her head in respect. Rielle nodded in reply.

The woman leaned forward. "How do you stand working with him?" she murmured, her gaze flickering towards Dahli.

Rielle shrugged. "I will not say it is easy, but it is necessary."

"You already know what they have to say," Hapre stated.

"Yes."

The woman straightened. "This had better be good information."

When all had settled, Qall turned to Zeke. "Tell us your story, Zeke."

The young inventor glanced around at the watching faces, then lowered his eyes. "Ah . . . as Qall said, Dahli and I had been working on a way to disable war machines, and we had finally come up with a viable method. Dahli had always warned me against travelling on my own to buy supplies, but I was excited by our new idea and too impatient to wait for him to join me. I was gathering parts when Kettin's followers found me.

"We knew that the inventors of the Liftre school of sorcery had formed an independent group dedicated to making machines for profit, including war machines, but we hadn't heard that they had a new leader. I asked one of the inventors why they had chosen her to become their leader, and he said she had chosen them. They had banned women from their ranks, but she simply ignored that rule and started bossing them around, getting away with it through a mixture of charm and threat and grand ideas.

"He couldn't or wouldn't tell me what her intentions were, but he believed she would make inventors the most powerful people in the worlds. They were superior to all existing rulers, she said, because they were more intelligent. Only their lesser magical ability stopped them from being in charge, but with machines they could weaken and control stronger sorcerers. They would have to do some terrible things for her, but it would bring about a new age where magical strength didn't determine who was superior. They would rule the worlds." Zeke shook his head. "Some of them believed in this; some didn't, but after seeing her strategy in action they figured she would be unstoppable and they had better take the side that would win."

He sighed. "I wasn't the only inventor who refused to be a part of what she was proposing. There were several. She didn't kill us; she put us to work. Each unwilling inventor has a partner whose task it is to guard us and read our thoughts. They present us with problems and watch for any solutions we think of. I knew of a possible weakness in my machine-combatting devices, so it wasn't long before I had unwillingly invented a way to exploit it. That got Kettin's attention.

"She questioned me and read from my mind that I had worked with Tyen once." Zeke glanced at Tyen. "She had my partner bring out a large box, and when it was opened I recognised a machine Tyen had made. It was a machine in the shape of a human – a humanoid. She told me to study it and then make another. When I had done that, she asked if I could put a mind in it." Zeke shook his head. "I didn't think it possible, but she insisted I start working on the problem. I've been working on it ever since – I mean, until I was rescued.

"At first I tried to make a mechanical mind. Though I had some success, it was many, many times larger than the humanoid's skull. Then one night I dreamed that the people around me were turning into machines, their clothes hiding mechanical limbs. She liked that idea and ordered me to pursue it. Instead of trying to create a human mind to put in a machine, I was to replace a human's limbs and organs until all that was left was their mind."

He shook his head. "If I tried not to think about it, they tortured people in front of me. If I did not do the work myself, my partner did it for me. Either way, many died. I lost count of how many. The more progress we made, the longer they lived, but, more often than not, that just extended their torment." He shuddered. "If I could have hidden my thoughts I'd have pretended to have had greater success, as Kettin was entranced by the idea of becoming a machine and eager to transform herself, and then we might have been rid of her."

He looked at Qall. "We'd had some success in replacing limbs with machine versions, but not organs. I can only assume that she had chosen me to work on the task because I was the best of the inventors, but I know there are other laboratories, as other inventors' partners spoke as if they were competing with at least three different groups."

He turned back to the audience. "All groups were working on weapons. Kettin believes that whatever sorcerers can do, machines will eventually be able to do as well. Reading minds. Travelling between worlds. Pattern-shifting. I saw no sign that anyone had come close to achieving these things, but I did catch glimpses of some very sophisticated machines. Some were being developed to attach to a person and feed them drugs, and cause them both pain and pleasure, as a way to control them. Other inventors were looking for faster ways to conquer a world, drain all the magic, extract materials and make more machines. Not long before I was rescued I heard they had developed a method that would enable a single sorcerer to fill an entire world with machines instantly rather than several transporting them in batches."

Zeke shook his head. "Every day Kettin's inventors find new and faster ways to destroy. Every day the possibility that she could be defeated grows smaller. It may seem that she is focused on simply spreading outwards, conquering worlds as she encounters them, but from the kinds of problems I saw inventors working to solve, she doesn't intend to keep doing that. Eventually she will target specific worlds. The sooner you deal with her, the easier it will be. And by easy I mean less impossible."

A hum of concern rose among the listeners, and many exchanged glances. The representatives of conquered and threatened worlds alike looked pointedly towards the generals and military strategists, who frowned but did not return the stares. Seeking minds, Rielle saw that some of the latter thought that Kettin was a threat that would remain far away for some time, so they had plenty of time to plan, study the enemy and gather support. But Zeke had sowed a seed of doubt.

Zeke turned back to Qall and nodded. "I think that is all."

Qall inclined his head. "Thank you, Zeke. Does anybody have questions for Zeke?"

A brief pause followed, in which glances were exchanged in order to check if someone more important was about to speak.

One ambassador, determined to make sure his people had a voice in this struggle, blurted out a question.

"She hates sorcerers, but she kills everyone in a world. Why?"

A shiver went through Zeke as he remembered the guards discussing this. "She believes that humans are just sophisticated animals. Most are savage, wild creatures that prey on each other. Some have the potential to be domesticated. By culling to the best people, she will tame the human race, and make it better."

A shocked silence followed. "This is worse than we feared," one of the generals said.

"The worlds have faced nothing like it," another replied. "Conquest for the sake of conquest seems strangely benign in comparison."

"You say she resents sorcerers their power," another ambassador said, "but she is one. How does she reason around that?"

Zeke grimaced. "My partner explained that she grew up in a near-dead world among people abused by those in power, and when her world was restored, the imbalance only became worse. When she found herself strong in magic, she despised herself for being more like her oppressors than her own people. She decided to use magic – and machines – to help others, placing those who are smarter but weak into the positions of authority they deserved." He swallowed. "Not just in her world, but all worlds."

"How long do *you* think it will take before she is able to start targeting specific worlds?"

"I can't guess." Zeke shook his head. "It could be days or a cycle. If she was waiting for me to make her into a machine, then my rescue may delay her. Or she may decide there's no reason to wait any longer."

"Do you know what vulnerabilities the inventors in your laboratory were working on?" Hapre asked.

Zeke nodded. "Some. Several were working on the problem of control. At the moment, machines have a trigger that, once turned on, can't be turned off. If commands or signals control them, a stronger sorcerer could read of them from the operator's mind and turn the machines off. Some more complicated machines are controlled with a device that uses sounds too high for a human to hear and self-destructs if it is removed from the operator, but there's still the risk the operator will be coerced into cooperating with an enemy."

"So the operators could easily become the victims of their own machines?" a general asked.

"I heard rumours that some were, in the beginning. Kettin lost a good inventor. She started sending out the less clever ones to attack worlds, along with sorcerers who joined her that aren't inventors. I know someone came up with a way of imprinting the operator's identity onto the machines so they ignore them. I don't know what it is, and I believe the operators don't know how it works either, so it can't be read from their minds."

"Do you know how many worlds Kettin has conquered so far?" another general asked.

Zeke shook his head. "Nobody spoke of that," he explained. "I only know what I overheard or the partners or guards told us."

"So you don't know of any weaknesses in her strategy for conquering worlds?"

"No." Zeke's shoulders lifted. "I wish I could be of more help."

"You have been already," Qall assured him. He looked at the general. "We have reports from worlds already conquered to illustrate Kettin's methods. Are there any more questions for Zeke?"

Several more questions came, tackling more specific details. Then a quiet fell over the room. Qall looked around and nodded.

"Zeke's information is a much-needed breakthrough after a half-cycle of frustrated attempts to learn more about Kettin and her followers. We have lost hundreds of scouts, and those few that have returned have given us limited knowledge. Though we have plenty of reports from refugees of conquered worlds, most escaped their world before or just after the conquest began and so have limited insight into how the machine army operates after the initial attack.

"During their mission, Dahli, Rielle and Tyen found that some displaced people have managed to get back to their worlds to start rebuilding their lives and homes. Kettin must know of this, so she is allowing it – for now. This sign that hosting refugees could be temporary may convince reluctant worlds that their kindness will not cost them more than they can give.

"As for Kettin . . . I am in agreement with Zeke and many of you here. We can't sit back and wait. We must gather an army and attack as soon as possible." He turned to Tyen. "At the same time, we must continue seeking a way to disable war machines. Tyen will be working on that problem. Zeke and Dahli will join him."

Looking at Tyen, Rielle saw him stiffen and look at Qall, his eyes narrowing and his mouth opening.

"We will take a break now to eat and discuss this," Qall finished. "If you have any ideas or additional information, please speak to me."

As he rose, the rest of the room followed suit. Tyen closed his mouth, approached Qall and grabbed his arm.

"We need to talk," he said. "Privately."

Qall smiled faintly. "I thought we might. Come into the next room."

Stepping around Dahli, Rielle followed them to a door opposite the main entrance of the room. As Qall opened it he looked back at Tyen, and his eyes flickered to Rielle.

"You too?" he asked, then beckoned. "Come on then."

She followed Tyen through. The door had barely closed when he spoke.

"I will *not* allow Dahli into my home world!"

Qall's eyebrows rose. "Do you not think it cruel to separate them when they've only just been united?"

"That's not reason enough to risk exposing my world and

spoiling our chances of finding a way to combat the war machines!"

"You exaggerate," Qall said calmly. "Dahli and Zeke spent five cycles searching for a way to stop war machines. Why would they do anything to foil that search now? And you know your world can't remain hidden for ever, Tyen. Yes, you would prefer to hide it until it is stronger, but I doubt it will be ready before Kettin reaches it. Your world's best chance now lies in finding a way to stop the war machines, and for that you need Zeke to be there and not distracted by worry about his lover."

Tyen scowled. "I don't need to be distracted by worrying about what Dahli is up to at the same time as leading the Academy, keeping the Emperor on side and finding a way to defeat the machines."

"Nobody needs any of this, Tyen," Qall said. "Did you think—"

He stopped at the sound of the door opening and closing. They all turned to find Zeke standing before it, staring at them defiantly. The young inventor's gaze moved from Rielle to Qall and settled on Tyen.

"I don't have to read your mind to know what this is about," he said. "You don't want Dahli in your world. I understand why. He has done terrible things. But you *have* to take him, Tyen. Not just because I won't be parted from him, but because he is not the man you believe him to be. Do you really think I would still be with him if he was?"

Tyen's steely gaze softened a little. "You're in love, Zeke. You only see—"

"That's rubbish, Tyen, and you know it," Zeke snapped. "He has told me some of what Valhan had him do. Things you can't even imagine. Things that would make anyone fall out of love with a person. I would have, but for knowing how much the memory of it torments him. Would it, if he was the person you think he is? He does not blame it all on the Raen, or use his love for the man as an excuse. He did it to survive. He could have chosen to die rather than do things he knew to be wrong, but he didn't. The only way he has been able to live with himself is by muting his memories – and he only did that because I made him do it." Zeke walked forward to stand in front of Tyen, his gaze direct and unwavering. "He will not harm your world. Not just because I don't want him to. He knows he wouldn't survive it."

Tyen stared back, searching and uncertain. Then he blinked and turned to look at Rielle. "What do you think?"

She hesitated, surprised that he was asking her. Looking at Zeke, she measured the certainty in his mind.

"Dahli *has* changed," she acknowledged. "Zeke has changed him."

"No." Zeke turned to her. "I have only helped him change *back* to who he really is: the man he was before Valhan's influence warped and distorted him. He has done all of the work, facing the worst of his memories, sacrificing strengths for vulnerabilities, resisting the instincts learned over hundreds of years."

She regarded him solemnly. "Even so, you don't know how much of this . . . reversion is due to you and how much due to him facing his conscience." She looked at Qall. "If Tyen doesn't want Dahli there, I support him. Tyen apologised for the harm he did, but Dahli has not."

Zeke opened his mouth to speak but stopped as the door opened again. Before they could turn to see who it was, a familiar voice revealed his identity.

"Stop it, Zeke," Dahli said. He closed the door, then looked at Tyen. "It's your world. If you don't want me there, that is your choice. If an apology is required, then I offer this: I am deeply sorry for the harm I've done to you, your friends and loved ones."

Tyen's gaze shifted to Dahli and his eyes narrowed. For a long moment the pair stared at each other. Tyen's lips pressed together, then relaxed. "You may accompany Zeke, but you must promise on his life that you will not harm my world or anyone in it, or reveal its location. Will you accept that condition?"

Dahli inclined his head. "I do."

"Don't make me regret this," Tyen warned. "If you do I will put aside my feelings about violence and hunt you down."

"I understand."

Frowning deeply, Tyen turned to Qall. "And I don't think our friendship would survive it," he added.

Qall nodded. "I would regret that for all my remaining years, Tyen. Please, trust me that I believe, having considered all that I know, that this decision is best. I only wish it was the most difficult one we are going to have to make in the days ahead." He sighed and turned towards the door. "Now, our allies have begun to wonder where I am, and if I intend to answer all their questions as I promised, not just yours, I had best talk to them. Let's return to the meeting room."

PART SIX

TYEN

CHAPTER 16

As the walls of the Grand Hall resolved around Tyen and his companions, they darkened to a shadowed gloom. The sound of feet landing on the floor, along with the heavy clunk of the crate Tyen had brought with him, signalled their arrival. He sought minds and found those of the two watchers he had employed to keep the hall clear of obstacles.

The room brightened as the pair realised someone had arrived. They immediately tensed as they saw the people surrounding Tyen, all with their heads covered with thick black sacks.

Reaching over to Zeke and Dahli, Tyen removed the coverings. The pair blinked and looked around.

"We're here?" Zeke asked.

"Yes," Tyen replied. "Welcome to the Academy." He raised his voice. "You may all take off your hoods."

The three other inventors divested themselves of the sacks and took in their surroundings. Tyen turned and beckoned to the watchers. They approached warily, eyeing these otherworld strangers with curiosity and a little fear. From their minds Tyen learned that it was early morning.

"I ordered that the hall be brightly lit at all times," Tyen reminded the young men, keeping his tone firm but not angry. "Why was it not?"

The pair winced. "Ah . . . I apologise, Director," one said. "We were told to avoid wasting magic."

Tyen checked the magic in the area. "There's still plenty here," he observed. "Safety is of greater importance. What if I had not been able to see someone walking across the hall as we arrived? They may have melded with this crate, or worse – with these visitors?"

The young man blanched. "It won't happen again, Director."

Tyen nodded and smiled. "I'm sure it won't. Now, could one of you please inform Halyn Wardlamp that I have arrived, then go on to find Tarren and bring him here."

"Halyn. Tarren." The watcher hurried away. Tyen continued reading the other watcher's mind. They had been worried that Tyen would be angry about the order to avoid wasting magic, as it had come from one of the professors who had left the Academy in protest. The man had returned and started rousing opposition to Tyen's leadership in the institution.

Taking advantage of my absence. How many are taking him seriously? Tyen wondered. *Have any of the others who left in protest returned?* Since they had left voluntarily, no rule prevented them from taking a place in the school, though they could not be reinstated to their former positions without his permission.

He would have the answers to his questions soon enough. Ushering Dahli and the inventors over to the crate, he asked one of them to help him open it. Soon they had exposed a carefully and compactly stacked pile of broken and depleted machines collected from conquered worlds. Stepping back to regard them, it struck him that they looked very different to anything his world had ever produced. Machine knowledge had evolved and expanded rapidly in the last ten cycles. The Academy could be too far behind now to find a solution to the machine threat. Was there any real benefit to having it work on the problem?

Perhaps the only reason to do so was because his world was, so far, a safe and hidden place.

The inventors had separated the machines into five neat piles when hurried footsteps drew Tyen's attention away. To his dismay, the very man who had ordered the watcher keep the Grand Hall dim was striding towards him. Professor Bargeman was followed by two teachers. One was reassuring himself that all three of them were strong sorcerers and surely would be equal to Tyen's strength. Tyen would have been more amused by that if it wasn't clear they had done enough in his absence that they expected him to grow angry enough to be a threat.

"Tyen Ironsmelter," Bargeman bellowed, his voice echoing in the hall. "I see you've deigned to return to us."

Tyen straightened and turned to face the men, keeping his posture relaxed and unthreatening. "Bargeman," he replied calmly. "It is good of you to welcome me home. I see you have decided to join us again."

Bargeman's chin lifted. "I have, as have many of my colleagues – many who were alarmed by your changes to this fine and ancient institution without consultation with and agreement from its members. We are arranging an investigation and require you to present yourself for questioning."

"If that is what is required to reassure everyone of their necessity, then I am happy to oblige." Tyen looked to the two teachers. Their attention had been captured by the machines, and one was thinking that they were the most sinister contraptions he'd ever seen. The other looked at Tyen, wondering if the new Director's true purpose was much darker than was apparent.

Tyen hid a smile. He had wondered how he might convince Academy members that a great deal of its resources should go towards finding a defence against Kettin's machines. Perhaps this teacher's reaction to the machines was a hint that he wouldn't have to do much more than show them what Kettin had created.

A new voice echoed in the hall. "Tyen Ironsmelter. Welcome home."

All turned to see a lean, tall man walking towards them from the entrance on the other side of the hall.

"Halyn Wardlamp," Tyen said as the man neared. "Thank you. Has the Academy been behaving itself in my absence?"

Halyn inclined his head towards the newcomers as he passed them and came to a stop before Tyen. "The place is still standing, as are most of its members and staff. A few squabbles here and there kept us entertained, and most sorted out. I'm sure you'll deal with the rest easily enough."

Tyen knew his choice of Halyn as stand-in Director while he was away had surprised many. The reasons for it were twofold. The Academy needed all its sorcerers and teachers engaged in study and instruction, especially now it had lost a few key members. Halyn wasn't a professor, teacher or sorcerer but a former assistant to one of the professors who had quit the Academy. Tyen had also been looking for someone efficient but not ambitious. Halyn had not worked for his former employer out of loyalty, but simply because it had been the best job he could get. He gained great pleasure in bringing order from chaos and believed the Academy's purpose should be to make sense out of the mysteries of the world. He would be the last person to let the institution fall into a heap while its Director was away.

I wonder . . . perhaps I should make this man my *assistant.*

Halyn glanced at the machines. "Would you like me to have these carried to the mechanical magic wing?"

Tyen shook his head. "Thank you for the offer, Halyn," he replied, "but they will stay here for now." Tyen gestured to the newcomers. "I have brought four inventors and a . . . ah, companion of one of them." It was not clear what Dahli's role would be. "Protector of Zeke" would require more explaining than Tyen needed right now, and the pair preferred to be assumed to be just friends when arriving in a new world, until they knew more about local customs.

He named the five men, then turned back to Halyn. "Now that I have returned, would you like to take the position of Director's assistant?"

Halyn's eyebrows rose. "I would be honoured."

"Excellent. Then your first task is to find accommodation for our new guests."

The man nodded, and his gaze shifted to Dahli. "I believe there is a room available in your hotel, Director."

Tyen nodded, amused to see that his new assistant thought Dahli looked like a man used to power and privilege.

"The inventors may wish to lodge with the those already here, however." Halyn turned back to Tyen. "The Emperor left orders that you report to him as soon as you return. No matter the hour."

"Of course he did. I will head to the palace as soon as I've spoken to Tarren."

Bargeman made a rude noise. "Running straight off to beg the Emperor's help, are we?"

Tyen looked over to the professor, and the two teachers, who were now looking awkward and embarrassed at their leader's outburst.

"Would you suggest I ignore his order?" Tyen asked. "Shall I tell him you expected me to report to him after everyone else?"

The professor flushed. "Of course not. But don't expect us to be swayed by royal favour. This institution is funded as much by generous donations from the aristocracy as from imperial coffers."

Tyen lifted his eyebrows. "Is it really?" He pretended to be considering that thoughtfully, which had the desired effect of making the professor wonder if his threat had actually given his enemy an idea.

"Yes." Bargeman took a step back. "We will summon you when we are ready to begin your interrogation."

Tyen merely nodded and, as the teachers began to edge towards the exit, turned his back. A last look into their thoughts revealed that one of the teachers had been reading Zeke's mind. *He wonders if we're fools*, the man thought. *The sort who are too blinded by our hurt pride and fear of losing power to see the greater danger we're in. What danger? What were those dark memories I glimpsed?* He glanced at the professor's back. *Am I on the wrong side?*

The idea that Zeke's memories might be a tangible way to show people the threat this world faced had already occurred to Tyen, but he didn't want to ask the young inventor to relive what he had endured. If he could convince them in other ways, then he would try those first. One might be to have Zeke touch Vella, who Qall had given back to Tyen on his return from their rescue mission.

He looked at Halyn. "So just another squabble, then?"

Halyn shrugged. "I didn't want to give him the satisfaction of anyone openly admitting his troublemaking is working."

"Fair enough. Has anybody else here requested a meeting?"

"The Librarian," Halyn replied. "As well as several professors and teachers."

Tyen had been expecting a long list of complaints, so it surprised him that Halyn had listed Rytan Kep first. "What does the Librarian want to discuss?"

"He didn't say."

"Anything else I should know?"

Halyn shook his head. "I'll show our guests their accommodation options, then?"

"Yes, please do."

The man turned to the newcomers and bowed. "Please follow me."

Zeke and the inventors obeyed. Dahli hesitated, then moved to Tyen's side.

"Leading suits you, Tyen Ironsmelter," he murmured.

Tyen blinked in surprise, then let out a quiet, bitter laugh. "Maybe one day I'll come to like it, too."

"Better to dislike it, than like it too much." Dahli stepped away and started after the inventors.

Tyen considered Dahli's words as the group entered the far corridor and moved out of sight. He had to admit, the man's praise had given him a small surge of pleasure. Which was immediately followed by doubt and the suspicion that Dahli was manipulating him. Clearly, Dahli had known the compliment would boost Tyen's confidence. After all, Dahli was hundreds of years old and had surely observed many leaders, good and bad.

But Tyen had seen no other intention in the man's mind. It

cost Dahli nothing to say it. *So, what more could it be?* Tyen asked himself.

Dahli's main desire now was to keep Zeke safe. And himself, of course. He hadn't lost his sense of self-preservation. Tyen had also felt a deep protectiveness of the worlds in Dahli, and horror at what Kettin was doing.

Perhaps that's all there was to it. Tyen resolved to put it from his mind until later. Instead, he sought out other minds within the Academy.

First, he found Tarren hurrying towards the Grand Hall. The old man had left several inventors and students studying machines, and they were coming close to a conclusion about them. Curious, Tyen sought out these and found a small group of students working together. Two were from Tyen's loyal circle, while two more were from the Academy. All had gained admiration for the others, for their intellect and different fields of knowledge. That there was unity and respect rather than division and enmity in the Academy lightened Tyen's heart.

Then his attention was drawn away by a voice.

"Tyen!" Tarren said as he entered the hall, speaking Traveller tongue. "Whoa! What is all this?"

Tyen turned to see the old man come to a stop, staring at the machines. "More of Kettin's creations."

"They've evolved." Tarren moved over to one and poked at it. "I fear they're developing faster than we can keep up."

"She has more inventors than we do," Tyen pointed out. "But we have taken one of her best from her. Rielle, Dahli and I rescued Zeke, and I have brought him and Dahli here along with three more inventors."

Tarren's eyes widened as he turned to face Tyen. "Zeke!" Then his brows lowered into a frown. "You bought *Dahli* here?"

"Yes. As Zeke's assistant and protector. Qall insisted it was—"

"Are you sure that's wise?" Tarren interrupted.

Tyen sighed. "Believe me, if I could have avoided it, I would have. This is my home world, after all. But the threat we face . . ." He shook his head. "Greater than the Raen. Greater than the mere proliferation of war machines. Kettin is . . ." He paused, then shook his head. "I don't have time to explain right now. The Emperor wants a report and I'm sure he'd rather I explained it all to him first."

"And we'll be able to do what we need to do much easier if he's on our side," Tarren finished. "But you wanted to see me first."

"Yes. Have you made any progress?"

The old man shrugged and nodded. "Lots of small discoveries. We understand better how the machines work. Components have been getting smaller as they are refined, allowing space for more sophistication. We can almost trace the evolution of the ideas behind them – three or four main branches of them."

"Zeke said Kettin had at least three laboratories containing both willing and captive inventors, all competing with the others."

Tarren nodded. "That would explain it. All the recent machines have an adaptation that seems designed to overcome a weakness. I think this may have been the idea Zeke had before he was captured." His lips stretched in a grim smile. "He will be a welcome addition to the team."

"Anything else the Emperor should know?"

"No. Other than that everyone in our department is getting along better than I expected. I hear that can't be said of others here, but that's nothing you need to deal with now. Go." He waved a hand. "Keep your Emperor happy."

Tyen smiled ruefully. "Oh, he won't be happy when he hears what I have to tell him, but he's no fool. He'll give us all the support he can. Thanks, Tarren."

"Do you want me to move these?" The old man gestured to the machines.

"No. Tell anyone who asks that I've ordered for them to remain where they are – and that nobody is to touch them."

Tarren rubbed together the fingers he'd used to poke at the machines and raised an eyebrow. "Oops. Bad me."

"You should know better, old man," Tyen scolded.

Tarren snorted and made a shooing gesture. "Get out of here, young scoundrel." He paused. "I think I'd better set a proper guard on them. You know some here are moving against you, don't you?"

Tyen smiled ruefully. "Of course. And yes, a guard would be a good idea."

He left, taking the same path Halyn and the newcomers had followed to the stables. There he found a carriage waiting and was told a messenger had been sent on ahead to the palace to warn of his arrival.

Definitely a good choice for my assistant, Tyen mused.

The busy streets of Beltonia outside his carriage were familiar and yet alien. It seemed like a hundred years since he had walked through this city, his concerns only those of a young boy or scholar. The idea of this place being destroyed in a matter of hours, after thousands of years of history, ought to be too incredible to grasp, but he had seen too much, both with his own eyes and through others'. He knew what was possible.

That brought a wave of regret and guilt. *If I hadn't come home, this world would still be poor in magic. Perhaps Kettin would have spared it.* Or not even found it, since the path he'd made when escaping fifteen cycles ago had faded out of existence.

He could leave and try to erase the single path he'd made in and out of the world. The faint traces of his smoothing would fade faster. Kettin's sorcerers might not even know to look for them. *No. If Zeke knows I can be tracked that way, then they know.*

Even so, he doubted that all, if any, of the otherworld sorcerers he'd brought here would want to be forever imprisoned in this world. Someone would eventually leave to see if Kettin still ruled the worlds. If they were found by Kettin or her followers, the location of Tyen's world would be read from their minds.

I could remove all the magic from this world and order the sorcerers who know how to travel between worlds to release their store of magic. It would require the cooperation of too many people, though . . .

The carriage slowed to a stop. He looked out of the window and realised he had arrived at the palace already. As he climbed down and made his way inside, he turned his mind to considering how best to inform the most powerful man in this world of the peril he and his people faced, and the role they must take in fighting it. Break the news gently, or deliver it without preamble?

He hadn't decided by the time he finally arrived at the private suite where their meetings usually took place. Omniten greeted him at the door with a broad smile.

"Tyen Ironsmelter," the man said. "I am glad to see you again, not least because it means you've survived this trouble you spoke of."

There was genuine concern and relief in the Emperor's mind, and for a moment Tyen was humbled and taken aback. Then he returned the smile easily. "It is good to be home," he replied as he bowed. "I only wish I didn't have to spoil the comfort of your good company with bad news."

Omniten made a small grimace. "Ah, I feared you would say that."

"You did?" Tyen smiled. "Who is the mind reader now?"

The man chuckled. "Certainly not me. I only guessed that if two of the most powerful sorcerers in the worlds were concerned, the source of their worry must be dire indeed." He led Tyen over to chairs, set before a gently flickering fire. "And I also ascertained that if you returned with bad news, then you must require help that only this world can provide." He sat down. "So, what is it you need from me?"

Once again, Tyen was taken aback. "But I have not even explained yet," he pointed out.

The Emperor smiled. "No. And I have not yet agreed to

anything. I have merely asked what you require. We shall see if I am able to provide it."

Tyen sat down. "Well then . . . we need the Academy to find ways to disable or defend against the enemy's war machines."

"That is all? Not sorcerers to fight by your side?"

Tyen spread his hands. "Leratia – and the Far South – may have sorcerers of great enough strength, but I fear their training is not yet of a standard to match those who have hundreds of years of experience in using magic, let alone a machine army capable of destroying them. There is no need to risk and sacrifice your people in battle." Tyen paused. "Though if the Academy finds a solution that requires an operator, those operators may have to venture into danger."

Omniten's expression grew serious. "I guess that will be an incentive to find a solution that doesn't require operators." He steepled his fingers and frowned at the fire. "So, tell me about this enemy. Tell me what we are facing."

Tyen nodded, took a deep breath and obeyed.

CHAPTER 17

T wo days later Tyen waited as the Grand Hall filled. Attendance was required of members of the Academy, past and present, who were living close enough to make the journey. Other people of power and influence had also been invited – mainly men, plus a few women, from the aristocracy – as an acknowledgement that they would have an influence upon, and a stake in, the decisions made today.

The room vibrated with the hum of hundreds of voices combined. Tyen skimmed minds, absorbing the general mood. That these few privileged Leratians should make decisions on the safety and future of an entire world seemed wrong, but time was short and the empire had no system in place to inform millions of ordinary citizens of an issue and then collect their responses to it.

He could only hope that these people would understand the danger their world was in, and react to it in a sensible manner.

Halyn emerged from the crowd and walked to Tyen's side. "I think everyone is here."

Tyen nodded. He took one last look at those standing nearby. To his left was a gathering of otherworlders comprising of his former students, Tarren and his students, the inventors Tyen had brought recently, and Zeke and Dahli. To Tyen's right, a large group of Academy students and teachers had formed, and he was pleased to see that they hadn't separated into cliques. Foreign and female students did tend to stand in small groups, but those were spread among the rest.

Tyen had chosen to stand near Kettin's machines, at the rear of the Grand Hall. Professor Bargeman and his supporters formed a small crowd in the middle of the hall, between Tyen and the main doors. Tyen knew from the minds he'd read that many of those opposing his leadership and changes to the Academy were circulating in the crowd, raising their objections with anyone willing to listen. Which meant that many, not knowing the reason for their summoning to this place, were assuming this was another challenge to Tyen's leadership.

A few of Tyen's supporters had noticed this and begun interrupting such conversations, arguing in the new Director's defence and pointing out that his worthiness was not under discussion today. One man in particular was quietly moving about, injecting into conversations that the Academy had best stop squabbling and focus on more important issues. When Tyen finally caught a glimpse of this man, he was surprised to see one of the two teachers who had appeared with Bargeman when Tyen had returned from rescuing Zeke. The one who had read Zeke's mind.

Taking a deep breath, Tyen let it out slowly and stepped into the space that had formed between his supporters and the crowd. He had been deliberating whether it would be better to attract everyone's attention with a flash of light or a loud noise, but he didn't have to do either. The nearest people stopped talking, and some called for the rest to hush.

When the room was quiet, Tyen spoke.

"Thank you, all, for coming here. I would not have called you from your work and your homes if I did not know, with great certainty, that the matter we must discuss and decide upon today is of vital importance, not just to the Academy, but to this entire world."

Bargeman muttered something. Another voice rose in reply but was shushed by those close by.

Tyen turned slowly, meeting gazes. "When I came back to this world, I sought not only to return to my home, but to establish a place of peace and safety in which to teach and study magic. I could have created a new school in the Far South, where I have friends, but I longed to be in my homeland, and the city in which I was raised, the great Beltonia.

"When the Academy generously accepted me as Director, it was more than I could have hoped for. I knew I could make this institution admired and respected not just in this world, but throughout all worlds. In return for this honour and responsibility I asked Rielle Lazuli, with the permission of Emperor Omniten, to restore magic here.

"This much you know. This much should have been all there was to know." Tyen paused to let out a small sigh. "This world should have had all the time it needed to catch up with the rest of the worlds before it took its place among them. Instead, we are going to be exposed to its dangers far sooner than I planned." He hardened his voice and straightened his back. "Because what is happening out in the worlds at this moment is not something anyone could have planned for. Because all of the worlds, both weak and powerful, face a terrible threat."

He grimaced. "Ironically, the source of the threat facing the worlds originated in this one." Tyen turned to gesture at the machines. "Mechanical magic."

He clasped his hands. "When I first left this world I soon learned that my grasp of magic was equal to that of a child compared to the sorcerers of most worlds. Less than a child's, even. I sought an education at the best school and I paid for that education with the only thing I possessed that was of value to it: the knowledge of mechanical magic.

"The sorcerers of the worlds learned and adapted that knowledge eagerly. Unfortunately, they also twisted it to darker purposes, creating machines of war. And while many set their minds to developing war machines, others . . ." Tyen gestured towards Dahli and Zeke. ". . . sought a way to combat them.

"Until now, the conflicts these machines were made for were small – wars that involved no more than a few worlds at most. The inventors of the war machines were motivated only by greed, but recently they acquired a new leader. Kettin united them, and directed their talents towards a grand and terrible purpose: the conquest of all the worlds. Those willing to follow this leader began to form an army of machines capable of destroying whole worlds. Those inventors unwilling to obey were imprisoned and forced to work, their ideas read from their minds.

"Kettin's armies began their conquest and expansion around a year ago, in this world's time. Each world attacked by her army was stripped of magic, which was then used to kill every occupant: man and woman, adult and child, sorcerer and non-sorcerer they can find. All butchered without mercy. Then the materials needed to create more machines are stripped from that world and used to enlarge the army. From there it moves on to the next world, and the next, and the next, growing larger each time. At this point, hundreds of worlds have been destroyed and conquered, and the army is expanding ever faster."

Tyen paused. A low murmur had risen among the listeners. He quickly scanned their minds. Many were frightened and worried, but the news was too fresh for the true horror to have sunk in yet. He caught a brief conversation between students.

"He said 'her'?" a Leratian boy repeated. "This leader is a woman?"

An otherworld student turned to him. "Oh, you had better believe it. Some of the worst tyrants in the history of the worlds have been women."

The Leratian thought of some of the fiercer female students. "I suppose I can believe that, though I wouldn't have until recently."

"Is anyone fighting this army?" someone called out.

Tyen nodded, and immediately the room quietened. "The Restorers. They are an alliance of the most powerful sorcerers, negotiators and military strategists of the worlds, and they have gathered to fight Kettin and her army. They need all the help they can get, and we have something unique to offer them."

"You want us to fight? But you said we weren't ready."

"No and no," Tyen replied. "Our task, if we take it on, is to find ways to disable or destroy these." He gestured to the machines. "Surely the world smart enough to invent mechanical magic can discover how to defend against it." He managed a half-smile. "I believe it can."

"That's all they want?" a woman asked.

Tyen turned towards the voice. "Do not think this will be an easy task. Kettin's machines have been designed by the best inventors of the worlds. They attack in such numbers that even the strongest sorcerers of the worlds are soon overwhelmed."

A murmur rose again, this time with an urgent pitch. Above this, a voice made itself heard.

"What proof do you have that all this is true?" Bargeman bellowed.

Tyen turned to face the man, inclined his head respectfully. "An important question and one I have thought about a great deal. I could take you, and a few other volunteers, out into the worlds to witness the destruction of Kettin's armies, but it would involve a great risk. If she or one of her followers were to read your minds, they would discover the location of this world. She would soon direct her attention to us, since the world where mechanical magic was invented would be a great prize to her."

He looked around the room again. "Instead, I have asked two of the otherworlders here to show you their memories. They have both spoken to survivors of Kettin's invasions and been present at some of the Restorer strategy meetings."

"But they haven't seen these machines in action? Or this Kettin woman?" Bargeman asked.

Tyen shook his head. "No. I restricted the—"

"I have."

Zeke stepped forward. He turned to Tyen. "I'm guessing you didn't want to cause me pain," he said haltingly in Leratian. "Don't spare me, Tyen. This is too important."

Tyen hesitated, then managed a sympathetic nod. "Are you sure?"

"Yes."

Zeke turned to Bargeman. "Read my mind." He looked around the hall. "Most of you who are sorcerers will be able to. I am not a powerful sorcerer. That's why I decided to study mechanical magic. Tyen was my teacher, back when I was at Liftre . . ."

As he told his tale Zeke let the memories rise. Good ones, to ease into the recollection of the bad. He skipped past his time working for Tyen and Dahli and lingered for a moment on his search for a way to combat machines before Kettin's followers abducted him. Then his memories became nightmarish. More so because of their harsh clarity. He recalled his solution to the war machines being read from his mind, and then fighting in vain to stop himself thinking of a defence to the solution. Then he remembered the developments he and the other inventers had made. A thousand ways to kill, one of them had said. Next came Kettin's visits, always wearing her sinister mask, and the monstrous things that had been done to people in her pursuit of becoming a machine.

And lastly, he spoke of the worlds he and Dahli had passed through on their way back to the Restorers, after his rescue. Smoking ruins. Bodies. Enormous factories. A world full of rows upon rows of machines awaiting transportation to the next victim of Kettin's mad dream. A world under attack. He had not seen his inventions in action until that moment, and he had sworn he would never invent anything again after he found a way to stop the machines.

By the time Zeke stopped, he was shaking and wiping away

tears. Dahli came forward, put his arm around the inventor and guided him back to the edge of the crowd. The Grand Hall had been quiet except for a low murmuring, but now the buzz of voices began to intensify as the audience discussed what they had heard and the sorcerers who had been able to read Zeke's mind confirmed he'd spoken the truth.

Tyen turned to Bargeman.

"Are you satisfied?"

The former professor was very pale. He swallowed, glanced at the sea of faces turned towards him, then straightened his back.

"Yes. But I find it hard to believe that we, isolated for centuries and with a great deal to catch up on – as you admit – can do anything against such an enemy." He pointed at Tyen. "You gained too much power here too quickly. You could be using this threat as an opportunity to gain even more." His hand opened in appeal to the audience. "How could this Restorer army, made up of the most powerful and intelligent sorcerers of the worlds, need us? I say we wait and see if they win, before we commit ourselves to serve a power we know nothing about."

Voices rose, some in agreement, and then others in argument. To Tyen's dismay, many were swayed by Bargeman's caution. Let us know more, before we entangle ourselves in other worlds' problems, some proposed. If we help the Restorers and they lose, Kettin will surely destroy us out of revenge.

When all had aired their doubts, Tyen raised his hands for their attention. "All I ask is that we examine Kettin's machines and look for ways to combat them. The Academy is a place of study and discovery, which is all I would have it be. If I had my way, we would be an institution that refused to involve itself in war and violence, but sometimes the only way to hold or gain peace is to study such things for defence." He shook his head. "I cannot order you to help. This is a matter for your own conscience. If that is not enough, consider this: if we find a defence against Kettin, all the surviving worlds will owe us their freedom and lives." Tyen paused and swept his gaze across the faces. "If we do not, it will not matter."

He took a step back. "I will give you an hour to discuss it."

"What will you do if we refuse?" Bargeman asked.

Tyen looked at him. "Take those who volunteer to help away with me. I have friends in the Far South who would assist."

"You'd join our enemy?"

"Who decided they were our enemy?" Tyen asked, raising his eyebrows.

"They are not part of the empire. They refused to join it."

"No," Tyen agreed. "But if we assume anything not in the Leratian Empire is our adversary, what will happen when we encounter someone or something stronger than us?" He deliberately turned and looked at the machines. "Though since Kettin is not of the empire, by your reasoning we should be fighting her."

"You twist my words," Bargeman objected.

"I only seek the truth in them," Tyen replied. "But don't waste them on me." He gestured to the crowd. "You have a whole room to use such reasoning on."

Turning away, Tyen walked back to Tarren and his supporters. The old man patted Tyen's shoulder. "Well done."

"You wouldn't say that if you could read everyone's minds," Tyen muttered.

"I can read enough, and it is not as bad as you fear."

Now he had to wait an hour while the gathering debated what they had learned and what should be done. Men and women, locals and otherworlders approached to offer their assurances and support. Humbled, Tyen could only murmur thanks in return. Then two professors suddenly broke off mid-sentence, their eyes widening with surprise at something over Tyen's shoulder. Turning, Tyen felt a small jolt of guilt as he saw the Librarian waiting there.

"Rytan Kep," he said. "I apologise. I have not had a chance to meet with you."

The Librarian smiled. "I understand. You have your hands full."

He moved a little closer, and as he glanced at the other people watching nearby they turned away and started conversations with their neighbours.

Tyen looked at the man closely. How had he never noticed that Kep was different? He had old eyes in a too-well-preserved body. As he puzzled over this, he suddenly realised he had never seen Kep in the company of more than a few others. The Librarian's agelessness was more obvious in the crowd. And that included the otherworld sorcerers – except for Dahli, of course.

"Are you able to contact Rielle Lazuli?" Kep asked.

It wasn't the question Tyen was expecting, though he wasn't sure what he had thought the man was about to say. "I can, but it would involve such a risk to this world that the cause would need to be extremely important."

"Ah," Kep said. He pursed his lips. "Well, perhaps you had better come down to the vault in her stead so you can judge that for yourself."

"For what reason?"

The Librarian shrugged. "That would be best discussed when you get there. Be assured, it is no threat to you or the Academy, and yet may be the most important and dangerous discovery the worlds have seen in millennia."

Tyen raised his eyebrows. "More than Kettin?"

Kep shrugged. "Perhaps. Or perhaps not."

Not sure whether the man was being obtuse because he did not know, or was reluctant to speak of the matter where others might hear, Tyen simply nodded. "I'll come as soon as I am able."

The man retreated, leaving Tyen free to be mobbed by alarmed and concerned questioners. The hour came to an end far sooner than he would have liked. A bell rang out, the crowd returned to its former arrangement, Tyen stepped back into the centre of the hall and waited until a near-silence fell, broken only by the shuffle of feet and the odd cough. Then he waited a little longer to allow the tension to rise.

"Let us decide," he said finally. "Those in favour of the Academy searching for ways to combat Kettin's machines, please stand behind me. Those not, please stand before me."

The rustle of clothing and tapping of shoes filled the room, then a voice cut across the noise.

"So, this is not to be an anonymous vote?" Bargeman stepped forward to stand twenty paces from Tyen.

"No," Tyen replied firmly. "Wouldn't you want to know, in the hour of defeat and destruction, who did not act when they could have saved the Leratian Empire and this world?"

Bargeman did not answer. His face was stiff and he watched the crowd intently, but he stayed in place as the last, hesitant ones chose their side.

Tyen looked behind, then in front, and nodded.

"I thank you," he said. "The challenge we face is great, but I have every confidence in the collective intellect and determination of the Academy and her supporters. We *will* find a way to defend ourselves and the worlds against Kettin."

And then he turned and walked back to join the slightly larger gathering of supporters standing between him and Kettin's machines, his heart racing. *We won*, he thought, *but not by much. Which means it will not take much for it to turn the other way.*

He would have to tread very carefully in the coming days, or all that he had built here would fall apart.

CHAPTER 18

Following the Librarian through the door, Tyen could not help feeling a shiver of nervousness at the void below his feet. Rytan Kep had created a platform of stilled air for them to stand on, and Tyen saw no ill intention in the man's mind, so he was not worried about falling. Maybe it was only that the wall of the circular room seemed to rise upwards, rather than that he and the Librarian were moving, as they slowly headed downwards.

"Before I returned with Rielle, what was the Academy planning to do about access to the vault when magic ran out?" he asked.

Kep shrugged. "They had no plans. The subject was raised now and then – usually when someone accompanied me down – but as far as I know, nobody truly believed the situation could get that bad." He let out a small huff of amusement. "Or realised I was using up my last supply of magic whenever I transported them in and out."

Examining the man's face, Tyen saw no sign of anger. Kep's calm exterior was not faked. He had resigned himself completely to ageing and inevitable death some years before, starting the search for a replacement Librarian who could handle the work and keep its secrets as well as meet with the Academy's approval. The search had proven fruitless so far, and he'd begun to wonder if the best protection for the most valuable items in the vault was for access to become impossible.

"There is much more down here than the former Directors knew," Tyen observed.

Kep nodded. "Ancient records they would have destroyed to hide ideas they didn't agree with. Objects that once belonged to sorcerers they considered dangerous."

One of these records was what the Librarian was taking Tyen to see. And a man. Tyen frowned at the Librarian's thought. A young sorcerer and researcher who had recently arrived from another world. Tyen drew in a sharp breath and searched for the visitor's mind, finding a young man waiting, radiating anxiety. His concern was that Tyen would be angry about him coming here, though he hadn't known the world was supposed to be hidden until he'd arrived. Tyen read no intention of harm.

"Don't be concerned," Kep said. "Our visitor understands the importance of this world's location remaining a secret and is willing to stay here for the rest of his life if that is what is needed to save the worlds."

Tyen looked down as the bottom of the drop appeared in the gloom. "I hope that won't be necessary."

The invisible platform supporting them dipped to one side, then rose upwards as the tunnel curved and became another shaft. They ascended this to the top, where another curve took them into a third shaft. They descended again, further than before. A flat floor appeared, drew closer, then met the soles of Tyen's shoes as they arrived.

Kep stepped up to a door, produced the odd cylindrical key Tyen recalled from his last visit to the vault and began working the lock. Watching the Librarian's thoughts, Tyen read the complicated formula that dictated how the combination of turns and reversals changed each time the door was opened. To his surprise, there was no magic involved. When the door opened, he followed Kep into the next chamber and waited as the man opened the second door.

The young sorcerer came forward. As Kep introduced Tyen, he bowed.

"Director Ironsmelter," he said, speaking the Traveller tongue. "I am Annad. Please forgive me for entering your world without permission."

"There is nothing to forgive," Tyen replied. "I have not forbidden anyone to enter it, nor do I have the right. But I am curious. How did you find it? Did you follow a path?"

Annad shook his head. "I followed a map of sorts. A very old coded map." Something to do with Rielle, Tyen saw in the man's mind. A favour for her.

"Did Rielle send you here?"

"No, I knew nothing about this world until I arrived, except that the neighbouring worlds believed it long dead."

"But you came anyway."

Annad nodded. "I gathered as much power as I could hold, hoping it would be enough."

"But you couldn't know it would be. Why take that risk?"

The young man's mouth twitched into a wry smile, and Rielle's face appeared in his mind – a memory distorted by time but still recognisable. *The Maker*, Annad thought. *She would follow the clues I left and find me, eventually.*

"I undertook a great task," the young man said, "to seek the source of an ancient belief. If I found it, and an explanation, it would not just satisfy my own curiosity, but go some way to show my world's gratitude to its saviour."

"Rielle," Tyen said.

Annad nodded. "The Maker."

"You've been looking for the truth behind Maker's Curse," Tyen saw.

"Yes." Annad smiled.

"Have you found it?"

Annad glanced at Kep. "Perhaps. We've found a mention of it in the vault's records. Can you bring Rielle here?"

"Not easily," Tyen replied. "She is helping the Restorers fight Kettin."

The young man frowned. "The one who wants to be the Successor?"

Tyen grimaced. "If Kettin knows of the prophecy, then yes, she will be doing what all conquerors do: use it to justify her methods. Which are more brutal than Valhan's, or Roporien's, ever were."

"Because she uses machines," Annad said.

"Because she uses them to kill all occupants of a world, then strip it of magic and take its resources to make more machines."

Annad's expression became serious. "I heard rumours of machine armies when I was travelling. I did not know they had grown to become such a threat until I arrived here." He frowned and looked at Kep. "You are looking for solutions to the machines, so we should not delay you too long."

The Librarian nodded. He gestured for Tyen to follow him, then led the way through the rows of shelving and chests to the far end of the vault. There they stopped before a bare stretch of wall. Kep extended a hand to the surface and pressed, and a fine dark crack appeared. It grew into an archway, then widened as a section of wall yielded to his push, softly sliding back into the rock. As the Librarian kept pushing, the wall retreated for several paces, until finally it passed a narrow gap on either side, too narrow on the right for a person to squeeze through, and barely wide enough to allow access on the left.

"I hope you're not claustrophobic," Annad said, smiling grimly at Tyen.

The young man created a spark of light and sent it into the left-hand gap. He followed it, edging sideways between the walls. Kep indicated that Tyen should go next. Creating his own light, Tyen entered the narrow space. From behind, Tyen heard the sound of clothing dragging over the rock, but he couldn't easily turn his head to look back. A quick read of Kep's mind confirmed that he was following. The sound stopped, then was replaced by the faint, soft sound of the sliding door, and he guessed that the Librarian was closing it again.

The crack appeared to be natural. The floor remained level, so he figured it must have been constructed that way deliberately. The gap grew wider and narrower as they travelled, and at one point they had to lean forward to slide on their fronts when the opening began to tilt.

They continued for some distance. Whenever the closeness of the rock began to bother Tyen he reminded himself that he could easily push out of the world, then skim up to the surface. Annad didn't consider himself a powerful sorcerer, but he clearly was strong enough to travel between worlds. Kep could read Annad's mind, so the three of them ought to be able to escape the confined space if they needed to.

The crack was now tilting in the other direction, and soon Annad and Tyen were sliding across one wall on their backs, moving their legs and then wiggling their torso along. As the angle grew more pronounced, Tyen wondered if he would end up upside down, walking on his hands. But then Annad stopped where the crack widened a little.

"We're here." He let out a deep sigh of relief. "Well, at the start of it."

Coming up beside him, Tyen waited for the young man to catch his breath, and for Kep to reach his side. Turning to smile at Tyen, Annad tilted his head towards the wall in front, which was now as much a ceiling as wall.

"Look up, above your head."

Doing as the young man suggested, Tyen first saw only plain rock. But as he sent his light further, he realised the rock surface was covered in patches of glass. The nearest was positioned higher than his head, and he could see the corner of something behind the glass. Something gold. Cautiously, he stilled air under his feet and pushed himself higher, his back sliding over the smooth rock.

Beyond the long, narrow sheet of glass was a gold cylinder taller than him, covered in markings. Looking closer, he saw notches and symbols that suggested sections of the staff could be twisted.

"What is it?"

"I'm not sure," Kep replied from below, his voice echoing strangely.

"Have you taken it out?"

The man nodded. "Quite a few times, a few centuries ago. It focuses light. At some settings so powerfully, it can burn through metal and stone."

"That would suggest a weapon."

"Or a signalling tool of some sort. Perhaps it had a creative use. Most inventions can be used for both good or ill." The man began to slide up the rock face. "Follow me."

Tyen waited for Kep to pass him. As the Librarian did, Tyen saw he was holding his back above the stone surface on a bed of stilled air. He quickly formed his own platform, and as he started after the Librarian he found he could move faster, keeping up with Kep as the man angled across the passage. It was also, he suspected, much kinder on his clothing.

The Librarian led Tyen to several other artefacts, some mysterious but most not. A jewel-encrusted cap of interlocking gold rings was labelled "Roporien's Crown", and when Tyen raised an eyebrow in doubt, the Librarian nodded and thought of the records he'd seen that described or pictured it exactly as the item appeared.

Most of the treasures were records, but few were made of paper. Those that had best survived the march of time had done so due to the toughness of the material they were made from. Sometimes a book lay beside them, containing a translation. More often the texts were so old they were unreadable, the language lost to time.

Kep stopped before a long cavity. It contained hundreds of plates of gold, joined by small links. No book lay behind the glass.

"This is what Annad travelled so far to find," the Librarian said. "It is called the Scroll of the Ancients. Roporien brought it here. As you know, he was a collector of knowledge. He built vaults like this throughout the worlds. Many have been destroyed; others forgotten." Kep smiled at Tyen. "Did you know the library existed before the Academy did? It was built here because this is the location of an ancient place of knowledge, presumed all but destroyed when Roporien died."

"But it wasn't destroyed," Tyen finished, looking around.

"No." Kep shrugged. "Though it may as well have been, since so much of what is here is useless because we can't read it. However, there is a way it might be accessed. A way that presented itself some years ago, but I didn't get the chance to try it before the opportunity was stolen away."

Tyen frowned. "By whom?"

The Librarian smiled. "You."

Tyen drew in a quick breath. At once, he became aware of the press of Vella's satchel against his chest. Unlike the satchels of the past, this one did not have holes in it to allow contact with his skin. He had grown wary of giving her constant access to his mind. In such a time of strife as this, and having taken on a position of responsibility, it was always possible he would learn something he must keep secret, even from Vella. It would take a very dangerous piece of information for him to stop talking to her completely – and he would never abandon her to permanent unconsciousness. If he ever had to keep her from absorbing a piece of information, he would get others to hold her for him.

Hopefully that would not begin today. He looked at the linked gold plates. "You believe this explains Maker's Curse?"

"We do," Kep replied.

Was that information too dangerous for Vella to contain? It might be. After all, it was said that if a Maker became ageless, he or she would tear apart the worlds. If this scroll described how it was done, then Vella could potentially contain instructions on how to destroy the worlds. While he trusted Rielle not to follow those instructions, he couldn't risk that Vella might one day fall into the hands of someone who was willing to. *Like Kettin.*

But what if Maker's Curse was wrong? Rielle might be able to become ageless again. If he didn't use Vella to translate the scroll, she would age and die.

Was that important enough to risk someone one day learning how to destroy the worlds?

One day? What about now? Kettin was already doing a fairly thorough job of killing worlds. *Would becoming ageless help Rielle stop her?* Tyen chewed on his lip. *She is the only Maker of her strength, and she is vulnerable. The better she can protect and defend herself, the better chance we have to stop Kettin.*

Of course, none of this would matter if Vella couldn't translate the scroll. Tyen drew in a deep breath and, as he let it out, examined the marks on the linked gold plates. Roporien had made Vella. Roporien had created this vault. If Roporien had known someone who could translate this scroll, surely he'd have had them hold Vella, and she would already know the truth of Maker's Curse. Since she didn't, the chances of her being able to translate it were small. She'd have had to have picked up the language after being owned by Roporien.

There was only one way to find out. Fortunately, he had room enough here to reach the satchel and draw it out. He was conscious of the Librarian watching, the man suppressing a small pang of desire for the famous book, but also a shiver at the thought that she could learn everything about him with a touch.

Tyen managed to bring Vella up to the level of his eyes and open her covers.

Tyen.

Vella. Can you read this text?

Yes, I can.

He blinked in surprise, then looked at the Librarian and Annad. "She says she can translate it."

The young man grinned with excitement, while Kep merely nodded. For a moment they said nothing as it dawned on them that this might be the first time in thousands of years that the scroll had been read. It occurred to Tyen that this was the sort of discovery he had dreamed of making when he had been a young archaeology student. Something beautiful, rare, which would expand the knowledge of the Academy. Who knew it was in the depths of the Academy's own vault?

Well, Kep did.

"So what does it say?" Annad asked, his voice barely louder than a whisper.

Tyen shifted until he was before the first panel and let his eyes trace the lines. When he had finished examining the first page, he looked down and read out the words that had appeared on Vella's pages. They were not quite what Tyen had expected. No introduction. No title. Just a warning that the original text had many words that had gained several meanings over time. He read it aloud.

"It's a translation," Kep said. "Possibly of a much older document." He moved closer so he could see the writing. "Vella, could you translate to Leratian? My Traveller tongue is a bit rusty."

The words vanished and were replaced by the language of Tyen's world. Looking back up at the scroll, Tyen continued reading but did not pause to speak the words aloud. Now that he had begun, he was eager to return to a more comfortable place to study the scroll's text.

He needed to focus on each character in sequence, which slowed the process, but he did not want to risk any mistranslations. They gradually slid along the wall, Tyen staring at the scroll, Kep reading the translation and Annad waiting patiently. Now and then the Librarian made a small noise of surprise or interest and muttered to himself, making it hard for Tyen to keep his focus on the original script.

When, at last, Tyen had examined every detail of the record, he suggested they return to the vault. Kep led the way back. Through the Librarian's mind, Tyen saw that the void behind the sliding door continued on into darkness. Kep had explored once but, when he found that the tunnel was flooded several thousand paces deeper, he had concluded that if any other records existed down here, they were likely long destroyed.

Not if they were made of durable material, Tyen mused. *But it would be a difficult task exploring underwater. I wonder if the tunnels could be drained . . .*

They each sighed with relief as they emerged into the passage. Tyen had returned Vella to her satchel, and as they entered the vault he drew her out again. Opening her covers, he set her down on top of a chest so they could all see her.

"So, Vella, can you sum up the contents of the record?" he asked.

As you noted, it is a translation of a much older text. This original source was in a bad state, with gaps in the information it provided. It dealt mainly with a long-dead race of sorcerers known as the Ancients at the time the original record was written. According to it, sorcerers of Valhan's strength were unremarkable in that time. The Ancients' abilities far surpassed his. They were typically born in isolated worlds, but as they came to power they joined their worlds with others.

"So it was these sorcerers who bound the worlds together?" Annad asked.

Yes.

"Does it say how?"

No. But it does say that to do so a sorcerer needs to be both ageless and a powerful Maker. Only with this combination can a sorcerer generate enough magic to enable worlds to be bound — or broken apart.

"Is that where Maker's Curse comes from?" Tyen asked. "It's not becoming ageless that causes a Maker to destroy worlds, it's just that they can break apart the binding between them at will?"

It appears so. The record tells of how the binding and separating of worlds was both traded or gifted or used as a threat by the Ancients. It says that the death of the last of the Ancients was an occasion of both sadness and celebration.

"Probably depending on which world you were from," Kep commented.

Tyen glanced at him and nodded. "Much as it was with Valhan's death."

The Librarian shrugged. "I have to admit I was a little relieved at the news. Sorcerers of my strength weren't of much interest to him, but the possibility that you would be collateral damage when someone did him a favour, or he did them one, always existed." Kep raised an eyebrow. "I'm surprised he let you live, considering your strength."

Tyen looked away. "I was more useful to him alive, at the time."

"For your knowledge of mechanical magic?"

Deciding not to answer, Tyen looked down at Vella's pages again. "If what we've learned is correct, Rielle has the potential to become one of these Ancients."

Annad nodded. "She could learn how to bind and break apart worlds, if she became ageless."

"She said the part of the mind that allows her to be a Maker is the same as the one that allows a sorcerer to be ageless. It can't be both. Vella, does the record shed any light on the method?"

No.

He muttered a weak curse. "So, it's up to her to discover it for herself. I was hoping to find another way to fight Kettin in all this, but I doubt Rielle could gain an Ancient's abilities particularly quickly, and her Making ability is vital to the Restorers right now."

"Perhaps there is a clue in the text," Annad said. "If we study it further . . ."

Tyen looked down at Vella, then up at the Librarian. "You'd need me to leave her with you."

The man nodded. His expression was serious. His thoughts acknowledged that he coveted the book a great deal, but he was adamant that he would not take her for himself. Tyen's impressions of the man had been one of an honest person who sought to protect both knowledge and people.

Annad watched them both, his loyalty to Rielle colouring all he thought.

It is a risk, Tyen thought. *But if we are to survive Kettin's conquest we need to take risks.* Then something else occurred to him. *If Kettin wins and Rielle, Qall and I die, Kep will be better placed to save Vella than anyone else.*

"Very well," Tyen said. "Let no other see her. If this world comes under attack, do not stay and fight. Take her and flee."

Kep nodded solemnly, a shiver of fear going through him as he realised the danger was great indeed if Tyen was willing to trust Vella to another's protection. "I will. Will you send a message to Rielle to tell her what we know?"

"Not yet." Tyen shook his head. "Though this is important to her, it is important to all the worlds that I do not risk bringing Kettin's attention to this world. As soon as I can safely do so, I'll tell her everything we've learned."

"I understand."

Looking down at Vella, Tyen hesitated, not wanting to break contact with her.

"And no asking questions about my personal life, or others'," he added.

"Of course not," Kep replied.

Tyen picked Vella up. *If we do not meet again, Vella, I wish you well.*

And I you, she replied in Doumian.

He smiled, closed her and set her satchel beside her. "If you discover anything, tell me right away."

"We will," Annad assured him.

Tyen took a step away, then sighed and looked up at the ceiling. "I'd like to stay and help, but I had better make sure civil war hasn't broken out above." Inclining his head to them both, he made himself turn and walk to the door, and started his journey back to the Academy above.

PART SEVEN

RIELLE

CHAPTER 19

Rielle knew they had reached the edge of Kettin's army when the first breath she took as they entered a world stank of fresh blood.

Too few bodies were scattered around the arrival place to explain the smell. Levitating above the Restorer army, Rielle and Qall soon located the rest. The arrival place had been the beginning of the carnage. They could trace the progress of the attack outwards by the arrangement. The closest ring of corpses was sparse – the first victims had been caught unaware or were unable to run. A gap separated this from a thicker band of bodies, where the machines had caught up with those fleeing. The gap was smaller where the streets narrowed and slowed progress, further away where there was more room.

The occupants of vehicles were next. Slow carts first, then faster ones. Next came the corpses of riders and the local beasts of burden, some clearly better bred for speed. None fast enough to escape the machines, however.

Many of the dead wore similar clothing. The most numerous type of uniform included armour, and victims wearing it were scattered through all groups. Less common was a kind of cape cinched at the waist with an embellished belt. The wearers of those did not carry weapons, but had fallen in lines that stretched across the road in a defensive manner, and were surrounded by the twisted and melted parts of machines. *Sorcerers*, Rielle guessed. More lay closer to the arrival place than further away.

Machines remnants lay among the once-living. "No whole machines," Rielle noted. "Just parts too broken to reuse. What had been salvageable had been carried away, but where to?"

"The east," Qall told her, his eyes focused on the horizon. "They are constructing a factory under the supervision of three of Kettin's followers." His eyes narrowed. "Two of whom are new to Kettin's ranks, and who are still shaken by what they saw here."

"Would they turn on their companion, if nudged?"

He shook his head. "They joined Kettin because they believe she is the Successor. This only proves it, in their minds."

Rielle sighed. "That ridiculous prophecy again."

Qall shrugged and turned back to her. "If we removed it from the minds of all the people of all the worlds, another almost exactly the same would replace it. It is in the nature of people to see patterns, but not to be able to interpret them realistically."

"Would they be able to if they lived long enough, I wonder?"

"Perhaps. Being ageless does not make you realistic, however. Or long-lived. A moment of bad luck or misjudgement can still kill you. Or not being on your guard. Or being surprised by an unexpected danger."

She looked at him. "During battles with unpredictable opponents – like machines that keep growing more sophisticated."

Qall grimaced. "Yes." He looked down at the Restorer army, which had moved out of the arrival place and into the courtyard next door. Unlike in the battles against Dahli, and the earlier one between the Rebels and the Raen, the army was not made up of a small number of strong sorcerers fortified by the magic gathered and delivered by weaker sorcerers. With Rielle able to provide a world's worth of magic in a short time, all fighters effectively had the stamina of powerful sorcerers – as long as it wasn't first taken by those positioned closer to Rielle.

Fighting large machine armies in dead worlds presented entirely new challenges to the Restorer army. Fighting with a Maker on their side was not as simple as it first seemed, either. Qall's advisers had considered how best to adapt to both. They'd suggested that many sorcerers were better than few, since the Restorers' targets were so numerous and they could aim accurately at only one or a few at the same time. Reports from refugees of defeated worlds supported this.

Tyen hadn't tried to fight the machines in Kettin's world, so he hadn't been able to advise on how to approach it. Rielle blinked as she remembered something he'd said.

"Tyen said he ran out of power quite suddenly. That the more magic you use the more abrupt and surprising it is coming to the end of it. We should be wary of that."

"Are you two together again?"

Startled by the change of subject, she raised an eyebrow at Qall. "So you haven't read my mind lately?"

"Of course, but your thoughts regarding him are . . . ambiguous. Something has changed. I'm wondering if you've been too busy to think about it."

She shook her head. "We're friends."

"You're more than that," he told her.

"Close friends. We have a lot in common."

"It's more than that," he insisted.

She sighed, exasperated. "Does it really matter to you what we do in our private lives?"

He shrugged and looked away. "I don't know. Maybe I'm interested in him myself."

She rolled her eyes. "Trying to make me jealous? I don't think he's interested in men, Qall."

"He wouldn't have to be. If I can change my appearance, I could be everything he's interested in."

She stared at him and, annoyingly, found she *was* jealous. And protective. To deceive Tyen like that would be—

He chuckled. "Don't worry, Rielle. I won't steal him from you."

He gave her a sidelong look. "On the other hand, I could try stealing you from him."

She let out a disbelieving huff. "You're like a son to me, Qall."

"You might feel differently in time."

"What, when I'm old and wrinkly?"

"You don't have to be. I can keep you young."

She shook her head. "I'm not sure I'd like to be constantly in debt to ageless sorcerers. Perhaps it's better to age and die like ordinary people. Besides, I may not even live through the next few hours." She looked towards the army. "What will you do if Kettin manages to kill me off?"

His smile vanished. "We leave. Don't worry. I am fully aware that having no source of magic will rapidly turn us all into ordinary, vulnerable human beings."

"Even you," she pointed out, relieved that he had returned to a less personal subject, though she suspected he had only been teasing her to find out how she regarded Tyen now.

"Yes. So much for being the most powerful sorcerer in the worlds." His shoulders lifted. "I need to be the smartest instead. And for my fighters to follow my orders, without Baluka here to show his support of me."

Baluka had returned with the news that the Travellers would not be joining the army. He had stayed behind, in charge of the base.

"Do you doubt they will?" Rielle asked.

He looked down, scanning the crowd. "Not at the moment. There are a few who aren't convinced about me, but if they don't trust me, they do trust those who are willing to trust me." He sighed and began lowering them to the ground. "I may have Valhan's knowledge, but I don't have his confidence in himself."

"You have courage."

"Is there any difference?"

"Yes. Bravery is what you have when you choose do something *despite* being afraid, not when you aren't afraid."

He raised one of his eyebrows. "How do you know whether I'm afraid or not?"

She smiled. "I knew you as a young man, when all your emotions were written on your face and in your gestures. You still give a little of that away, though nobody else can see it but me."

The corner of his mouth twitched. "I'll have to try harder to hide them."

They were nearly at the ground, landing in the centre of the army. Rielle waited until her feet were on the pavement before she spoke again. "Must you? Can't you leave me one small advantage?"

Qall didn't answer. Something had caught his attention. He was looking upwards, his gaze moving back and forth. The chatter among the Restorers began to fade. Rielle searched the aqua-blue of the sky, wondering what he had noticed.

Then she saw it. A shadow so large her mind had not been able to make sense of it. It was like a moon hovering over the arrival place, the base nearly touching the ground and the top disappearing behind clouds high above.

"Link!" Qall shouted.

Rielle tore her eyes away from the enormous globe as the army obeyed. The fighters drew close together, taking hold of a neighbour or two. She took hold of Qall's arm and grabbed the shoulder of the closest sorcerer.

"That's incredible," Qall breathed, still looking upwards. "So many machines. They must already be carrying magic, since there's almost none here for them to take. When they get here we'll have to — ah!"

Machines? Rielle looked up again. Details of the globe were now visible. Limbless machines nestled against other machines, like a giant round puzzle. All were exactly the same: grey, smoothly metallic and double the size of a human head. As she stared, the gaps between them grew darker . . .

Then gasps and curses came from the Restorers as the globe

suddenly fragmented. The closest machines blurred as they passed through people and buildings into the ground. A dizzying impression of shapes spreading outwards followed, and as this expansion slowed Rielle was able to see fine cables stretching between the machines, forming a massive ball-like net expanding to surround not just the Restorers, but the entire world.

"Why aren't we leaving?" someone asked.

"Because if we do, we'll encounter whatever that is in the place between worlds," another voice replied.

The net was hollow, so only the skin of it settled into place above and around them. But that skin was made of so many machines it was thick enough to fill the air between the city and the clouds. When the cables between each machine were stretched out fully, the machines were spaced about a hundred paces apart, in a formation not unlike the one Rielle, Tyen and Dahli had encountered in Kettin's world.

"They're arriving!" Qall shouted. "Check your position! Check your neighbour's position!"

Looking down, Rielle saw that a cable appeared to pass through her leg. She took a step aside, out of its way. The sound of shuffling feet and spoken warnings broke the eerie silence of the dead city. Most had to let go of their fellow sorcerers. Looking further afield, she saw that Restorers were moving not just out of the way of the arriving machines, but to surround individual ones.

The grey metal invaders turned black.

"Attack!" Qall called.

The air exploded. Deafening noise and flashes of light assailed Rielle's senses. Attacks came from all sides, making the shield of stilled air she held about her body vibrate. The scream of metal distorting and breaking joined the cacophony, as well as human shrieks of pain. Not all the fighters had stayed out of the way of the arriving machines. Not all had withstood the first attack.

This was not the formation the advisers had suggested. It was exactly what they had warned against.

"Don't stay on the ground. A clear space all around will allow you to see what is arriving from the place between, be that obstacles or assassins hoping to get within your shield."

But it was not long before the attacks on Rielle's shield lessened as the closest machines used up their store of magic and were smashed by the Restorers. The remaining assault was coming from the swarms of machines that were crowding down from above, no longer linked by cables.

"Levitate!" Qall ordered.

The fighters began to rise as one. Rielle concentrated on the shield she held around herself and moved it upwards in synch with the army. Levitation would use up more magic than standing on the ground, but this wouldn't matter once she began producing more.

Which I should be doing now, she realised, looking towards Qall.

"Now?" she asked.

He glanced at her, then nodded. "Yes. Let's see if the machines understand what you are doing and single you out."

She looked up. "Is no sorcerer controlling them?"

He shook his head. "Whoever brought them left before I could find their mind. Perhaps to bring another one of those . . . things."

Rielle shuddered at the prospect. "Then I'll get to it."

Qall move away a little to give her space. "Formation!" he shouted.

"Keep Rielle in the centre, not just to protect her but so that your army can take all the magic she generates and none goes to the enemy," the advisers had said.

Drawing upon a little more of her store of power, Rielle started creating sparks of light. As each began to glow, she set it on a little dance that followed in the path of the previous one, until she had several threads of them, like strings of beads, swirling around her. It was strange to be doing this in the midst of a battle. She didn't want to be doing it. The Restorers were forming a protective sphere around her, and she wanted to watch to see if it proved as effective a strategy as the advisers hoped. She wanted to smash the machines, too. Though the prospect of fighting always filled her with dread and reluctance, machines were not people. She could destroy them without shouldering the burden of guilt that had increased every time she had killed someone.

But generation was her role here, not destruction. Nobody else could do what she did. She drew in a deep breath, closed her eyes for a moment, then opened them and focused on the sparks. On the designs she created. On trying new and interesting patterns. Twirling lights would not produce magic without her will behind them. Only creativity generated magic.

The battle intruded. It was impossible to ignore the rare scream. Each time she could not help trying to see if someone had been killed or injured. Each time she was relieved to see that the Restorers were doing a fine job of dispatching machines, overall. As each device depleted its store of magic, it could be smashed or melted or torn apart. The fragments fell, sometimes bouncing off the shields of the sorcerers below them, to a steadily growing mound of them below. The strategists would be proud.

"*Destroy the machines, so they can't be revived with more magic and sent against you again,*" they'd said.

"Link on my signal! We are moving on!"

Rielle looked at Qall in surprise. He was holding a hand out to her.

"I think we've proven we can hold our own under this sort of attack," he said as she took it. "Time to see how close we can get to Kettin's world."

The order was being repeated so that all would hear it. Fighters moved closer together, those above dropping and those below rising to the same level. The machines crowded in, still attacking. When all the fighters were close enough to easily take hold of a neighbour, Qall called out again.

"Anyone not ready?" he asked.

No answer came.

412

The world faded. Machine attacks that had been aimed at Restorers struck other machines. More fell from the sky, but the scene faded out of sight before any reached the ground.

"Take the fight to Kettin," the advisers had recommended. *"The machines aren't your target, the controllers of them are, and Kettin is the foremost controller."*

Rielle stretched out her senses, searching for presences beyond the army. She detected a pair retreating. Too far away to see. Qall took the army down towards the arrival place, found the path they'd arrived along and a different one leading away. The last shadows of the freshly conquered world disappeared as he started down the latter.

The next world emerged from the whiteness. A vast depression in the earth, perfectly round as if a bowl had been pressed into it, stretched below them. Rielle recalled the size and shape of the sphere of machines and guessed it had been the cause. All around the depression were tracks radiating outwards. Or, more likely, inwards if the machines were the source. Smoke or steam wafted up from the soil and pooled in the base of the depression. Qall paused just before arriving, perhaps wary of this. Rielle sensed another path and felt him direct everyone along it rather than entering the world.

The next world's arrival place was within another ruined city. Huge pointed structures with five sides remained standing amid a flat plain of rubble. A red river choked by debris curved like a slash of paint or blood through all. Qall brought them into this world long enough for Rielle and the other mortal sorcerers to catch their breath, then pushed out of it again.

This time Rielle sensed several presences in the place between. They kept their distance, tracking the army's progress. Two worlds later, a shifting darkness appeared on the path ahead. It was travelling quickly towards them and, as it neared, the shadow expanded. Rielle recognised the same moonlike structure as before, like a vast net hoping to enclose the Restorers.

Qall swerved around it. The net changed direction too slowly to touch them. It followed as the Restorer army continued towards the next world.

When we arrive we'll have to get out of its way quickly, Rielle thought. But they didn't enter the world. Qall abruptly skimmed the army to one side, using the advantage of superior magical ability to outrun the net. He brought the Restorers into the world on a sandy shore scattered with washed-up vessels of many different sizes and shapes, their crews lying on deck or floating at the high-tide mark.

"Stay linked," he called.

Rielle breathed in and out as quickly and deeply as she could, wincing at the smell of death. The Restorers looked around, searching for signs of the machine sphere's approach.

One moment the sky was clear, the next a dark network surrounded them. Only this sphere did not expand to match the curvature of the worlds. It remained closely connected, the gaps between the machines kept small to make it harder for the Restorers to slip through, and shifted to surround the army.

Rielle glanced at Qall. *Are we not going to levitate?* she thought, knowing he'd hear the question. He did not take his eyes off the sphere, but gave a tiny shake of his head.

The sphere arrived, sending sand and water surging out in all directions and blocking out most of the light.

And in the next moments the army was back in the place between worlds. Rielle could sense a presence close by, but it rapidly moved away to join others in the distance. She itched to give chase, or see someone else do so, but the importance of remaining together had been stressed during the tactical meetings and preparations.

Qall skimmed them around the world, seeking another arrival place or path to the next world. The presences faded, unable to keep up. He found no other arrival place before they had to stop for Rielle and the other mortal fighters to breathe. She read frustration in Qall's face. He had only allowed non-ageless sorcerers to join the army because it would be slowed down by Rielle anyway.

Oh, what I'd do to become ageless again right now! But then she would be of no more use than everyone else here.

At last they came upon a lightly used path. Qall sped along it without hesitation. The next world was weak but had been spared Kettin's conquest. A stepping stone, Rielle guessed. Sure enough, it led them through two more destroyed worlds to another pristine one, then three before the next undisturbed oasis. The path remained a minor one, and Rielle began to wonder if it was one that followers of Kettin used to travel to and from her base. Perhaps even Kettin herself used it.

No moonlike clusters of machines assailed them. No sorcerers kept pace with them. It was all too easy. Rielle looked at Qall to see him frowning with worry. Had the same possibility occurred to him?

Then a world began to emerge that was already surrounded by a network of machines, without a web connecting them. The arrival place was on a rooftop of a small city that showed no sign of damage. Qall looked at her, his eyebrows rising in query.

She shrugged. They would not know if it was Kettin's world until they arrived.

He took the army upwards to hover far above the city.

"Separate!" he ordered. *"Be ready to shield when you arrive. Clear a space among the machines and we will regroup."*

The Restorers obeyed, spreading out as they parted. The nearest machines turned as the first fighters arrived, sensing movement.

Qall turned to Rielle. *"Shield and start generating magic immediately."* He didn't wait to see her nod, instead turning to look around at the army. *"Enter the world!"* he called.

To Rielle's relief, none of the fighters screamed or fell as they did, but the sounds of battle immediately battered her senses.

"Do your thing, Maker," Qall ordered, flashing a quick smile as he moved away.

She obeyed, trying to ignore the rapidly expanding battle as she created lights and set them moving. In the periphery of her vision she saw that thousands of machines were breaking formation and swarming upon the invaders. Focusing on the magic she was creating, she saw it being snatched up by the sorcerers around her in no organised pattern, unintentionally depriving some so that all too soon a scream reached her, and she glimpsed a body fall in the corner of her sight.

Her stomach sank. *We were warned about that.*

But the advisers had not been certain how they could prevent it. Nobody has ever fought like this before. The urge to smash at the machines rose again, but with the Restorers protectively surrounding her it was as likely she'd strike them as hit a machine. *Stick to what you're here for*, she told herself, and set about just that.

The air darkened, then filled with black lines.

"More arriving!" someone shouted.

"Check your position!" Qall roared.

Rielle paused from her light show to avoid the shadow of a machine and the cables connecting it to its fellows. She and Qall attacked it simultaneously, shattering its shield and boring holes in its body. It sagged in the net of cables, then, as the network unlinked, fell. Drawing Rielle's attention down, she saw it punch a hole through the roof of a house below. Her stomach sank again. The streets of the town had filled with people, some staring up at the battle, others fleeing the machines raining down on them.

"Should we move away from the city?" she asked.

Qall didn't answer. Looking up, Rielle saw that he was scanning the horizon. "Where is she?" he muttered.

"Shall I search so you can focus on the battle?" she asked.

He glanced at her and shook his head. "No. Make magic."

Once again, she forced her attention away from her surroundings and began the dance of lights. Her heart wasn't in it, and she could feel very little magic spilling from her. Every machine that dropped made her heart skip, and she couldn't help looking to see where it landed. When one struck a man, she tore her eyes away. "We have to move, Qall."

"We will when I find her," he growled.

"More arriving!" Hapre shouted. The woman was hovering nearby.

Qall looked up and around, his lip curling with annoyance as he saw another tangle of machines about to arrive. He stretched out an arm and faded a little, but she could still see him as his hand encountered part of the oncoming network of machines. Rielle gasped out a laugh as she saw the simple brilliance of his ploy. He was bound to be stronger than any of Kettin's controllers.

But he did not know how to collapse the network. Instead he moved it up and away from the Restorer army. It tilted, one side dipping into the ground far below, then grew abruptly more distinct. Puffs of dirt exploded up from the ground. Qall had brought the great sphere of machines into the world partly buried. As the surviving ones disconnected and began to swarm, Qall skimmed back to Rielle's side.

"Let them try that again!" he said smugly.

"They are," she told him as another cable appeared, faint but now familiar, in the air between them.

He sighed and faded again. This time, as he took hold of the approaching network, it turned upside down. At first Rielle wondered if the sorcerer trying to bring it into the world had managed to regain some control, but as the machines arrived and uncoupled, she realised that most of them would have emerged far, far above, in the darkness beyond the sky.

"More magic!" someone called.

Rielle's heart skipped. She cursed and set her attention to making magic again. If people were calling for it, they must be running dangerously low. She turned her mind to shaping a more complex light pattern. When a machine fell past her, she sent lights chasing it down in a dance of triumph.

Suddenly Qall was back beside her. "There are more coming,"

he said. "I think they aim to crowd the place between worlds with them so we can't leave."

"Let some of us clear them away," Hapre advised. "While you stay and search for Kettin."

He nodded. "Pick our strongest to do it."

Hapre moved off through the fighters. Qall's attention returned to the distance, his expression searching. Rielle returned to making magic and her focus was not interrupted again, though she paused now and then to check how the battle was progressing. Each time she did, the swarms of machines attacking them were a little denser. Though the sorcerers Hapre had enlisted were successfully copying Qall's ploy, each time a sphere arrived plenty of machines survived to join those already in the fight. They seemed to be accumulating faster than the army could destroy them.

"I've . . . found her!" Qall exclaimed.

Catching a hesitation in his voice, Rielle glanced at him.

"But . . .?"

"Only by searching for her in other people's minds. I can't see her mind."

"She's *that* strong?"

"Perhaps," he said. "You'll see what I mean when they arrive."

"'They?'"

"She's bringing her own sorcerers to fight. Or rather, *they're* bringing *her*."

As she began searching for minds, Qall drew in a sharp breath.

"No. Generate magic," he said. "We may need it."

Turning her attention back to her light show was difficult, but she forced herself to concentrate. What pattern should she create to greet Kettin? What might inspire the Restorer army? Kettin was all about destruction and death. So Rielle made her creations about life, mimicking swirling flocks of flying creatures, the growth and blossoming of plants, seeds bursting out of pods and petals spiralling towards the ground.

"They're here," Qall said, his voice breathy and harsh. Rielle

418

paused to see where he was looking just as Hapre appeared beside him.

"There are too many machines now," she said. "They're overcoming our defences more and more."

Qall nodded. "Then let's bring the fight to Kettin."

As Hapre followed the direction of his gaze, Rielle did so as well. Beyond the Restorers was a swarm of machines too thick to see through, but she could sense hundreds of minds on the other side of it. Focusing on one, she learned that he was one of Kettin's sorcerers.

The man was dragging his eyes away from the enormous cloud of attacking machines to what now seemed like a tiny army of sorcerers arranged around Kettin. Hundreds of golden masks tilted up towards the battle. He did not know Kettin's plan. She had never required her sorcerers to fight beside her before. "Protect the controllers," one of Kettin's generals snapped. The man drew in a deep breath and readied himself for a fight.

Hapre's voice cut across the thoughts Rielle was reading.

"The core of them have controls for the machines. They can stop them attacking."

"I see," Qall replied. "They are to stop the battle if . . . ah. Interesting. It is a secondary defence. The masks should tell the machines not to attack the wearer, but they aren't certain it will work."

"If they do, we need to remove them. Take them for ourselves."

"Yes. They are expecting us to attack from above, but I don't think they've considered what would happen if we simply skimmed down and arrived among them."

"Drawing the machine's attacks upon them as well." Hapre paused, then laughed. "None are considering the possibility, as far as I can see."

"Link!" Qall shouted. The call was repeated, spreading outwards. Rielle placed a hand on Qall's shoulder, her heart racing.

"Give me a line of sight," Qall ordered. Immediately a gap

appeared as sorcerers moved out of the way. A wall of machines appeared.

"What about me?" Rielle murmured. "What do I do when we get there?"

"Protect yourself," Qall replied. "Make magic. Don't try to fight anyone."

"They'll take the magic too."

"We'll have to be faster." He looked around. *I must time this carefully, between arriving spheres.* "Anyone not ready?"

A faint reply came. A moment later, an affirmation of readiness followed. The swarms of machines faded as Qall took the army out of the world a little, then blurred as he sent everyone through them. As they emerged from the cloud, Qall did not slow. A larger golden shape drew Rielle's attention to the centre of Kettin's army. Someone was wearing not just a gold mask, but gold armour as well. Details grew clear as they sped closer, and she realised that the figure was not *wearing* gold armour. It *was* gold.

She, Rielle corrected, as the humanoid held an arm up, signalling to her army.

Kettin's new body was more feminine than the one Tyen had made, more than five cycles ago. Its curves were strangely ludicrous. A body of metal did not need breasts or wide hips. Nor did it need fine clothing draped over its metallic skin. Bright jewel eyes reflected the sun as the humanoid looked up at the Restorer army.

Eyes that seemed to fix upon Rielle. Or Qall.

Qall slowed their descent. "*She's done it,*" he said, speaking in the place between worlds. "*I couldn't read her mind because she is no longer human.*"

"*She didn't do it,*" Rielle pointed out. "*Her inventors did, willing and unwilling.*"

"*All these other machines can't hold much magic,*" Hapre said. "*Neither can she, I'd wager. If she had solved that problem, she'd have applied the solution to all her machines.*"

"Unless she hasn't had time to modify her machines yet," Rielle added. *"Maybe it is so costly and difficult it was only worth it for her new body."*

The three of them exchanged glances. Rielle looked back. The great mass of machines was close behind them, following them down. A new sphere was approaching in the place between.

"We will soon find out," Qall said.

Kettin remained still as he neared, no emotion discernible on her rigid face, her arm still raised. Only when the Restorers were almost upon her did she drop it.

Her followers hesitated, then surged up into the air.

Through Qall's army, still slightly outside of the world.

Their confusion was clear to see as they came to a halt and turned about, belatedly realising that the Restorers had been slightly out of the world, and that they were now wedged between the machines and their enemy. Qall brought his army to a stop just above the ground. The enemy sorcerers hovered, attacked by machines that could no longer see the masks now that their backs were turned. The controllers among them activated their switches to stop the machines attacking. All paused, and quickly realised that it had not worked. The machines' attack continued, only now Kettin's army bore the brunt of it.

"Separate!" Qall ordered. *"Arrive, levitate and fight."*

As Rielle let go of his shoulder, he turned and took her hand. *"Their inexperience and reliance on machines is their weakness. Start making magic as soon as you can."*

Air touched her face. She sucked it in, taking deep breaths, and created lights. The familiar sensations of sorcerous battle began as the Restorers rose to attack Kettin's followers. Sorcerer fighting sorcerer. Or two against one. She saw a follower aim at the back of a Restorer hard pressed by two adversaries. In a reflexive move to protect him she sent one of her lights towards him, bright with her anger but otherwise ineffectual. She cursed her foolishness, yet at the same time wondered if this was the moment her determination to not kill would break. *Except in defence*, she reminded herself. *If there was no other choice.*

The follower's attack went wide. He shaded his eyes but could not see past the light.

Maybe . . . I can be a part of this battle! And fight at the same time as Making! Creating more lights, she sent them in swarms at the enemy, blinding and distracting them. She shaped them into machines to confuse them, or into glowing figures that startled and frightened. Magic spilled from her, stronger as she created a new shape with which to distract and dazzle.

"Stop, Rielle!" Qall said, spinning about and grabbing her arm. "Stop now!"

She did. "But it's helping, and I'm making magic at the same time."

"And they're taking it too," he told her. He looked around, shaking his head. "This was a mistake. We've lost our advantage and we can't link."

"But we are winning." The voice was Hapre's. The woman dropped down from above. "They have lost their advantage, too. The machines are attacking them. And their army is weaker."

Looking around, Rielle saw that it was true. Though the size of the combined armies was smaller, both sides having lost many fighters, more of the Restorers had survived than their enemy. She looked for Kettin. The gold figure hovered between two followers. Looking into the pair's minds, Rielle saw that they, too, had realised their side was losing. The pair nervously exchanged a glance.

"She's not used magic," Qall said. "Let's see what she does when directly threatened."

He began to move towards Kettin, bringing Rielle and Hapre with him. The two followers only noticed when Qall had halved the gap between them. The jaw of one clenched and he stood straighter. The other's eyes widened. He looked at his companion and spoke. Then he quickly faded from sight. A moment later, the other vanished too.

The gold figure fell.

A ripple went through the battle as the followers noticed. All fighting stopped as the humanoid plunged towards the ground. She landed with a dully metallic thud. The head broke from the body and rolled into a nearby depression, the eyes not quite staring upwards.

And then those eyes flashed, rapidly.

The followers began to vanish. One after another, then simultaneously.

"Shall we give chase?" someone called.

"No," Qall replied. "Let them go." He looked around at the Restorers, who were still, shielding against the continuing machine attack, and raised his voice. "Be ready to link!"

He moved into the place between worlds and dove towards Kettin, Rielle and Hapre following, and landed several paces from Kettin's head. Arriving beside him, Rielle stared down at the strange replica of a human face. The jewelled eyes seemed to glow.

"Is she alive?" she asked.

"I don't know," he admitted.

Hapre glanced at Qall. "Is it a trap?"

"Perhaps. But if there's any chance she could be repaired, we must destroy this. If it's really her."

The jewel eyes moved, swivelling towards Qall. A voice came out of the head.

"Fooled you."

Rielle tensed, increasing the strength of her shield. The air misted with cold as Qall did so as well.

And then the light behind the humanoid eyes died.

They did not move for a long moment, then Qall shook his head. "No," he muttered. "Surely she wouldn't."

"Was it Kettin or not?" Hapre asked.

Qall looked around at the fallen followers. "Her supporters thought so. Surely she isn't willing to sacrifice them for the sake of a . . . a . . ."

"A joke?" Rielle replied. "Or a trick?"

"Or a distraction?" Hapre suggested.

A hollow feeling bloomed in Rielle's gut. "From what?"

The three of them exchanged glances, then looked up. The mass of machines swarmed between them and the sun, blotting out the light.

"The Restorer base," Qall said.

Rielle caught her breath. "Baluka!"

Hapre's eyes widened. "Of course. Affen. It's what I'd do . . ."

Qall bent and scooped up the humanoid head, then straightened and pointed to one of the nearby fallen machines. "Grab one of those," he told Hapre, then he took Rielle's arm and lifted them into the air, hurrying back towards the Restorers.

"Link!" he shouted as he reached them. Hapre appeared at his side, holding the broken machine.

"You should smash that," she said, looking at the head.

"It's nothing. A decoy," Qall replied. "It was never Kettin. She knew we were coming. She's planned this all along. But Tyen may learn something useful from it, which might make this whole battle worthwhile." He looked around. "Anyone not ready?"

No reply came. The army was barely visible in the shadow of the attacking machines. Rielle took a deep breath.

And then everyone was drawn into whiteness.

CHAPTER 20

O nce all the Restorer fighters knew the reason for their hasty flight, few had spoken. Not even when they stopped to wait for Rielle and the other mortal sorcerers to catch their breath. Rielle knew she was slowing them down and tried to convince Qall to leave her behind. While she wanted to help, if the base was, indeed, under attack, she did not want to be the reason they didn't arrive on time. Qall replied with a flat "no". They would not last long against another machine army if she did not generate magic for them.

They paused a world before Affen so she could do just that. The idea of making pretty light patterns in the middle of a tense, impatient army felt strange and inappropriate, so she drew out some paper and drawing sticks and sketched a few faces instead. Qall moved about answering questions and reassuring everyone that people would be sent back to gather the bodies of the fallen. Those with family or friends awaiting their return in the Restorers' base were anxious to move on, but all were afraid they would not survive another battle with the machines.

They'd lost a quarter of their number.

The faces she drew were lined with worry. As she finished a sketch and put it aside, a hand touched her arm. Qall's.

"That will do, I think," he said. "We could always be stronger, but I don't want to wait any longer."

"Are you sure? I thought nobody would die as long as I created enough magic, but we've lost so many."

He met her gaze, his own steady and serious. "Their deaths are not your fault, Rielle. We had all the magic we needed."

"But—"

"Mistakes and surprises," he said. "If we'd had a chance to refine our strategy further, more might have lived, but we didn't have time."

He sounded older. Worried. Her heart clenched. This would all be affecting him too. He was so young, had taken on a huge responsibility, and this was his first battle. He was doing well, but at what cost? She sighed and began packing away her drawings and implements. Qall straightened, and his voice rose over the murmurs of the waiting sorcerers.

"It is time," he told them. "We don't know what we'll find. It may be death and devastation. It may be a battle. It may be a trap. Kettin may have some dreadful new weapon awaiting us." He paused. "We are not as numerous as we were, but we are still strong and the Maker is with us. Kettin is far from her home world and many of her supporters have died. Our chances are good. Even so, if anyone does not wish to go you may leave us now, with our thanks for your help."

Not one sorcerer stirred, though Rielle could not know if anyone outside of her view had faded out of sight.

Qall nodded. "Thank you. We go in. Be prepared for nasty surprises. Link."

Connections were remade. Rielle slung her pack onto her back and took Qall's hand.

"Anyone not ready?" he asked.

Silence. Rielle took a deep breath.

The world faded from sight.

The place between was empty of other presences. When details of the Restorers' world began to emerge, she thought, for a moment, that all was well. Then shadows on the ground gained detail, and she recognised the all-too-familiar sight of corpses. Among them were many, many objects moving with the precise and relentless ease of mechanisation.

As air surrounded her, her stomach sank and twisted with nausea. She drew in a deep breath, watching as the nearest machines stopped moving and turned to face the arrivals.

"Levitate," Qall ordered. "In formation."

As one, the army began to rise, fighters taking positions above, below and around Rielle. Several machines rose up to follow and attack. Qall stopped not far above the city. He turned to Rielle.

"Help me gather information," he murmured. "I want to know if anyone is alive before we waste too much of our energy fighting machines."

Rielle grimaced in agreement. Looking in the direction of the Restorers' base, she immediately found several minds in the area.

"The base has been levelled," she said.

"Yes. There are people hiding underground."

She looked below ground and found the minds of the building's occupants immediately. A few were freshly buried, in pain and terror and with not enough magic to push out of the world and skim to safety. *Hold on,* she thought at them. *Rescue will come.* Other sorcerers were uninjured and hiding in the levels below. Looking deeper, she found the minds of two sorcerers that did not belong there. Kettin's followers, their thoughts revealed. They were hunting for more of the Restorer leadership to kill, confident that as the strongest of Kettin's followers they'd succeed. Rielle's heart lodged in her throat. She skipped from mind to mind, then let out a gasp of relief when she found a familiar one, sitting in the meeting room.

"I've found Baluka."

"As have I," Qall replied darkly. "He has company."

Looking through Baluka's eyes, Rielle saw a woman's face. Something was oddly familiar about it, and when she read the

427

woman's identity from Baluka she realised why. The humanoid had been modelled on it. It had the same inhuman beauty.

"Kettin," she hissed.

"They won't try to save me," Baluka was saying. "I'm not their leader any more."

"Oh, but they value you greatly," Kettin replied. "They won't want to abandon someone so famous. It would be demoralising. And the Maker is your friend. What sort of friend would she be if she lets you die?"

Baluka shook his head. Kettin had told him that if anyone but Rielle approached them she would kill him. He could see no good end to this situation. He could not hope that rescuers would read his mind and learn of the danger, because then Rielle would fall into whatever trap Kettin was laying. Yet he could not wish that rescuers wouldn't read his mind because not only would he die, but they would too.

He didn't know what Kettin intended to do if Rielle arrived. Rielle looked into the woman's mind . . . and found no answer. If Kettin had a plan she must have found a way to prevent herself thinking about it. She truly believed that all she wanted to do was talk to Rielle.

"What are you going to do to her?" Baluka asked.

"I told you," Kettin replied. "I just want to have a chat."

Rielle looked at Qall. He frowned as he met her eyes. "She must be able to hide her memories as Dahli can, and trigger their return at the right moment."

It's going to be so interesting to see her thoughts, Kettin was thinking. *It's possible she doesn't know why she's such a strong Maker, or else she does and it's impossible to replicate. Otherwise the worlds would be full of Makers of her strength.*

"She thinks she is stronger than me," Rielle observed. "She has underestimated me." She met Qall's eyes again. "I think I can rescue Baluka."

His frown deepened. "It is a risk. And we need you here."

"The magic I generated before we arrived will last a while, and it will not take long for me to dash in there, grab Baluka and leave."

Qall shook his head. "She'll say something that will force you to stay and listen to her."

"If I don't stop long enough for her to, she won't get the chance."

"We can't risk losing you—"

"And we can risk losing Baluka?" she snapped. He winced and she regretted her tone, but this was no time to be gentle. "The moment I start making magic here she'll sense it. If any of her followers have spotted us, they will be rushing to tell her. Once she knows I'm here she'll torture Baluka in order to force me to go to her. Our only chance to save Baluka is to surprise her, right *now*."

Qall stared back at her. His lips pressed together. His eyes reflected doubt.

Then he nodded once. "Just . . . be careful. I'll be watching. If she tries to blackmail you, I'll come fetch you myself."

Rielle squeezed his hand. "Thanks."

She let go of him. Looking back in the direction of the Restorers' building to orientate herself, she pushed out of the world and propelled herself towards it. Skimming to the top of the ruins, she paused to take a deep breath and get her bearings, then she left the world again and plunged downwards.

She counted the floors, aiming to stop in the room above the meeting room. Several of the floors below were still illuminated by lamps, helping her find her way. She moved carefully, all too aware that Kettin would be alert to the thoughts of everyone in the building and would notice any shadows they saw. A stretch of rubble passed . . .

. . . then she passed through the ceiling of a familiar room, one occupant facing away from her, the other sitting at a long table, his gaze lowered. The latter was Baluka, so the former must be Kettin.

Silently cursing, Rielle dropped quickly down through the floor and was relieved to find the next room empty. The collapsed floors above had put out her count of floor by one, and she had nearly materialised in the same room as Kettin and Baluka. Arriving, she searched for the two minds above, found Baluka's and confirmed he had not seen her. Neither had Kettin.

Rielle let out a deep sigh of relief. Then, moving forward, she considered what to do next. She wanted to arrive out of sight but within reach of Baluka. She smiled briefly as she realised where the best place was.

Positioning herself carefully, she pushed out of the world again. Skimming slowly upwards, she let her head pass though the ceiling and up through the floor of the room above until her eyes entered the room. As she hoped, she could see legs: the table's, chairs' — and those of two humans.

Swivelling her body to a horizontal position, she rose upwards until she was fully within the room, lying on her side. Carefully checking and adjusting until none of the chair legs were within her body, she brought herself into the world.

At once, gravity settled her onto the ground with a soft thud. Her heart lurched. Was it loud enough to alert Kettin? Reaching out, she grabbed Baluka's ankle and quickly pushed out of the world again.

And rapidly propelled them away.

Upwards first. In moments, the ruined building was gone and they were shooting into the sky. A startled Baluka threw out his arms, then looked around and, as he saw her, blinked at her in surprise. She extended her other hand towards him and he reached down to grasp it. They pushed, pulled and adjusted their position so that they now faced each other.

"Rielle Lazuli."

The voice was feminine. They looked down towards the base. A figure shot up from the Restorers' building. It moved fast, and before Rielle could skim away, Kettin was beside her, grasping her arm. Rielle felt a light, ineffectual tugging.

430

Kettin's triumphant smile faded, and a crease appeared between her perfect eyebrows as the feminine voice spoke again. "*You're stronger than me!*"

Keeping a firm hold on Baluka, Rielle placed herself between him and the woman. She stared back at Kettin. The woman could not stop Rielle returning to Qall, but she might follow her back to the Restorer army. Still, that might be a good thing. Kettin on her own was not a great threat. Perhaps Rielle should try to lure her there. Would capturing Kettin bring about the end of the machine conquest or would she have made sure her followers would continue destroying worlds if she was killed or imprisoned? She doubted Kettin would be so easily caught, though. And rescuing Baluka was Rielle's priority right now.

"*Let go of me,*" Rielle ordered.

Kettin blinked, then smiled. "*But I want to talk to you.*"

Remembering Qall's warning about blackmail, Rielle grabbed Kettin's wrist and forced her hand off her arm. "*I don't want to talk to you.*"

"*Wait!*" Kettin protested. "*Don't you want to know what I have to say? Why I'm doing all this?*"

"*No,*" Rielle replied, pushing the woman away. "*There is no excuse that could justify it.*" She propelled herself and Baluka towards Qall.

"*You and I are the same,*" Kettin said, following. "*We both came from dead worlds. We were both raised to believe magic is evil. We are both criminals in the minds of our people.*"

Rielle risked a glance away, looking for Qall and the army. "*You know nothing about me, if you believe that to be true.*"

Kettin smiled. "*Ah, but I have been to your world. I know they think you are an Angel now, and that you gave them permission to use the magic you gave them.*"

Had she not been between worlds, Rielle might have felt a pang of worry or flare of anger. She was grateful for the detachment, as she was able to control her expression and not betray her feelings. Kettin might be lying. She might not. If the woman thought Rielle cared that much about her home world then she truly did not understand her.

Glancing away again, feigning distain, Rielle finally spotted a ball of dark shapes – the Restorers obscured by the machines attacking them. A nagging feeling reminded her that she and Baluka could not remain in the place between worlds much longer. Yet she looked back at Kettin.

"Call off your machines and I will listen."

Kettin glanced at the battle. Her shoulders rose and she grimaced. *"I'm afraid I can't do that. Once animated there is no way to recall them."*

Rielle narrowed her eyes at the woman. She did not think this was a lie. Zeke had said as much.

"Then there is no reason to stay." Turning, she skimmed towards the army.

"Listen to me!" Kettin called from not far behind.

That the woman was still following surprised Rielle. She imagined Kettin chasing her all the way back to Qall. And then Qall killing Kettin. *Could I live with knowing I led this woman to her death?* Perhaps with *this* woman, she could. But if she could do that, why not kill Kettin herself?

"Magic is evil." Kettin's voice remained close behind. *"It is the manifestation of all the darkness within humans. It too easily allows us to subjugate and kill each other. Without magic, we would all be equal. I aim to reduce the magic in the worlds. To free them from the rule of sorcerers."*

Baluka looked back. *"If you are so against magic, why do you use it? And if you consider killing to be wrong, why do you slaughter everyone when you conquer a world, whether they have magical ability or not? Why do you kill the subjugated as well as the subjugator?"*

"For a big evil you need a big weapon, and a big weapon is bound to strike more than the target." Kettin sounded sad, but determined. *"To cleanse the worlds of magic there have to be sacrifices. It will be better afterwards. I will make sure of that."*

Rielle could think of a hundred things to say to that, but the need to get herself and Baluka to air was more urgent. The woman was either mad or . . . *What? I'm not sure. But definitely not worth suffocating within worlds for.* The Restorers' army floated before her now, beset by machines from above and below. She propelled herself towards it.

Kettin's voice grew more distant.

"I was going to invite you to join me," she called. *"Then I could keep the worlds in check with rewards as well as control them with threats. I could offer magic to those who are worthy."*

Rielle reached the edge of machines attacking the Restorers. She paused and looked back.

"I would never join you."

"I'm not inviting you." Kettin's smile was gone. *"I said I was going to. Not now. You are stronger than me, and a Maker. That makes you more dangerous than any sorcerer that has lived. More dangerous than me, even. You could destroy all the worlds."*

Rielle frowned. Was Kettin speaking of Maker's Curse? If she was . . . how much more destruction would she wreak if she believed it was her duty to eliminate Rielle? Would she still do so, if she knew Rielle was not ageless? It would reveal a vulnerability, but it might be worth the risk . . .

"Only if I become ageless again," Rielle told her.

"'Again'," Kettin repeated, unsurprised. *"If you already know how to, you will do it again. You won't be able to resist the temptation when you're dying of old age. I'm not prepared to wait and see. I'm going to have to kill you, Rielle Lazuli."*

"That doesn't change much, from my perspective."

"It changes everything," the woman said. *"We will meet again."*

And then she quickly faded out of sight.

PART EIGHT

TYEN

CHAPTER 19

"To be honest, I'm surprised at our progress. I thought it would all fall apart within a few days," Tyen admitted.

Halyn nodded. "Well, only a few days have passed since the vote."

Tyen glanced at his calendar. "Yes, it just seems far longer." He nodded at the sorcerers practising beyond the window. "And too early to give Tarren the credit for providing my detractors reason to cooperate."

"His offer to train anyone in the fine arts of sorcerous warfare was no accident," Halyn replied. "He knew it would have that effect. Who could resist the lure of learning from a famous teacher of the worlds?"

"Yes, and he's had plenty of practice at keeping sorcerers, be they students or teachers, in line. When I was at Liftre he was mostly retired, but everyone in charge admired and respected him, even if they didn't always agree with him."

"We're lucky to have him then. He has asked why no women have entered his class, and was surprised when told that Leratian women are not interested in fighting."

"Not yet." Tyen smiled wryly, as he thought of the subjects the Empress had expressed desire to learn. "They will in future. Did you check in with Zeke?"

"Yes. He's taken to being in charge of the machine investigations well. They all seem to respect him and are happy to follow his orders.

"Does he have any good news for us?"

Halyn shook his head. "Not yet. He hasn't submitted the daily reports you requested."

Tyen shrugged. "No, he was never one for keeping records. But then, I'm there half the day, helping out, so he doesn't really need to."

"Not if they are solely to inform you, but there are others interested in their progress," Halyn pointed out.

"Academy sorcerers?"

"Mostly."

"And the rest? Sorcerers outside the Academy?"

"None have yet requested them."

"Then who?" Tyen looked up. "The Emperor?"

"Of course. And others who are concerned about threats to this world."

"Who will be receiving reports from me, not Zeke." Tyen turned away from the window and regarded his chair. "Which I should get around to writing. Is there anything else we need to discuss?"

Halyn sighed. "Well there's . . ."

A knock at the door interrupted him.

"Come in," he called.

The door opened and one of the watchers from the Grand Hall stepped into the room, his gaze flickering to Halyn before returning to Tyen.

"Visitors have appeared in the hall," the young man said.

"Visitors?" Tyen repeated. He cast his mind out, searching for the minds of otherworld sorcerers. "Did they introduce themselves?"

"Yes. Rielle Lazuli and Qall. Just Qall. No surname, apparently."

Tyen's heart lifted, then sank as quickly. If Qall had risked the safety of this world by coming here, something important must have happened. Unless it was someone else . . . Looking into the watcher's mind, he saw a memory of a figure that did, indeed, look like the Restorers' new leader. Standing up, Tyen stepped around the desk. "Sorry, Halyn. Whatever you were about to raise will have to wait."

His assistant's eyes were wide. "Is that the Qall who rules all the worlds?"

"Yes and no," Tyen replied as he strode to the door. "He doesn't *rule* all the worlds. He leads the Restorers, who work to keep the worlds from descending into chaos." He turned to the watcher. "Where are our guests now?"

Halyn blinked in surprise, thinking that Tyen never asked where people were. He always seemed to know. Which meant . . . these newcomers could be even more powerful than Tyen. And Halyn had just demanded their names and purpose. Had he been too officious?

"Waiting in the hall," he replied weakly.

Tyen nodded and started in that direction.

"What protocols are there for greeting the most powerful man in the worlds?" came Halyn's voice from behind him.

Glancing back, Tyen found his assistant following close behind. "None. The Restorers discourage the kinds of elaborate ceremony and ritual that strengthen the divisions of class and hierarchy. Most of their founders came from places where power was abused, so they see such things as manifestations of inequality."

"I see." Halyn was quiet for a stretch, then as Tyen neared the hall he spoke again. "If everyone's equal, how is it that there is a leader?"

Tyen chuckled. "Practicality. They do have a hierarchy but it's there to aid communication and representation, not strengthen hereditary systems of power or ideas that one race is somehow naturally better than another."

"Sounds fascinating," Halyn murmured.

Arriving at the hall, Tyen looked for and found two figures standing where the pile of machines had been before it had been taken to the mechanical magic wing for study. At their feet lay a single machine – something similar to the ones that had attacked him in Kettin's world. Qall had obviously sensed Tyen approaching, as he and Rielle were facing the doorway. They were smiling, he noted with relief.

"Qall," he said as he strode towards them. "Rielle. It is good to see you both again." As he reached them he inclined his head to show Qall this was the customary greeting. The young man returned the gesture of respect.

"Tyen." Qall's gaze moved to Tyen's shadow. "And Halyn. Yes, I am as young as I look."

Tyen glanced at his assistant in time to see the man hide his embarrassment.

"Stop it, Qall," Rielle murmured in the Traveller tongue. Her smile had vanished into such a serious expression it made Tyen's heart skip a beat. *All is not well*, he thought, and his earlier foreboding returned.

Qall turned to her. "He doesn't mind."

"Yet," she said. "Tyen's world is new to mind reading, and you should not take advantage of Halyn's awe of you to show off. We can't risk offending this world's people." She turned to Tyen and switched to Leratian. "You're probably wondering why I brought Qall here. Is there somewhere we can talk in private?"

Her expression sent a chill down Tyen's spine. "Of course," he replied. "Would you like some refreshments?"

"That would be most welcome," she replied. "We dared not stop and seek out any in case we were recognised."

"Come to the visitors' room." He gestured to indicate that they should follow, then led the way, Halyn nodding once before slipping away to fetch food and drink.

The visitors' room was now across the corridor from the hall. It had been used as a storeroom until Tyen had chosen it as a place to meet with important and powerful visitors. The fine decoration told of a less humble past, and arrangements were being made to have the paint and gilding refreshed. A dining table and chairs filled the far end, and a suite of comfortable seats surrounded a low table nearer the entrance. All were quality pieces made of fine materials and decorated in good taste. Good enough for a visit by the Emperor, but not so indulgent as to make it seem that Tyen was wasting Academy funds.

He directed Qall and Rielle to the seats, then sat opposite them. Both had brought well-filled packs, he noted, as if prepared to travel for some time.

"You wouldn't be carrying those if it were good news," he pointed out. "So, what has happened?"

"We brought the fight to Kettin," Qall told him. The young man described the whole battle, and his care in explaining the success and failure of both sides' strategies hinted that he thought Tyen would need to draw upon the lessons they'd learned in future, despite the fact that they won the battle. Hearing that Kettin's fighters had been led by a humanoid chilled Tyen, but he'd thought many times about how she might succeed in becoming a machine and what it could cost her. It did not surprise him to hear that she had not used magic, or that the humanoid proved not to be her, and was easily destroyed.

". . . but when we examined her body we found the humanoid's head, though detached from its body, was still animated," Qall continued. He leaned down and opened his pack, bringing out a gleaming metallic head and setting it on the table. "And a voice from within it said, 'Fooled you.'"

Tyen stared at the head. It was nothing like that of the humanoid he'd made more than five cycles ago, hoping it might house Vella's mind. Were these features modelled on Kettin's face?

"If this wasn't her, then where was she?" He drew in a sharp breath as he saw the obvious answer. "It was a distraction. They were attacking you elsewhere. The base?"

"Yes," Qall replied. "When we returned a great deal of damage had already been done. Several Restorers and thousands upon thousands of Affen's inhabitants had died. We concentrated on evacuating as many survivors as possible, then we scattered. Since then, Kettin has been attacking worlds randomly . . . well, not entirely randomly, as she is targeting worlds important to us too, but her followers and machines are no longer solely spreading outwards from her world in a ring formation as they did in the past."

"So the Restorers have no base now." Tyen's heart lurched. "Is Baluka still alive?"

Qall looked at Rielle. "It would be best he heard this from you."

Tyen's stomach sank and filled with dread.

"Don't worry. Baluka is fine," she assured him. She drew in a little breath, then let it out. "He was in charge of the base while we were gone. I found him by his mind, trapped in the meeting room with Kettin. She had told him that if anyone but me tried to rescue him she'd kill him. I managed to enter the room underneath the table, grab Baluka's ankle and transport him away. She followed, and told me she had intended to invite me to join her."

Tyen frowned. "Do you believe that?"

Rielle's shoulders lifted. "I'm not sure. She seemed earnest. She said we were alike: both from dead worlds where we were regarded as criminals. That magic is evil – the manifestation of darkness in humans. It allows us to oppress and kill. She intended to strip most worlds of it in order to make people more equal, and wanted me to join her so she could reward worlds with magic as well as punish them by removing it." She smiled thinly as Tyen raised his eyebrows at the hypocrisy. "When Baluka questioned her killing of innocent people she said she needed a big weapon to defeat a big evil, and that sacrifices had to be made. But it would be better afterwards."

"How can killing all the people within a world make their life better?"

Rielle spread her hands. "I don't know. It was strange talking to her. Without her mask . . . it made her more human somehow. I could not help wondering, later, what had driven her to become

442

so ruthless. She thought she could convince me to join her, despite all she has done. But then, her attitude switched direction suddenly. She had assumed that I would be weaker than her, because I am a Maker and therefore not strong enough to become ageless. When she realised I was stronger, she no longer wanted me to join her, because if I was this powerful I could became ageless, which made me too dangerous . . . which suggests she really does care about the worlds."

A thrill ran down Tyen's back. "She knows of Maker's Curse."

"Yes." Rielle tilted her head a little and narrowed her eyes. "What about that made you sit up all straight and alert?"

He smiled. "Do you remember a young sorcerer named Annad?"

She blinked. "Yes. He is trying to find a lost library containing information about Maker's Curse."

"He found it." Tyen grinned. "Here, under the Academy, in one of Roporien's secret vaults."

Qall straightened and leaned forward. "The vaults. Yes. Valhan sought them out. He knew he'd never found them all."

Tyen turned to stare at the young man. "He did?" Qall nodded. "Well, I suppose he would. Roporien was a seeker of knowledge. It's possible he's the true founder of the Academy. It is said to have grown out of a school based in Beltonia more than thirteen hundred years ago, and we know from Vella that he was in this world around then." Tyen turned to Rielle. "Annad told the Librarian of his quest. Kep saw that his intentions were good and, well, he likes you, so he took Annad into the tunnels below the Academy vault, and they found the record Annad was seeking. But they couldn't translate it."

Tyen tried not to smile at the disappointment in Rielle's eyes.

"They came to me hoping that Vella knew the ancient language," he continued. "She does, and has stored the record. I've left her with Kep, so the two of them can study it."

"And what did it say?" Qall prompted.

"It describes sorcerers known as the Ancients. They were very powerful – probably more powerful than us – and knew how to connect and separate worlds. The warning that should a Maker become ageless the worlds will be torn apart is a mistranslation of a passage. All it is saying is that a Maker who becomes ageless can link and part worlds."

Rielle's eyes went wide. She looked from Tyen to Qall. "I could do that?"

"According to this record," Tyen replied. He looked at Qall. "It occurred to me that if Rielle could do this, we could isolate Kettin's worlds." He paused. "Though if she has abandoned them and is roaming around striking worlds at random that will not work any more."

"No," Qall agreed. "But we could lure her into a world, then isolate it."

"It would have to be somewhere uninhabited."

"And she must believe it is important to us."

Rielle reached out to grab Qall and Tyen's sleeves. "You can work that out later. Does the record say *how* I can become ageless without losing my Maker ability?"

Tyen grimaced. "No, I'm afraid it doesn't. I guess you'll have to work it out yourself."

She sighed. "If it were that easy, surely other Makers would have stumbled upon it in the thousands of years since these Ancients lived."

"Unless it has been that long since a Maker of your strength emerged," Qall pointed out. "Valhan never met anyone like you."

"I want to see this record for myself," Rielle declared. "Perhaps there is some code in it. And you should come, Qall. It may be something that only someone with Valhan's memories could unlock."

"Tyen has all of Valhan's knowledge, in Vella," Qall reminded him.

"Yes, but that is different to knowing how he thought," she replied.

He looked from her to Tyen. "Well then. Can we see it?"

"I can't see why not." As Tyen rose, they got to their feet. "Follow me."

He led them out into the corridor. As they passed one of the hall entrances, Tyen glanced in and saw Zeke and a few other inventors examining the machine. "When we come back, tell Zeke how it was used in the battle," he said to Rielle and Qall. "It might help."

"We will," Qall assured him.

They passed a handful of Academy members and staff on the way to the Library. These eyed Qall with curiosity but not alarm. They were used to otherworld newcomers appearing in the institution's corridors now. Most noted how handsome Qall was, and it amused Tyen to see how this made them more inclined to trust him. He then began to wonder how much of Qall's adopted appearance had been chosen to have this effect. *Or is it more for his own benefit, because he wants to feel he is a friendly, easily trusted person? It would certainly be easier than constantly seeing people assessing you and deciding you're suspicious.*

That reminded him of the hunt for a place to settle that had led him to Doum. No matter where he went, he was an outsider and stranger. Only in Leratia was he truly home. He'd never thought he'd be welcome here again. That he was made him even more determined to protect his world. If it was destroyed, he would have lost his home.

As he led Qall and Rielle into the library, he sought and found Kep and Annad's minds. They were down in the vault already, studying other rare records. He took Qall and Rielle through the tunnels and locked door, noting their amusement at the safeguards.

"Yes, this is definitely Roporien's work," Qall said as they arrived in the vault. "Valhan would have recognised it."

Kep had looked up as they'd entered, and now he stared at Qall intently. As he opened his mouth to speak, Annad spoke.

"Rielle Lazuli!" he exclaimed. "You're here at last!"

"I am," she replied, smiling and coming forward to meet him. "I hear you have succeeded in your search. Tyen has told me what you've learned."

He nodded and looked at Tyen. Taking advantage of the pause, Tyen made the introductions.

"I thought you might be," Kep said as Tyen announced Qall's name and responsibilities. "Nobody else could be so certain about the Raen's memories."

Qall's eyebrows rose. "Rielle told you of my past."

"Vella did. Not all of it, I'm guessing."

Qall nodded. "We are here to see the record that contains information about Maker's Curse." Qall glanced at Rielle. "I think we'd like to see the record itself, before we read Vella's translation."

Kep nodded, then turned to Tyen. "As Director, it's your decision who may see the inner vaults." A habitual reluctance to reveal the secret store had risen in him. He wanted to be sure Tyen was considering carefully who had access to them.

"I give permission for you to show them," Tyen replied.

The Librarian nodded, then beckoned and led the way to the secret door.

"I'll stay here," Annad said. "So it won't get too crowded in there."

Once again, the Librarian opened the sliding door and led them into the crack in the rock.

"Well, this is not for the faint-hearted," Rielle muttered as they slid along the narrow space. Tyen noted that Qall was eyeing other protected alcoves containing tablets, carvings and various objects. Kep stopped beside the Scroll of the Ancients, giving Rielle and Qall room to lie under it. The linked gold plates gleamed softly in the magical lights floating above their heads.

Qall stared at the scroll in silence for some time before he spoke.

"Some of the characters seem familiar, but I can't make sense of it." He sounded disappointed. "I doubt Valhan would have."

"But Vella can," Rielle reminded him. "She must have picked up the language from someone."

"From a scholar," Kep told them. "More than thirteen hundred years ago."

"So what's on the other side of these gold pages?" Qall asked. "Have you turned them over?"

"Ah . . . I'd not thought of that," Kep admitted. "I am afraid to move it though, in case I break it. Sometimes ancient things look perfectly solid but disintegrate at a touch."

"The plates are gold and quite thick," Qall noted. "Even the links are gold." He looked at Tyen. "I think it is worth the risk, but the decision is yours."

Tyen nodded. "If there's a chance Rielle can become ageless again, we must try." He looked at Kep. "It may be all that we need to stop Kettin destroying the worlds. We have everything on this side of the plates recorded in Vella. We won't lose the information if they are destroyed."

The Librarian swallowed, then sighed. "As Qall said, it's your choice, Director."

Tyen turned back to the record. "Then I say it should be done. As the Librarian and expert on ancient treasures of the Academy, you should do it, Rytan Kep. Carefully."

"Of course." The Librarian slid along the rock until he was central to the alcove, Qall and Rielle moving out of the way. He stared intently at the record. Turning to watch the gold plates, Tyen held his breath as the leftmost one began to move. As it slowly revolved, the links tightened and the next plate began to turn, and as that turned it moved the next. In this way, from the left to the right, Kep slowly flipped the whole record over.

The rear of the first two plates were blank, sending a stab of disappointment through Tyen. The third held one glyph. The fourth, however, revealed writing of the same size as that on the front of the plates. Tyen let his breath out slowly as more and more of the text was revealed. Turning his head, he called back to Annad.

447

"Bring Vella!"

"Yes, Director!" the young man replied.

A short silence followed, then the sound of Annad's clothes scraping across stone. As he reached Tyen he lifted the strap of Vella's satchel off his head and handed it over. With slightly trembly hands, Tyen drew her out, held her up and began examining the marks closely.

Qall moved closer so he could see the text forming on Vella's pages. The young man remained silent, not giving anything away. Tyen worked as fast as he dared, wanting answers but wary of missing something. When his gaze had finally settled on the last character, he let out a sigh of relief.

"What does it say? What does it say?" Rielle whispered.

Tyen looked eagerly at the pages before him.

What do you make of it, Vella?

Letters formed.

It is upside down, of course, she replied. *But otherwise the same script as before. I will translate from here . . .*

He read the words aloud for the others' benefit. In several places they interrupted to seek clarification, and a few times he paused to exchange a puzzled look with them. When he'd finished, Rielle let out a small huff of frustration.

"I expect it will only make sense when you do it," Tyen told her.

"I hope so," Qall agreed. "Because if someone wanted to destroy a Maker, this would be a clever way to do so."

A chill ran down Tyen's spine as he saw the truth of that. The method was not dissimilar to that for learning pattern-shifting, which would make Rielle ageless but also remove her Maker ability. The instructions claimed that the differences would allow her to retain her particular gift. They said that she would have a new part added to her mind, and in doing so she would not quite be human any more. The tone of the text held a hint of warning, perhaps even disapproval, calling the change unnatural.

"It may have been written for a Maker who has never been

ageless before," Rielle pointed out. "I've been ageless, then returned to being a Maker. In fact, I made myself a far stronger Maker." She pursed her lips. "I think I could restore my Maker ability again, if I failed."

"If you haven't used all the magic of a world trying to follow these instructions," Tyen pointed out.

She shook her head. "All I had to do last time was sketch on a wall to generate enough magic to do it." She smiled at him. "As you know, it's the learning of pattern-shifting that takes so much magic. Using it takes not much at all."

Tyen nodded. "That's true. But will you need plenty of magic to *relearn* pattern-shifting?"

She frowned. "Yes. Fortunately, while I have my Maker ability I create more than enough to do that."

Qall shifted restlessly. "Let's return to a more comfortable room to speculate on this." He looked over to Kep. "I suggest you turn the plates over again. It would be wise to hide instructions on how to become a god, even if the circumstances in which it can occur prove to be extremely rare."

"A god?" Rielle shook her head. "I wouldn't be a god."

"You wouldn't be human any more," Qall pointed out.

"But not a god. Just a slightly altered human."

"Some cultures would consider you a demon," Kep added quietly. He shrugged as they all looked at him. "People's ideas are as diverse as the worlds are infinite and diverse."

"Then let's hope *that* idea isn't a common one," Tyen said.

Kep nodded. He shifted towards Tyen, preparing to take his place and flip the scroll back over. "You can find your way back?"

Once in the vault again, Rielle and Qall did not speak, both standing silent and preoccupied. Annad regarded them nervously, wondering how he'd had the fortune, good or bad, to be in this place and moment, with three of the worlds' most powerful sorcerers, all rendered speechless by what they had just learned. Eventually, Rielle shrugged.

"I have to try this," she said. "It might be our only way to stop Kettin."

"It's too risky," Qall disagreed. "We can't risk losing your unique skills right now. We will find another way to defeat Kettin. She is not as strong as we. She can be killed. Her machines will be an ongoing threat, but they can be defeated." He looked at Tyen. "And the inventors may still come up with a mechanical solution."

Rielle turned to face Qall. "Yes, it's a risk, but if it leads to fewer people being killed it's worth taking."

"Not if it leaves the worlds without a Maker."

"It won't. I can always change back if I fail."

"You can't be sure of that." He took a step towards her. "At least take some time to consider the implications."

"How long? Each moment we wait, thousands die."

"That is not your fault."

"No, but doing nothing when I could have helped is almost as bad," she told him. "This is my decision. You know that I'll try it eventually, when I'm old and dying." Her lips pressed into a stubborn line. "Kettin was right about that. So I may as well try it now."

Qall straightened. "You'll need an ageless sorcerer to help you," he pointed out. "Someone more powerful than you."

"More, or equal," Rielle reminded him, moving closer to Tyen.

Qall looked from her to Tyen. "Tyen needs to stay here and work on the machine solution."

Rielle looked at Tyen expectantly. He regarded them both, considering their views, weighing his options.

"Actually, I don't," he told Qall. "I have people far smarter than me working on the problem, and with a common threat to unite and occupy the Academy, it is back to running itself quite well."

Qall scowled. "If it is a long process, who will protect or evacuate your world should Kettin invade in the meantime?"

"I had hoped you—"

"On my own?" Qall's eyebrows rose in disbelief.

"Well, if *you* can't, what hope have *I* got?"

"Not much, but you do have one advantage: your people will follow you. Not me." Qall glanced at Rielle. "Just as you could not unite and lead the Restorers again as easily as Rielle and I can. We can't hang about here. We must gather our allies and continue the fight or there will soon be nobody left to use your inventors' solution on the machines."

"Perhaps Tyen and I could work the change here," Rielle injected. "There would be no risk of us being recognised and our path traced back to this world. Tyen could watch over the inventors at the same time and—"

"No," Qall said firmly. "If you do this, you must go to an unoccupied world."

Tyen winced. He turned to Rielle. "He has a point. If you fail, you leave my world vulnerable."

She looked at Tyen, her lips twitching as if she wanted to object, then turned back to Qall. "I'm not going with you. I will stay here, so that if Tyen's world is attacked it has some hope of surviving long enough to find a solution to the machines."

"But we need your ability to make magic!"

"Not until you go into battle. You don't need my help in gathering the Restorers together. Or to make plans for how to fight Kettin. But when you do, don't dismiss Tyen's idea of trapping her in an isolated world. It might be the best idea we have. Or the worst." The stare she levelled at him was challenging. "In the end, it's my decision, so you had better come back with a good argument for me not becoming an Ancient . . . or demon . . . or whatever we decide to call it."

Qall held her gaze for a few moments before nodding. "I'll consider it. As long as you also consider the possible pitfalls, and alternatives, to what you want to do before you try anything."

She crossed her arms. "Of course I will. Do you really think I wouldn't?"

"I'm not sure," Qall replied softly, his eye narrowing. "At least agree to wait until I've had time to think it over – until I come back."

Rielle nodded reluctantly. "Very well. I'll wait."

Qall smiled, somehow instantly shifting back into his usual friendly, obliging demeanour.

"Well then," he said. He turned to Tyen. "Is there anything else you need to know or want to tell me before I go?"

Tyen considered, then shook his head. "But please do leave from the same path you entered along."

Qall nodded. "Of course." He glanced up. "I should talk to Zeke before I go."

"No need," Rielle said. "I'll do it."

The young man's lips pressed together. "Then I guess I shouldn't delay leaving any longer."

CHAPTER 20

Tyen paused to look around the Grand Hall, taking advantage of a rare moment of quiet to be still for a moment. Little sounds he would not normally notice soon came to his attention. The shuffle of the watchers as they wondered why he was still standing there. The distant hum of the city. A muffled buzz from somewhere beyond the Academy walls he couldn't place.

He thought back to the last conversation he'd had with Qall a few days ago, before the young man had left.

Looking around the hall, Qall had sighed. "She's mad at me," he'd said. "I thought she'd see me off before she went to talk to Zeke. Do you think I am wrong, telling her not to attempt the transformation?"

Tyen had smiled. "No. But I'm not sure you have the right to tell her what to do, either."

"Not as the leader of the Restorers?"

"Did she swear loyalty to them?"

"No." Lines of worry creased Qall's brow. "I guess I took it for granted. I took her for granted. Have I lost her support?"

"I don't think so," Tyen had assured him. "She will always feel a little responsible for you."

Qall had let out a small snort. "Yes, well, I'm not that foolish young man she took to the edges of the worlds. She's not my guardian any more."

"That doesn't automatically make you her leader, either," Tyen had pointed out. "I'd say you have to earn that right, but I have to ask: does she want or need someone telling her what to do? I think she's had enough of that from Baluka."

The young man's eyebrows had risen as he'd considered that. "You're right." His lips had pressed together into a grim line. "Others need me to be that leader more than she does. I must work with what I have." He'd then drawn in a deep breath, then let it out. "I can't wait any longer. The sooner I go, the sooner I'll find and reunite the Restorers."

And then he had gone, leaving the hall as empty as it was now. And Tyen had paused to notice the quietness then . . .

. . . which had not included the distant buzzing noise he was picking up now. It was not the sort of sound normally associated with the city. As it continued, he realised it must be considerably louder outside. Extending his senses, he sought and found the mind of someone outside on the street.

They were gazing in awe and fear at a contraption circling above the city. It was no aircart, since instead of a capsule above the chassis there was a flat, broad paddle-like shape. At once, a memory leapt into Tyen's mind of a similar contraption sliding off a ramp over a precipice. He drew in a sharp breath, then hurried towards the main doors.

At the same time, he searched for minds above. His heart leapt as he found them, and he laughed out loud with joy. Mig, and the young man's wife, perched within the glider's capsule, were searching the ground for a place to land. In Mig's mind Tyen read what they needed: a long flat area. And if they didn't find one soon, they'd have to fly away and hope to find something in the surrounding country.

Tyen reached the doors, pushed through and scanned the sky. He found the small craft circling above the Academy. Glancing around, he realised that nothing within the city matched their requirements. Unless . . .

A crowd of onlookers had filled the street before the Academy, effectively stopping the traffic. Tyen hurried down the stairs. He did not stop to wonder how he would persuade hundreds of people to obey him. If he hesitated, he might lose confidence. Instead, as he arrived at the Academy gates, he drew a deep breath and pushed through them.

"Back!" he shouted. "Make room!"

The closest people heard and turned to stare at him. As he repeated the order they began to retreat. Some even started instructing the people behind them. Slowly, then faster as more realised what was happening, a gap formed in the centre of the road.

More voices rose above the buzz of the glider and crowd. He looked around to see familiar faces among those urging people to get off the road: professors, teachers and other Academy staff – and even a group of the Emperor's guards. A small crowd had formed on the steps of the institution as other Academy members emerged to see what was going on.

Now the clearing progressed more swiftly. Tyen paused to look up, seeking Mig's mind. The young man was watching, thinking that even if Tyen managed to get the whole street clear he was not going to have much space to land, particularly as a sign for a store projected over the street about halfway along.

Seeking the obstacle, Tyen found it easily. He gathered magic and sent out a push of air. The signposts groaned as they were forced aside.

Mig silently thanked Tyen, drew a deep breath and told his wife to hang on.

The glider circled away, turned, aligned with the street and began a rapid descent. It skimmed over the tops of the buildings, then dove. The crowd gave a collective gasp as the flying contraption swooped down and levelled out; then people surged back as they realised the wide paddle-like arms were going to pass very close by. Surprisingly small and delicate-looking wheels, extending from the vehicle's underside, touched the ground. The glider bounced a few times, then settled down. There did not appear to be a brake, or any method of halting the vehicle except letting it roll to a stop, and yet it did slow, the means becoming clear as Tyen read Mig's gratitude to his wife, Delt, who had skilfully thickened the air in front of them with magic to halt the glider gently.

Tyen hurried forward, smiling broadly. The buzz was still coming from the glider, but it abruptly quietened and the source was revealed to be propellers that had been spinning so quickly they'd blurred out of sight. A hatch opened in the side of the chassis and a folding ladder flipped out, then the front top half of the capsule hinged upwards, revealing the two drivers.

A cheer broke from the crowd, making Mig and Delt start and look around. They both began to grin and wave.

"Mig! Delt!" Tyen exclaimed as he reached the glider. "Welcome to Beltonia!"

The young man looked down. "Thank you, Director Ironsmelter!" He caught his wife's sleeve. "This is Tyen," he said in their native tongue. "You met briefly when you were at Spirecastle."

She shook her head. "I don't remember," she replied. "It is good to meet you again," she said to Tyen, then she turned back to her husband and murmured, "Can we get out? I have no feeling from my butt down."

Mig chuckled and held out a hand to steady her as she stepped backwards out of the capsule, finding the rungs of the ladder, then nimbly descending. He followed, wincing and rubbing his rump as soon as his feet were on the ground, earning a laugh from the crowd. Then he took a small wooden triangular block of wood from a compartment in the side of the glider and wedged it behind a wheel.

"We're not here on a social visit," he said as he walked over to Tyen. He lowered his voice. "We heard that our world was in danger, so we're here to help."

"How did you . . .?" Tyen began, then left the question

unfinished as he read the answer in Mig's mind. Spies. The south liked to keep an eye on matters in the north. "Any assistance will be most welcome, though I will have to seek the Emperor's permission before I make that official."

"Of course."

The noise of the crowd was growing louder, and people had begun to edge forward to get a closer look at the glider. Tyen beckoned to the Emperor's guards, who immediately hurried over.

"Watch over this machine," Tyen ordered. "Don't let anybody touch it."

The pair nodded gravely, then positioned themselves between the vehicle and the crowd, who read the warning in their stance and backed away.

Tyen turned back to Mig. "May I have my people move the glider into the Academy?"

Mig nodded. "Of course. It clearly can't stay here. Delt will move it, though. She is very protective of it. Just get them to show her where."

"I will." Looking around, he spotted Halyn standing nearby. At a quick jerk of Tyen's head the man came forward and waited as formal introductions were made. When they were done, Tyen turned to his assistant.

"Is there somewhere safe we can store Mig and Delt's glider?"

Halyn's eyes narrowed as he summed up the machine. "It should fit in one of the guest aircart hangars."

"Delt will move it herself. Make sure nobody tries to touch it unless she requests help."

The man nodded. "I understand." He turned to Delt and inclined his head. "I am Halyn. I will show you where to take your vehicle."

She looked at him closely, no doubt reading his mind, then nodded. "See you soon," she told Mig. "I'll meet you when I'm done."

As she walked away, Tyen gestured towards the Academy gate. "Let me introduce you to everyone and give you a tour."

Mig grinned and eagerly followed Tyen to the stairs. After many introductions, Tyen freed the young man from the attention of the curious and led him up the stairs to the Grand Hall. Mig gazed around the big room, impressed by the size and richness of decoration.

"Now I wonder if you even need our help," he admitted.

"Everyone can contribute in some way," Tyen assured Mig. "But you must have something in mind other than sorcery."

"Yes," Mig agreed. "It was when I heard that you had brought inventors here from other worlds that I decided to come. I guessed that you needed clever minds." He paused, then reached into his jacket and brought out a small, gleaming object. Tyen caught his breath as he saw it was a miniature copy of Beetle. "This does not have magic, but it can fly," Mig explained. He turned the beetle over and twisted a small protrusion a few times, then set it on his palm and flicked at one of the antennae. Immediately the wing covers opened and inner wings emerged. These blurred into life and the insect rose from Mig's hand, flew in circles above them, then dropped into the young man's palm again. He held it out to Tyen.

Tyen took it and examined it closely. "That is exceedingly clever."

"You need clever minds," Mig said, shrugging. "I have one."

"Do you have any understanding of mechanical magic?"

Mig shook his head.

Tyen considered the beetle. How much use was an inventor who didn't understand mechanical magic in the hunt for a weapon against war machines? *Perhaps what is a weakness will be strength.* A beetle that didn't require magic to work had an advantage over one that did, in a world with no magic.

"I may have a little difficulty convincing the others that you have something to contribute, but I will remind them that a different perspective can be beneficial," he said, hoping that it was true and Mig hadn't wasted a very long journey.

The young man nodded. "I'm used to sorcerers doubting my

value," he said, his voice deepening with determination. "I've fought that prejudice all my life."

"Come. Let me show you around."

Tyen led Mig down the hall and into the side corridor. Before they had walked far, Mig glanced at Tyen.

"I would love to have another look at your beetle," he said.

Tyen nodded. "Sure. Zeke has it at the moment. I'll tell him you can examine it."

"Thank you." He smiled. "It is wonderful just to be here. I've heard so much about this place. I am a little sad you didn't join our school in the south, but if the threat to this world is as great as I've been told, it is better that you took charge here, where mechanical magic was invented. Can you tell me more about Kettin?"

Tyen filled the young man in as he showed him around. When they neared the inventors' wing, he noticed for the first time he could have easily found it with his eyes closed. Buzzes, bangs, clangs and pipes echoed in the halls, and the smell of hot metal, oil and other chemicals tainted the air.

They found Zeke in a room full of steam. The inventor greeted Mig warmly as Tyen introduced him and explained that Mig had flown up from the south to help them.

"So, you invented that capsule-less aircart we saw flying overhead before?"

Mig nodded.

"I'd love to check it out when I have time." Zeke turned to Tyen. "No, there's nothing new to report."

Tyen chuckled. "At least give me the chance to ask."

"It saved time, didn't it?" Zeke smiled. "Are you joining us today?"

Tyen sighed. "No. Too many Academy matters to attend to."

Zeke shrugged. "There always are."

"Could you show Beetle to Mig?" Tyen asked. "He has made one of his own, only it does not need magic."

Zeke's eyebrows rose. "Interesting." He put a hand on Mig's shoulder and steered him away. "I'd love to see that. Come this way."

"Before you go," Tyen added. The pair paused and looked back. "Mig may not be familiar with mechanical magic, but he has an impressive grasp of machines that don't use magic. That may prove to be an advantage somehow."

"Don't worry," Zeke assured him. "We have a saying here: no ideas are bad ideas." He made a shooing gesture. "Go away, Tyen. We have work to do."

On the way back to his office, Tyen spied a clock and marvelled that the day had barely begun, yet plenty had already happened. Qall leaving. Mig and Delt arriving. Having two southerners helping the Academy would be, at the least, good for relations between the two regions. That reminded him that he ought to have sought the Emperor's permission before allowing someone from outside the empire to work within the Academy. Then there was the matter of housing Mig and Delt. He realised that he hadn't given Halyn instructions on that matter. Well, the man would no doubt come to the office straight after finding a place to stow the glider.

As Tyen neared his office he saw the door was slightly open. He didn't know how his assistant had managed to get the glider into the hangar and return so quickly. Smiling to himself, Tyen pushed through.

Instead of his assistant, it was Rielle waiting in the room. She rose from the chair she had been waiting in.

"Tyen," she said. "Has Qall gone?"

"Yes. He was disappointed you weren't there when he left."

She sighed and shook her head. "It's petty, I know, but I'm still angry at him."

"He isn't just concerned about losing a Maker," Tyen pointed out gently. "He does care about you."

She met his gaze, then smiled crookedly. "But it is his job to worry more about stopping Kettin than my safety. Do you agree with him?"

He moved to his chair and sat down. "On what, exactly?"

"That I shouldn't attempt to become ageless," she clarified, returning to her seat.

Tyen considered how to reply. "I do and I don't. Losing the worlds' most powerful Maker would be a terrible setback right now. Even if we had another way to fight Kettin, I'd hesitate to say it was worth that risk. Many worlds will need restoring, whether we win or not. We don't know how long it will take you to learn how to separate worlds. You might succeed, only to find Kettin has used the time to take control of all the worlds."

Her lips pressed into a thin line and her brow creased.

"But," he continued, "it would be better if the worlds' most powerful Maker could heal herself and not easily suffocate between worlds. As you said yourself, the instructions appear to be for a Maker who has never learned pattern-shifting. You have regained your Maker ability before, so if all you achieve is to relearn pattern-shifting you ought to be able to become a Maker again."

"And if I somehow lose both?"

"I've been thinking about ways to reduce that risk. Qall or I could copy the pattern of the part of your mind that contains the Maker ability into magic, as you did with Valhan's pattern during the first part of his resurrection. If you fail, then that pattern could be imprinted on your mind again."

Rielle's eyes widened. "That's brilliant! Why didn't I think of that?" She rose and began to pace the room. "That lessens the risk considerably." She stopped and turned to him. "We have to go after Qall. Surely this would convince him." Then she shook her head and turned away again. "No. We wouldn't catch up before he left this world, and we'd risk attracting attention to it." Once again, she rounded on him. "Would you do it? Would you help me make the change?"

Tyen blinked, then nodded. "Yes."

She frowned and returned to her seat. "Without waiting for Qall's agreement?"

"Yes."

Her eyebrows rose. "But what of your work here?" Her brows knitted together. "And we'd have to leave this world."

"It would be worth the risk if you succeeded."

She paused, then leaned forward. "Is there a world nearby that would be suitable for us?"

He nodded. "I believe so."

"But . . . if you left this world it would be vulnerable."

Tyen spread his hands. "If Kettin invaded now I doubt I could stop her. Still, I wouldn't want my people to think I'd abandoned them. The Emperor will need to know what we're doing and why. Someone must be able to fetch us quickly, and rescue us in case your transformation fails and we end up stuck in a dead world."

Rielle nodded. "Who?"

Tyen considered. "It would have to be someone who knows how to travel between worlds, who is strong enough to enter and leave a dead world. Not one of the sorcerers working on the machines or training Academy sorcerers, as we need them focused on that." He frowned as he realised there was only one sorcerer who wasn't. "It'll have to be Dahli."

Rielle's brow wrinkled. "Do you trust him?"

He nodded slowly. "We can trust his desire for Zeke to be safe. What do you think?"

"I . . . think we can." She grimaced. "Mostly because of Zeke, but he does genuinely appear to have changed. He does want to help the worlds."

"This will be his chance, then."

She said nothing, her expression suddenly full of doubt.

"Are you sure you want to do this?" he asked.

Her shoulders rose and fell, then she sighed. "It does frighten me. But then, I know I'll try it eventually. Why grow old and die if I don't have to? Especially now we know it wouldn't destroy

462

the worlds if I did. The power it might give me scares me too, but there is the potential for good as well as bad in it. I also like that it gives us a way to stop Kettin that doesn't involve killing." She looked at him. "Do you want me to try it?"

He met her gaze levelly. "No. But that's only fear – and a purely selfish one."

"What do you mean?"

The urge to look away came. He resisted it. "I don't fear you will fail as much as I fear you will succeed, and no longer be you."

She leaned closer, her gaze intense and questioning. "So why are you helping me?"

"Because it's your choice," he told her. "Your life. Your body. Your risk to take. You're not just the Maker. You are Rielle."

A look of wonder came into her eyes. She stared at him for a long moment, then her eyes began to sparkle and her mouth spread into a broad smile.

Then she stepped out of her seat, leaned over the desk and kissed him.

PART NINE

RIELLE

CHAPTER 21

In the centre of the hall a small, tense crowd had gathered. Rielle would have preferred for her and Tyen to leave discreetly, but she understood it was important that he did not seem to be sneaking away. Impatience rose as Tyen spoke to each of the men who'd come to see them depart, but she suppressed it. This was his world. Whatever time he needed to ensure everything here would keep running smoothly in his absence she would never begrudge.

A deep feeling stirred within her, part respect, part admiration, and she studied it carefully. Like her, he feared becoming too involved in the problems of a world, yet here he was, involving himself not just in *any* world's troubles, but in his *own* world's. The potential for heartbreak was even greater.

It wasn't that he didn't care about the consequences to himself, or felt he had no choice. He had voluntarily accepted the personal risks of his involvement. Which was an act of bravery she wasn't sure she was capable of. Although she had interfered in her own world, she was already exiled from it. Tyen had a lot more to lose.

For some mysterious reason, it made her want to help him. To support him when things went badly, and console him if it all went wrong – or, better still, watch him succeed, with her help or without it, and celebrate when he did.

And he was willing to help her, even though it meant leaving his world, even though he was not sure if it was the right thing to do.

Which was why she had kissed him.

Was she in love? She did not feel the same way towards him as she had before, but she definitely wanted to be with him. Perhaps different was a good thing. If everything was the same, it would end the same way.

Halyn had arrived soon after the kiss, before she and Tyen could get over their surprise. Since then, Tyen had been too busy organising to leave. They'd had no private moment to broach the subject. She kept finding herself musing at how Qall would want to know if they were together again. He was becoming almost as much of a nosy gossip as Tarren.

Almost.

"Keep training them," Tyen told Tarren. "Push them hard. I've done everything I can to avoid attracting attention to this world, but if Annad found his way here without help, then one of Kettin's followers could do the same. I fear it is only a matter of time before she finds us."

Tarren nodded. "We will watch the skies for invaders, day and night."

Tyen turned to Zeke. "I wish I could stay and join you but, in all honesty, I have had little time to apply myself to invention these last five cycles, what with teaching and Liftre's inventors constantly chasing us. You are far better suited to the task."

"I don't agree," Zeke replied, "but if whatever you're doing now can only be done by you, then you must do it. Just do it quickly."

"If I can, I will. But before we go: how is Mig?"

Zeke shrugged. "We are pursuing a new idea, thanks to him. His belief that the solution to the war machines wouldn't involve magic received scepticism at first, but nobody could argue against the fact that machines that don't need it would have an advantage over those that do in a dead world. Whether that theory can work in practice is another matter. Especially as this idea we are pursuing would require us to make several machines for every one of Kettin's."

"It is the use of a great number of weapons that would individually be no threat that allows Kettin to defeat sorcerers," Tyen pointed out. "The same principle may work for us against machines."

Zeke nodded, then smiled. "See? You do still have something to contribute."

Dahli chuckled. As all eyes shifted to him, the man's expression became serious. "I will protect your world as best I can, if the need arises," he assured Tyen. He turned to Rielle. "I wish you success. Not only because the worlds need you to help fight Kettin, and repair the damage she has done if we win, but because they will be diminished without you. I hope the cost for attempting to save them is not too high."

Rielle blinked in surprise. Expressing such sentiment was so uncharacteristic of the old Dahli, she immediately looked into his mind for deceit. Instead she saw only genuine affection. She managed a smile. "Thank you, Dahli."

She turned to Tyen. Surely all that needed to be said had been said. "Are you ready to go?"

He nodded and held out his hand. "I will transport us for the first leg, if you like?"

She took his hand, drew in a breath and nodded to show she was ready. He pushed them out of the world. The Grand Hall and its occupants vanished as he followed the path leading away.

Tyen took over directing their journey when they reached the ruins of Spirecastle. Once they were out of his world, he forged a new path between worlds, avoiding arrival places. Every moment they spent in the place between, she stretched her senses for other presences, but found only the occasional distant traveller, too far away to detect her. In each of the worlds they passed through, they paused to check nearby minds. The few who saw them were not Kettin's followers, did not recognise her and Tyen, and had no intentions of tracking anyone.

How dangerous had the worlds become since the Restorer base had been destroyed? Rielle would not be surprised to learn Kettin had gained many more followers as the news spread that Affen was now a ruin and the Restorers scattered. People would conclude that former alliances were over and many would try to make new ones with this frightening new power, in the hopes of saving their worlds from her machines.

After three worlds, Tyen brought them close to a city to search the minds within. They learned of a rumour that Kettin wanted to find the Maker and the leader of the Restorers. Tyen offered to change her appearance, but Rielle was wary that any alteration to her body's pattern might affect the transformation. They moved on.

"This is it," Tyen said a few worlds later. "A small world, weak in magic. It was powerful a few hundred cycles ago, when it was the base world of a civilisation. I spent a few days here during my original journey to Liftre. You can find remnants of their food crops growing wild, so we can add fresh fruit and vegetables to our supplies. Other travellers occasionally stop here for the same reason, so we should keep an eye out when gathering food and stay away from the arrival place."

He led her across the paved circle – an oasis of tidiness in a ruin overrun by plants – and out into the abandoned streets. Within a few hundred steps, they were well hidden behind vegetation and crumbling walls. Tyen continued on and after some time they reached a wall. Passing through a gap where the rusty remains of gates still protruded, they entered a sparse forest, fine grasses like fur growing in the space between trunks.

Narrow winding paths led in all directions, marked with animal prints. From time to time they passed signs of past human habitation in the undergrowth: a crumbling cottage, a long-fallen bridge, and even a broad circular space surrounded by a short wall on which carved figures engaged in a forgotten ball game. She had been in many ruined cities and they always fascinated her. It was like walking in a vast puzzle.

But she had no time to study this one. As they walked she searched for other minds but found none. They were the only people between here and the horizon in all directions, but even in this former rural area, the marks of people gave the world an eerie feeling. The rustle of wind in the grass and chirp of animals meant it was not silent, and yet the absence of human noise made it seem very quiet.

They reached a patchy road and ascended towards low hills. The day grew older and the sun's heat grew less comfortable. She wanted to suggest they levitate to move faster but trusted that Tyen would have already suggested it if it were safe to do so.

The hills drew closer, like arms drawing in on either side. They entered a cosy valley, the road surface succumbing to so much plant invasion it forced them to follow a small stream instead.

"Is that sunfruit?" Rielle asked as she spotted orange globes hanging from a tree. She plucked one and sniffed. "It certainly smells like it."

"In my world we call it depple," Tyen told her. "There are several edible species here that I've seen in cultivation in other worlds. I've seen decorations and lettering on the walls in the city that remind me of an ancient civilisation that once occupied part of my world. I suspect the same people lived here. Maybe the people of my world originally came from here."

"If this place is still capable of producing food, why is it deserted?"

"It's not entirely deserted," Tyen told her. "There are remnant populations far from here, but they have reverted to simpler and somewhat barbaric ways of life. In neighbouring worlds, they tell stories of how the people here died from five calamities: drought, sickness of crops and animals, starvation, human diseases, and warfare." He shook his head. "Of course, they also blame various groups or races for offending the gods."

"What do you think was the cause?"

Tyen shrugged. "Too many people. They couldn't feed everyone, so they either left and colonised other worlds or they starved."

She looked at the sunfruit. "And now there is food but nobody to eat it."

They continued a little further, then stopped to eat and drink at the edge of a pond.

"Will this do, do you think?" Tyen asked.

Rielle looked around and nodded. It was a quiet area, protected from wind by the steep banks of the valley. The water and food would help sustain them if her transformation attempt took longer than planned. Shrugging off her pack, she walked over to a rock beside the pool and sat down. From there she had a view down the valley to the city, with the creek meandering in the foreground.

"It's been a while since I painted a landscape," she said. "This should be challenging – which will definitely put me in the right frame of mind. You may as well get comfortable. I want to make plenty of magic."

Tyen pulled a blanket out of his pack, draped it on the ground nearby and sat down. She set up a small easel and placed a cloth-covered frame upon it, then set out her paints. Tyen had taken her to a tiny shop in Beltonia that catered to artists. Oily paint had been developed centuries before and was available in convenient pre-mixed form in tins. The cloth-covered boards were a surface that she hadn't used before, but the shopkeeper had enthused about the springy surface so much that she had given in to his urges to try it.

As she started to work, Tyen gave a quiet gasp. She knew he was detecting the magic that was flowing out of her, but she kept her attention on her work.

If anyone does visit this world now, they'll definitely know I'm here, she mused. Nothing could be done about that. Nothing except work fast, so that she would use up the magic as soon as possible.

The scene was as challenging as she'd expected. She had not painted a landscape in a long time and was unfamiliar with the frames, but the oily paint allowed her to throw down colour without having to worry about it drying too quickly to blend. When the colours in one area blended too much and became muddy, she scraped them off and started again. Then she couldn't get the texture of the grass to look convincing, so she grabbed a twig and tried scratching grooves in the paint.

Finally, she reached that point where she knew that if she worked much more, she would spoil the areas that were working well. She'd just have to accept the areas that weren't. Turning away from the painting, she began cleaning her brushes. A soft scrape reminded her of Tyen's presence, and she looked up to find him peering at the frame and easel from the side.

"Can I have a look?"

"Of course." She stepped aside, rubbing and stretching stiff muscles. Sunlight was no longer beating down from above but filtering through trees on one side of the valley. Soon the space they were in would be filled with shadows.

"It's really good."

"No, it isn't."

"You're too critical."

She laughed softly. "You're too easy to please!"

He straightened, his head tilting a little to one side. "Would you rather I was harder to please?"

A teasing look had entered his eyes. Her heart skipped a beat and she looked away. She almost cursed Qall for putting ideas into her head. *But I've been falling back in love with Tyen for some time now*, she realised. *Maybe I never properly fell out of love; I just resisted it because I was so angry with him, even though I knew why he did what he did, and thought I'd forgiven him.* She recalled the words that had chased away the last of her distrust. *"Because it's your choice. Your life. Your body. Your risk to take. You're not just the Maker. You are Rielle."*

"You're better at portraits," he amended, "but I'm sure that's only because it's what you paint most of the time."

She nodded and glanced towards the sun. "And the light source doesn't move and change everything. We should eat before it gets dark."

Which meant her transformation must begin at night. A hollow, nervous feeling bloomed in her stomach. Had she made enough magic? She focused on the magic within the world. An intense brightness surrounded her, so dazzling that she could not sense any depth to it. "That's strange. I can't sense how far the magic stretches."

A laugh burst from Tyen. "That's because there is so much it overwhelms the senses." He paused. "I wonder what would happen if we left the world like this?"

Rielle shook her head. "Even if I don't need all this magic, I'll leave this world as we found it. If worlds that have been weak for a long time produce strong sorcerers when they're restored, I could create another Kettin."

"You and I also come from weak worlds. We aren't murderous world-conquerors."

"Perhaps we are the exceptions. But even if we aren't, one Kettin has a much greater effect on the worlds than a hundred Rielles or Tyens."

"That is true."

She sighed. "Well, we had better get started. If someone passes through and notices how powerful this world is now, they might look around for the reason and find us."

Tyen examined the ground. "Are you okay with sitting on a blanket?"

She nodded. Tyen left the easel and they walked over to the blanket together. They sat facing each other, close enough to link hands.

"What next?" Tyen asked.

"I will open my mind to yours and begin creating. Hopefully you'll be able to see the part of my pattern that makes me a Maker. Once you see it, copy it into the magic of this world." She smiled.

"If you're not sure how, I'll think about what I did at the start of Valhan's resurrection."

Tyen looked doubtful, perhaps even a little afraid.

"Don't worry," she told him. "This bit is easy. Ready?"

He nodded. "You?"

"As ready as I'll ever be." She straightened her back and closed her eyes. "Let's get started."

Opening her mind was surprisingly difficult, because she couldn't detect when it was. She had to ask Tyen several times if he could see her thoughts before she got it right. Her natural urge to close it again took over then and it was a battle to keep it open. She was too used to having privacy, and only Qall being able to see her thoughts. She told herself to imagine it was Qall reading her mind instead of Tyen and was amused to find her mind gave up trying to block her thoughts as if it couldn't be bothered doing so when there was nothing to gain.

To ensure she would not lapse into blocking Tyen at some vital moment, she waited to see if it would close again. As she did this, she spent a while thinking through what she needed to do next. Five cycles had passed since she had been able to pattern-shift, and it was ten cycles since she had begun her attempt to resurrect Valhan, so her memory of both was fuzzy. To her surprise, Tyen opened his mind to confirm and correct what she recalled of the former, and allow her to see if he understood her explanation of the latter.

Once they were sure they each understood both processes, they paused – and shared an almost wordless feeling of affection for each other, as if each other's mind had sensed love and leapt forward to say "me too!"

Yet the moment was refracted an instant later by fear. She saw that he was afraid of what this transformation would do to her, but as she examined his anxiety, she was relieved to see it wasn't a fear *of* her, but fear *for* her. He wanted her to become ageless again. He still wished for a long life together, and though he could extend her life as they had both been doing for Tarren, he did not know how long that could be sustained without unintentional alterations changing her.

And yet . . . to become ageless and retain her Maker ability would alter her too. It would make her more than human. He feared she would become a different person. Someone he wouldn't like. Someone who wouldn't like him.

Everything we do, everything we see, everything done to us changes us, she told him. *You can't stop that change.*

I know, but I don't have to be happy about it.

Perhaps if we change together . . .

You want me to make this transformation too? Is that even possible?

It might be. She had changed herself into a powerful Maker. Why wouldn't she be able to change someone else into one? Even as she thought it, she sensed Tyen's dislike of the idea.

Being a Maker of your strength stops you doing what you love – creating – because you might make too much magic, he thought. *I would not wish that on you, and I think you would not wish that on me.*

No, she agreed. With that thought came a pang of both fondness and sadness. He understood this about her, but so long as she was the sole Maker she would be one of a kind. Alone.

Not alone, he told her. *Just . . . unique.*

As we all are, really, she added. She sensed his agreement, and acceptance. And the nagging tension that was his worry for his world, and all the worlds. *Let's delay no longer. It is time to begin. Look for the part of my mind that makes magic as I create.*

Opening her eyes, she created sparks and sent them swirling in patterns.

I see it, Tyen told her.

That was quick!

The next bit won't be.

She continued Making, slowly and steadily. She couldn't sense Tyen copying her pattern into the magic of the world, so she concentrated only on making patterns. Time stretched on. She stopped trying to guess how much slipped by and stretched before them. After a while Tyen asked her to do something different, so she drew lines in the dirt beside the blanket. She hoped this meant he was testing his work, and was nearly done, but he said nothing more. Over and over she smoothed the dirt and started tracing a new pattern until she had lost count of how many times she'd begun again. A calm spread through her not unlike what she'd sensed in the minds of monks and priestesses meditating. The dangers of the world existed elsewhere. It was comforting, and she began to wish Tyen wouldn't finish and disturb it. But eventually he would . . .

"I think that's it."

Reluctantly, she looked up at him. "You're done?"

He nodded. "I muddled it a few times and had to begin again. Fortunately, you made so much magic before that it didn't matter. And you were making more, so that helped too. What next?"

She yawned. "You have to duplicate the Maker part of my mind. The instructions said I'd do it, but I can't see how when I've lost the understanding of pattern-shifting and the Maker part would be gone if I had regained it."

"We'll work it out." He paused. "It's cold. I'll get your blanket."

She glanced around them. It was dark. An intense band of stars dominated the sky. She stared at them, the lingering calm drawing her into their patterns. Tyen jolted her back into awareness as he draped the blanket around her shoulders. With the weight of it came a sense of urgency.

I can't waste time, she reminded herself. *Tyen needs to get back to his world. Kettin is out there destroying everything.*

She drew in a deep breath, let it out and turned her attention to the present. Tyen, reading her thought, saw that she was ready.

I think this will be easier for you if the Maker part of your mind isn't active, he suggested.

Taking his advice, she focused on the thing furthest from her own mind: his thoughts. She saw him push aside fear and doubt and draw magic to use. He looked at the pattern of her mind and understood it, and through his mind, for the first time in five cycles, so did she.

They both drew in a sharp breath of realisation. *This* was how she would duplicate her mind. She would use *his* understanding of it to make the change.

A spark of excitement enlivened their thoughts. She set to work. He looked where she needed him to look, enabling her to change and alter. Their first attempts were failures, but nothing they could not undo together. Finally, they hit upon a method that worked. It was the oddest sensation, her concentration and will undisturbed by a simultaneous blooming new awareness. This understanding matched and mirrored Tyen's, and it was deeply familiar.

And then it was all *there*, new but as natural as all the other parts of her mind that allowed her to do everything from simple tasks to drawing and using magic. Once again, she understood how to change patterns – her own or that of other living things'.

Once again, she was ageless.

She opened her eyes, met Tyen's gaze and smiled. His eyes were bright, but his returning smile was hesitant.

Are you sure you can still make magic? he asked.

Lowering her gaze to the ground, she traced a new pattern.

He sucked in a breath. "Oh, that's definitely a yes."

Stilling her hand, she looked around and sensed a brightness around them. It was spreading outwards into a void. Their work had, indeed, taken most of the magic she had created.

"We did it," she gasped. "It actually worked." Pushing to her feet, she let the blanket fall and felt the stiffness from sitting in the same position for a long time melt away as she automatically healed herself.

"How does it feel?" Tyen asked, looking up.

She closed her eyes. "Good. I'd forgotten how *healthy* it feels to be ageless."

Something about the texture of the air tickled her skin, and she realised what it was. "You can let go of the Maker pattern now."

Tyen rose. "Are you sure?"

She created a few sparks and concentrated with her new senses on that part of her mind. "Fascinating. It's as though I could understand what magic is if I looked closely enough." She resisted the urge and turned her senses outwards. "Oh!"

Tyen frowned anxiously. "What?"

She tore her mind from her surroundings to him, then grinned at what she saw. "Everything has a pattern. *Everything!* It's like . . . I can see in the dark."

Curiosity lit in his eyes. "So . . . now that you can understand pattern-shifting again you can use that to understand your Maker ability?"

"Yes, and more." She paused as a thought occurred to her. "I think there are other ways to gain this understanding. I think Valhan may have been close. I will have to ask Qall." She paused, then grimaced. "He's not going to be very happy with us. With me, for going against our agreement."

"No," Tyen agreed. "But I think he'll forgive you. And he'll have to get used to the idea that someone is more powerful than him, too."

She shook her head. "Not stronger. Just different. Which he should be used to already with me. All I have to do now is work out how to sever a link between worlds." She paused. The ridges of the valley were now outlined by orange light. She realised this was no magical effect. Dawn had come. Was it the next day, or a dawn several days later? She was not sure.

"How long did this take?"

"Most of the night." His expression shifted, lines of worry returning. She realised his mind was no longer open. Neither was hers. She was not sure when the boundaries had gone back up, or who had raised them first. It made her a little sad, and yet she did not resent it.

"We should be getting back," she said.

Tyen nodded. "Yes. I wish we could stay here longer." He stood and reached out to take her hand, squeezing it gently, then letting it go. "Perhaps another time."

As he bent to pick up the blanket, she walked over to the easel and began returning her new art materials to her pack. When she was done she slung it onto her back, picked up the painting and walked back to Tyen. She held the piece out to him.

"It's yours," she said.

Smiling, he took it carefully so as to not smudge the paint. "Thank you. I will frame it and hang it in my office."

"I expect no less," she told him, then leaned in to kiss him. "Tell me we don't have to walk all the way back."

He grinned. "But it's all downhill."

She raised her eyebrows at him, and he laughed. "No, there's no reason to sneak around now. Though we will still have to be careful of watchers and pursuit."

"Of course." She took his hand. "Take me home, Tyen Ironsmelter. We must save the worlds and that is going to take quite a bit of planning."

CHAPTER 22

"Trapping Kettin in an isolated world will not stop her machines," Rielle pointed out as she struggled with the buttons on the back of her dress. "Though I'd rather do that than kill her. It's more important to lure her machines into one."

Her words seemed distant and unimportant, eclipsed by the sight of her brown skin contrasting with the white of her bustband. He rose and went over to her, sliding a hand under the dress and pushing the shoulders off so it fell to the floor. Looking over to the standing mirror, he watched as her inhalation pushed her breasts against the undergarment. She closed her eyes, a small smile beginning, then frowned and shook her head.

"Stop distracting me," she told him, pushing him gently away. "I've arranged to meet with Delt this morning."

"You looked like you needed some help."

"To put my clothes on, not take them off. And it would be much easier to put my clothes on if they didn't fasten in such ridiculous, difficult-to-get-to places."

"You're meant to leave that to servants."

"If we had servants you wouldn't be here watching me dress."

"That's true. So let me help you dress."

"No. You clearly don't know the meaning of the word 'dress'. Sit down and let me sort this out."

Shrugging, he returned to the chair he'd been watching her from, wondering how he could be so lucky to have the affections of such a woman. A second time. Despite every bad decision he'd ever made.

"What was I saying before you interrupted?" she wondered aloud.

"Kettin. Trapping her in a world." He paused to consider. "If the world was full of her machines that would probably lead to her death anyway. The world would be dead. She'd be as vulnerable as any ordinary woman."

Rielle winced. "That depends on how hospitable the world is. People and animals would have been destroyed by the machines, but not crops. But her death is not what we're trying to achieve."

"To avoid killing anyone." He nodded. "I disagree that luring her machines into a trap is more important. For a start, I doubt she would – or could – send every war machine in existence into one world, and she would just make more if she lost them anyway. Without her, machines will still be made, but the purpose of using them to destroy and control all the worlds would be gone."

"Unless someone stepped into her place." Her eyebrows lowered. "Whatever lure we use has to be enough to draw her, all her followers and all the machines. She wants to kill me and the Restorers, and all strong sorcerers." Turning her back to the mirror, she looked over her shoulder and narrowed her eyes at her reflection. The hems of her dress began to overlap, buttons slowly pushing through buttonholes. "Together we are a great enough lure to attract everything we want to get rid of."

Tyen waited until she was finished so as to not break her concentration. "So, we put out a rumour that the Restorers have a secret new base, and you and I are there."

She nodded and turned to face him. "Then let some of her people discover the location. How do I look?"

He nodded in both agreement and approval. She'd not explained why she wanted to dress as a local woman now, and he'd expected it to seem odd. Instead she looked very fine indeed. The dressmaker had adapted current fashion to Rielle's build extremely well, capturing her grace and celebrating the curves that the last five cycles of true ageing had enhanced – curves he was pleased she hadn't used pattern-shifting to remove. The colour of the fabric suited her brown skin and dark hair. He brought his attention back to the subject with an effort.

"But would Kettin suspect a trick if all of her targets were coincidentally found in one location?" he asked.

Rielle pursed her lips in thought. "Probably. I would if I were her. I'd want the information verified before I risked approaching."

"Then all we need to do is let a spy or two into the world and make sure it convincingly looks like the new base."

"And a stronger one than before, so that she has to bring all of her machines and followers."

"If we could create a sense of urgency, she'd attack sooner. Perhaps not wait for confirmation."

She sat down and slipped on her shoes. "A rumour that I've become ageless?"

"No, that would make her more cautious."

"A rumour that I am trying to become ageless, then."

"Hmm. We should be very cautious about even hinting that you might be. The risk that you may succeed might make her hesitate."

"Is there something else we could use?" She rose and walked over to the bedroom door and opened it.

Tyen followed but did not get a chance to reply.

"Oh, you look very nice this morning, Rielle," a familiar voice said from the direction of the dining setting. Tyen smiled, then smoothed his expression and strode through. "Good morning, Father. You've let yourself in again, I see."

Deid smiled. "Well, if I'd known you two were now *that* sort of friends, I'd have had my breakfast alone."

Tyen opened his mouth to deny it, then realised he was responding automatically, as if to Tarren's teasing. *I should introduce*

Tarren to my father, he found himself thinking, then immediately changed his mind.

"It's lovely of you to have arranged such a fine breakfast, Deid," Rielle said, glancing at Tyen. She moved over to the dining setting, which was covered in plates of food, and sat down. "Any interesting news?"

Deid lifted the newssheet in his hands. "Plenty of speculation about you two and the Academy."

"Not surprisingly, considering the quality of *that* newssheet," Tyen muttered.

"Indeed. But they do note that the meeting between the southerner couple and the Emperor went well, apparently." Deid flicked through a few pages. "Then it returns to the usual gossip and complaints. I keep waiting for them to get bored with you lot but—"

A knock at the main door to the apartment interrupted him. Tyen had reached one of the empty dining chairs but not yet sat down, so he answered the door. A young woman – one of the students he'd first brought to this world – stood outside, deep shadows under her eyes.

"Zeke wishes to speak to you as soon as possible, Director," she told him. Her mind told him a great deal more, but fragmented and fuzzed by weariness. His heart leapt into a faster beat.

He nodded. "Thank you." Closing the door, he moved back to the dining table, picked up a piece of toast and spooned bluedrop conserve on it. "I'm afraid I can't stay and discuss the gossip, Father," he said. "The inventors have made some sort of breakthrough."

Rielle put down her cup and rose. "Really? I'll come with you."

Deid shrugged, barely raising his eyes from the paper. "When such important news calls you away, I can't complain."

"Thank you for arranging breakfast," Tyen said. "I do wish I could have enjoyed it with you."

"Another day. Go save the world." Deid paused. "Worlds."

Rielle laid a hand briefly on the old man's shoulder, then followed Tyen out of the apartment. Once in the corridor Tyen quickly ate his toast. He increased his stride when he was done. There had been no urgency in the student's thoughts, only a tired excitement and, inexplicably, disappointment.

"Should we seek out Zeke's mind?" Rielle asked.

Tyen shook his head. "I suspect he wants to explain in person, or to demonstrate something, or he'd have sent a clearer message."

Since the hotel was not far from the Academy and it was still early, it was faster to walk than order a carriage. The streets were busy despite the hour, but not so crowded that anyone who noticed them couldn't make a little space. At the main Academy doors, Halyn waited. He knew Zeke had requested Tyen visit, but not why.

"Anything urgent I need to attend to first?" Tyen asked. Halyn shook his head. "Come with me."

The three of them made their way through the Academy to the mechanical magic wing. The rooms were uncharacteristically empty and quiet. Zeke stepped out of a doorway several steps away.

"Tyen. Rielle. I hope I didn't interrupt your breakfast."

Rielle chuckled. "There will be other breakfasts."

"Many more, if we are right about this." Zeke beckoned them into the room. Unlike the student messenger, he showed no signs of fatigue, Tyen noted. Perhaps Dahli had healed it away.

When Tyen and Rielle stepped inside, they both paused, taking in a strange sight. Machine pieces littered the floor. A buzzing drew Tyen's attention to a swarm of metallic insects circling above them.

"Miniature Beetles." Mig stepped into view. "Come closer and we'll show you what they can do."

Noting Dahli standing at the back of the room, Tyen inclined his head. The man returned the gesture of respect. Zeke moved to a shelf and took one of Kettin's less developed machines down.

He placed it on the floor, then manipulated something under its casing.

It sprang to life, hobbling forward with one bent segmented leg.

A high peep came from something in Mig's hand. The swarm of insects dove. As each tiny mechanism landed on the machine, it began to scurry over the casing. Their numbers decreased rapidly, and Tyen understood why when he noticed one disappear into the seam where a leg met the body.

The machine stopped and began to let out a series of creaks and pops.

And then it convulsed. Legs froze. The sensors that gave it machine sight popped out of their fittings. The body seams popped open and the casing clattered apart.

"They cut wires, undo screws and inject glue or shrapnel to clog up moving parts," Mig explained. "Kettin's machines can't sense them. They're too small to be detected and they use very little magic."

Tyen nodded. "How do they get past the machine's shield?"

"They land on top of the shield and wait until the machine switches from shielding to attacking."

"They're fast enough?"

"Just."

Rielle shook her head. "So Kettin's machines can't shield and attack simultaneously?"

"No," Zeke answered. "It's not as great a weakness as you might think because it happens too quickly for an attacker to take advantage of it. Sometimes a lucky shot has landed at the right moment, but it's so rare, and the number of machines in a battle so large, that it makes little difference."

"Why don't they shield and attack simultaneously?" she asked.

"To take magic into two reservoirs would require doubling the components," Mig answered. "The machine would weigh more, and therefore spend more magic on levitating."

"More likely it's because they aren't sophisticated enough yet," Zeke disagreed. "As you know, in order to push stilled air or heat outwards while shielding you must create holes in your shield for it to pass through. Since those holes only exist while a strike is passing through, a point of weakness isn't created. Even if machines could attack and shield at the same time, they aren't yet able to shape their shields as we can."

"Yet." Rielle looked from Zeke to Mig and back. "Sounds like those are weaknesses that would eventually be overcome."

The pair nodded. "War invention is always a race of ideas," Zeke said, then smiled at Mig. "Sometimes all you need to get the upper hand is a fresh idea. Mig's original insectoid didn't use magic but a kind of mechanism that stored energy in springs. It didn't run for long however. We considered how to use magic to extend that, then realised we were looking at the wrong part of his idea to adapt. Our usual way of storing magic is more efficient, but instead of that magic being used to still, move, heat or chill outside the machine, we use it almost exclusively to move parts within the insectoid. In effect, we're aiming to use magic as little as possible rather than take Kettin's approach of getting machines to do everything humans can."

"The hard part was finding a way for the insects to find the right target," Mig added, "so they don't destroy all the machines in this world. It was a modification Zeke came up with to improve Kettin's machines that turned out to be their weakness." His expression became grave. "Her machines detect and target the heat and movement of living things. Once they find it, they signal to others. The communication isn't audible to humans, but it's unique to Kettin's machines. We've designed our swarms to home in on that."

Tyen looked around the room. "Have you tried your swarm on the repaired machine Rielle brought back from the battle?"

"Not yet," Zeke replied. "We have only one of them, and once it is destroyed it may be harder to study it."

Tyen nodded. "How many insectoids do you have?"

"Just these right now," Mig replied. "But they are quick to assemble when you have the right components on hand."

Tyen looked from him to Zeke. "We're going to need a lot more."

Zeke nodded. "At least two for each of Kettin's machines. Preferably ten."

Drawing in a deep breath, Tyen considered the size of the task. He could order all members of the Academy to begin assembling them, but that wouldn't come close to enough people. Much of the work could be done by non-sorcerers, but sorcerers would have to supervise. He'd need all of the machine makers of the city, and possibly of the entire empire. It was unlikely nobody would protest, when every machine-part maker in Leratia had to put aside current orders and turn their expertise and factories to manufacturing insectoids. But if cities and countries outside Beltonia were told it was for their own defence, they would be more cooperative.

"Halyn, send a message to the palace. I have a request to make of the Emperor."

"Right away, Director."

As the sound of his assistant's footsteps faded, Tyen turned to Rielle. "We need to get a message to Qall."

She nodded, her eyes widening a little. "I'll change my appearance."

"No, you stay. I'll go. Kettin doesn't want me dead, as far as I know."

"But you—"

"I'll go."

They turned to regard Dahli. "Kettin's watchers might read your mind," Tyen said.

"If they do they won't find any memory of the location of this world or the threat to Kettin's machines," Dahli replied. He looked at Rielle. "You must stay here. If I can notice the change in you, others will too."

Her eyes widened. "You'd better hide that memory, too."

"Oh, I definitely will," he assured her.

Zeke looked puzzled at the exchange, but as Dahli looked at him, he shrugged. "I won't ask, but . . . you said we should stick together."

Dahli nodded. "I know. You will be safer here than coming with me. Don't worry, I won't be recognised and I won't be away for long."

Zeke did not look happy, but he did not argue either. He turned to Rielle. "How high above the ground do Kettin's machines extend to when they enter worlds?"

She paused to consider. "Four, five hundred paces maybe."

He straightened, glanced at Mig, then turned to Tyen. "Have you ever transported an aircart between worlds before?"

"No," Tyen replied.

"The swarms would be most efficiently released from above. If the Academy sorcerers who know how to fly them were willing to join in the battle, they may prove very useful."

Tyen looked at Rielle. She guessed what he was thinking: if their plan to lure Kettin and her machines into a world and isolate it went ahead, no Academy sorcerers need risk their lives, but he couldn't reveal that now. "If they are willing, and the Emperor approves."

"Of course." Zeke shrugged.

Tyen nodded. "In the meantime, you and your helpers need to draw up specifications for making machine parts and instructions for assembly, as well as make some to test on Kettin's most recent machine." He looked at Dahli. "The sooner we contact Qall the better. I'll send a messenger when I'm back from the palace." Next, he turned to Rielle. "You wanted to speak to Kep and Annad," he reminded her.

"Yes, I'll do that now before I am too busy to see them."

"Give them my regards." Tyen nodded to Dahli. "I'll see you soon." He headed for the door, but when he got there he noted that Rielle was not following and looked back. She smiled and waved him away, so he entered the corridor alone.

His footsteps echoed in the quiet. *Two breakthroughs*, he thought. *Two sources of hope. But Rielle doesn't yet know how to isolate a world, and we can't be sure if Mig's insectoids can bring down one of those spheres of machines, let alone several of them.*

Then another thing occurred to him. *If Mig's insectoids can, Rielle didn't need to become ageless after all.* The words "of course she did" rang in his mind. He was immensely relieved to find the woman he loved had not disappeared, replaced by someone strange and inhuman – a god or demon or something else. If she'd changed so dramatically, he would have grieved and regretted his decision. *But if what she became was what she was meant to be, I had no right to stop it. Unless it was truly going to destroy all the worlds, that is.*

The only person who seemed bent on doing that was Kettin.

They had two possible weapons against her and her machines now: an ageless Maker and Mig's insectoids. Hopefully that would mollify Qall when he found out that Rielle had not kept her side of their agreement, and Tyen had helped her.

PART TEN

RIELLE

The easiest way to tell a native of the city of Beltonia from everyone else was to wait until the sun came out. Even in summer, periods of sunshine were short in the city, the only difference being a greater frequency of them. So when the sun came out, the locals did too, and if they couldn't they grew restless. Even Tarren had commented that it was hard to get his students to concentrate whenever the clouds parted.

For more than thirty days now, Tyen had been occupied from early morning to late in the night with organising the manufacture of Mig's insects. The Grand Hall was filling with boxes of them. He'd taken the design to countries around the world, including the south, and shown the locals how to make and deploy them. It was a benefit of the great spread of the Leratian Empire that he was able to find people and materials for making the insects anywhere within its territories. In the Far South the only places where people were capable were in the city beneath the ruins of Spirecastle, and the school of sorcery.

With Tyen occupied, Rielle had taken over the instruction of the Empress and those of her cohort of royal companions who had magical ability. They, in return, were teaching her the finer details of local etiquette. She'd had to, regretfully, decline lessons in decorative stitching and botanic painting, run by a group of women who had, having embraced the truth about creativity generating magic, started the Society of Magical Generation

Through Handcraft and Art. Though all the women she'd met were stoic and confident on the surface, they felt the same tension everyone in Beltonia was enduring. Would their world's isolation protect it from Kettin's machines? How long before enough of Mig's beetles were made to defend against an invasion? If this world was going to manufacture beetles to sell to other worlds, would it soon run out of metals? Could they import materials? How would selling beetles to worlds outside this one affect the value of local currency?

Today's lesson with the Empress would not begin until the afternoon, leaving Rielle a rare few hours of free time. Craving a little warmth on her skin too, Rielle headed for the courtyard Tarren used as a training ground, settling on a bench seat. He soon noticed her watching and decided it was time he gave the class a break.

"I thought you'd be with Tyen," he said as he sat beside her, a familiar glint entering his gaze.

She patted the seat beside him. "I hardly see him, he's so busy. And I have been too. I'm only here because the Empress had to cancel her magic lesson."

"How is that going?"

Rielle shrugged. "Good, I think. I've never taught a raw beginner before. Any tips?"

"Nothing was set alight?"

"No."

"You're doing fine." He smiled. "She's an Empress. What matters is whether she is pleased with her progress."

"Yes."

"Then you're doing remarkably well."

Rielle chuckled. "How are the Academy sorcerers doing?"

"Very well. They take their learning seriously, and since they never expected to be able to do much with their abilities, they are grateful for any guidance. Very different to the spoilt youngsters I so often have to deal with." He raised an eyebrow at her.

She ignored his attempt to tease her. "You've been teaching them world travelling. Didn't Tyen want to avoid that for now?"

"He changed his mind. We need sorcerers who can move beetles above the machines, and the fastest way to do that is through skimming."

"Which is why you're teaching them to levitate today." She pursed her lips. "Need any help?"

He nodded. "I do, actually." His gaze moved past her shoulder and he frowned. "But I think you're wanted elsewhere."

She turned to see Qall approaching. As always, since his return a few days ago, he frowned as she met his gaze. He claimed not to be bothered about her transformation, just disappointed that she went against his wishes, but his manner spoke otherwise.

"Rielle," he said. "I wanted to speak to you before I left."

"I'll leave you to it," Tarren said. "Come join us when you can, Rielle." He smiled, then rose and strode away.

Rielle turned back to Qall and patted the bench. "No need to loom over me."

Qall hesitated, then folded himself down onto the bench. "Zeke says we need to lure Kettin into attacking us with all her forces. Once she knows about the beetles, she will have her inventors work on a defence against them, so it's likely we'll only get to use them in a few battles, possibly only one. He says it wouldn't be difficult to modify the method of shielding on her machines to make it constant." He grimaced. "We should assume we get one chance at this."

"Tyen and I came to much the same conclusion, though more because we need to weaken her and her followers enough that we can go on to destroy the remaining machines without much opposition." She smiled as she saw Tarren herding reluctant students back into the courtyard to resume their lesson. "Do you have a world in mind for the confrontation?"

His frown deepened. "Yes."

"And I am to be the bait?"

"Yes, if you are willing."

"I am, but I have one condition: make sure it's a world only linked to one other."

He stared at her without speaking for a long moment, then looked away. "I'd rather you didn't even try it."

"I'd rather not have to, but we shouldn't dismiss it as a possibility."

"A possibility not tested. What if you get it wrong and become trapped in that world? What if you destroy all the worlds, as Maker's Curse warned?"

She sighed. "The Ancients learned to do it without destroying all the worlds. I will too, Qall. It may as well be now, when we need it, than later, when we don't. The only reason I haven't left to try it yet is because the more trips made in and out of this world the greater the chance of drawing attention to it."

He nodded. "Then . . . when you do, could you test your powers as far away from the habitable worlds as possible?"

"It took us half a cycle to reach the edge of the world last time, Qall. Do the worlds have that much time?" He shook his head. "If the only alternative means Kettin destroying the worlds anyway, I may as well try my luck." She paused. "You know my senses have changed. That I perceive pattern in everything. I remember sensing pattern in stone when Dahli taught me pattern-shifting, but this is clearer, somehow. Changing those patterns seems . . ." She searched for a word, but the only one that came to her was not quite satisfactory. "Possible."

"No, I didn't know that," he said. "I can't read your mind any more, Rielle."

It was her turn to stare.

"What you just said terrifies me," he added. "I don't want it to seem possible to anyone to change the pattern in anything. Or the links between worlds. Not even you."

She heard what he said, but surprise had shifted to curiosity and she began to wonder . . . could she read his mind now? She blinked, then searched for his thoughts and found nothing. Then she looked at his pattern and . . .

. . . wish I hadn't suggested we flip over the record . . .

She swallowed and looked away. What did this mean? Was she more powerful than Qall now? Or was she simply . . . different?

"I'm the same person you knew before," she told him. "I've not changed."

"The person who ignored me and went ahead with the transformation," he pointed out. "I'm afraid that doesn't reassure m—"

"MACHINES! MACHINES IN THE SKY!"

Qall jumped and Rielle's heart lurched at the same time. They both looked up, then leapt to their feet as they saw a pattern of interconnected ellipses spreading across the sky. More shouts broke out as Tarren's warning spread, then a bell began to ring, soon joined by others across the city.

"No," Qall muttered. "Not now."

Rielle extended her senses in time to feel all the magic of the world vanish, from a hundred paces above the ground to the furthest extent of it in the sky.

"I hope that was part of Tyen's plan," Qall said, "and that sorcerers around the world haven't suddenly found themselves unable to fight."

She looked down and found Qall regarding her with one eyebrow raised.

"Of course it is," she replied. "A few days ago Tyen sent a warning to sorcerers around the world telling them that it would happen if we were attacked, and they should hold a store of magic at all times."

"A few days ago? There can't have been time for the messengers to reach all of them."

"Oh, Tyen has put it in the Leratian papers," she assured him. "They spread faster than you'd expect. And he made a quick visit to the Far South."

Qall looked up. "What did he say to do next?"

She followed his gaze. The pattern of linked machines was still expanding. She and Tyen had discussed whether one of them should push into the place between worlds and wrest control of the machines away from the sorcerer bringing them in, as Qall had done during the battle in Kettin's world. It might gain them a little extra time but it had disadvantages – if Tyen did it he'd be separated from the fighters he needed to lead, and there wasn't anywhere they could safely put the machines. Bringing them into this world partially within the ground risked killing people at the surface. Taking them to a neighbouring world would make an enemy, unnecessarily.

Tackling the sorcerers might prevent more machines being delivered, however, and if they were brought into this world their minds could be read. It could be ascertained whether the invader knew this was Tyen's world, or had arrived by chance.

"Distribute beetles," she replied, just as a familiar voice began to speak close by.

"Take as many boxes as you can manipulate easily and skim up above the machines," Tyen instructed. Rielle and Qall turned to find him standing behind them in front of a neatly stacked pile of boxes almost as large as the Grand Hall. He must have transported them to the courtyard so they could be more easily reached. He was talking to the closest of the crowd of sorcerers still flooding out of the Academy buildings. "When you're in position, shake the box to activate the beetles, then open it and tip them out. Try to spread them around."

Sorcerers grabbed two or three boxes each, then stepped out of the way. Watching one, Rielle saw him pause, take a deep breath, then fade a little before shooting upwards. She moved over to Tyen.

"Should I stay here or seek out the controller?"

He looked at her, his gaze slightly distracted as he considered. "Find him. Or her. Come straight back here. Once we start fighting we'll need your magic."

She took hold of a stack of five boxes, then pushed out of the world. As she did, her new senses tempted her with information she had never been able to see before. What came with her into the place between was controlled by her will and the same sense that detected the location of magic, otherwise she'd be trying to take the entire world with her. Until now she hadn't grasped how that worked. When she extended her will, she made the boxes vibrate in tune with her own pattern. It was fascinating.

But she had no time to study the phenomenon. She skimmed upwards. The machines were still within the place between worlds, so she had to weave through them and their linking cables to get higher. Once above them she paused to consider which way to move next.

The invading sorcerer had most likely found one of the two paths in and out of this world: the one she and Tyen used in the Far South or the one Annad had made when he'd travelled here. Studying the movement of the machines, she saw that they were expanding from a point a considerable distance from Beltonia, but not in the Far South, suggesting they'd found Annad's path.

She skimmed away, high above the machines. As she increased her speed the world below her seem to spin. Tyen had suggested she memorise a globe replica of the world, though it included only a sketchy, inaccurate depiction of the Far South, paying most attention to the coastline and mountainous features. Using what she remembered, she managed to travel two-thirds around the world before the machines below her suddenly faded a little, telling her that they had arrived in the world.

Which meant she was too late. The sorcerer who had brought the machines had arrived too. It was unlikely they'd stay long, since the machines would attack them as well. The likelihood of her finding their path was slim.

She considered the boxes of beetles. While instructions for their creation had been sent to other cities around the world, and hopefully were being distributed as widely as possible, it was likely broad stretches of the world did not have any to deploy. If she abandoned searching for the sorcerer she could, at least, deliver them to a few places under attack.

Hurrying on, she scanned the horizon for signs of battle. The machines guided her, reacting to the signals of machines further away that had sensed movement and heat. Soon she was hovering over a small town under siege.

She stopped and emerged into the world. Taking the topmost box, she shook it vigorously, then opened it and scattered the beetles in all directions with magic. They buzzed as they activated, then headed for the nearest machines. Then she pushed out of the world a little, saving her strength as she watched to see what would happen.

At first the machines seemed oblivious to the tiny invaders. They continued to attack the city, some falling as sorcerers below struck back at them. Then the nearest machines to Rielle began to behave strangely. Some stilled, a few began to spin on the spot, while others careened into their neighbours.

Then they began to fall.

Three more times she stopped and distributed beetles. Three more towns under attack had a small reprieve. Too small, she feared. How much difference would one box of beetles – maybe a few hundred – against thousands of machines? As she dumped the contents of her last box over the swarming machines above a small city, she pushed out of the world ready to skim back to Beltonia.

A disturbance in the place between caught her attention. Focusing on it, she saw that the substance of it was moving.

She had noticed the effect when she and Tyen had returned from the world in which she had transformed. Paths were like a hole pushed through very thick syrup that immediately began to shrink as the substance slowly seeped back to fill the gap. It was not unlike magic flowing back in to fill the void created when a sorcerer took it. The drift of that magic towards the void was detectable, and now she was sensing a drift in the substance of the place between. But towards what?

She followed the drift. It quickened a little, then she sensed the sharp edges of a recently made path. She could even sense which direction the creator had been travelling in.

It was not difficult to guess who had made it.

Propelling along it, she stretched her senses before her. As she passed the midway point to the next world, she sensed a presence ahead. Concentrating, she found she could make out information that would normally be outside her grasp.

It was a man, she saw with relief. Not Kettin, but one of her followers. He was wondering what Kettin would make of the world he'd just dropped machines into. A world that already contained machines, but had turned them to uses he hadn't seen before. Transport, crop harvesting. Yet they looked old in design and make.

Shock and surprise nearly made Rielle stop. *I'm reading his mind!* That should not be possible between worlds. But by focusing on his pattern, as she had done with Qall, she had seen and deciphered the workings of his mind.

The man was now considering whether he should have ignored his orders – to seek magically powerful worlds and deposit cleansing spheres in them – and report this world to Kettin instead. She'd also said to keep an eye out for paths to worlds believed to be dead. He'd heard in a neighbouring world that the one he'd just visited was dead, so when he'd stumbled upon a recent path and found a world that wasn't just strong, but full of machines, he'd been surprised.

Rielle increased her speed, determined to catch up with him before he reached the next world. She could not let him escape. When he described Tyen's world to Kettin she would guess that it was the original source of machines, and come to see what remained of it. Though that might be a good lure, Kettin was unlikely to bring all her forces with her, and Tyen's world was not a good trap world. Even if Tyen wanted to have his world isolated from all others, it had several neighbours, giving Kettin an easy escape if she realised what was happening.

The shadows of a new world were growing more distinct. The sorcerer's presence snapped out of her senses as he arrived in it. She saw him standing in the arrival place for an instant before he blinked out of sight, heading down another path. She arrived, sought that new path, found it and followed.

She was close enough that he sensed her. At once, her pursuit turned into a chase. He was fast, suggesting that he was powerful, but she was faster. She had nearly caught up with him when he reached the midpoint between worlds. Then two new presences entered the place between. They headed towards the sorcerer and joined him. Rielle slowed and searched for their minds.

A voice echoed in the place between worlds.

"It's her! The Maker!" one said.

"Ah! The world I just came from had machines like the ones Tyen originally made."

"Scatter!" one of the others ordered. "One of us must tell Kettin!"

They fled in three directions. Rielle cast about, cursing silently as she realised she couldn't catch up and grab all three. If only she could reach out and stop them. Perhaps she could. She focused on one, reaching out through the place between and pulling.

And the substance of it parted in a way entirely different to making a path.

A gash opened between the men and the next world. It widened rapidly, like black lightning. A savage, patternless nothingness. The sorcerers' eyes and mouths went wide with surprise and horror but their screams made no sound.

Then the hole snapped outwards in all directions.

The men disappeared.

And something slammed into Rielle, propelling her backwards through the place between, faster than her senses could comprehend. She tumbled, but with no sense of gravity or direction.

Then she was falling. Air filled her lungs. Realising she was within a world, she tried to create a platform of stilled air beneath her body, but wasn't fast enough. Slamming into the ground, she felt the pain of breaking bones, then the instant fire of them healing.

She lay there a moment, stunned. Then she pushed herself up onto her elbows and looked around. She was in the arrival place of the previous world. Her head throbbed with pain. The sunlight was too bright. The silence deafening. Balance, clarity and sound returned all too quickly as her body healed. She sat up, her quick breathing now only due to shock, as the memory returned of three men screaming as the darkness consumed them.

I think I just killed them!

She hadn't meant to, which only made it more frightening. As did the realisation that she had no idea what she had done.

No, that was a lie. She did have an idea, but she was struggling to believe it.

Did I just separate two worlds?

She had to know. Gathering her courage, she stood up, brushed off her clothes and pushed into the place between.

No sign remained of the rend she had made. The path the sorcerer had taken was no longer detectable either. She could still sense the one leading back towards Tyen's world, however. Stretching her new senses, she examined the pattern of the whiteness. She could feel the world behind her. It was like the presence of a person, but immense. No corresponding presence existed in front of her.

A disturbing question now came to her. Had she removed the link between worlds, or had she destroyed that world along with the sorcerers?

I could try to reach it from another direction . . .

But that would take time. Tyen needed her to return to Beltonia, and she had already been away longer than she'd intended. He needed to know that Kettin hadn't found his world, after all. That there would be no additional spheres of machines following the first.

That she could tear apart the substance of the place between worlds.

That last part didn't feel like such good news now. For the first time she wished she had obeyed Qall, and not undergone the transformation to an ageless Maker. Three more deaths on her hands. Starting back towards Tyen's world, she braced herself for the guilt that would come when she emerged into a world again.

TYEN

"We will rebuild," the Emperor assured Tyen. "If not for you and your otherworld friends, this entire world would have become a home only to the dead."

He had invited Tyen to accompany him as he inspected the damage to Beltonia – a demonstration that he did not blame the Academy Director for the invasion. Perhaps one in ten buildings was in ruins. Thousands were dead. Tyen knew it could have been far, far worse. He felt a terrible guilt – more than after Spirecastle fell, when he knew its destruction was not his fault, and Doum's invasion of Murai, which he'd failed to prevent.

"If I had never come home to this world, never asked Rielle to strengthen it, we would not have been attacked," he lamented.

"That is true, but it is also irrelevant," Omniten replied. "I believe it would not have been long before we realised our mistake in regards to magic and creativity. Once we had, we'd have set about restoring our world ourselves. We would have relearned to travel between worlds. Leratians may be stubborn, but when we set our minds to fixing something, that weakness becomes a strength."

"And who is to say that Kettin won't attack weak worlds when she is done with strong?" the Empress added. She tucked her free hand under Tyen's forearm in a gesture of reassurance – one the watching public would note. "She seems a very unstable person."

"This is an age of progress and invention," Omniten said. "To remain a dead world when it could be alive is not the Leratian way. We know that progress does not come without a price. We may not like it, but we accept it."

Tyen sighed. "The price is very high this time."

"Perhaps," the Empress agreed. "But it could have been higher, and now we know our new defensive method works."

The Emperor stopped to regard an apartment block, half of it rubble. After a moment he turned to face Tyen. "This problem is ours to fix, Tyen Ironsmelter. Yours is to work against it happening again. That is not something many could hope to attempt. I appreciate you joining me today. It was necessary. But what it was meant to achieve has been achieved, and you need to set your mind to preventing it happening again, here and anywhere else. Go deal with this woman and her machine armies."

"Go with our blessing and hopes," the Empress added, slipping her hand out from under Tyen's arm and patting his shoulder before she moved to the Emperor's side.

Tyen knew a dismissal when he'd heard it. He gave the Empress a smile of gratitude, then bowed to the Emperor. "Thank you, your Imperial Highness. I will do my best."

The pair nodded. Tyen pushed out of the world a little and skimmed back to the Academy. Arriving in the Grand Hall, he hurried to the meeting room, where he found Rielle, Qall and Dahli.

"Did I miss anything?" he asked as he joined them around the table.

"Only Rielle failing to talk Dahli out of his part in this," Qall replied. "Again."

Rielle looked up at Tyen. "I know you're as troubled as I am."

Tyen nodded. Her accidental killing of the three sorcerers had shaken her, and now she was rethinking everything she had intended to do. He understood her horror. He'd have felt the same. Something else about it had shocked her, too. Something about the violence of the unlinking of worlds had disturbed her even more deeply.

After telling him what had happened, she'd said, "*Perhaps Annad is right. Perhaps I have become more like a demon than a god.*"

He'd told her if she was a demon, she'd not be feeling any concern right now. They'd then argued half-heartedly about different cultures' ideas of demons, and whether any were believed to have a conscience, neither coming to any certain conclusion, but at least it had lightened her mood.

"It is Dahli's choice," Tyen reminded her. "And Zeke's. It's not as though they're sacrificing their lives."

"And it was their idea," Qall added.

She turned back to Dahli. "But the *best* outcome means the two of you will be alone and trapped in a dead world."

Dahli shrugged. "We spent five cycles mostly alone on the edge of the habitable worlds before, and we found it suited us. You've given us an enormous amount of magic to carry, so we won't be in a dead world for long." His mouth twitched into a crooked smile. "And there's nothing like guilt to drive a person into working out how to do something. That's why I trust you to find a way to re-link the worlds and free us."

Qall chuckled at that. Rielle sent him a worried look. "And if I can't?"

"We live out our lives in peaceful isolation," Dahli replied calmly.

She shook her head. "There are plenty of ways this could go wrong. We could be the ones stranded in a dead world while Kettin goes free. I don't know exactly what I did when I unlinked those worlds. Until yesterday, when the scouts we sent located it from another direction, I couldn't even be sure if the world I unlinked still existed."

"But it does," Qall assured her. He smiled wryly. "How is this any different to you becoming ageless again? You couldn't be sure that would work, either."

She scowled. "That only risked harming me, not other people. And not, well, people I know."

Dahli shrugged. "I am flattered that you care, Rielle."

She glanced at him, then away. "I am surprised that I do – and that I seem to have forgiven you. You're frustratingly hard to hold a grudge against, Dahli."

He gave her the ghost of a smile. "Thank you for your forgiveness, Rielle."

She opened her mouth but no words came out. A silence filled the room. Qall looked at each of them, his gaze finally setting on Tyen.

"Well, I don't see any reason to delay. Everything is in place. Protocol has been followed, the Emperor informed."

Rielle blinked, her gaze shifting to Tyen. She had told him she could read his and Qall's mind now, but only if she concentrated. He was surprised to find he wasn't bothered by it. After all, every time he'd spoken to Vella she'd read all of his memories, not just his thoughts. He'd even thought of a few ways Rielle reading his mind could be used to their advantage.

"Then it is time I changed," Dahli said, pushing his chair out and standing. He turned to face Rielle and raised a mirror, and his gaze began moving from her face to his reflection and back again.

The room fell silent. Rielle looked uncomfortable, and she glanced at Tyen and Qall before her shoulders straightened and she returned Dahli's stare. Tyen considered engaging Qall in conversation to ease her discomfort, but he did not want to distract Dahli. It was too important that the man got Rielle's likeness right.

Looking at the man's face, Tyen's skin chilled. The changes were already obvious. At first it seemed like Dahli was failing, his face becoming only a more feminine version of his own. Then Tyen began to recognise the shape of Rielle's mouth and the angle of her nose as Dahli refined the details.

Strangest of all was the point near to Dahli achieving her appearance, where he looked like a slightly wrong version of Rielle.

Thankfully, that did not last long and soon it appeared that two Rielles stood facing each other in the room. Before he could stop himself, Tyen let his gaze drop to Dahli's body, wondering how convincingly the man had changed the rest of him. Too convincingly, Tyen decided as he recognised curves he was becoming more familiar with each time he and Rielle seized a free moment alone together. *Don't think about that*, he told himself, remembering that Qall could read his thoughts. *That's Dahli, not Rielle.*

"Well, that was quite an experience," Rielle murmured.

Dahli smiled, and her face twitched as if compelled to reflect the expression.

"Your turn," he said, handing her the mirror. To Tyen's relief, Dahli's voice had not changed. "Have you done this before?"

She shook her head. Holding the mirror up beside his face, she looked from it to Dahli. Then she dropped her arm.

"I don't need this."

Dahli's eyebrows rose. "You may be an artist but . . ." He stopped, then laughed as he realised the real reason she did not need the mirror. "Three hundred and seventy years old and I still miss the obvious. You can't copy me because I already look like you."

She smiled and shook her head. "No. But that's not why I don't need the mirror. I don't need to use my eyes to do this."

The change was swift, and more disturbing because of that. Her face and body appeared to contort and spasm, and then Dahli was standing in her place. Dahli's masculine features had now erased her own. Her chest had flattened and her shoulders grown wider. Tyen could not tell how accurate the changes were, since her clothing was loose and masculine, but he was sure she would not resemble the woman who had come to his bed every night since her transformation, and the thought was as disturbing as seeing Dahli taking her form.

Dahli's mouth had dropped open. "How?"

"I copied your pattern," she said. Her voice had also remained her own, and sounded strange coming from what looked like his body. They both had donned identical clothing – a simple tunic-and-trousers combination. She raised a hand to her hair, now reddish and curly but long, and a cascade of cuttings fell to the floor as she trimmed it with magic. She looked at Tyen. "Close enough?"

He realised he had been staring at her. Part of his mind was frozen with horror and fear at seeing her disappear and be replaced by Dahli. Somehow he managed a nod. *Tell me you can reverse this as easily*, he thought. She smiled and nodded.

The expression on Dahli's face was one Tyen had never seen on Rielle's before. Calculating, but not unfriendly. Looking closer, Tyen saw that the man was contemplating a future where more people existed who could do the things Rielle could do now. *The first few hundred years of my life may be the least interesting, if I survive this*, he was thinking. *Perhaps I do want her to free Zeke and me from isolation, so I can find out how this story plays out.* He drew a deep breath to speak.

"Time to for me to go."

Rielle nodded. "Be careful. Remember, you only need to let one of Kettin's followers follow you to the fake base, so he or she can report back to her where I am. Don't try to bait the woman herself. If she reads your mind, she'll know it's a trap."

"Don't worry. I have no intention of making her acquaintance," he replied.

"Travel safe," Qall added.

As Dahli faded from sight, Tyen looked at Qall, who was frowning and chewing his lip, reminding Tyen that for all his seeming self-assurance, Qall was still just a young man whose mind was only ten cycles old. If not for Valhan's memories and the ability to read minds, Qall would never have been able to handle himself and others so well.

Which he does, Tyen realised. *Quite well, most of the time.*

He drew in a deep breath. "This has all been arranged so

fast. Are there any lingering doubts? Weaknesses we haven't considered?"

Qall shrugged. "I see many, many small ways this could go wrong, but that is true of all plans. Mostly I worry that Kettin won't fall for it." He smiled without humour. "It would be simpler to kill her." As Tyen opened his mouth, Qall forestalled him with raised hands. "I know, I know. Kill her without destroying her machines as well and another could step into her place. I doubt anybody could, and I suspect there are more machines in the worlds now than what could be physically sent into a single world."

Tyen nodded. "We will have to seek and destroy the rest while her followers are still weakened by her disappearance."

Rielle frowned. "Dahli and Zeke can survive for years on the supplies Qall put in place for him, but if she makes the world uninhabitable, she and her followers will starve."

"If she doesn't, they could live out a normal mortal lifespan. Unless Dahli releases the magic he holds. Then she will be ageless. But I doubt Dahli will do so until he knows he and Zeke are safe," Tyen said.

"They won't be completely safe while she is alive."

"No."

"He won't hesitate to kill her."

"Probably not."

"So we *are* killing her." She shook her head. "I wish we knew why she is like she is, and if we could help her. We gave Dahli a second chance. Why not her?"

"Because if we don't do this, far more people will die," Qall pointed out. "Dahli wasn't slaughtering whole worlds of people. All he wanted was to resurrect one man."

Tyen nodded. "I agree with you in principle," he told her. "But even if Kettin is the victim of the most horrible, unjust torture and suffering, does that excuse what she has done and continues to do? If she has a choice in how she acts, we must stop her. If she can't stop herself doing what she does, we still must stop her.

At least there is a chance she will survive this way. If not for your ability to isolate worlds, the only other choice the Restorers have is to try to kill her."

Qall rose and extended one hand to Rielle, and the other to Tyen. "Decide."

Tyen exchanged a glance with Rielle, then took Qall's hand. Rielle looked at Tyen searchingly, then accepted the other. As she offered her free hand to Tyen, completing their circle, she straightened her back and her expression became set and grim. The sensation of cool air on Tyen's skin disappeared and the room slowly faded from view.

They took the usual route out of the world, skimming to the Far South and leaving from high above the ruins of Spirecastle. The fake base was further away than the one Rielle had transformed in, but only by a few worlds. Tyen would have preferred the trap to be laid far from home, but at least this way it would not take long to get back to his world, if news came of another invasion.

The trap world had a single neighbour, so Rielle only needed to undo one link in order to isolate Kettin. It had been the heart of a great civilisation that had expired more than a thousand years before. Smaller populations had occupied it since, occasionally trading with its neighbouring world, until a war during the chaos following Valhan's death had all but stripped it of magic and occupants. It hadn't been devoid of human habitation when Qall chose it. A few communities had survived. They had a belief as old as the lost empire that the gods would one day take them to a better world. Though Qall had told them he was no god, they had embraced his offer to settle them in one of the many worlds stripped of occupants by Kettin's machines.

In the largest town, the Restorers had occupied the fanciest building and, unaware this base was to be sacrificed, started setting it up. At Qall's orders some of them had brought in food, seeds and domestic animals. These were for Dahli and Zeke to use, if they survived.

The arrival place near the fake Restorer base was well guarded. Tyen nodded to the watchers to convey his respect. They believed this was the new base and, while they knew they were volunteering for a dangerous job, they didn't know how dangerous. It Kettin arrived here, they might easily be her first victims, but it was more likely she would enter the world in the sky along with her machines, as her followers usually did.

Their headquarters was a few streets away. Qall led them to it, introducing them to a group of generals and advisers made up of old faces and a few new ones to replace those who had fallen in the recent battles.

"You have done well here," Qall told them when introductions were over. "But be alert and ready to leave at any moment. Kettin's watchers are everywhere. Tyen, Dahli and I have matters to discuss," Qall told them. "Do not disturb us."

The men and women nodded, then strode off in different directions to resume their tasks. Qall led Tyen and Rielle through the building, then out into a large area at the centre. It was filled with plants. Large-winged insects of bright colours and patterns flitted among the leaves. Worm-like creatures with frilled necks curled around branches, and Rielle jumped as one of them lunged at an insect, catching it with a very long tongue.

At the centre of the garden was a large, flat slab of rock set into the ground. They stepped on it. Qall held out his hands to Rielle and Tyen. They took them and the world faded to white.

He returned to the path they'd arrived along and took them back to the neighbouring world. The arrival place was in a sink-hole from which a maze of tunnels and smaller caves extended. Tyen looked up. The circle of sky visible at the top was clear and a purplish blue. Qall created a light, beckoned, then led them into the tunnels a little way to a room filled with old, dusty and faded furniture. As they sat down, he smiled grimly.

"Now we wait, and hope she takes the bait."

RIELLE

Time passed slowly. When they grew hungry Qall brought out some stores he'd arranged to be put here. They ate, talked, rested and grew hungry again. Rielle could barely eat the second meal, too worried that Kettin had caught Dahli and their plan had fallen to pieces at the first stage. Then, in a few moments, the wait went from too long to too short.

"Someone's in the arrival place," Qall said. "Dahli." He paused. "Kettin is on her way."

The three of them stood and turned to the cave entrance. Footsteps echoed in the passage beyond, then a woman stepped into view. Rielle stared at the newcomer. It was like looking at a three-dimensional, moving reflection – but not for long. The face, so personal and familiar, began to distort. Soon Dahli's features were recognisable, his body matching his voice as he spoke to Rielle.

"Your turn."

She snapped out of her fascinated trance and turned her attention to her body. All but her mind was held in a copy of Dahli's pattern. As she relaxed that hold, her mind automatically changed her pattern back to her own, bringing a brief sensation that was not exactly pain, but was as intense.

"Then this is goodbye," Qall said, standing. "Thank you, Dahli. We owe you more than we can repay."

Dahli shrugged. "Not if you get this right. So . . . get this right." He looked at Rielle. "We don't have much time. She is quite determined to catch you. It took all the tricks I know to keep ahead of her. Be wary."

"I will," Rielle replied. "Look after Zeke."

He smiled. "Always."

"I promise I will do everything I can to work out how to re-link the worlds."

"I know you will." He looked at Tyen. "Look after her."

Tyen could not help smiling. "She can look after herself. But if she needs help, I'll be there. As I'm sure she will be for me."

Dahli turned to Qall, nodded, then turned on his heel and hurried away, his footsteps breaking into a rapid beat as he sprinted back to the arrival place. Rielle's stomach sank as she realised what that meant. *He fears she is close enough that she might catch up before he can travel on to the fake base. I hope he has time to warn the volunteers.* Following him by his mind, she breathed a sigh of relief when he reached the cave and his mind disappeared from her senses.

A long, tense stretch of time followed, then Qall drew in a quick breath. His eyes were focused elsewhere.

"She's here. Or rather, the leading edge of her army."

Stretching out her senses again, Rielle found the mind of one of Kettin's followers. He was holding a sphere of machines, not yet activated, within the confines of the enormous cave. Some of it had fused with the wall. He was admiring the Restorers for this good initial defensive strategy, but now that he knew the arrival place was in a cave he could go back and warn Kettin to skim up to the world's surface. His mind faded away.

Then several minds appeared: the Restorer volunteers, who'd had to skim out of the way of the giant machine sphere stuck in the sinkhole. Hundreds appeared in the space, then retreated to the edges to allow room for others to arrive. They deliberated briefly whether to continue on or hide here, but the thought of encountering Kettin and her followers sent them scurrying towards a tunnel entrance. One looked up, then stopped and gasped. Through his eyes Rielle saw several circular shadows against a chink of the sky, some close and large and others small and distant.

"So many," she whispered.

Qall laughed sourly. "Overkill for one world. I guess we needn't worry whether she's taken the bait."

The spheres were breaking apart and expanding as they arrived, their lattice pattern matching and overlapping. Soon the sky had been blotted out, and a darkness deeper than night had the Restorers wondering if they could risk creating a light.

Then the sky flashed bright white, and as the volunteers' eyesight recovered they saw only sky above them again.

"Gone," Tyen muttered. "To the next world."

Imagining how the solid black sphere of machines would look as it arrived in the trap world sent a shiver down Rielle's spine. *Be careful, Dahli. There are a LOT of machines coming your way.*

"Now we go after her," Qall said as he got to his feet.

Rielle dragged her attention back to her surrounds. Qall and Tyen had linked hands and were extending their free ones towards her. She pushed a rising foreboding aside and took them. The room faded.

As Qall sent them into the place between worlds, Rielle stretched her senses out, searching for other presences. Kettin would most likely hang back to watch the effect her blanket of war machines had on her enemy's world. She'd be looking for Rielle, too. Dahli's words echoed in her memory. *"She is quite determined to catch you."*

All she found were the many presences of the woman's followers, hovering behind the interlocking spheres of machines. Which was like coming upon an enormous black wall within thick fog. It loomed before them, effectively blocking access to the entire world. She looked closer, using her newer senses, and detected the vibration of their pattern. Could she change the machines while between worlds? Perhaps render them useless?

She dared not try. Not only was there a risk the sorcerer controlling them would detect it, but it had been her previous attempt to move someone in the place between that had triggered the separation of worlds.

The great looming mass of machines faded from her new senses, though it was still visible. It had arrived in the trap world. The presences of the sorcerers had vanished too.

All but one. As Rielle focused on it, she recognised it, and knew that it had detected her, Tyen and Qall.

Kettin.

The woman headed towards them. Qall started to retreat, then stopped. Looking at him, Rielle read that he did not want to draw Kettin away from the trap world.

The woman halted a distance away.

"*Rielle Lazuli!*" she said, removing her mask. Her gaze shifted to Tyen and Qall. "*And my other two favourite magic users: Qall, Leader of Restorers, and Tyen, Inventor of Machines.*"

I could unlink the world now, Rielle thought. *But Kettin will die. And I don't know what will happen to Tyen and Qall.* They were supposed to retreat to the previous world once they confirmed that Kettin was in the trap world, so there was no chance they'd be harmed. But they made no move to leave.

"Kettin," Qall replied. "*What are you calling yourself now? Destroyer of Worlds?*"

The woman shook her head. "*No, I think we ought to put that one in reserve for Rielle here.*" Though she smiled, her eyes were hard. "*You haven't yet torn the worlds apart, have you? Why not?*"

"*Perhaps because, unlike you, I don't want to,*" Rielle replied. She looked at Qall and Tyen, but their attention was fixed on Kettin. *I can't tell them to go or Kettin will wonder why.* They might be thrown out of the place between worlds, as she had been last time, if they were behind her when she made the tear. But she couldn't be sure, and didn't want to take the risk.

"*I don't want to destroy the worlds!*" Kettin rolled her eyes. "*I want to free them from the evils of magic. I see my conversation with Rielle did nothing to convince you of the need. But I didn't expect it to. You have so much to lose. So I have a new proposal for Rielle."*

Blunt words came to Rielle's mind, but she held them back. *"What is it this time?"*

"It is only for you," Kettin added, giving Qall and Tyen a haughty look. *"Your friends will have to leave."*

Hope sparked in Rielle's mind. She turned to them. *"Go back."*

"No," Qall said.

Tyen let go of Rielle's hand and took Qall's forearm.

"Rielle is stronger," Tyen reminded him.

"She is," Kettin acknowledged. *"The risk is all mine."*

Rielle turned to face Qall. *"I have to hear what she has to say,"* she told him. Then, making sure her back was to Kettin, she winked.

Qall's eyes narrowed a fraction. Reluctantly, he let go of her hand. *"Don't take too long,"* he warned as Tyen drew him away.

Rielle did not reply. As Qall and Tyen passed the midpoint between worlds, she turned to Kettin.

"Well?"

The woman looked past Rielle. *"A bit longer. I want to make sure they can't hear us."*

"Are you trying to suffocate me?" Rielle asked.

Kettin blinked. *"No. I am serious. I will be quick."* Her expression became earnest. *"I have to admit, I don't know that much about Maker's Curse, and what I do know could be wrong. And I realise that you'd hardly agree to an alliance, for ideological reasons. So, I'm proposing a truce of sorts. I will conquer no more worlds if you agree to restore those I select."*

"How do I know if you will hold to such a deal?"

Kettin nodded. *"Well, if you come with me to the next world, you could read my mind and know I don't intend to go back on my word."*

"To a world full of your machines and followers? Alone?"

"If we go to the previous world, how can I be sure your friends won't kill me?"

"Because, unlike you, they are not murderers," Rielle replied.

A look of confusion and disbelief crossed Kettin's face. It was such an odd response, Rielle began to focus on the woman's pattern.

Thoughts emerged. Cold, calculating thoughts. Kettin did, indeed, plan to set all her forces – machine and sorcerer – on Rielle as soon as they arrived, whether it be in either world. Then she would hunt down Qall and Tyen. Then continue her domination of the worlds. She felt no remorse or shame. Only a belief that if she could do something, she should. The fact that she had got away with so much already was a source of great satisfaction. She could do anything she wanted – or would be able to once the only sorcerers more powerful than her were gone – and intended to.

Rielle had never encountered a mind like it. But it was not entirely unique. She had encountered people with no conscience before, though most were neither as clever nor as powerful as Kettin. She shook her head slowly. *"Go back to your machines and followers and find what satisfaction you can in them, Kettin."*

Kettin's eyebrows rose and her mouth twisted. *"That's disappointing. Though no great loss, really. You would have been a useful ally, but I don't need you, Rielle Lazuli, and you have terrible taste in friends."*

The woman did not move. Rielle waited. After a long pause, Kettin smiled. "Oh, I'm not going to leave until you have."

Well, I can wait as long as she does, Rielle thought. But then she would reveal that she had become ageless again, and Kettin would suspect Rielle had more dangerous abilities. *If I retreat, will she follow?* Pushing back towards the sinkhole world, Rielle silently cursed as Kettin began to follow. They passed the halfway point. Details of the sinkhole world began to emerge. Flashes and movement surrounded them, and Rielle made out the cause she saw that the sphere of machines in the sinkhole was gone and a battle had taken its place. Tyen, Qall and the Restorers crowded together in the arrival place, taking advantage of the constricted space to lessen the number of machines that could attack at any time.

"Did you really think I wouldn't guess you had an escape plan?" Kettin asked. *"Or that I'd let your friends go? I have more walls of machines preventing them from reaching the worlds beyond. And more waiting beyond that. My followers will keep transporting machines in until the Restorers run out of magic. And you won't be able to create it fast enough to help them. You're trapped."*

Rielle stopped and turned back to face Kettin. The woman's smile was feral, eyes bright with anticipation. Rielle was glad of the detachment between worlds, as she saw which of two terrible choices she must make.

"You'd better hurry and join them, or they won't last very long at all," Kettin added.

"They'll last long enough," Rielle told her.

Focusing on the substance of the place between worlds, she willed part of it to come towards her. This time she pulled carefully, increasing the strength of it until she felt the substance tear.

As before, the impression of the split only lasted a moment, before blackness gaped wide. The substance of the place between worlds rippled and bucked. She thought she saw eddies of it pouring into the darkness. She lost all sense of Kettin's presence, and she could not tell if the woman had slipped into the hole or fled.

Then, once again, a force knocked her backwards. As she careened towards the sinkhole world, half-dazed by the force she'd unleashed, she thought of Dahli and Zeke, and the sacrifice they'd made. *Be safe*, she thought at them. *I will find a way to retrieve you.*

And then she was kneeling on the ground, feeling her strength returning as her body healed. Qall and Tyen hovered close, anxious and protective, their questions tangling together. The battle still raged overhead.

She got to her feet. Dusted herself off. And nodded.

"It's done. The world is isolated."

"Kettin?" Qall asked.

"I couldn't tell if she survived."

"So she is either dead or isolated," Tyen concluded.

Qall nodded and let out a relieved sigh. "The worlds no longer need to fear her."

Rielle looked up. "Just her machines."

Tyen and Qall exchanged a grim but satisfied look.

"Let's get out of here," Qall said, holding out his hands to them.

"Kettin has more of those walls of machines blocking your exit," Rielle warned as she took one of them.

He nodded. "And we three are strong enough to move them. I've had stores of Tyen's beetles placed in all the local worlds, ready to deal with any further attacks."

Tyen looked at Qall in surprise. "You *have* been busy."

"Not as busy as their makers."

Tyen took Qall's other hand. "But they're not really my machines. I had little to do with their design."

Qall smiled. "But without you they'd have never been created. The worlds need to know who saved them, Tyen."

Tyen looked at Rielle. "Then they should know it was Rielle."

Qall looked at her and nodded. "She did, indeed."

Rielle grimaced. "Well, in return I have one request."

Qall's eyebrows rose. "Yes?"

"Never, *ever*, ask me to do something like that again."

"Of course not," Tyen replied.

"I won't," Qall promised. Then one of his eyebrows quirked upwards. "Not if the worlds face a danger equally as terrible?"

She frowned. "It would have to be at least as bad."

"You're not now opposed to re-linking worlds, are you?"

She thought of Dahli and Zeke, starting a new life in what was probably now a magically dead, machine-filled empty world. Though if Kettin's followers had survived, they wouldn't be completely alone. And if Kettin had . . . She smiled grimly. Dahli could take care of himself. And Zeke.

Rielle shook her head. "No," she answered. "I made a promise to Dahli to free him and Zeke, and I intend to keep it."

Qall nodded, then raised his head. "Link!"

The Restorers immediately took hold of each other.

"Anyone not ready?"

No reply came.

The sinkhole and the milling machines within it faded a little, then faded to white.

EPILOGUE

TYEN

Despite knowing she could levitate and hold objects in the air, Rielle had never been completely at ease in an aircart. Tyen, however, was like an excited boy when he was in a flying contraption, whether one of the Academy's small aircarts or one of Mig's gliding vehicles. The aircart they were in now was nothing like either of those agile, sleek contraptions. It was a big-bellied thing with generous glass windows affording a view of the city below. Within, it was wide enough to fit a set of chairs and tables on either side of an aisle, and long enough for twenty tables in total, and a tiny kitchen at the far end.

Only their table was occupied today, so no hum of conversation covered the sound of the propellers.

"A restaurant aircart," Tyen said yet again. "Genius idea."

"Yes," Rielle agreed, her tone betraying her doubt.

The light in his eyes dimmed a little. "You're not enjoying this."

She waved a hand. "I'm not hating it either. It's just not the thrill to me that it is to you."

"I'm sorry. If it bothers you, don't look down," he advised.

She glanced at the oval of glass next to their chairs. A section of Beltonia was captured within the frame. An impressive amount of rebuilding had been done in the last quarter-cycle, some of it taking advantage of the damage from the invasion to simplify the maze of streets.

"It's not that," she said. "I'd have no trouble levitating this high. It's more the idea of being stuck in the middle of so much wood and glass and fabric if this thing fell that bothers me."

Her stomach swooped as the aircart was buffeted by wind.

"And there's that, too," she added.

"Yes," he agreed ruefully. "It does take a strong stomach to eat on an aircart in windy weather."

Looking over his shoulder, she saw a waiter heading their way, slim glasses balanced on a tray. The man paused and rode out another disturbance with practised ease. When the floor was relatively still again, he continued to their table, set down the three glasses and filled them without spilling a drop.

"That was well done," Tyen told him.

"I spent many years serving on the royal ship, Director," the man replied.

As the waiter walked away, Tyen checked his clock pendant and frowned, for the fifth time since they'd arrived.

Rielle smiled sympathetically. "Don't get your hopes too high, Tyen. Aside from the difficulties in calculating time difference between worlds, Qall has a lot of work to do now the war is over."

"Over?" a familiar voice said. "Who said it was over?"

They turned to see Qall standing in the aisle. He grinned and nodded to a man standing beside him.

"Baluka!" Rielle rose to her feet. Qall had sent several messages to arrange a meeting since their confrontation with Kettin, but hadn't managed to attend any. Now not only had he finally made it to one, but he had brought Baluka as well. She kissed them both on the cheek.

"It is good to see you, Baluka."

His smile widened. "And you, Rielle."

"Come join us," she invited.

The waiter hurried over to place a chair beside the one they'd reserved for Qall. As the pair sat down, he poured wine for the newcomers.

"I don't know that you can call a war 'over' when there are still plenty of attacks on worlds," Qall said.

"Your last messenger said the Restorers had dealt with most of Kettin's followers," Rielle pointed out.

"That's what I want the worlds to think. The truth is, a group of them went into hiding and are trying to establish their own little empire." Qall shrugged. "We need to extinguish that little fire while they're only made up of minor sorcerers." He picked up his glass and sipped, then nodded in approval. "This is good. I wish I could stay and enjoy the rest of it."

"You're not staying?" Rielle asked.

"I can't, unfortunately." Qall grimaced. "I would have cancelled but for the fact that Baluka wanted to come."

Baluka straightened. "I am here to say goodbye," he said. "I am leaving the Restorers, as you know I have planned for some time."

Rielle and Tyen nodded, Tyen's expression reflecting Rielle's sadness.

"Have you found somewhere to settle?" Tyen asked.

Baluka shrugged. "Not yet."

"We won't see you again, will we?" Rielle asked, though she knew the answer. With too many enemies likely to seek revenge if Baluka did not have the protection of the Restorers, he would have to start a new life away from everybody who'd known him. That included her, Tyen and Qall, and even the Travellers.

He shook his head. "Probably not." Then he smiled. "But who knows? I might sneak into your world and visit you one day."

"We'd like that," Tyen said.

Baluka looked at Qall. "I'm done. You can make your proposal now."

Rielle and Tyen exchanged a look. He smiled faintly, as if to say 'I told you so'.

Qall's gaze moved from Tyen to her and back again. "The worlds need you. Both of you. And I don't just mean to make machine-destroying beetles. There are over a thousand dead worlds to restore and countless broken machines to dismantle so that others can't repair and use them. Surely everything is under control here now."

Rielle smiled.

"We thought you'd say that." She looked at Tyen, who met her gaze and nodded. They'd discussed this many times in the days since they'd last seen Qall. "We want to help, to restore worlds and clean up the machines. But we don't want to work with the Restorers."

Qall's eye widened in surprise. Clearly, he hadn't been reading Tyen's mind, Rielle mused.

"If we work with you, your enemies will become ours," Tyen explained. "Since we've agreed we won't do anything that will endanger my world," Tyen glanced at Rielle – "*our* world," he corrected – "we have to remain independent."

Qall opened his mouth but no words came out. He looked from her to Tyen and back again, then closed his mouth again. His eyes narrowed.

"So what are you suggesting?"

"You appeal to us when worlds come to you for help," Tyen answered. "But we also help worlds that come to us directly."

Qall nodded slowly. "That could work. But people already think of you as Restorers." He frowned. "Do you want us to have a public disagreement, to make sure it's known you are independent?"

Rielle shook her head. "No, if people think we're enemies that will cause problems too. It will all be in the way you refer to us, and us to you. Perhaps you could ask us to help someone we clearly wouldn't help, so that we can be seen to refuse. But mostly we'll just give it time. People will work it out eventually."

Qall's nods slowed to a stop. He looked at them in turn, an odd expression on his face. "Did you know that people have started calling us the Three. Rielle is still 'the Maker' and Tyen is now 'the Builder'."

From the way Baluka's eyebrows rose, he didn't know about this.

"Well, that's a change from 'the Spy'," Tyen said.

"What are you, then, Qall?" Rielle asked.

"The Successor?" Baluka guessed.

Qall shook his head. He looked a little embarrassed. "The closest translation is 'the Fixer'." He sighed. "They are building temples to us in some worlds."

Rielle winced. "You're discouraging that, I hope."

"I'm trying to. When people believe you are gods, they will only be disappointed when it becomes clear you are human."

Except, I'm more than human, Rielle thought. *Yet definitely not a god. I'm much closer to human than god.* The word "demon" rose in the back of her mind, but she pushed it away. Instead she thought of Annad, who had returned to his world intending to create a library of knowledge. He'd asked her to visit, but she was worried she'd be recognised as the goddess Rel and that would make life hard for him.

She sighed. "It wouldn't be so bad if we could do good as gods, then return and live our ordinary human lives in peace."

Tyen straightened a little. "I wonder, could we do that? Well, not claim to be gods, but take on a different identity when we help a world. If we changed our appearance, people wouldn't recognise us when we were ourselves again. It would help to protect Leratia."

"But then nobody will recognise you as the Maker or Builder when you go out in the worlds," Baluka pointed out.

Tyen shrugged. "Most people in the worlds don't know what we look like anyway. In time the memory of our true likenesses will fade and our adopted ones would be what we're known for."

Qall smiled crookedly. "If I did the same, it would allow me to help people when being the head of the Restorers restrains me. It is an interesting idea." He rubbed his hands together, then got to his feet, the rest of them following suit. "Well, I'd best get back to the Restorers, before they send someone out to drag me away. Why did I ever agree to lead a bunch of contrary, bossy sorcerers?"

"It's not like you didn't know what you were taking on," Baluka reminded him.

"Yes, I did and I don't regret it yet." Qall chuckled, then kissed Rielle on the cheek and reached out to pat Tyen's shoulder. "Take care, old friend."

Tyen frowned. "Who are you calling 'old'?"

Qall grinned. "No matter how old I get, you'll always be older."

Rolling her eyes, Rielle turned and enveloped Baluka in a hug. "Take care, Baluka."

"Always." He hugged her back, then stepped away and was embraced, somewhat awkwardly, by Tyen. "You be careful too."

"We always are," Tyen assured him. "I hope you find happiness wherever you settle."

"Thank you." Baluka stepped back, then took Qall's offered hand.

The pair slowly faded from sight. When Rielle could not make them out any more, she sighed and turned to Tyen. "Meal first, then home to make arrangements to restore and clean up the machines?"

He smiled. "I've always found I am much more effective at saving worlds on a full stomach."

She sat down. "Then let's not disappoint the chef; there are some fine aromas coming from that kitchen."

Tyen reached out and took her hand. "So by 'home', do you mean my world?"

She smiled. "Yes. I'm staying, if you want me."

He leaned forward and kissed her. "It would make me very happy."

RIELLE

Machines rained down from the sky.

A few bounced off Tyen's shield and landed on those that had already fallen. A ring-shaped pile was growing around him as the beetles he'd released far above them did their work. Soon he and Rielle would have to move or sweep away the accumulated debris, or they'd be buried.

They'd come to this world to restore it, after representatives of its former occupants had appealed to Rielle for help. Though reconstruction was underway, the magic that ought to be generated by people rebuilding and making repairs was drained away as fast as it was generated, and now and then a machine came back to life and attacked someone. It was a common problem. Machines that had simply run out of magic were revived whenever magic returned to a world, making restoration a difficult and dangerous task.

But it just happened that Rielle and Tyen had the right match of skills to tackle it.

He drew in more of the magic Rielle was generating to strengthen his shield, then blasted a swathe of machines out of the sky.

"Another," Rielle said.

Tyen paused and opened a gap in his shield for long enough to let a dead machine tumble through. Before it landed, Rielle had seized it with magic and drawn it close. The carapace split open. Five beetles fell out. Rielle swept them towards Tyen with magic.

He caught and inspected them in turn. Three were easily repaired, one just needed recharging with magic, and the last was beyond repair. Selecting what he needed from a box at his feet, he set to work, tossing the restored beetles into another box.

"Another."

When she split open the next machine, only one beetle fell out, so after he'd dealt with it he stopped to watch her work. She stared intently at the machine's remains. Soon they began to glow. The parts melted and blended together until it had become a molten mass. That mass began to twist and stretch, rising in the air and moving towards the sculpture she was creating. In this case, a life-sized metal tree. The cooling remains of the machine slotted into existing limbs, becoming another branch.

They could have simply let the dead machines pile up, then transport them away when all had expired, but in order to generate the magic needed to deliver the beetles, defend themselves and fight the machines, Rielle needed to be creative.

Rielle paused to look up at the tree. She frowned, and leaves and flowers began to sprout from it.

"You're getting very good at this," he said.

She glanced at him and smiled. "Not as good as you. I've always worked flat. You're far better at sculpture."

"A few badly thrown pots doesn't compare to this."

"I'm not talking about pots," she told him. "The machines you make are more than just practical items. They have beauty in them. And the pots aren't too bad, either."

"Perhaps, but I am better at making insectoids than working with clay."

"Insectoids?" She raised her eyebrows, in her gaze a challenge. "You've been far more creative than that."

He thought back to the objects he had once made. Contraptions his father had kept. Toys. Clocks. Music boxes. *She has a point.*

She paused to look up at him. "Why don't you let the beetles do their job for a while and take the opportunity to make something?"

Endless machine smashing had been satisfying at first, but it *had* grown boring. Letting another machine fall through his shield for her to reshape, he allowed a second in and began to work. Soon he had lost himself in melting and fusing. At first, he missed his tools, and standardised screw and cog sizes, but once he let such restrictions go and made parts the size they needed to be he felt freer. When he had finished, a music machine the size of a cart stood before him.

Rielle's voice spoke at his shoulder. "You're quite a strong maker when you get involved."

He turned to regard her. "Not as strong as you."

"Of course not. My ability was enhanced." She tilted her head a little to the side. "As yours could be if you wanted. The offer still stands, you know."

"I know."

"And?"

"Becoming an Ancient seems like something I shouldn't do just for my own benefit. I'd rather wait until the worlds need it. Though it doesn't seem fair that I'm free to create without making too much magic when you aren't. If you'd rather I—"

She pulled him close and pressed her lips against his. Delighted by her sudden passion, he let the machine part he'd been holding fall. As it clanged to the ground, she pulled away, her expression slightly apologetic. "Oops. Sorry. I didn't mean to distract you."

"Yes, you did."

She laughed. "Well, it wasn't my main purpose."

"Which was?"

She shrugged. "Nothing more than to remind you that I love you."

He drew her closer. "Then I should remind you how much I love you."

She placed a hand on his chest. "As much as I would enjoy that, any further delay may see us buried by machines."

He glanced at the pile of dead machines forming around them, held back by his shield. Only a small hole remained at the top. "You have a point."

As she stepped away, he gathered magic and thrust his shield up and away with great force. Machines were flung off in all directions. Without their bodies blocking the light, the area suddenly seemed brighter. He looked over to see if Rielle was ready to take another one to dismantle, and found that she had turned the leaves of the tree into hundreds of little books.

He thought of Vella, now safely in the possession of the Librarian, absorbing all the knowledge in the Academy. And Beetle, the toy that had inspired a solution to Kettin's machines, now kept in a display cabinet dedicated to significant Academy inventions. He recalled Mig's admiration of it. The southerner had taken over from Zeke as the most admired inventor in the Academy, despite not having any magical ability.

That brought his train of thought around to Zeke and Dahli. He hoped that the pair were still alive, surviving on their isolated world. Rielle had not yet attempted to re-link the world. Dahli had told her to wait at least five cycles before attempting it, in case Kettin survived. Rielle had decided that, when she did, she would travel to the furthest edge of the habitable worlds. Which would mean she would be away from him for at least a cycle – something he wasn't looking forward do.

It had better be worth it, he thought. Linking worlds had to be possible. It had been done many, many times before, as the great number of linked worlds proved. Tyen suspected it would not be easy, though. All too often, it was far easier and faster to destroy something than to make it.

Rielle was the Maker, however. If anyone could do it, she could. He looked over to her, to find her sitting on the ground staring at nothing, her expression one of intense concentration.

"Rielle?" he asked, concerned.

She blinked, but her eyes did not focus on him. "We've been

here quite a while now," she observed. "Have you looked at how much magic we've made?"

"No. I'm sure if I do, my senses will be overwhelmed."

"Well . . . I've always wondered what would happen if I kept filling a world with magic. I think I've just found out."

Tyen looked around. The world was, indeed, saturated with so much magic it was dazzling. "I can't see anything but magic. What do you sense?"

"I . . . I don't know. The magic doesn't stop at the edges of this world now. It seems to have reached a point where the force that keeps it close to this world no longer contains it. It has . . . gone beyond." She shook her head. "It's . . . amazing. I can see the distances between worlds. They are, in a physical sense, immense."

He drew in a sharp breath. "You can sense other worlds?"

"Yes." She blinked, then her eyes focused on his, bright with excitement. "I think I know how to link worlds."

He drew in a quick breath. "You can free Dahli and Zeke!"

"Yes. But . . . not for some time."

"Well, yes. He said to wait."

"Oh, not because of that." She got to her feet, dusted off her clothes. "It's going to take at least that long to generate enough magic to forge a link. And all that magic has to be in one world."

"Well, then, you have no excuse not to practise your painting now."

She smiled. "None but the fact that if we stop restoring the dead worlds and getting rid of the war machines so I can paint, it won't go down so well with most people of the worlds."

"No, but most of the work is in dealing with machines. If worlds were stripped of them before you arrived, all you'd need to do is restore the magic."

She looked thoughtful. "But if I create enough magic, we can lure the ones still functional to a single location, ready to transport. But where would we put them?"

"A dead world, where they could be dealt with safely, taking as much time as required."

"Who is going to do that?"

Tyen chuckled. "In a few years the Academy will have more graduates than it can cope with. We have to keep them out of trouble somehow."

She laughed. "I'm sure they'll be delighted to find they've become otherworld cleaning staff."

"They'll do anything to finally get to travel the worlds."

"And what will they do with all that metal?"

Tyen considered. "Give it back to the worlds it came from?"

Rielle nodded. "That seems the right thing to do." She smiled and took his hand. "Well, I see no reason to wait. Let's see if we can find a nearby dead world to store these machines in."

He picked up the box of beetles and pushed out of the world – and as his shield was removed, the pile of machines collapsed in on itself. Together they headed into the whiteness.

DAHLI

O f the forty or fifty sorcerers who had followed Kettin into the trap, only twenty-three remained as far as Dahli could tell.

Twenty-four now, he corrected, watching one of the two younger women playing with a baby. The group had settled near the equator, where the weather was warm though subject to violent seasonal storms. Fruit was available for most of the year and they'd learned which sea creatures were safe to eat through trial and a few fatal errors.

Maybe in a few centuries their descendants would retell the story of their arrival in this world. Maybe those tales would include Kettin as some mythic godlike figure.

Dahli hadn't seen any sign of the woman. He hoped she was dead, but in the absence of a body to prove it, he dared not release all the magic he held. From time to time he ventured to the other side of the world to check on the survivors, forced to levitate and "fly" there since there was no place between the worlds now, but they hadn't seen their former leader either.

On the day of the unlinking he'd been safe underground with Zeke. For fifty-one days afterwards, they'd slept when they were tired and explored the caves when they weren't. On the fifty-first day they'd stumbled upon another exit to the caves and crept out to find a world littered with dead machines. A little released magic had revived the closest, and Dahli had quickly smashed it.

"Hmm," Zeke had said, looking out over the countless dark

shapes. "I could fix them so they don't wake up when you release magic."

"It could take a lifetime," Dahli had pointed out. "Maybe several."

The young man had shrugged. "I have a lifetime to fill."

"I'm sorry. It's not what you wanted."

Zeke had laughed. "I have you and a world full of machines to play with! It doesn't get any better. At least for me it doesn't. For you it's going to get very boring."

Dahli smiled at the memory as he levitated and propelled himself back towards the house they had built. Zeke was perceptive, but to truly understand what it meant to have lived more than three hundred cycles, you had to have lived them. Zeke could not appreciate why Dahli would never be bored around him, despite having served a man as desirable and elusive as the Raen.

Because Dahli had never felt *affection* for Valhan. His respect had been part fear, which was not respect at all. Zeke was always himself: clever, sometimes foolish, honest, forgiving. He made Dahli a better, happier person.

That, alone, could sustain him for many more lifetimes.

He smiled as he moved through clouds, above a glittering sea. If Rielle never found a way to re-link this world to the rest, he wouldn't care. The past was far behind him. A better future lay ahead.

For the first time in his life, he was content.

ACKNOWLEDGEMENTS

First up, a big thank you to the team at Orbit, from the editors who knock my books into shape, to the designers and illustrators who make them look fabulous, to the publicity folk who come up with fun and effective ways to bring the books to the attention of readers, to the people who have, over the years, written lovely notes and inserted them in reprint copies to send my way. I appreciate all your hard work and creativity.

Next, a big hug for my agents, especially the wonderful Fran Bryson, who has stuck by me for all these years and the lovely agents I've worked with at Abner Stein, but not forgetting all the overseas agents who represent me around the world.

Thanks also to Stephanie Smith, Liz Kemp, Heidi Schwegler, Donna Hanson and Kerri Valkova for beta reading and editing, catching all those inevitable mistakes and inconsistencies and enthusing about the story.

Thanks also to Mum and Dad. Always.

And Paul, for support during the bad times and assistance celebrating the good.

Lastly, as always, a huge thank you to all the fans of my books. Your enthusiasm and patience have kept me going in the tough times. I have had a lot of fun writing my books and it is an extra, awesome bonus to know other people are enjoying reading them. And rereading them. Thanks for coming along the adventure with me. You're the best travel companions ever!

extras

www.orbitbooks.net

about the author

Trudi Canavan published her first story in 1999 and it received an Aurealis Award for Best Fantast Short Story. Her debut series, the Black Magician trilogy, made her an international success, and all three volumes of her Age of the Five trilogy were Sunday Times bestsellers. Trudi Canavan lives with her partner in Melbourne, Australia, and spends her time writing, painting and weaving.

Find out more about Trudi Canavan and other Orbit authors by registering online for the free monthly newsletter at www.orbitbooks.net.

if you enjoyed
MAKER'S CURSE

look out for

THE MASK OF MIRRORS
Rook and Rose:
Book One

by

M. A. Carrick

Nightmares are creeping through the city of dreams . . .

Renata Virdaux is a con artist who has come to the sparkling city of Nadezra — the city of dreams — with one goal: to trick her way into a noble house and secure her fortune and her sister's future.

But as she's drawn into the aristocratic world of House Traementis, she realises her masquerade is just one of many surrounding her. And as corrupted magic begins to weave its way through Nadezra, the poisonous feuds of its aristocrats and the shadowy dangers of its impoverished underbelly become tangled — with Ren at their heart.

Prologue

The lodging house had many kinds of quiet. There was the quiet of sleep, children packed shoulder to shoulder on the threadbare carpets of the various rooms, with only an occasional snore or rustle to break the silence. There was the quiet of daytime, when the house was all but deserted; then they were not children but Fingers, sent out to pluck as many birds as they could, not coming home until they had purses and fans and handkerchiefs and more to show for their efforts.

Then there was the quiet of fear.

Everyone knew what had happened. Ondrakja had made sure of that: In case they'd somehow missed the screams, she'd dragged Sedge's body past them all, bloody and broken, with Simlin forcing an empty-eyed Ren along in Ondrakja's wake. When they came back a little while later, Ondrakja's stained hands were empty, and she stood in the mildewed front hall of the lodging house, with the rest of the Fingers watching from the doorways and the splintered railings of the stairs.

"Next time," Ondrakja said to Ren in that low, pleasant voice they all knew to dread, "I'll hit you somewhere softer." And her gaze went, with unerring malice, to Tess.

Simlin let go of Ren, Ondrakja went upstairs, and after that the lodging house was silent. Even the floorboards didn't creak, because the Fingers found places to huddle and stayed there.

Sedge wasn't the first. They said Ondrakja picked someone at random every so often, just to keep the rest in line. She was the leader of their knot; it was her right to cut someone out of it.

But everyone knew this time wasn't random. Ren had fucked up, and Sedge had paid the price.

Because Ren was too valuable to waste.

Three days like that. Three days of terror-quiet, of no one being sure if Ondrakja's temper had settled, of Ren and Tess clinging to each other while the others stayed clear.

On the third day, Ren got told to bring Ondrakja her tea.

She carried it up the stairs with careful hands and a grace most of the Fingers couldn't touch. Her steps were so smooth that when she knelt and offered the cup to Ondrakja, its inner walls were still dry, the tea as calm and unrippled as a mirror.

Ondrakja didn't take the cup right away. Her hand slid over the charm of knotted cord around Ren's wrist, then along her head, lacquered nails combing through the thick, dark hair like she was petting a cat. "Little Renyi," she murmured. "You're a clever one . . . but not clever enough. That is why you need me."

"Yes, Ondrakja," Ren whispered.

The room was empty, except for the two of them. No Fingers crouching on the carpet to play audience to Ondrakja's performance. Just Ren, and the stained floorboards in the corner where Sedge had died.

"Haven't I tried to teach you?" Ondrakja said. "I see such promise in you, in your pretty face. You're better than the others; you could be as good as me, someday. But only if you listen and obey— and stop trying to *hide things from me*."

Her fingernails dug in. Ren lifted her chin and met Ondrakja's gaze with dry eyes. "I understand. I will never try to hide anything from you again."

"Good girl." Ondrakja took the tea and drank.

The hours passed with excruciating slowness. Second earth. Third earth. Fourth. Most of the Fingers were asleep, except those out on night work.

Ren and Tess were not out, nor asleep. They sat tucked under the staircase, listening, Ren's hand clamped hard over the charm on her wrist. "Please," Tess begged, "we can just go—"

"No. Not yet."

Ren's voice didn't waver, but inside she shook like a pinkie on her first lift. *What if it didn't work?*

She knew they should run. If they didn't, they might miss their chance. When people found out what she'd done, there wouldn't be a street in Nadežra that would grant her refuge.

But she stayed for Sedge.

A creak in the hallway above made Tess squeak. Footsteps on the stairs became Simlin rounding the corner. He jerked to a halt when he saw them in the alcove. "There you are," he said, as if he'd been searching for an hour. "Upstairs. Ondrakja wants you."

Ren eased herself out, not taking her eyes from Simlin. At thirteen he wasn't as big as Sedge, but he was far more vicious. "Why?"

"Dunno. Didn't ask." Then, before Ren could start climbing the stairs: "She said both of you."

Next time, I'll hit you somewhere softer.

They should have run. But with Simlin standing just an arm's reach away, there wasn't any hope now. He dragged Tess out of the alcove, ignoring her whimper, and shoved them both up the stairs.

The fire in the parlour had burned low, and the shadows pressed in close from the ceiling and walls. Ondrakja's big chair was turned with its back to the door so they had to circle around to face her, Tess gripping Ren's hand so tight the bones ached.

Ondrakja was the picture of Lacewater elegance. Despite the late hour, she'd changed into a rich gown, a Liganti-style surcoat over a fine linen underdress—a dress Ren herself had stolen off a laundry line. Her hair was upswept and pinned, and with the high back of the chair rising behind her, she looked like one of the Cinquerat on their thrones.

A few hours ago she'd petted Ren and praised her skills. But Ren saw the murderous glitter in Ondrakja's eyes and knew that would never happen again.

"Treacherous little bitch," Ondrakja hissed. "Was this your revenge for that piece of trash I threw out? Putting something in my tea? It should have been a knife in my back—but you don't have the guts for that. The only thing worse than a traitor is a *spineless* one."

Ren stood paralyzed, Tess cowering behind her. She'd put in as much extract of meadow saffron as she could afford, paying the apothecary with the coin that was supposed to help her and Tess and Sedge escape Ondrakja forever. It should have worked.

"I am going to make you pay," Ondrakja promised, her voice cold with venom. "But this time it won't be as quick. Everyone will know you betrayed your knot. They'll hold you down while I go to work on your little sister there. I'll keep her alive for days, and you'll have to watch every—"

She was rising as she spoke, looming over Ren like some Primordial demon, but mid-threat she lurched. One hand went to her stomach—and then, without any more warning, she vomited onto the carpet.

As her head came up, Ren saw what the shadows of the chair had helped conceal. The glitter in Ondrakja's eyes wasn't just fury; it was fever. Her face was sickly sallow, her skin dewed with cold sweat.

The poison *had* taken effect. And its work wasn't done.

Ren danced back as Ondrakja reached for her. The woman who'd knotted the Fingers into her fist stumbled, going down onto one knee. Quick as a snake, Ren kicked her in the face, and Ondrakja fell backward.

"That's for Sedge," Ren spat, darting in to stomp on Ondrakja's tender stomach. The woman vomited again, but kept wit enough to grab at Ren's leg. Ren twisted clear, and Ondrakja clutched her own throat, gasping.

A yank at the charm on Ren's wrist broke the cord, and she hurled it into the woman's spew. Tess followed an instant later. That swiftly, they weren't Fingers anymore.

Ondrakja reached out again, and Ren stamped on her wrist, snapping bone. She would have kept going, but Tess seized Ren's arm, dragging her toward the door. "She's already dead. Come on, or we will be, too—"

"Come back here!" Ondrakja snarled, but her voice had withered to a hoarse gasp. "I will make you fucking *pay*..."

Her words dissolved into another fit of retching. Ren broke at last, tearing the door open and barreling into Simlin on the other side, knocking him down before he could react. Then down the stairs to the alcove, where a loose floorboard concealed two bags containing everything they owned in the world. Ren took one and threw the other at Tess, and they were out the door of the lodging house, into the narrow, stinking streets of Lacewater, leaving dying Ondrakja and the Fingers and the past behind them.